D1525601

THEIR BRIDGEWATER BRIDES BOXED SET

BRIDGEWATER MENAGE SERIES - BOOKS 1-3

VANESSA VALE

Cover design: Bridger Media

Cover photos: Bigstock- Lenor; Period Images

GET A FREE BOOK!

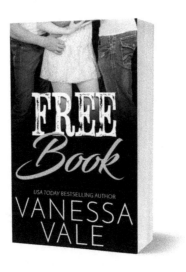

THEIR KIDNAPPED BRIDE - BOOK 1

1

MMA

"You may do with her as you wish. I wash my hands of her."

These were the words that I first comprehended as I awoke, my mind unusually foggy. Everything that came before was garbled as if I had cotton stuffed in my ears. My eyes felt as if lead weights were pressed upon them, too heavy to open, and a bitter taste coated my tongue. My head thumped in time with my beating heart. I didn't want to surface from the safe warmth of my slumber.

"Surely she could be spoken for easily enough. A hasty marriage. Her face and body are more than appealing to any man." A woman responded to the man's insistent words.

"No," his tone was emphatic, sharp. "That will not suffice. My money, if you please."

My head was clearing enough to recognize the voice. It was my step-brother, Thomas. Who was he speaking with, and why? The topic was odd. Everything was odd. Why were they talking in my bedroom while I slept? It was time to discern the answer.

Stirring, I pushed up from the bed to sit, my eyes fluttering open, then widening in surprise. This wasn't my bedroom! The walls were not robin's egg blue, but a garish ruby red. The room was gaudy and softly lit, equally red velvet drapes hung at the windows. The room imbued decadence, extravagance. Tawdry deeds. I rubbed at my sleepy eyes, making sure I was not dreaming, taking a moment to clear my head.

Thomas stood tall with his erect bearing by the door, palm out, speaking with a woman over a foot shorter. She wore an emerald green satin gown that had her ample cleavage all but spilling over the top and showcased a narrow waist. Her jet black hair was piled high, creatively so, in the latest of styles with artful curls down her nape. She was beautiful, her skin an alabaster white, her lips tinged with coloring, her eyes darkened with kohl. She was as decadent as her surroundings.

She moved gracefully to a large desk, situated before an unlit fireplace and smoothly opened the top drawer. Her eyes shifted to me and made notice that I was awake, but made no mention of it. She removed a small stack of bills and handed them to Thomas. He was a big man, broad and imposing, and could easily make the strongest of men nervous. But not this woman. She didn't cower. She didn't simper. She only tilted her chin up in a haughty way at the transaction.

"Thomas." My voice came out scratchy and I cleared my throat. "Thomas," I repeated. "What is happening?"

His dark eyes narrowed as he fixed his gaze on me. Only hatred showed in their inky depths. It had been disinterest that was usually there, this anger was new. His father married my mother when I was five and Thomas fifteen, both parents widowed years prior. The union was more for money than affection and when they died – he of a fall from a horse and she a year later of consumption – I was left under the guardianship of Thomas. Although he had never been affectionate or overly interested in me, I had wanted for nothing.

"You are awake," he grumbled, his mouth turned down in a frown. "The laudanum dose was not as substantial as I expected."

My mouth fell open. Laudanum? It was no wonder I struggled to comprehend. "What – I don't understand." I ran my hand over my hair, my severe bun having lost several of its pins and some long tendrils brushed along my neck. Licking my dry lips, I glanced between the strange woman and my Thomas.

My step-brother was an attractive man, in a conservative, severe fashion. He was precise, concise and exacting. Strict would also be apt, as would severe. His suit was black, his dark hair slicked and shiny with pomade, his mustache full, yet fiercely maintained. Some said we looked similarly, even though we were not formally related, our eyes the same bright blue, hair dark as night, however our countenance was quite different. Thomas's emotions matched his attire: austere and tense, a trait also found in his father. I, however, was considered to be more placid, the peacemaker in the family. With our parents dead, I lived with Thomas and his wife, Mary, and their three children. A part of a hectic household, I was always able to maintain some semblance of lightheartedness in contrast to my sibling's less generous nature.

Thomas sighed, as if wasting time on a recalcitrant child. "This is Mrs. Pratt. I relinquish my guardianship of you to her."

Mrs. Pratt did not look like any married woman that I'd ever known. None I knew of wore a dress in such a color, sheen of fabric, or daring cut. Her expression remained neutral, as if she did not wish to be involved in this conversation.

"I don't need a guardian, Thomas." I shifted to swing my legs over the side of the chaise on which I'd been sleeping. Not sleeping, drugged. The piece of furniture was an odd feature in what I surmised was Mrs. Pratt's office. This was not a topic of conversation to have lying down and I felt at a complete disadvantage. I straightened my dress and tried to tidy myself, but there was not much I could do without a mirror and a comb. "If you feel the house is too crowded, I can certainly find a home of my own. I am not without means."

Our father had been the owner of a gold mine on the outskirts of

Virginia City and money had, for a time, poured in. With well placed investments, our family wanted for nothing. Every extravagance was brought in by railroad, even to such a remote and small town in Montana. This fortune had even helped fund Thomas's position in the town's government. His interest in politics, and a future in Washington, called for the well-placed spending of these funds.

"No. Your money is gone." He glanced down at the nails on one hand.

I stood at his words, stunned. The room spun for a moment and I grabbed hold of the chaise for support. The money was gone? The account was ample for anything I could ever need. "Gone? How?"

He shrugged negligibly, flicking his gaze to mine for the briefest of moments. "I took it."

"You can't take my money." My eyes widened, my stomach flipped, as much from the sour effects of the opiate laced drug as to my brother's words and banal tone.

"I can and I have. As your guardian, it is within my rights to manage your funds. The bank cannot stop me."

"Why?" I asked, incredulous. He knew I was not asking after the bank, but his claim on my inheritance.

Mrs. Pratt just stood and listened, her hands clasped together at her waist. It seemed I had no champion.

"You witnessed something you shouldn't have. I need you gone."

"Wit–" I shut my mouth after I realized his insinuation. I *had* seen something I shouldn't. The other morning, Mary and I had taken the children to school before joining the women's auxiliary to discuss the plans for the summer town picnic. One of the children had forgotten their lunch pail and I volunteered to return to the house and retrieve it while Mary continued on to the meeting. Tedious as those functions were, I was thankful for a reprieve from the matchmaking older women. At twenty-two, my unmarried state was their pet project. It was their goal to see me wed before my next birthday. I, on the other hand, was not in such a rush, especially based on the supercilious and unappealing men who were under consideration.

Instead of finding Cook in the kitchen, I found Clara, the upstairs maid, lying upon the kitchen table. Her gray uniform was bunched up about her waist, her white cotton drawers dangling from one ankle as Allen, Thomas's personal secretary, stood between her spread thighs. His pants had been open to expose his manhood, which he thrust into Clara with vigor. I remained quiet and hidden in the doorway, the couple unaware of my presence, and watched their carnal actions. I knew of what happened between a man and woman in general terms, but had never seen it firsthand, and nothing like this. Not on a kitchen table!

From what my mother had told me before she'd died it was done at night, in the dark, with only a minimal amount – and then only what was required – of skin exposed. By the intensity and vigor of Allen's motions, I thought Clara would complain or be in pain, but the look on her face, the way she tossed her head back and thrashed upon the wood surface had me thinking otherwise. He was pleasuring her. *She liked it!* Mother had said it was something to be endured, but Clara proved her statement false. The look of ecstasy upon her face could not be feigned.

I'd felt a tingling between my legs at the idea of a man filling me in such a way, making me lost to everything but what he was doing. When Clara ran her hand over her covered breasts, my nipples had tightened, ached to be touched. She hadn't just been enjoying Allen's attentions. The way she arched her back and screamed, she'd *loved* it. I wanted to feel as she did. I wanted to scream in pleasure. I was aroused by the idea of being handled thusly by a man. Unfamiliar wetness had seeped from my woman's core and I'd reached down to run my hand over the swollen flesh, even through the thick fabric of my dress. When I felt an unfamiliar jolt of pleasure from the motion, I removed my hand in stunned surprise. If my touch alone had felt so heavenly, what would it feel like being taken care of by a virile man?

Allen had thrust a few more times, and then stiffened, groaning as if injured. When he pulled his plum colored member, glistening and wet, from Clara's body, I saw not only her womanly folds, but copious white cream as well. He'd placed her feet on the very edge of the table so she was exposed and vulnerable, however the young woman didn't seem to care, either too well pleasured to bother with modesty, or she had none.

I'd licked my lips at the sight of her wantonness, her sated body replete and well used. *I* wanted to feel that way and I wanted a man to do it. Not Allen, but a man that would be mine.

My desire had been quickly doused when Thomas, previously hidden from view, came to take Allen's place between Clara's thighs. Leaning forward, he grabbed the front of her bodice and ripped, buttons skittering across the room. He lowered his head to her exposed nipples and suckled on one, then the other. I had no idea a man would do such a thing.

His hands had moved to the button on his pants and pulled his own member free. It was bigger than Allen's, longer, and wetness seeped from the tip. The secretary stood to the side, his pants set back to rights and watched, arms over his chest. Thomas lined himself up and shifted his hips so that he thrust deep into Clara's body. The woman's back arched off the table as Thomas filled her, her moan of pleasure filling the room.

I must have made a sound, a gasp, some noise that was different than the woman with whom he was fornicating because he turned his head and saw me peeking around the doorway. Instead of stopping, he pumped into her even harder, the woman's head thrashing about on the hard surface.

"Watch, I don't mind," Thomas told me, grinning, placing his palms on the table to go even deeper. "In fact, I might like knowing a virgin is learning something."

At his words I'd fled, the lunch pail forgotten.

That had been a few days ago and I'd barely seen Thomas since, out of sheer avoidance on my part. I didn't know what to say to him, nor how I could even look him in the eye knowing he not only took women with his secretary, but had broken his marriage vows. Did Mary know of his indiscretions, for I could only assume this wasn't his first. The duo seemed to be comfortable in their endeavors in a way that indicated long term familiarity. I'd readily distanced myself from Clara and Allen as well.

"I see you know to what I speak. I can't have you blathering about what you saw to the entire town. Besides, your voyeuristic tendencies are not normal for a woman of your station. I can't rightly marry you off to a friend of mine with such indecent proclivities."

2

MMA

He hissed the last words as if I was the one who'd been involved in those base sexual acts instead of him. I was being accused of indecent proclivities? He was the one who had careless disregard for his wife!

"Voyeurism? I wouldn't have watched if I'd known. It was the kitchen mid-morning. Thomas, I'd never–"

He sliced a hand through the air, cutting off my words. "It is irrelevant anyway. Having you about is not a risk I can take with my career. One utterance of impropriety and my chances for Washington are dashed."

"Men have mistresses, Thomas. It would come as no surprise," I countered. "Surely, Mary must know."

He laughed coldly. "Mary? I'm not worried about my *wife* and what she thinks. She would not speak ill of me. I am within my rights to ensure that."

I cringed at the thought of how he ensured her silence. Mary was a meek woman and I was coming to discover why. Mary had no grounds to protest or complain about a husband's peccadillo. A wife was completely at the mercy of her husband.

"Surely you're worried that Allen or Clara would tell tales as well." I wasn't the only one who could reveal his extramarital tendencies.

Thomas rolled his eyes. "Please, Clara was easily dispensable and Allen knows his place. He's just as driven as I am to be in Washington."

I could only imagine how he'd *dispensed* of Clara if turning me over to Mrs. Pratt was how he dealt with a member of his own family. I began to wring my hands. Thomas seemed as serious about this as everything else, removing any problem or impediment from his way with ruthless precision. It appeared he was taking care of me in just such a fashion.

I did not have to stay here and listen to him. I walked toward the door to leave, but he held up a hand. "You have no money, no connections. Only the clothes upon your back."

I shook my head in doubt. "This is insanity, Thomas!" I waved my hands in the air, frustrated. "I have friends, a sister-in-law, neighbors! I have Father's money! I can just walk out that door and see someone on the street I know and they will help me."

"Besides your lack of money, we're not in Helena."

My arms fell to my side. My stomach plummeted. "What? You can't. I'm of age."

"True, but your father's will stated I maintained control until you reach the age of twenty-five or upon your marriage. Since you have yet to wed, I can do what I wish with the money."

"You've turned all my suitors away!" I cried out, realizing right then and there his master plan. "You've planned this all."

He smiled, albeit coldly. "We are in Simms, in Mrs. Pratt's establishment. If you walk out that door, you will be on the streets of a strange town with no one to vouch for you, with no alternative but to return to her to survive. Besides, I doubt she would let you leave. Isn't that right, Mrs. Pratt?" He didn't wait for the woman to answer. "She has paid me a tidy sum for you and I have no doubt you will need to earn your keep on your back." He sniffed. "The way you seemed to enjoy Clara's sexual awakening, I trust this will be a perfect fit for you." He eyed me from head to toe, then turned his attention to Mrs. Pratt. "Thank you for your business."

"Mr. James," she replied with a small head nod, holding the door open for him. She was going to let him go?

Thomas left, his void as big as the emptiness of my emotions. I'd been sold to a brothel! The very idea was ludicrous, unimaginable, yet here I was. Tears filled my eyes.

"It's not all that bad, Miss James. You're no longer under that odious man's thumb." She pursed her lips as she shut the door behind him. It was as if life as I'd known it had ended, the door closed on it, a new one beginning. That was what was most fearful. What did my new life entail? Would I have to service men like Clara had Allen, or would I have to suffer beneath the cruel hands of a man such as Thomas? This was insanity!

I wiped frantically at my wet cheeks. "Little consolation," I replied, looking down at the decadent Oriental rug. "The alternative, the way Thomas painted it, is not appealing either."

"That man, your step-brother, *sold* you to me." She pointed toward the closed door. "He is not a man worthy of our attentions. I say good riddance." Her soft voice held a note of iron as she waved her hand through the air with finality.

"Then why did you accept his business? Why did you *buy* me?"

Her skirts swished as she crossed the room. "To make money, of course. Yet I have a soft spot for women whose lives have become endangered. Trust me, you are better off here with me than to linger another night beneath that man's roof."

I tilted up my chin, not as confident in my situation as she. "I suspect it is dependent on what you wish to do with me."

"You are a virgin," she stated.

I blushed furiously, my cheeks hot.

"Yes, I can see by your reaction to that word alone that you are," she replied, going over to her desk, sitting down at the chair beside it. Her back was straight and she adjusted her full skirts. She might be a Madame, but she had the mannerisms of a lady.

I looked down at the pale blue morning dress I'd donned just this morning. I thought back, realizing Thomas must have laced my coffee with the laudanum. I took it black, so the bitter taste would have been well masked. The last I remember was eating a piece of toast with marmalade in the dining room.

"I suppose virginity is quite a commodity in your line of work. You are a Madame, are you not?" I countered, wanting to confirm her profession. I doubted she arranged for governesses.

She nodded once. "I am. Unlike your Mr. James, I offer you two choices."

I arched a brow as I waited to hear them. My options, which I doubted were going to be to my liking, might be better heard sitting down, so I returned to the end of the velvet covered chaise on which I awoke.

"You may work here to pay off your debt. As you are innocent, you will be quite popular, I assure you. You are also quite lovely, which will make your long-term appeal guaranteed. This is the finest brothel between Kansas City and San Francisco and we cater to more *unusual* requests. The other girls will teach you all that you need to know above and beyond basic fucking with regards to meeting the men's needs."

My mouth fell open at her base language, but I supposed it was relevant to her profession and part of her everyday conversation.

I glanced down at my hands in my lap trying to collect my thoughts. A dull throb filled my head, the lingering after effects of Thomas's deviousness, it made clear thinking difficult. "And...the other choice?"

"You can pay off your debt in one evening. Tonight, in fact."

This sounded appealing, but I knew there would be a high personal price. She might be selling carnal pleasures, but this was all business.

"Oh?" I queried, very nervous about what she would say.

"A marriage auction."

I paused and stared at Mrs. Pratt. Did she say marriage and auction together? As in I would be auctioned off to a potential groom?

"I beg your pardon?" I replied, confused.

Mrs. Pratt smiled softly. "I know of several men who are seeking a wife who can handle their more intense sexual natures and dominant personalities."

I frowned. I most certainly couldn't meet those requirements. "As you've said yourself, I am a virgin. I don't know anything about...intense sexual natures."

"Good." She gave a decisive head nod. "I didn't say you needed to *know* anything about that, but that you could *handle* it."

I frowned. "There's a difference?"

"Vastly." I waited for her to clarify, but she remained silent.

"How are you so sure I can *handle* these...expectations?"

"From what Mr. James mentioned, you were aroused by the sight of a woman being fucked. Is this an accurate statement?"

I tried my best not to squirm. To admit I'd been aroused by witnessing Clara's pleasure would mean I was just like any of Mrs. Pratt's girls. It meant I truly was a voyeur, a whore even. Perhaps I did belong in a brothel.

"Well?" Mrs. Pratt asked.

"The woman was pleasured by both men. I had no idea such things were possible."

Her eyes widened slightly. "There were two men then? And you were aroused as you watched this? Interesting." When I remained silent, afraid to let any more secrets slip, she continued. "So you *were* aroused?" She'd twisted my words around to fit her needs. "Come, Miss James, there's no need to fear speaking your feelings with me. I am a Madame. I've seen and heard it all. Nothing you, a virgin, could admit would shock me."

I couldn't voice the words, but nodded.

"Did you like watching?"

I nodded again. "I liked seeing the first man and the woman. I could have done without watching my stepbrother engaged in such activities."

"Wished it had been you that was being fucked?"

I met her clear gaze. Held it. "Yes," I whispered.

She stood, the satin sheen of her dress catching the light. "What choice do you make? Work here or marry the highest bidder?" Her blue eyes watched me. Waited.

Her words made my life seem so negligible, as if the choice were easy. I'd only woken up to this situation only minutes ago, my head still pounded from the after effects. I was now to choose my fate? "I will not marry myself to a man such as Thomas." I clenched my hands in my lap. "A multitude of men using my body is nothing in comparison to a lifetime of dishonesty, indifference and infidelity. It would be a prison without any means of escape. You met him. To suggest a permanent arrangement with the likes of him would make you of the same ilk."

A hint of emotion shown in the woman's eye. Admiration? Surprise? I couldn't be sure. "I would never marry a woman to a man who was anything but generous and caring. I am stringent in the men to whom I serve, yet protective of the women I provide. Remember, being dominant in the bedroom is quite the opposite of being cruel."

I didn't know what she meant by the last. "Why marriage? Why not just sell my virginity?"

"You would gain nothing after the first man breaching your maidenhead. You would be tarnished and your value would be that of every other girl in my employ. You would then be unmarriageable and your fate sealed. Marriage will maintain your respectability. I don't stand for men who only take from women and give nothing in return. Or you may remain here and work to earn your keep."

I had no interest in becoming a prostitute, the idea made me want to vomit, but I could only accept the woman's reassurance that I would not be shackled to a man such as Thomas on blind faith. Her oddly placed values – the need to marry me off to make money all the while maintaining my virtue – was an odd twist on my scenario and painted her in a slightly different light.

"I can imagine the life of a wife readily enough. Perhaps you can describe my other choice."

Her lip quirked up at my request. "Most girls work from six at night until six in the morning, servicing as many as twenty men. You'll soon discover your best skills and be known for them. At first, of course, it will be your innocence, but once that fades, you'll have to decide." She shrugged negligently. "Some go for straight fucking, others are known for their cock sucking. A few enjoy being fucked in the ass. Then there's being tied up, role playing, ménage, the list is quite long really."

I held up my hand, not able to keep up with her long list of services. In fact, I was still considering twenty men a night. Clearly, she was forcing my hand toward marriage. That, most likely, was her intention all along, allowing me to believe I had a choice. Licking my lips, I asked the relevant question. "How much money did you pay Thomas for me?"

"Seven hundred dollars."

My brows went up. That amount of money was a drop in the bucket for the James family and I could have paid her readily enough after a quick trip to the bank, although not any longer.

"At less than a dollar a roll, that would be hundreds of men. You'll most assuredly be here for a lengthy duration. After that...." She shrugged her shoulders and let what she didn't say speak for itself. "Or you could be gone tonight."

I pursed my lips. She, in a perverse and roundabout sort of way, was helping me. She couldn't just let me leave; too much money was at stake. Marriage helped me while she helped herself. There really wasn't much choice. The groom himself wasn't a choice either. It seemed Mrs. Pratt would decide that, or at least narrow the choices to a small cadre of eligible men who had the means to offer her the money she wanted. Based on her profession and business sense, their initial requirements included baser sexual needs and wealth. "You can guarantee the man I marry is not a drunk, geriatric or a beater?"

Her blue eyes met mine. "I can."

"I'll...um...I'll take the marriage auction."

"A wise choice." She moved and opened the door. "As I said, these men want you to fulfill very distinct, very clear needs. Being dominant is not akin to being cruel. Remembering that will serve you well."

3

MMA

Hours later, I stood before a group of men in just my shift, the new one I'd purchased with such eagerness earlier in the week. Mrs. Pratt, while seemingly kind, felt it prudent to let the bidders see more of me than what my dress exposed. Now, I was berating the very feature I'd so admired, as the material was so fine as to be translucent. I couldn't look at any of the men, seeing the looks on their faces as they looked at my body as if inspecting a horse for purchase. I kept my focus lowered to the floor.

Looking down, it prompted me to what they could see of me. The color of my nipples was plainly visible, the tight tips poking out. My shift fell to the middle of my thighs and I was sure the dark color of the hair between my legs was clearly discernible. The fine embroidery detail along the hem only drew the men's eyes to the short length. It had been pleasurable to me to wear such decadence beneath my modest dresses, with secret knowledge of what was beneath, but to be exposed in such a way to a roomful of men was mortifying. Humiliating. Downright scary.

It was almost impossible not to cover myself with my arms, to tug on the hem with trembling fingers, but Mrs. Pratt had made it clear that my future husband wanted a good glimpse of what he would purchase. If this were the case, I should be naked, however I most certainly wasn't going to suggest such an idea. Fortunately, the small room wasn't overly bright, only lit by a few lamps, which cast a muted yellow glow. It wasn't cold, but goose flesh rose on my arms nonetheless. The slight odor of kerosene combined with tobacco filled the air.

And so I stood, hands by my side, fingertips rubbing together, eyes averted from all of the men as murmurs filled the air. Mrs. Pratt was the only other person in the room and I knew all eyes were on me, the men sitting in chairs in a semicircle around me. They could have any woman below stairs, so why me? Why an inexperienced virgin when a veritable courtesan could meet their every need without the burden of wedlock? Clearly, with that option available and not taken, these men were serious about their intentions. I'd briefly glimpsed four men as I entered, but refused to meet any of their eyes. It wasn't as if I was afraid I'd be an acquaintance of any of the men – the chances were remarkably slim being in Simms, and not Helena – but I didn't want to see their looks as they took in my *dishabillé*. I didn't want to see their expressions as they gazed upon me.

"She is a virgin?" a man asked to my right.

Mrs. Pratt, who stood behind me, spoke, her words clipped and surprisingly sharp. "Do not question the integrity of my auctions, Mr. Pierce."

The man made a sound in his throat of dissatisfaction, but did not reply.

"I want her naked," another man added.

"Emma," Mrs. Pratt addressed me instead of responding to the request. "What has a man seen of your body?"

I turned my head toward her voice, looked up at her through lowered lashes. "Ma'am?" I asked, my voice barely above a whisper.

"Has a man ever seen your ankles?"

I flushed hotly at the very idea. "No." I dropped my gaze and concentrated on the carpet beneath my feet.

"A wrist?"

I shook my head. "No."

"This is the first time a man has seen you in just a shift?"

Why did she have to point out the extent of my innocence? I took a deep breath to calm my racing heart. It felt as if it would beat right out of my chest. Licking my lips, I responded. "Yes, ma'am."

"Then, Mr. Rivers, to witness her reaction to being naked with a man will be saved solely for her husband. Bid the highest and that man will be you."

A voice spoke from my left. "She has been trained to meet her husband's needs?"

"Of course not, Mr. Potter. Her training is her husband's responsibility."

"And pleasure." This man's voice came from directly in front of me. It was deep in timbre, rough, yet assured. I saw only his feet and lower legs. Leather boots, black pants. I refused to look higher. Pleasure, he'd said? This man would find pleasure in training me to meet his needs? A vision of Clara, her legs spread wide and being pleasured by Allen, came to mind. Had the maid been doing what the man wanted?

"Precisely," Mrs. Pratt added, her words returning me to the present. "Shall we begin? The bidding starts at one thousand dollars."

The price made me gasp. That much? No wonder Mrs. Pratt wanted to sell me to the highest bidder. She easily recouped her losses and would make a tidy profit.

The price climbed readily enough. I didn't dare to look up and see who bid. The weight of the situation was not lost on me. These voices were of men who wanted to marry me. *Marry.* And they were willing to offer a small fortune to do so. There was no courtship, no dinners, walks, or chaperoned outings. No whispered confidences, flirty smiles, stolen kisses. The men were bidding on me because of my purity, my looks and Mrs. Pratt's assurance that I would meet their sexual needs. I ran my fingers over my shift at my sides as I continued to study the paisley pattern in the carpet, willing my breath to even. This was stripping my ideals of marrying for love and replacing them with something seedy, something tawdry.

"Sold!" Mrs. Pratt said with finality, making me jump. It was over? It had happened so quickly, perhaps only a minute or two, yet my life had changed irrevocably. I was too frightened to look up and see the man who'd bid the highest. In fact, I wasn't sure who had won. Seeing his face would make it all the more real. "Mr. Kane, Mr. Monroe, congratulations. Please follow me. The doctor and Justice Of The Peace are waiting in my office."

Did she mention two men? That couldn't be. The woman took my arm and led me from the room. As we walked down the hallway I noticed the man with the boots and dark pants following. He was Mr. Kane? He was to be my husband? When we turned a corner I observed a second man following a little further behind. It was all so overwhelming, confusing. Quick. It seemed we were to wed immediately. Mrs. Pratt was a shrewd businesswoman and most certainly didn't want any chance of this man, Mr. Kane, backing out of the arrangement. Most assuredly wedding vows would see to that.

The Justice Of The Peace was a short, rotund man with a thin mustache. He had more hair above his lip than on his head. Bible in hand, he stood at our appearance. So did the doctor, or so I assumed. He was tall and trim, lanky in build, yet attractive in his dark suit. I glanced past the man with dark pants and boots, afraid that if I looked at him, all this would become real. The man who followed moved to stand unassuming in the corner. His clothes were less formal; dark pants, white shirt. His hair was longer than *de rigeur* and his skin was tanned as if he spent ample time outdoors. The color of his hair reminded me of a wheat field, where the locks were lightened by the summer sun. With his piercing green eyes focused directly on me, I felt exposed, a reminder I wore solely my shift. It was as if he could see through the fabric to my untouched skin. When his gaze held mine, I felt he could see into me, to read my very thoughts. I couldn't help but cross my arms over my chest in an attempt at modesty.

I felt my cheeks heat, my nipples tighten at the knowledge he was looking me over. When I glimpsed, from my periphery, the corner of his mouth tilting up, I knew he would not be my savior in this farce of a marriage.

"Doctor Carmichael, we will start with your examination," Mrs. Pratt said, and my gaze darted to hers.

I froze in place. Examination? Here? With these men? Curling up my shoulders, I tried to shield myself as much as possible. The doctor took a step toward me and I jumped back.

"Wait," Mr. Kane interrupted, holding up his hand, halting the other man's steps. I recognized his voice from the auction. "Don't you want to see the man you're marrying?" The man's voice was deep and stern and I realized he was speaking to me. A British accent laced his words, the vowels short and clipped. What was an Englishman doing so far from home, and in a brothel and wedding a complete stranger? The way he'd ignored not only Mrs. Pratt but the doctor as well, was indicative of his power, which had me curious about the man and fearful at the same time.

I shut my eyes briefly and swallowed. I couldn't avoid him any longer. Turning, I looked forward, but only looked upon the buttons of his white shirt. Tilting my chin up, I took the first glimpse of my groom, and sucked in a breath. The first thing I observed was his eyes. Dark, so dark as to be black, with a strong brow. He looked upon me with such intensity, such possession, that it was hard to even glance away. His hair was equally dark, so black as almost to have a blue cast. It was close cut on the sides, longer on top to fall over his forehead. His nose was narrow, but had a slight crook in it, as if being broken at some point. His jaw was wide, angular with a hint of dark whiskers. His lips were full and the corner tipped up as if he knew I was impressed by what I saw.

He was handsome, so very handsome. And tall – well over six feet – and also quite large. His shoulders were wide and defined beneath his white shirt, his chest broad, tapering to a narrow waist. His legs were long and blatantly muscular, something I hadn't noticed in the other room. If he hadn't spoken, I would not have known he was a foreigner.

In comparison to his large size, I was small, dainty even. This man, *my groom,* could hurt me easily if that was his desire, however the smoldering look in his eyes told me he wanted to fulfill other desires. With me. I gulped.

"There now. I can see your face. For such dark hair, your eyes are a surprising blue."

His cultured voice, although rough and a deep baritone, had an undercurrent of something – tenderness, perhaps – which unexpected. His lip turned up at the corner and a dimple formed in his cheek.

"What is your name?" he queried.

"Emma. Emma James," I replied, his soft tone compelling it from me.

"I am Whitmore Kane, but everyone calls me Kane."

Kane. My groom's name was Kane and he was English. Would he take me off to England to live? The idea struck fear in me. I knew nothing about England, nothing about life outside of the Montana Territory.

"Ian," he said. The man in the corner stepped forward, pulled a folded stack of bills from his pants pocket, counted out an outlandish sum, then handed it to Mrs. Pratt. Was this man Kane's secretary just like Allen was for Thomas?

"We will not require the doctor's services," the man called Ian said to Mrs. Pratt once the transaction was complete. He was tall and broad as well, with light hair and serious eyes.

"You do not wish for me examine her to verify her virginity?" the doctor asked, as if I weren't even in the room. "It is a simple task. She will lie upon the chaise holding her knees up to her chest. I will put my fingers within to feel for the barrier. Surely you'll want proof after the tidy sum you've paid."

I blanched at the very idea the doctor presented. He wanted to touch me with three other men looking on, plus Mrs. Pratt? I took a step back and bumped into Ian. Thankfully, he was the one who'd said that unpleasant task was not necessary. Even so, I gasped at the contact and moved away. The room was too small!

"I assure you I can examine her myself," Kane countered.

The doctor did not look bothered by the response, only nodded his head in understanding. "Certainly."

"Let me get the door for ye, Doctor, so ye can be on yer way," Ian said congenially, his brogue thick.

Dr. Carmichael took a black satchel from Mrs. Pratt's desk and exited the door that Ian held open for him, then closed it firmly behind him.

I exhaled a pent up breath. Just having that man from the room eased some of my tension.

Mrs. Pratt turned to the Justice Of The Peace. "It appears we are ready for you, Mr. Molesly."

No, the tension had not diminished after all. I was going to marry a strange Englishman.

"After, I'd be happy to take you downstairs to avail yourself of one of my girls."

"Is Rachelle available?" he asked, his eyes bright with eagerness.

Mrs. Pratt nodded. "Most assuredly. She has been asking after you."

The man puffed up like a peacock at the flattering, yet most likely false, words. It did make the man eager to complete his task, however. It only led me to question to depth of his calling. He cleared his throat and began. "Dearly beloved...."

This morning I was an heiress eating her breakfast. And now, I stood in nothing but my shift and married a handsome stranger who had bought me at auction in the upstairs of a brothel.

4

MMA

"You wish to inspect your purchase now, I'm sure," Mrs. Pratt commented. She'd ushered the Justice Of The Peace downstairs and in the direction of Rachelle. He had no qualms about performing the unusual ceremony, a task he'd most likely done before; no doubt Rachelle's services were always complimentary after.

Ian moved to stand beside Kane. Both were tall, broad shouldered. I had no knowledge of their profession, but it was most certainly something that involved using their muscles as they were both well formed. Brawny, even. These were not typical gentlemen who sat idly. By their bearing, the intensity they exuded, they were powerful men. And one of them was my husband. The other, he looked upon me in the same possessive glint. I also found them both very handsome.

"I do," Kane replied.

My eyes widened and my mouth fell open, and I retreated, a hand out in a poor reflection of defense. "Surely you don't expect–"

Kane held up his own hand to halt my words. "Wedding me

undoubtedly prevented you from an unsavory situation in which you found yourself. I paid a hefty sum in doing so. Therefore, I have earned the right to inspect the merchandise."

Merchandise? My cheeks heated this time not from humiliation but indignation. "I am not some prized mare purchased for breeding."

Kane's dark brow arched. He pierced me with his equally dark eyes. "Aren't you?"

His words left me speechless and I turned away, not able to look at him.

"Here." Mrs. Pratt offered a glass jar to Ian. "This will ease the way."

"No need," Kane replied. "Her cunny will be wet when I check her."

Cunny? I'd never heard that term before, yet I knew it to be crude and an English euphemism for my woman's core. I pressed my legs together. He was going to stick his fingers in me. *There.* I had no idea what he was saying about being wet, but the man seemed confident.

"Nay worries, lass. Kane will have ye likin' it, to be sure. Leave us, please, Mrs. Pratt," Ian said. Not Kane, but Ian. He meant to remain within? Now? I swallowed down my fear of this dominant duo.

Us? I highly doubted I would like Kane to touch me as he planned. Handsome or not, I was wary, and rightly so. Today was too great a transition for me to be anything but.

Mrs. Pratt left readily enough; she'd made her money and was rid of me very tidily. With the vows said, not only legal but binding in God's eyes as well, Kane couldn't change his mind.

The three of us remained, the room less crowded, yet with Kane and Ian's large size, I felt overly small. Threatened, overpowered.

"You are displeased in your husband?" Kane asked, humor lacing his voice.

The tone had me spinning around to face him, but saw from his expression that was what he'd intended. He wanted me to look at him. At both of them.

"With what you intend to do, yes."

"We are your husbands. We *will* touch you."

My eyes widened and I stepped away, now truly fearful. "*We*? Both of you? I must have misheard."

Both men shook their heads. "You did not." Kane pointed to himself, then at Ian. "*We* are your husbands."

That was preposterous and I was sure the expression on my face showed that. "I can't have *two* husbands!"

"Ye are legally wed to Kane, lass, yet ye are mine as well. I am Ian Stewart." Ian's voice was deeper than Kane's, darker and had a stronger accent.

I shook my head, the tears I'd held at bay for so long now filled my eyes, spilled over to run down my cheeks. "Why? I don't understand."

"As you can tell by our accents, we are British."

"Speak for yerself," Ian muttered. "I'm a Scot."

"I...I don't want to live in England," I said, shaking my head vehemently as I did so.

"Neither do we. We might be from another country, but we are home here in the Montana Territory."

He didn't seem the type of man to deceive, so I felt a small kernel of hope that I would not be living in a foreign country. I was only *married* to foreigners. What an insane notion!

Kane crossed his arms over his broad chest. "We're army men. Our lives have been spent defending the realm for Queen and country. This included a stretch in the small middle eastern country of Mohamir which broadened our perspective on the treatment and ownership of women."

Mohamir? I'd never heard of it, however I was not familiar with the further reaches of geography. "Ownership?"

Ian casually tossed the jar from hand to hand as he would a snowball in winter. "A wife belongs to her husband, ye ken? He can do with her as he sees fit. Abuse her, beat her, treat her poorly. Nothing can stop him, neither law nor God can protect a woman from her husband."

I felt all color drain from my face and I stumbled back. These men were like Thomas. Mrs. Pratt promised I would not suffer the fate Ian detailed. He stepped forward and took my elbow, his grip surprisingly gentle considering his size, his grim words.

"Easy, lass," he murmured.

"Please...please don't hurt me," I whispered, my face turned away, flinching from whatever the man would do to me next. I couldn't survive two men abusing me.

Kane stepped closer and I lifted my hand to cover my face.

"Emma. Emma, lass, look at me." Ian's voice was insistent, yet his hold remained gentle. Turning my head ever so slightly, I glanced at him – them – through my lashes. Both observed me intently, their jaws clamped tightly, a cord in Ian's neck bulging.

"We will never beat ye. Never be cruel," Ian vowed. "We will value and respect ye in the ways of the East. Ye will be cherished and protected."

"By both of us," Kane added, his words solemn. "As our wife, you belong to us. It is our job to keep you safe, to see to your happiness, to your pleasure. Beginning now."

"By validating my virginity. You doubt me and Mrs. Pratt," I countered.

"You will find pleasure when I find that validation, I guarantee." Kane sighed, probably when he saw the skepticism on my face. "Mrs. Pratt would not have left the room if she acted falsely, but I will know the truth. We will not leave this place until I do so."

"Why?" I asked, confused. Why did he need confirmation? "We are married and there's no undoing the vows. I am your wife, virgin or not." I glanced at both men as I said the last.

"We must know if you are a virgin so when we take you the first time, we do it right."

Not knowing what he meant, I asked, "You won't take my word on the matter?"

"We don't know you," Kane countered. "And we will change that readily enough."

I retreated a step, looked up at the man to whom I now belonged, eyes wide with fear. "You...you would force me?"

Ian and Kane glanced at each other, speaking without words, it seemed. Ian looked at the glass jar in his hand, considered something, then placed it on the desk.

"I will say this again," Kane repeated. "I am your husband. Ian is your husband. You will do as we bid in all things, but I can assure you, as can Ian, there will be no need for force. You will be well satisfied before we are done."

So arrogant! "Oh? And why is that?"

"Because you will be wet and want our hands on you. I am going to sink my fingers into your cunny to find your maidenhead and you will want them there. Then I will give you your first pleasure. Are you wet now?"

"You keep talking about being wet." I furrowed my brow in confusion. "I...I don't know what you mean."

Instead of approaching me, he moved to the comfortable chair in the corner and sat down. He leaned back, his forearms resting casually on the padded arms, his legs wide and stretched out before him.

"Mrs. Pratt said you watched a couple fucking and this is why you are here." My eyes widened, but he continued. "Were they in bed?"

"No! You are insinuating I snuck in and hid."

"They let you watch then?" Ian asked, still standing beside me.

"No!" I repeated, becoming fretful at the two men hounding me with their words. "I returned to the house and found them...in the kitchen."

"Ah. Did you see his cock?"

I didn't know how to answer this. Of course I saw his cock. They'd been...fucking! Would it make me soiled goods if I said yes?

"Was he fucking her cunny? Her mouth? Her arse?" Kane wondered.

"Mr. Kane, please!" I cried, my cheeks heating. I covered them with my palms. How could they talk about this so readily?

"Was her cunny wet, lass?" Ian prodded.

"I don't know–"

"Betwixt her legs." He cut me off, his voice deep. "Was she wet betwixt her legs?"

"Yes," I replied, frustrated and unused to being verbally bullied.

"Right now, is your cunny wet like hers was?"

I took another step back and I bumped into the desk. Grabbing hold, I clenched the wooden edge behind me. It was steadying – something to hold onto while my world spun around me. The question was, would it ever right itself?

"Of course not."

"Then I will get you wet so my fingers can slide in easily," Kane replied confidently.

"Why is it so important, this...being wet?" I asked, waving my hand before me.

"It tells us you are aroused. It is a sign, an indication of what arouses you, even when you may tell us otherwise."

"What? No." When he didn't move, didn't say anything, I continued. "I didn't want this. I didn't ask to be here. Thomas drugged me and I woke up here, the only option was to work for Mrs. Pratt or to marry you. I didn't want to do either, nor marry either of you. *Both* of you. How can you expect me to be aroused when it was not my choice?"

"Who is Thomas?" Ian asked, his eyes narrowed.

"My step-brother."

"He's the one you saw fucking?" Kane asked.

I licked my lips. "I saw his secretary first with one of the maids, then when he was done, Thomas took his turn, but I was caught and fled before I witnessed much of that."

Ian nodded. "I ken now. Your step-brother dinna sound like an honorable man. There's nay wonder ye are wary of men."

"You may not want it – this marriage or anything we do to you – your mind may be telling you to resist out of how you perceive you should react, but your body will show us the truth," Kane said.

I was skeptical. Doubtful. Was this what he spoke of? How my mind was questioning him, but could my body go against my very wishes and act at his command? It was impossible, yet so was being married to two men. I could control myself. I crossed my arms firmly over my chest. "How?"

"I know you're afraid." He paused, watched me closely. When I took a deep breath and nodded, he continued. "Answer my questions.

I won't even touch you as I do so." He leaned forward, hands on knees and looked up at me, his dark gaze engaging.

"You won't touch me?" I repeated, wanting him to confirm what he said. It raised my hopes, but I let my pessimism show on my face, especially when I looked to Ian.

"Neither of us will. Yet," he clarified. "When your body is ready, then I will find your maidenhead."

I continued to eye him skeptically, doubting him as my body would never be ready, but he was so confident in this!

"Tell me, Emma, what did ye like about watching the couple fuck?" Ian asked. He moved to lean against the wall, ankles crossed, his stance relaxed. Positioned as he was by the door, there was no escape. "Nay your step-brother. The other."

I glanced at a letter opener on the table, my bare feet, the unlit fireplace, everywhere but at him. Them. My sensibilities were being tested.

"Answer me, please."

I couldn't avoid a response. It appeared he had a well of patience and would get what he wanted. They both did. As they said, I belonged to them. Oh dear lord, *them*! Kane's tone – the way he positioned himself across the room, the way Ian stood so casually – made them unthreatening, as if this was their intention. Even so, it was impossible to forget their purpose. This gentle approach was a plan to win me over, and it was only a matter of time before their real ways would come to light. This couldn't be as simple as just two men wanting me.

"I was returning for a child's lunch pail and at first didn't know what I was witnessing." When they quietly watched me with penetrating, dark gazes but did not respond, I continued. "It caught me by surprise. I never expected, never *knew*, this could occur in the kitchen."

"You didn't answer my question, but I'll let it pass. How was he fucking her?" Kane asked.

I closed my eyes briefly, completely unaccustomed to this line of query. "She was...on her back on the table. He held her ankles up and spread wide. His member–"

"Cock." I jumped when Ian said the word, interrupting me. "His cock. Say it, lass."

I licked my lips. "His...cock was big and hard and red and he was putting it in her, over and over."

"He was fucking her cunny with his cock." He said the words I couldn't.

I pushed a curl back from my face. "Yes."

"The woman was enjoying his attentions?"

I looked to Kane at his question, met his stare. "Yes. Yes, she was."

"Did you enjoy watching?"

I pushed off the edge of the desk, paced the small room, from the unlit fireplace to the bookshelf and back, steering clear of Ian. I couldn't tell them the truth. What would they think of me? I would be just like the girls below stairs if I admitted I'd felt...need course through me at their actions.

"Emma?"

"No. No, I didn't," I replied, averting my gaze.

"Emma." This time, when he said my name, it was laced with harshness, disappointment. "I will offer you this one opportunity to lie to me. In the future, if you lie, I promise you will not enjoy the consequences."

5

MMA

"How do you know I'm lying?" I waved my arms in the air. "Isn't it possible that I didn't like what I'd witnessed?"

"As I said before, your body doesn't lie. Look at your nipples, they're hard."

I glanced down. They were.

"Your eyes, they're not a pale blue now, but a deep, stormy gray. I'd say just thinking about what the secretary did to the woman has you aroused. Answer the question, Emma."

I spun around, faced Kane, narrowing my eyes. I didn't need to glance down at my breasts to know the tips were hard. I could feel them, painfully erect. I was not one to let my ire show – no lady of good breeding did – but I'd had quite the day and they'd pushed me too far. "Yes! I enjoyed it. I felt...something when I watched them." I tightened my hands into fists. "Now you know the truth, but it's too late." My breasts were rising and falling beneath my thin shift and the material chafed my sensitive nipples.

Kane only arched a brow at my heated response. Why did he have to be so calm? "Too late?"

"You're married to a woman who is just as her step-brother painted: a voyeur with the moral leanings of a prostitute. Why you would want me, both of you, is beyond me. There's no escaping marriage to me now." No doubt he could hear the bitterness in my tone.

My words did not have the effect I expected. Instead of anger, they were both amused. Kane smiled, broadly, showing off his straight, white teeth. He was even more handsome, and that irked me.

"That's true. You are mine." He still rested his forearms on his knees. "You are Ian's as well." He let those words settle for a moment, perhaps trying to ease my worries. It was not working.

"I will make this even easier for you. Answer yes or no to my questions, all right?"

I took a deep breath and stood before him, yet still too far away for him to reach. Either man could move quickly and grab me, hit me, hurt me, but they remained still. My heart pounded, my breathing deep from my outburst.

"Close your eyes. Go on, close them," Kane added when I didn't respond immediately.

The darkness was like a protective barrier, something I could hide behind. I didn't have to look at Kane or Ian, see their handsome faces, feel their scrutiny with my eyes closed. It was...easier.

"Good girl. Picture the couple. The secretary and the maid. Did your body warm watching them?" His voice slowed, went smoother.

"Yes."

"Did your nipples tighten?"

"Yes."

"Did you want the man to fuck you?" Ian asked, his voice coming from my side.

I pictured Allen and what I saw. *He* hadn't appealed to me, what he'd been doing had. I hadn't wanted him to fuck me, but a man of my own. "No."

33

"But you wanted to be fucked, to know what it felt like when his cock was buried deep. What the woman felt?"

I saw Clara's head tossed back, eyes closed, mouth open, back arched off the table. She'd been lost in her pleasure in that moment. "Yes."

I heard Kane stand, walk behind me. Circle me.

"Keep your eyes closed." His voice came from the right. "Your cunny – your pussy, that place between your thighs, does it ache at the idea of cock?"

It did. Oh, it did. "Yes."

I heard Ian move next, coming from my left to stand behind me. "I can see your nipples, all tight and erect." He was close enough to where I could feel his breath on my shoulder. "Do they need to be touched?"

My head fell back, as I became entranced by his deep voice. "Yes."

"Answer my question again, Emma. Are you wet?" Kane asked.

Now, I knew to what he spoke. That place at the juncture of my legs, my woman's place, was...wet. I could feel the hotness of it, the way my folds were swollen and coated in a slick essence brought about by the men's words, the mental pictures they'd elicited, their voices, their very presence.

I was surrounded. I felt the heat from their bodies, the way they took away all the air from the room. With my eyes closed, I didn't feel threatened – overwhelmed, assuredly – but protected instead.

It was dark with my lids closed, only a soft flickering of orange light seeped through. I could block out the world, everything that had happened to me, everything around me except Kane and Ian. Their words, their deep, almost hypnotic voices with the lovely accents. This was why I felt at liberty to answer, to respond to how they made me feel.

I heard Kane sink back into the chair in front of me. Waiting.

"Yes," I uttered.

"Open your eyes," Kane commanded.

My lashes fluttered open as I looked down at him first, then glanced over my shoulder at Ian whose gaze was dark and lust filled.

He was close, only a foot away, but he did not touch me. Neither had yet to touch me except for when Ian caught my stumble.

"Come here," Kane ordered. He gestured with his hand to the space before him, his knees wide, the fabric of his pants stretched taut and defined over his muscular thighs.

I approached him slowly and stood where he bid. He met my eyes, then his head lowered, taking in my breasts and tight nipples, the transparent shift, my bare thighs.

"Spread your legs."

I moved my left leg so my stance was wider, my thigh bumping against his knee, and waited. What did he intend? He still hadn't touched me in any way. My modesty was losing to curiosity. Neither had done anything for me to fear, so on bated breath, I waited.

Slowly, he lifted his right hand and slipped it between my legs, up beneath the short hem of my shift to touch me. *There.*

I startled at the contact. The one finger brushed over me in the lightest of touches, yet it felt like I was being branded, the heat that it wrought searing. I gasped and met his piercing, dark gaze, but didn't move, afraid that if I did he might stop. With a feather light touch, he slid over my folds, slowly, watching me. The corner of his mouth tipped up in something akin to triumph all the while learning my flesh.

"I haven't held your hand. I haven't kissed you. I like knowing that the first place I touch your body is your delectable cunny."

When his finger flicked over the place that throbbed, that had pulsed and come to life when I'd witnessed Clara and Allen, a moan slipped from my lips. Panic flared in my eyes at the illicit feelings, the way I found pleasure in a stranger's intimate touch. That barest of caresses felt so incredibly...amazing, that I feared it. Feared what he was doing to me. How could a man I didn't know bring about such carnal feelings with the barest of touches? It wasn't proper. It was wrong.

I started to step back, but just one word from his lips kept me still.

"No." Somehow, after only a few minutes, he was able to sense my emotions. "I will give you your pleasure. Do not fear it, or me." His jaw was tight, his gaze hooded as his fingers became bolder, parting my folds and running over the slippery, swollen flesh. Finding my virgin opening, he circled it, nudging in just a fraction and my body clenched down on it.

"She's so tight, Ian," he murmured.

I'd forgotten about the other man.

The finger dipped in even further, then slid back out to slide up my folds to the bundle of nerves. I exhaled harshly and placed my hands on Kane's solid shoulders for balance. My knees weakened and I needed to hold on to stay upright. Just the very tip of his finger on me had me off kilter. Even through the jacket of his suit, I could feel his warmth, the very strength of him.

When his finger moved back to my opening, another finger joined and two slipped inside. I shifted my hips and lifted up onto my toes at the onslaught. My tissues burned at the stretching and yet, it felt...exquisite. I could hear how wet I was, the sound of his fingers probing me filled the space between us.

"There." His eyes held mine. I couldn't look away. I felt the pressure and pain of his digits as they tried to push even further into me, but couldn't. I clenched his shoulders and winced. "I can feel her maidenhead."

"I...." I licked my lips. "I told you I was a virgin."

"Yes, yes you did. Now I have to decide what to do about it." He pulled his fingers completely from me and I was bereft, lost. Empty.

His fingers were glistening and slick with my wetness and I watched as Kane put them in his mouth and licked them. "So sweet. Like honey." His gaze heated, his skin flushing in what I recognized as desire. "Taste."

My eyes widened. "Your fingers?"

He shook his head. "No. Kiss me."

I leaned forward ever so slightly and Kane came the rest of the way so his mouth covered mine. It wasn't a tentative, chaste kiss, for his mouth opened over mine and his tongue delved deep. He tasted musky and sweet and deliciously male, perhaps a combination of my woman's essence and his own personal flavor. I sank into the kiss, I could do nothing but, for he was quite skilled at it. My body heated and softened, my skin warming and becoming sensitive to the cool air. Finally, after an interminable length of time, Kane sat back.

"Run your fingers over your pussy. Good girl. Now feed them to Ian. Let him taste you, too."

I pulled my hand from between my trembling thighs and looked at my coated fingers. My arousal was warm and slick. Ian took my hand in his and lifted it to his mouth, sucking on my wet digits. His pale eyes darkened as I felt him suck on the tips of my fingers. My mouth fell open as I watched him.

"Aye, like honey," he said when he lowered my hand back to my side. His voice was darker, more gravelly than before, his accent stronger. "Have you ever come before?"

I didn't know to what he spoke, but I had no doubt the answer was no, so I shook my head as I licked my lips.

"Then for being such a good girl, you will have a treat," Kane promised.

Both of his hands moved beneath my shift and over my cunny, or the other word he'd used, my pussy. Fingers dipped inside of me, just bumping into my maidenhead, while his other hand moved to circle and flick at the bundle of nerves that had my eyes slipping closed, my head falling back and mouth opening to let a moan of pleasure escape.

This was what Clara had been feeling: sheer, unadulterated bliss. Kane was masterfully working my body as a weapon against my strongest of mental defenses. One flick of a well skilled finger and my mind emptied of every reason why this was wrong.

This was something I couldn't control. In this moment, my body did not belong to me. It belonged to Kane.

I shook my head at that revelation. "No, please. I'm scared," I cried out, my hands pushing on his shoulders one moment, then gripping and clinging to him the next.

"There's nothing to fear, lass," Ian murmured from behind me.

"I've got you," Kane added. "You are safe and in this moment, your body belongs to me."

It was too much. The pleasure was building, growing. Kane was masterful in working my body. My skin was damp, my knees were weak, my nipples tight peaks. I felt engulfed in flames and with each stroke of Kane's fingers he threw more fuel on the fire, until....

"Come, Emma," Ian ordered. "Let us see your pleasure."

His commanding voice pushed me over some precipice and I was falling, falling into nothingness. The intensity of it all was so grand that I screamed and clawed at Kane's shoulders. With letting go, giving over to what he was doing to me, I'd found the most amazing pleasure I never knew was possible.

No wonder Clara had spread her legs. No wonder she let herself be taken on the kitchen table. With this one demonstration of Kane's power, I was addicted. I wanted more. I wanted it again. I *needed* what he'd just done to me. Again and again.

Kane's fingers continued to gently stroke and work my body until I'd taken a deep breath and opened my eyes. Kane watched me and the corner of his mouth turned up, dimple appearing. "Like that, did you?"

I almost purred like a cat and couldn't help but grin. "Oh, yes."

Pulling his hands free, he showed me the evidence of my desire, what I tasted even now on my tongue from our kiss. "You dripped all over my hands. You will always be wet for me."

6

ANE

The simple shift so seductively wrapping Emma's body was more alluring than any lacy garb worn by Mrs. Pratt's girls. If I hadn't just found the proof of her innocence, I would think her a temptress. Her coral nipples poked at the thin fabric, the soft swells of her breasts were plump above the plain edge. Her skin was pale and creamy, most assuredly silky to the touch.

"I want to see all of ye, lass. Let's take off your shift," Ian told her.

Her skin was damp and flushed with desire, her eyes cloudy with her first pleasure. There was no doubt that had been her first orgasm, for she'd been so quick to arouse, so fearful of the pleasure. And yet, when she came, she succumbed to it beautifully. Emma looked at me now with those bewitching blue eyes for a moment, a small frown marring her smooth skin.

"Show us what's ours, Emma."

But I hadn't touched. I hadn't touched her anywhere but her cunny and kissed her delectable mouth. Her skittishness endeared her to me and I felt a swift and ruthless wave of possessiveness at the very first glimpse. When I tasted her essence from her fingers, my cock pulsed against my pants because her scent, the taste of her cunny had me wanting to sink into her sweet depths. I knew Ian felt the same way, although neither of us had said as much.

Mrs. Pratt's auction was known to only a small group of men who traveled in similar circles as Ian and I. Landowners, ranchers, mine owners, railroad magnates whose actions were often outside the parameters of the law – men able to keep silent about their lives, about how they, or their fellow businessmen, acquired their wives. Ian and I had secrets – that's why we settled as far from England as possible and in such a remote a location.

All bidders were wealthy men who sought more than a quick fuck. Malcolm Pierce was looking for a bride to be his little girl, to dress her up and treat her as a child, yet fuck like a woman. Alfred Potter's mansion in Billings was filled with female servants who tended to more than just the house. Since he needed an heir, a bride was required, but she would be only one of several women who serviced him in his household. John Rivers liked doling out pain more than pleasure and his bride would need a strong constitution and a wild spirit.

We'd heard about the auction while playing cards downstairs as several of Mrs. Pratt's girls shared their attentions with Ian and me. It was Mrs. Pratt's invitation to claim a virgin bride that had piqued our interest, especially when we learned of the other bidders. An auction of this type was common in the Mohamir where we'd been stationed for several years – an auction for a woman trained from birth to please several husbands, to submit to them for their protection as well as their pleasure. Those women knew the men who would win them would treat them with honor. This auction could offer no such guarantee.

Our years abroad in the army reinforced the idea this antiquated approach was, for Ian and me, as well as a handful of other members of our regiment, the best option. Life as a soldier was short; having more than one husband offered protection and stability to the woman and their children. These unusual ways swayed us from following the strict Victorian dictates and morals of our country. But it was the actions of our superiors that had us leaving the ranks, abandoning our positions in the British army and escaping to the United States.

When I first laid eyes on Emma, I knew she was for us. The other men could find their own woman another time.

When she was too slow to comply to my command to remove her shift, Ian stepped forward, his fingers dipping to the hem of the barrier that prevented us from seeing her body. As his fingers slid the material up her thighs, she jerked in surprise, but held still.

Slowly, Ian lifted the material up to show off her shapely legs, the dark hair at the apex of her thighs that glistened with her desire, her narrow waist, flat belly, full breasts with large, tight nipples. The soft cotton caught on her hair and a long curl fell free as Ian tossed the shift onto the floor.

Seeing her naked, I knew we'd made the right choice. This was our first auction, and most definitely our last. Where Mrs. Pratt found her women to be sold off was not asked, but it was clear to both Ian and me that Emma was as innocent as could be. Seeing her dark hair, her creamy skin, the slightly hidden delights of her body, she was perfection. Seeing the fear and shame on her face had every protective and possessive instinct screaming to save her. The reason was clear, at least to me. She wasn't meant for the other men at the auction. This woman was ours. And so I bid, and bid well.

When the doctor had prepared to inspect Emma, to put his fingers in her cunny, I saw red. Ian would not have allowed another man to touch her either, especially now when every soft inch of her was visible. I knew Carmichael well. He was a skilled doctor who tended to patients all over the area, but he also enjoyed new flesh. That bent was fine for other women, but Emma's cunny was for Ian and me alone. I wanted our hands upon her to be the first. Her last. What we planned for her wasn't always gentle, wasn't tame or legal by society's standards, but we'd kill any man who touched our bride. A Mohamiran woman was never abused, never mistreated, only treasured. We would give Emma the same honor. She was scared of us now, but once she learned of our intentions, was trained to our ways, she'd see our devotion.

She stood naked within the circle of my legs. Her skin was unmarred and porcelain white and I itched to feel its silkiness. Her breasts were a handful, teardrop shaped with nipples I longed to suck and nip. But none of that was the prize. It was at the juncture of her thighs, hidden well in the dark curls. I could just make out the pink cunny lips, all swollen and slick from my touch. Her clit protruded, a hard, pink nub that was the epicenter of her desire.

Emma would be responsive; I had no doubt. She might have been skittish as we'd visually inspected her, then bid on her, but her passion couldn't be hidden. And once I'd won the bidding and she'd looked at me, I was certain. The way her eyes sparked with indignation, frustration and then ultimately desire – I hadn't been mistaken. Ian saw it, too. I recognized the need for her in his eyes, the tense jaw, the fisted hands, for all of his actions mirrored mine. I was the one who had legally wed her, but Ian would claim her in the most elemental of ways and Emma would never doubt his possession of her.

She would make the perfect wife, responsive and eager to please without even realizing. She just needed some guidance from her men. Since I showed her first pleasure, let her see how I controlled her body, it was time for her to tend to me. My cock was hard enough to pound nails in a fence post and my wife's first lesson would be how to slake my need. Ian would have his turn next.

"Have you ever touched a cock before?" Ian asked, his voice husky.

I undid my belt, the placket of my pants. Emma tilted her head and watched as I pulled my cock free. I couldn't help the sigh that escaped as it bobbed free from the tight confines of my pants.

"No," she whispered, eyes wide. "You...you're...you're so big." She darted a glance over her shoulder at Ian. He was still clothed, but the thick outline of his cock was evident beneath his pants and I knew by Emma's deep inhale that she hadn't missed it.

I smiled wickedly and met her gaze when she turned her head back. "The vows have been said, Emma. There's no need for flattery."

"That's supposed to...to go in me?" She looked at me with equal measures of surprise and concern.

"Will. It *will* go in you. Right now, in fact." Wrapping one hand around her waist, I pulled her forward as I leaned back, settled into the chair. She gasped as she lost her balance. "Sit astride me."

Placing her hand once again on my shoulder, she placed one knee on the outside of my thigh, then the other, her breasts directly in front of my face. I couldn't deny such a tempting offer and pulled one pink tip into my mouth. The tip was soft at first, but hardened quickly against my tongue. Her skin was warm, her taste sweet, her response a delight.

"Oh!" she cried as my hand on her waist held her in place, sucking and drawing on the hard tip. Her hands moved to my shoulders, her fingers digging into the tense muscles there.

Her skin smelled of flowers and arousal, a heady combination. At one extra strong suck, Emma's fingers slid upward to tangle in my hair, holding my head in place. Her breath escaped in little pants as I trailed kisses from one breast to the other, ensuring that each nipple received the same attentions. Her hips began to shift of their own volition and her knees squeezed against my sides.

"She's ready," Ian said gruffly. He looked at me from over Emma's shoulder just before he lowered his mouth to kiss and nibble at her neck.

I pulled away and saw that her nipples were wet and bright pink from my mouth. "Emma, look at me. Look at me when I make you mine."

My hand slid from her waist and down to the soft globe of her arse as I lined my cock up. My blunt head slipped through her drenched folds and settled at her virgin opening and I gritted my teeth at the scalding hot feel of her. Ian didn't stop running his hands over her body, his mouth on her heated skin.

Emma's eyes opened at the placement and looked at me, uncertainty flaring. "Kane, I don't think–"

"Don't think, love. Feel. Feel Ian's mouth on your skin, feel his hands run over your body, cup your breasts."

Her eyes slipped closed as she did just that. "You're too big. You won't fit. And Ian's watching!"

I pushed her down onto my cock as I thrust my hips up, filling her only with the head, her maidenhead blocking further penetration. Her eyes widened at the feel of being stretched wide.

"I'll fit, and Ian will claim you next."

Ian's hands came around to cup her breasts, to pinch her nipples.

She shook her head and frantically pushed up with her knees, fighting me. "No! It's too much."

Her squirming wasn't going to have me pull out. In fact, quite the opposite. Her writhing had her inner walls clenching and squeezing down on the tip of my cock, driving me insane.

"Stop," Ian commanded. Realizing she was panicking, he spanked her arse, her skin quivering beneath his palm.

She froze in place and cried out. Stunned. "He spanked me!"

"He bloody well did, and he will do it again if you continue to resist. Oh, you liked it. Ian, she's dripping onto my lap."

"No, I don't like it!" she cried out, but her juices dripping onto my cock said otherwise.

Ian gave her another mild spank. "Do not lie, lass."

Her inner walls clenched down on the head of my cock. I gritted my teeth. "You are not in control here. We are. I assure you my cock will fit and your body is most assuredly wet and ready. It is your maidenhead that is blocking the way. I will solve that problem right now."

"But–"

Before she could protest anymore, I pressed her down with both hands on her arse, thrusting up, deliberately hard, claiming her. She was more fearful of the idea than the act itself, therefore I resolved the problem at hand. I breached her maidenhead with that one thrust and my cock pushed through from just the entrance all the way in to the hilt. She cried out and stiffened, her face contorting in pain, her eyes as wide as saucers at being stuffed so completely. She held still, but her fingers dug little furrows into my shoulders.

The feel of being embedded within her hot cunny was so incredible that I groaned. Her walls milked my cock, the wetness almost scalding. I could feel the entrance to her womb nudging against my wide head. I was so deep and she was so tight.

"I fit," I hissed.

Swallowing visibly, she replied, "Yes. Yes, you do. Is that it? Are you done?" She was panting, as if afraid to breathe too deeply.

"Done?" Ian asked, his hands soothing her as if she were a skittish mare. "You're just getting started, lass."

I grinned at her naïveté. "Now you ride me."

"Ride you? But it hurt." She pouted, clearly afraid to move.

With my palms, I guided her, showing her how. With each slick slide of my cock against her cunny walls, I was close to coming. There was nothing to prevent my balls from tightening, my cock thickening and swelling within her. This would be a fast fuck; she'd tempted me too much.

"Oh," she gasped, the sound escaping was of pleasure, no longer pain.

"Only pleasure now, Emma," Ian promised.

"She's so tight," I murmured, my teeth clenching.

She was a quick learner, shifting her hips and lifting up and down on her knees to ride my cock. I was her stallion and she was the timid mare. As she found her rhythm, I moved my hands to her breasts, cupping them, feeling their weight as I plucked and tugged on the hard-tipped nipples. Ian knelt down behind her and reached around between her spread thighs to touch her clit.

"Kane, I...oh my," she sighed, her head falling back. Her hair was a wild tangle down her back.

"See, lass, no more pain. Only pleasure," Ian reiterated as he worked her hard, little nub.

"Come again, baby. Come on my cock."

She was a natural at taking orders when her mind was distracted, for she came on command, her cunny walls milking me, strangling my cock in its pulsating grip. I came too, my hips driving up into her hard as my cock spurted thick ropes from my body, filling her with my seed.

The fit was so tight that as she shifted, my cum dripped out, coating her thighs along with her virgin's blood. She slumped down upon me, a warm weight upon my chest. She was a lusty one, easily to orgasm and most certainly claimed. I glanced up at Ian, his need to fuck Emma evident in every line of his body. He nodded his head in silent agreement. She was ours, and his turn was next.

7

AN

The sun was shining when Emma finally stirred. She was on her side, her back curled up against my front. She made a sound in her throat and stretched before stiffening, remembering that she was not alone. I'd enjoyed the past few minutes just staring at her, amazed she was mine – mine and Kane's.

After Kane claimed her the night before, we bundled Emma into a long dressing gown supplied by Mrs. Pratt and slipped into the back entrance of the hotel. Neither Kane nor I had had any intention of spending the night in the brothel, no matter how easy it would have been to find an empty room and fuck our bride all night long. Instead, I'd carried her to my hotel room, sight unseen. We hadn't anticipated a bride when we'd taken the trip into town and Kane's room was down the hall. Since he'd claimed her first, she'd been mine for the night. Sharing wasn't an option at the hotel. We ken our marital ways to be honorable, but the people of Simms would not agree. Once on the ranch, however, the two husbands to one bride dynamic would not be hidden.

I'd stripped Emma, who was too tired to put up much of a fight, and helped her beneath the covers before she fell directly asleep. We didna ken her life story prior to the auction other than that of a bastard step-brother, but whatever her day had been like, it had exhausted her. Or perhaps it had been her initiation into fucking that had tired her so. I spent a long night with my cock hard and throbbing, waiting to claim her for myself.

"Good morning, wife," I murmured in her ear. I saw goose flesh rise on her arm above the sheet as my breath fanned over her nape. I smiled into her soft, heated skin.

Once we'd heard of the auction, our sole goal had been to recognize whether the woman up for bid was in danger of the other men, or if it was all an act. One look at her and we'd both known. She'd needed our help. She couldna have not fall into the clutches of the others. She would be ours.

It had been very late when Kane finally fucked her and I'd watched as he took her virginity. The look on her face when she'd been breached by Kane's cock would be something I remembered forever – the look of surprise, a hint of pain and the instant knowledge that she'd been claimed. When she came riding him, her head thrown back, her dark hair spilling down her back, breasts thrust forward, she was the most beautiful thing I'd ever seen.

As I watched her sleep during the night, I considered her safety. It reassured me to ken that Kane would be there for her if the bastard Evers tracked me. We'd crossed an ocean and a continent to avoid the man and the crimes he'd pinned on me years ago. The others in the regiment who'd joined us here in the Montana Territory also had sullied reputations and lost rank, but they weren't wanted as I was. I kent, deep down I kent, Evers would find me. He'd find me and drag me back for trial. There was no question it would be soon. Finding a wife and settling into the happiness I knew would follow, was a luxury Evers would find a way to take from me. And so, my time with her was most assuredly short, and I was reassured to ken that Emma would be safe with Kane.

Many women had come before, for Kane and me, but there was no question Emma was different. Not only did she arouse every sexual need to a point where my balls ached with impatience to have her, but every protective, possessive desire as well. She wasn't a woman to fuck and leave. She was a woman to cherish, to protect, to possess, to dominate. I ran my fingers over her dark curls, silky soft. She was so very dainty. Sweet. Sexy as hell. Fucking her wouldn't be enough. We'd spend time training her to meet our every need, and her every pleasure. This is what husbands did for their wife. It was our job, our responsibility.

She began to stir, and twas time to make her mine. Finally! Later, the training would begin. My cock throbbed against the curve of her arse. When she stiffened in my arms, recognizing she was most certainly not alone and definitely naked, I shifted so that she lay beneath me, her soft breasts pillowing against my chest, her nipples hardening at the contact. I nudged one of my legs between hers and I felt the heat of her cunny against my thigh.

"Oh," she gasped in surprise. Her hands came up to push against my chest. She was so lovely when she awoke, her dark hair spread over the pillow, her pale eyes soft and sleepy.

"Expecting Kane?"

She nodded warily, licked her lips. I bit back a groan at the idea of what that little pink tongue could do.

"Dinna fear any jealousy or Kane's ire. Ye are my wife just as ye are his and he expects ye to be well fucked when we board the stage. By me."

Her eyes widened at my words. I wasn't going to soften them because of her innocence. I would speak and act as I planned to proceed. I would be gentle, however she would know my dominance. Shifting my hips, I nudged my cock against her inner thigh. The skin there was so satiny soft it made my cock pulse.

"We must rise for the stage, but first, I will fuck you, make you mine just as much as Kane's." My voice was deep with desire. "Every morning while ye are still abed, Emma, ye will be fucked either by me or Kane, or both of us together. Trust me in saying that ye will be quite eager for this soon enough as are we. For now, let me get ye ready." I nudged her legs wider and reached between to test her readiness. She gasped in surprise and pushed at me, trying to lift me off. She'd ridden Kane when he took her. This was the first time she was beneath a man. I'd need to take it slow, to wake her body to desire just like she awoke from sleep. When I found her clit, her reticence slipped away, just as her hands dropped to her sides.

Propping myself up onto one arm, I leaned down and kissed her, brushing my lips across her softness, then slipped my tongue in to touch hers. I played with her slick cunny, brushed over her clit all the while I kissed her. Slowly. Leisurely. I felt every tense line of her body soften, felt her skin heat beneath my touch. I brushed her hair off her face then kissed my way across her jaw to her ear, licked the dainty swirl.

"Mmm," I whispered, my cock hardening painfully as I found her dripping wet. Her heat practically scorched my fingers. "You're slick with Kane's seed. I love to ken your cunny's filled like this. It is my turn to add to it. I have been waiting all night to make you mine."

"Why...." She cleared her throat. "Why didn't you do it last night?" she whispered, tilting her head to the side to give me better access to nuzzle at the frantic pulse beating at her neck. Her scent was so sweet. Tempting. Her hands gripped tightly on my biceps. "Ye were asleep, Emma. I want ye wide awake when we fuck." I moved between her thighs, spread her wide with my palms. "When ye call out my name. Kane may have taken yer virginity, but ye are mine, too."

I looked down her body, noticed her tight nipples and had to taste them. I laved a turgid tip then took it fully into my mouth as I slowly, gently even, slipped a finger deep inside her.

"Ian!" she cried and I relished in hearing my name from her lips, especially in such an aroused tone. I shifted from one breast to the other, the rasp of my beard leaving a hint of red skin in its wake. Her skin was so delicate, almost tender, yet I wanted to fuck her hard. My cock ached to sink into her delicious heat. The way her inner walls were clenching down on my finger, I knew she'd be tight and perfect around my cock.

Her hips began to shift, her skin flushed and dewy, the wetness copious on her thighs. She was ready.

Lifting my head, I looked down into her eyes and saw only pleasure there. No fear, no pain, nothing but need. Lowering my head, I kissed her as I aligned my cock up to nudge at her tight entrance and slid into her in one deep stroke. I swallowed the moan that escaped her lips. She was so tight, her body clamping down on me like a vice, rippling around me. Her hands gripped my back, her nails digging in as I began to move. Neither of us could kiss any longer, focused solely on how we were connected, the way it felt. I grabbed her arse, tilted her up so I penetrated her even deeper. Completely.

Her back arched, her head tilting back as I took her. Her breath escaped in little pants, her eyes closed.

"Look at me, lass."

Her blue eyes fluttered open as I continued to thrust into her. Her hands were once again on my chest trying to push me away. Pull me in. She couldn't decide.

"This isn't right," she moaned, a little frown forming on her brow, confusion warring with the pleasure on her face.

"What?" I rasped.

"This. You. Kane." She exhaled each time I filled her.

"You're going to come, baby. I can feel your walls squeezing me. What shame is there in your pleasure when it is your husbands that give it to you?" Sweat beaded my brow as I held off coming until Emma did. She was close, right on the edge, but she was thinking too much.

"I can't want two men. It makes me...it makes me a harlot."

I grinned at her words. She wanted both of us and that pleased me immensely. My orgasm built at the base of my spine and into my balls. My seed all but boiled and was ready to escape. Not being able to wait any longer, I moved my hand between us so I could rub my thumb over her little distended nub. Breaking her of her inhibitions, her doubts of having two husbands, was not something that I could resolve now. But I could pleasure her, let her see how good it was, not only with Kane, but with me as well. She would ken we were both well satisfied with her, and she in return. So I worked her clit faster as

I filled her over and over. A drop of sweat dripped from my brow and onto an upturned breast.

"No, not a harlot. It makes you our wife," I all but growled as she came. I had to cover her mouth with mine once again to stifle her scream. I wanted to keep her pleasure just for me, like a secret gift I would not share with anyone, most especially the other hotel guests along the hall. She might be modest and uncomfortable in her passion, but when she let go of her inhibitions, she was incredible. So responsive, so sensitive. My own orgasm could not be held back any longer and my seed joined Kane's. My base instinct to claim, to mark, to fill was complete.

8

$\mathcal{I}$AN

"How were you able to claim the coach just for us?" Emma asked, her body shifting and swaying with the poorly sprung motions of the stagecoach. She sat across from both of us, her posture erect, her hands clasped primly in her lap. She hadn't been prim an hour ago. The only outward indication that she'd been recently fucked was a slight flush to her cheeks.

"Money," I replied. The leather flaps were open on only a few of the windows to minimize dust and the interior was warm. The three of us were alone, a large purse to the driver ensured we had privacy for the duration of our journey, not that there was much room for other passengers.

Emma wore a blue silk dress, the bodice low cut enough that the swells of her breasts were plump and full above the lace trimmed edge. The sleeves were long, the waist trim. The fabric and color were decadent and impractical for travel, but certainly showcased our wife's eyes and other attributes. Mrs. Pratt had done as requested and delivered something to wear to the hotel, but it was not the least bit serviceable. When Emma had questioned what had happened to her very serviceable dress she'd been wearing upon her arrival at the brothel, Mrs. Pratt only replied that the alternate dress might please Kane and me more. It certainly kept us focused on her assets. The appreciative look from the coach driver hadn't been missed by me or Kane. We were not the only ones that found Emma beautiful.

"Where is it we are headed?" she asked, her gaze turned towards the window.

"Travis Point," Kane told her. "From there, we will ride the rest of the way to Bridgewater, our ranch, by horse. We have a few hours to fill and there are many very pleasant ways to pass the time."

She sat directly across from me, our knees bumping on occasion. "Pleasant ways? You mean what we did last night?" Her gaze shifted to meet Kane's, then mine. "Or what we did earlier?"

The sun shifted and filled the stage, Emma's body swathed in a stripe of bright sunshine. She was so lovely, so endearing when she looked at us with such questioning glances. Knowing we'd saved her from a less appealing fate made her innocence even more precious.

"There is so much more, lass. Undo the buttons on your dress and show us your beautiful breasts," I commanded.

Her plump lower lip fell open as she looked around. "Here? Now?"

"We are quite alone for the moment and I wish to see your beautiful breasts. Kane?"

"Yes. Your breasts are lovely and shouldn't be hidden from us."

"But–"

"Do not question us, baby. It will please us to see you so," Kane countered, the tone of his voice shifted to commanding. If we wished to see her breasts, we would not be deterred.

She must have heard the sharp bite in his voice because her fingers went up to undo the tiny buttons that ran down the length of her bodice. Slowly, the two sides flapped open, revealing her white corset. I had ensured the fit was quite snug when I dressed her, pulling the laces tight, so I knew her nipples were just below the edge. In fact, I could see the upper curve of one pink tip peeking out above the top.

"Lift your breasts out," I told her. She belonged to both of us – in all things – and the quicker she acclimated to having two men to please, the better. Two men to please, two men to obey. The ranch was a rugged place, where dangers abounded. The land was harsh and rugged. *We* were rugged. She would obey us in the bedroom for her pleasure and outside of it to keep her safe.

As she held my gaze, she tugged the front of the corset down to sit at the bottom curve of her breasts. Cupping herself, she adjusted her soft flesh until it was fully exposed. With the tight corset beneath, her creamy globes were lifted high and thrust out, the soft pink tips plump and pointing straight towards us. I kent how they tasted, how they felt against my tongue. My mouth watered to suckle at them again, but I wanted something else from her first.

"On your knees, lass." I gestured with my chin to the floor between my wide stretched legs.

"Ian," she countered, her eyes flitting left and right, but I arched a brow.

"I can spank you for your disobeying Ian, but you will still end up on your knees before him," Kane said.

Her eyes flared in surprise at his words. "Disobey? You mean–"

"Yes, we would spank you," Kane reiterated.

Licking her lips, she slid off the bench seat, knelt on the wooden floor, and placed her small hands on my thighs. She swayed with the motion of the stage, her face upturned to look at me with sweet innocence. In this position, she was a sight to behold.

Lowering my head, I kissed her, but only chastely and briefly. I wanted to deepen the kiss, but she had a lesson in cock sucking and I didn't want to divert from that. I didn't want anything to delay her hot little mouth around my cock. Her skin was flushed, her breasts were out and on delightful display, her eyes innocent as to what was to come. I loved her submissive placement between my legs, her mouth only inches from my from my–

"Take out my cock." My words were deep, my need obvious not only in my voice but in the thick length pressed against my pants.

With small, fumbling fingers, Emma undid the placket on my pants and pulled me out. I was incredibly hard, the tip oozing clear liquid in a steady stream. I'd fucked her only an hour before, yet I was ready for her again. What man could resist a wife on her knees before him?

"First lesson, lass, is sucking cock."

Her eyes flared as she understood my cruder terminology. "How?"

"Lick the tip. See how it's dripping for you? Clean it off."

She did. Her dainty little tongue lapped at it, swirling around the plum shaped head. My breath hissed out through clenched teeth at the hot lick.

"How do I taste?"

I watched her throat work as she swallowed. "Salty."

"Good girl. Now take it all the way into your mouth."

As instructed, she engulfed me in her hot warmth as far as she could go, which was not all that far, only half of me filled her. Her eyes widened and she coughed, pulling back. "You're too big!" she gasped, her eyes watering.

"Ye will ken soon enough, lass. Ye are doing fine. For now, take me as far as ye can go."

She did, licking and sucking with a sweet innocence that had my hips coming off the seat. "Grab hold of the base." I ground my teeth together as her grip tightened around me. "Good," I growled. "Now fuck my cock with your mouth."

Lowering her head, she took me into her mouth as far as she could comfortably go then pulled back, over and over. Her mouth was so wet and so hot that she all but seared my flesh. She was so earnest, so eager to comply with my instruction that my balls tightened, my orgasm close.

"Her mouth is as tight and perfect as her cunny," I told Kane, savoring the tight suction. I wouldn't last long, the need to come so intense.

"She's being a very good girl," Kane praised as he watched Emma take my cock. His big hand ran over her head, stroked her silky hair in reassurance.

I closed my eyes and gave in to the pleasure of her tentative tongue, the hot licks, the sweet sucking until I was almost there. "I'm going to come in your mouth, lass. Ye need to take it all. Our seed belongs in ye. Your cunny, your mouth, your ass. Swallow it all down."

My hips thrust up to join with the ministrations of her mouth and culminated in the most intense release that I groaned, my fingers gripping the hard bench seat, as my seed shot into the back of Emma's throat. Pulse after pulse, I throbbed against her tongue. She was sucking me dry all the while trying to swallow my seed. All she accomplished with her unskilled actions was choking on the copious seed before backing off my cock, the final white ropes of my cum spurting onto her upturned breasts. My release was explosive and did not seem to end. Some thick cream dripped down her chin and one large glob landed on her plump nipple. The erotic sight of her being marked in such a way prevented my cock from softening.

She'd done an impressive, albeit sloppy job. I came quickly and reveled in her first mouth fucking, my body sated. I had to catch my breath, for she had the ability to render my body useless until I could recover.

Even though she did beautifully, there was a lesson here for Emma to learn and I couldna veer from teaching her what we expected of her just because of her eagerness to please. However, I was too replete to do anything, the haze of lust and release overwhelming. My cock rested half erect against my open pants, wet and shiny from Emma's mouth. My shoulders slid across the seat back with the sway of the coach. Fortunately, Kane recognized my state and took over.

He shook his head in disappointment.

She glanced up at him through her lashes as she lifted her hand to wipe her chin.

"Don't," he told her. He leaned forward and ran his finger over the cooling seed and fed it to her. "Lick." Her lips closed over his finger and she sucked it as if it were a cock. "You disobeyed, Emma."

He pushed a second finger in her mouth to join the first, sliding the digits in and out like I did my cock. Slowly, he worked the fingers further and further back until met with her instinctive reaction to choke. Pressing down on her tongue, he held his fingers in place. "You must adjust to taking a cock. All the way."

Her hands wrapped around his wrist as her eyes widened in panic. She was breathing, air going in and out quickly through her nose, but she fought him and the innate reaction for something to be so deep in her mouth.

"Shh. Settle," Kane murmured, his tone calming her. After only a few seconds, he pulled back, slipped his fingers from her mouth.

"You didn't swallow his seed, baby." He glanced down at her exposed breasts and the viscous cream spread in random pulses across her pale flesh. I liked seeing my seed mark her this way, a stain of possession.

Emma lowered her head to see for herself. "I'm sorry, Kane, Ian, but it was too much. It...it surprised me."

She was correct; my seed had been plentiful. Her lush mouth had pulled it all from me.

"It is your job to do our bidding and you did not."

Her brow furrowed. "I had no idea it would be so...copious. I now know what to expect, therefore I will do better next time."

Kane stroked her hair again and she tilted her head into the caress, clearly savoring, and even craving, the affection. "Of course you will, but you must be punished."

She sat back on her heels, a frown marring her brow. "Punished? Why?"

"Because you did not swallow Ian's seed."

"But–"

He held up his hand and she quieted. Pulling a handkerchief from the pocket of his suit jacket, Kane wiped at her breasts, smearing away all traces of my emissions.

"Over my lap, please."

9

AN

She shook her head. "Kane, no. I will be good."

"You were a very good girl, sucking his cock, but we do not take disobedience lightly. We will no longer be in a large town but on a ranch where it is wild and untamed. Following rules can save your life, therefore we must know that you will obey us in all things. It is our job to keep you safe, but your job to listen so we may do so. Now, over my knees." He deepened his voice and hardened his gaze.

She glanced at me, perhaps seeking a pardon.

"Your delay has added five additional strikes of Kane's palm," I told her. "Would ye like to delay longer and make it ten?"

She scurried to obey, realizing the consequence was growing. When she positioned herself correctly, her belly pressing into Kane's thighs, her feet just touched the floor of the stage on one side, her hair a curtain about her head on the other. I could see her breasts pointing downwards, the nipples tight and furled. I had to shift my legs out of the way to make room for hers. Lifting her dress, Kane tugged it up to bunch around her waist. Her legs were covered in stockings with pale blue ribbons securing them on her thighs. Her drawers, however, were a hindrance.

Using both hands, Kane ripped the delicate material exposing the pale globes of her arse. He'd strategically placed her so I could get a good glimpse. He let the torn material fall to the wooden floor below her head so she could look at them. "No more drawers, baby. Your cunny must be available to us at all times. Spread your legs, please."

She shook her head in defiance.

Kane spanked her, his palm landing in a firm strike against her left cheek.

"Kane!"

She jolted and cried out more in surprise than in pain. The strike hadn't been overly hard; it was more of a warning and introduction than true punishment.

Quickly realizing Kane was very serious, she widened her legs and I could see her cunny clearly as Kane began to spank her. Even though I'd just come, my cock hardened at the sweet sight, her lips there red and swollen from being fucked twice. "Count, please."

Each strike landed someplace new on her untried bottom, the skin turning a light pink, yet quickly turning darker as she counted. It was the most arousing of sights. When she called out the tenth strike, she was crying, yet the fight had left her. Instead of kicking out and wiggling her hips, she'd given up and took her punishment, her body lax. Kane's strikes weren't overly hard, but solely for her to learn the consequences of her actions. She would be turned over a knee as needed, especially if she did something that would put her safety in jeopardy.

Seeing her accept the error of her ways was a sweet sight. Her submission was beautiful and I was very pleased. Kane, no doubt, was as well.

"Fifteen," she sobbed.

Gently, Kane caressed her hot flesh, soothing her with words. "You did beautifully, sweetheart, taking your punishment like a good girl."

Once she settled, her breaths coming evenly and slowly, Kane helped her up and onto the bench seat across from us once again, brushing the hair back from her face and kissing her brow gently. It was a mild spanking and she would quickly recover, however the hard seat and the bumpy ride would keep her mind on her transgression.

"Put yer feet up on our knees," I said.

She frowned at me in confusion, so I patted the bend in my leg where I intended. "Give me your foot." I held out my hands, palms up.

She lifted her foot and I placed it against the front of my knee. Once she saw what I expected, she placed the other one in Kane's hand and he placed it against his own knee. This position had her sitting lower on the bench so her arse was off the edge, keeping the brunt of her weight off her sore flesh.

"There. That's better, isn't it? Your arse will be sore for a little while, but sitting this way should ease your discomfort," I said, stroking my hand up and down her stocking covered calf.

It was also an unladylike position, her shoulders slumped, her legs wide, her breasts uncovered and thrust out. My smeared seed had dried upon them leaving a dappled haze on her creamy skin. Emma was most certainly a lady, but neither Kane nor I were gentleman, at least not when we were alone with her. "Pull your skirt up. Show me my cunny, or as ye say here in America, pussy."

When she didn't comply to my request, I arched my brow. Her eyes lowered and she complied, although her dislike of the action was obvious. Slowly, her fingers pulled the blue silk up higher and higher so it pooled at her waist. I moved my knee wider, which opened her legs further. We had the perfect vantage of her body.

"You are so beautiful, Emma. Every inch of you." I couldn't help but stare at her delectable cunny and the way the tops of her creamy thighs were at full advantage above the edge of her stockings.

Her cheeks heated and her hands gripped the edge of her seat, her knuckles white.

"Ye dinna ken so?" I asked.

She looked shocked by my question. "My breasts are exposed and my legs are apart and you can see...everything!"

Both of us grinned.

"Your body belongs to us and we will look at it as we wish. Your cunny is all swollen from our cocks, your lips there are open. Your arousal is obvious, lass. You doubt me, but your thighs, they're glistening with your desire. You liked the spanking."

She tried to move her legs together but I gripped her ankle, Kane the other. "I did not!" she replied, full of indignation.

"Your body doesn't lie, sweetheart," Kane said. "Your nipples are tight pink buds."

She pursed her lips, her eyes bright with anger.

"I allow ye to like it, lass," I told her, my voice soothing.

"Allow me?" Her voice dripped with sarcasm.

"Aye. Ye are allowed to enjoy showing your gorgeous cunny to your men. Ye are allowed to be aroused by it, for we most certainly are. Touch yourself. Make yourself come."

"What?" she squeaked.

"Touch your cunny with your fingers until you come."

"I don't want to," she countered as she shook her head.

"Your mind dinna want to, but your body is desperate for release. As I said, I allow ye to like it. In fact, ye have nay choice. Ye will stay just like this until you come. I would assume we are close to Travis Point, which means the stage will stop."

"But the driver!" she cried.

We would never share the view of her delectable body with a stranger like the stage driver. Her body was precious. *She* was precious to us. "It's your choice. Show us how ye pleasure yourself or get another spanking beforehand."

She pulled against our hold on her ankles, but we would not release her. This was the time for her to learn to obey me. Both of us. Punishment would be plentiful because of her willful spirit, but she'd quickly learn that we always pleasured her when she was good.

"Five minutes to Travis Point! Five minutes," the stage driver yelled, his voice loud even over the rumbling of the wheels.

Emma gasped in surprise and her right hand flew to her cunny, her fingers rubbing over it in untried ways.

"Find your clit," Kane instructed. We wanted her to succeed. She'd earned a sweet release. We wanted to watch her as she came for it was a most beautiful sight. "Remember that place I touched you yesterday with my fingers? Yes, I can see you found it. Now, small circles. Just like that."

We might force her to pleasure herself, but that didn't mean we couldn't guide her. She was inexperienced and it was our job to tell her what to do.

Her cunny was slippery and wet and soon her fingers were shiny and coated with her arousal. Her eyes fell closed and she relaxed into the seat, giving in to our demands and focusing on her cunny.

"Good girl. We can see what makes ye feel good. Oh, tiny circles on your clit? What about your cunny, your pussy, does it feel empty? Ye can slip your fingers of your other hand in, ye ken. Aye, like that." I talked to her all the while she played with herself. Her nipples softened, her back bowed and her mouth parted and I knew she was close. She was a glorious sight and perhaps we would have her sit on display like this every time we were in a stage.

"Come for us, lass. Show us your pleasure."

She shook her head back and forth, her hand continuing to move. "I can't, I can't do it!" she cried out.

Kane shifted, placing her foot on the edge of the bench seat and moved to sit beside her. He ran his hands over her puckered nipples and played with them as he leaned in and murmured in her ear. "Let go and come, baby. This isn't your decision. You don't have to like what you're doing, but you are allowed to feel pleasure in it. Feel pleasure knowing we are watching. You are so beautiful. Good girl."

Her body tensed and her eyes flared open in surprise. She cried out as she came, her back bowing, her fingers slipping over her clit persistently. Her skin flushed a pretty pink all the way down to her upturned breasts, her skin bright with a sheen of perspiration. When the tremors left her body, when her heart rate slowed, she remained slumped upon the seat, her eyes closed and a small smile on her lips. Her hand rested over her used cunny, her fingers glistening. We each held an ankle and enjoyed the view until the stage began to slow. There was nothing like a woman sated and replete from her pleasure, especially when the woman belonged to us.

10

MMA

The ride from Travis Point to the men's ranch was several hours in duration. The exact length I was unsure of, but it felt interminable. I was sore...there, from the spanking, but also inside where my maidenhead used to be. They'd permitted me to button up the front of my dress so I appeared to the stage driver and any passerby that I was a modest, demure woman, although I now knew better.

Kane had insisted I ride upon his lap as it was horses only from Travis Point on. I'd objected at first, but he'd placed me sideways across his muscular thighs and the discomfort wasn't as terrible. He'd held me securely in the circle of his arms, the sway of the animal lulling me. I shouldn't have found comfort as I was, but I did.

The side of my face rested against his chest and I could hear the steady beat of his heart. He smelled good, radiated warmth and I felt...safe. With Ian riding beside us, I knew nothing could happen to me. Neither Thomas nor any other man would harm me again. And yet, was I safe from these men? They'd touched me, used me, punished me in ways I never imagined. It had all been so illicit, so carnal, so wrong. Everything I'd done in the stage was beyond my scope of imagination, but would probably be an everyday occurrence with them. The way they'd made me find pleasure in what I'd done had me confused, frightened even, by my own reactions. I'd liked it! Even after being so debased, I'd come, harder than any previous time and it had been incredibly *good*. All that had been missing was a cock filling me.

We rode up to a large house built solely of logs. It was two stories and vast, with a covered porch that wrapped all the way around. Ian tied his lead to a rail then came over and helped me down from Kane's lap. Various buildings were scattered about the land in the distance. A barn, with a hayloft was attached to a longer, one story stable. A fenced paddock with several horses grazing was beside it. Further away, several smaller structures, and in the distance, set upon rises in the landscape, were other houses, discernible by their porches, stone chimneys and windows. Our arrival must have been witnessed or heard as several men approached.

I smoothed out my dress as the men shook hands, caught up on the happenings at the ranch, too nervous to look any of them in the eye. Could they tell that I wore no drawers and had thick seed dried on my thighs? Would they know what Kane and Ian had forced me to do in the stage or that I had found my pleasure while doing so? I was certainly travel worn and unkempt, but would they associate part of that state to being on my knees servicing Ian or my head thrashing about as used my hand to make myself come?

All my concerns were irrelevant, as I quickly became the center of attention, completely surrounded by very large, very commanding men. There was something about their bearing that was identical – shoulders back, eyes assessing and sharp, bodies honed with muscle and strength. It was quite overwhelming. I glanced at Ian and Kane, whose looks included blatant possessiveness that I found surprisingly reassuring.

Kane moved to stand beside me and took my elbow, Ian did the same on the other side. "This is Emma, our bride."

With this pronouncement, the men's gazes shifted to scrutiny and I felt as naked and exposed as I had on the stage. My eyes widened, realizing that Kane had introduced me as *our bride*. Not his bride, not Ian's bride. Not one man seemed surprised. Had they missed his very specific wording?

"Emma, the bloke on the left is Mason." Kane indicated with his chin. "Next to him is Brody. Simon and Rhys are the dark-haired lads. You will discover as soon as they speak that they were members of our regiment as well. The last is Cross, who is as American as you are. We each own a stretch of land, but the ranch, Bridgewater, is our common goal."

I nodded my head and gave a smile, finally reassured I would not be taken to the other side of the world.

"Ann is expecting you two for the noon meal, although Emma will be quite a surprise." If I remembered correctly, it was Mason who spoke. He appeared a few years younger than both Kane and Ian, with black hair and a neatly trimmed beard.

I tugged on Kane's sleeve and he leaned down. "Do they know...I mean–"

My whispered words were cut off by Ian. "They know ye belong to us. To ensure there is nay doubt, I'll repeat it for ye. Emma is our bride." The man puffed up with pride at the words and it felt very reassuring. "The men ken our ways, lass, because they share them as well. Ann is married to Robert and Andrew, who are off somewhere, but ye will meet them later."

My mouth fell open and stared at the large bunch of men before me. "You all, I mean, I belong to all of you?" I stepped back, eyes wide with fear. I felt the blood drain from my face. What had I gotten myself into? I couldn't handle all of these men. What was expected...?

"Emma," Kane's loud voice sliced through my thoughts. He grabbed my shoulders and lowered his head so his eyes held mine. "You belong to Ian and me. The other men, they will find their own wives."

"Wives?" I asked, licking my dry lips.

"Mason and Brody will claim a wife and Simon, Rhys and Cross another. In time."

He raised his brows as he watched me, asking without words if I understood. I nodded. "Ann? Does she know about–"

"As I said, she's married to Robert *and* Andrew. They are the foremen here. Their house is over there." He pointed over my shoulder and I turned to see a house in the distance, set off on its own by a meandering creek. "There is nothing to worry about. Nothing to fear."

"We will ensure your safety."

I couldn't see who spoke as Kane blocked my view. He stood and Ian pulled me in for a hug, my cheek resting against his hard chest.

"There is no need to worry about anything but being our wife."

"You may belong to Kane and Ian, but you are one of us now. We will protect you as our own," another man added.

I didn't understand their ways. These weren't British ways, which I knew to be even more severe than in the American West; some other deeply rooted moral code was at work here. Their conviction for several of them to marry one woman was unusual, to say the least. But they believed it, were impassioned by it. They did not seem to sway, but held firm to this, and somehow, this set me at ease, at least somewhat so.

Kane kissed my hair. "There. Better?"

I nodded against his shirt quite relieved, yet completely overwhelmed.

———

KANE

One of the luxuries we added to the house when we built it was a water closet, complete with hip tub. We knew any woman would thrill in such a feature, especially during the harsh winter months. As we helped undress Emma and held her hand as she slipped into the warm water, just the look of sheer bliss on her face made all the effort worth it.

Sounds drifted up from downstairs as the noon meal was prepared, but we were far removed tending to Emma. She leaned against the high back, her hair swirling on the surface of the steaming water about her, her breasts bobbing on the surface and her pink nipples plump and lush. Ian glanced at me, his jaw clenching as he shifted his cock in his pants. I knew just how uncomfortable he felt. A hard cock would be a permanent state now.

We'd been gentle with her, but as a virgin, she did not have much chance to come to terms with her new role. Surely being married to two lusty men, living on a ranch with other men with similar leanings and notions, would require adjustment of mind. Her own story would need to be told, but not now, not when everything was so overwhelming. I wanted to know about her bastard step-brother, Thomas, so I could track him down and beat him bloody. He'd done her wrong. She wouldn't have ended up in Mrs. Pratt's auction otherwise. As her husbands, we'd ensure he never harmed Emma ever again. I was reassured knowing she was away from the man and safe at Bridgewater.

After her hair had been washed and her body cleaned, we helped her from the tub and dried her.

"I can do this all myself," she replied, trying to cover body.

"I assure you," I murmured as I rubbed her pink skin with a bath cloth. "This is no hardship."

"Come," Ian said, taking her hand and tugging her out into the hall.

"Ian, I'm naked!" She dug in her heels, but that was not enough resistance to stop the man. All it did was make her breasts sway and that only had me more intent than ever.

"Just the way I like you." He grinned at her over his shoulder. "You will have to learn to appreciate two men seeing how beautiful you are."

I grabbed the shaving supplies and a clean cloth and followed the duo into Ian's room. When I joined them, Emma was held within the firm hold of Ian's arms and they were kissing, his hands roaming up and down her back, then cupping the perfect globes of her arse. When finally he pulled back, Emma's eyes were dark like a stormy sea, her lips pink and swollen.

"I could do that all day, but we have things to do." He gave her one last peck on the lips. "Lay down, lass."

It wasn't hard for Ian to get her onto her back as the man's kiss seemed to have robbed her of all reasonable thought. Which was just the way we needed her for what we were about to do. Ian climbed onto the bed after her, moving so he leaned back against the pillows, pulling Emma up so she was lying against him. Her back to his front.

"Ian, what are you doing?" she asked, tilting her head to the side and glancing up at him. He took this opportunity to give her a lingering kiss.

"Ian is to hold you while I shave you," I told her.

Placing the shaving supplies on the side table, I grabbed the soapy brush and razor and sat down on the large bed as well.

"Shaving?" she asked, her brow furrowed.

Ian's hands slid down her body, taking a moment to cup and then play with her breasts before grabbing her inner thighs and pulling her knees up and back.

"Ian!" She tried to shift from his hold, but leaning against him as she was, she had no leverage.

"Shh," he soothed, kissing her ear and along her neck.

Ian did an excellent job of spreading her open for me, her knees up at the sides of her breasts. I shifted into position between her thighs and quickly began coating her in thick lather.

"I am shaving your cunny."

"Why?" she asked, confused and embarrassed. It was doubtful she realized she tilted her head to the side to give Ian better access to her long neck.

"Because your pretty pink lips are hidden beneath these dark curls and I want to feel every slick inch of you when I take you with my mouth." Placing the brush on the table, I picked up the razor. "Don't move now."

I tended to the task as Emma didn't move a muscle. Slipping my finger over the shaved area, it was so smooth, so slick to the touch.

"Kane? Ian?"

The shout came from downstairs. Mason. Most likely calling us to eat. I heard other footfall below, as the other men went to the dining room for the noon meal. The house was large, the dining area a distance from the bedrooms upstairs.

"We're up here," Ian called back.

Heavy footfalls made their way up the steps and I pulled the razor from between Emma's legs, stood and met the man at the door before he could enter. Mason stopped just outside the doorway, hat in hand, and took in the razor and cloth in my hands. My body blocked his view of Emma's very exposed body. It was for our eyes only, not Mason's or any other man's. His mouth quirked knowing what we were doing.

"Keep your bloody thoughts off our wife," I growled in possessiveness. Instead of wiping the small smile from his face, it only made him grin as he held up his hands in surrender.

"Sorry for interrupting, but I've got kitchen duty with Ann. We eat in ten minutes."

"Ian, let me go!" she whispered loudly. I knew Ian would not relent on his hold until we were done and we were far from it. Her resistance was futile.

I nodded at Mason, stepped back and shut the door in the man's face. I could hear his chuckle through the wood.

I turned to look at Emma, whose head was turned away from the doorway, her eyes closed. I moved back into position between her spread thighs.

"Don't move, baby." I went back to work, removing the last bits of dark hair from between her thighs, her pink, lush cunny more and more apparent with each stroke. "You are ours, baby. Only Ian and I will touch you. The men know what happens between men and their woman. They will know your pussy is being shaved. They will hear you when you come, for we will take you regularly and in places –

albeit private ones – where you might be overheard. They may even hear you being spanked if warranted."

"But–"

"It is our job to train you to be our wife, to teach you what is expected. Becoming comfortable with others knowing how much you please us and are pleasured by us is something to which you must accustom."

"You *are* beautiful, lass," Ian said, his voice reassuring.

"I've been wondering what you taste like, baby." I glanced at Ian, then at Emma's wide-eyed stare. "I think I'll find out."

Shifting, I lowered my head between her thighs and licked her from arse to clit, my tongue feather light, only brushing over her newly exposed flesh.

"Kane!" she shouted, her eyes lowering to watch me. "What are you–"

Using my fingers, I spread her bare cunny lips, slick now with her cream. "Now doesn't that feel better?"

Her little pink pearl was hard and erect and begging for my tongue. Lapping away all of her arousal, my tongue flicked over her clit. Once. Twice. Her body jerked and she cried out.

"She tastes sweet. Like honey."

"She's fighting my hold," Ian added.

"You don't like your reward, Emma? You've been such a good girl. Stay still or you will be spanked."

11

KANE

I watched her from my position between her thighs. Her breathing made her flat belly rise and fall; her nipples were puffy pink tips, her skin was flushed. Long tendrils of damp hair clung to her forehead and neck. Her pale eyes were a misty blue, her emotions evident; arousal, fear, embarrassment.

"Is your cunny sore?" Ian whispered, her eyes falling shut as he licked the round shell of her ear. I heard a whimper escape her lips.

Carefully, I slipped a finger into her. She was slick and hot, her passage so very tight. My fingers only delved in about an inch, then pulled out and I added a second to the first. I watched her closely and when I slipped in to the second knuckle, her eyes opened and she winced slightly.

"Poor lass," Ian soothed. "Two big cocks took your maidenhead and stretched you wide. Your sore cunny needs time to heal, so instead of fucking you, we can start your training."

As he spoke, I returned to my task, flicking just the tip of my tongue over her clit. Her small hands pushed against Ian's thighs, trying to move away. She tasted sweet, tangy and her scent lifted from her heated skin to fill the air around us. My cock pulsed painfully against the placard of my pants. All it wanted to do was sink deep into her, sore cunny or not. I bloody hell wasn't going to hurt Emma with my baser needs so I took a deep breath, lowered my head and focused solely on my new wife's pleasure.

"Kane, it's...it's too much!"

My brow arched as I looked up her naked body. This was the first time a man's head was between her thighs and the pleasure would be different, perhaps even more intense than one of our cocks. "Am I hurting you?"

Her head thrashed. "No." She swallowed.

"Then I will continue, for I wish to see you come." And I did, lapping at her, sucking on her little nub, nipping it gently with my teeth.

"No, please. I don't like this!" she cried out.

I didn't stop as Ian asked her, "It doesn't feel good?" His hands cupped her breasts once again, played with them.

She sighed as I flicked her clit just right. The little nub was hard and very sensitive against the tip of my tongue. "Yes, but–"

"You don't want to come?"

"Not...no, I can't like it!" Her damp hair clung to the sides of her face, in long tendrils over Ian's chest.

I didn't stop, only added a finger to just the very opening of her cunny, letting it move in the smallest of circles, around and around. I loved having her hairless here. So smooth, so pink. Luscious.

"Why not, lass?" Ian murmured as he kissed the thrumming pulse at her neck.

"Because...there's two of you."

I lifted my head from between her luscious thighs. Her inner walls were greedily squeezing at the tip of my finger, trying to pull it in. Her clit had grown bigger and harder beneath my tongue, her cream slipping from her to coat my chin. There was no question she was about to come, but her mind was too diverted by the morality of it all. This was a barrier we would break through, just like I had her maidenhead. It would take time, but it was one of the most important aspects being married to Ian and I. She would accustom herself to being pleasured by both of us. Together.

Because of this, I slowly wiped the back of my hand across my chin. "Then I will stop."

Her eyes opened and met mine, her body still. "What?" she asked, now more confused than ever.

"If you do not wish to come, then I will stop," I repeated, moving off the bed. My cock was hard as a rock, but tending to it would have to wait.

Ian released her legs and she sat up, confusion warring with arousal on her face. She had no idea how pretty she was with her hair damp and down her back, long tangles of curl fell over her shoulder and onto an upturned breast. Her skin was flushed and the way she sat, her legs curled, her bare cunny was exposed. The swollen pink folds couldn't be missed.

Shifting from behind her, Ian moved from the bed to his dresser and took a small box that held handcrafted butt plugs. Opening it, he took the smallest size from the selection along with a small glass jar of slick lubricant. I had the honor of taking her virginity and the first to sample the sweetness between her thighs. Therefore, it was Ian's turn to work her body, teaching Emma we would both tend to her, one at a time, for now.

Ian sat on the edge of the bed. "Over my knee, lass."

Her eyes widened and she dashed off the far side of the bed, pressing her back against the wall. In this position, she only showcased her assets for us even more. I was reveling in her bare cunny and just stared at it while Ian took over. I leaned against the doorway, relaxed and ready to watch what came next. Just looking at her all mussed and naked had me adjusting my hard length in my pants.

"You're not spanking me. I've done nothing wrong!"

"Nay, lass. You've behaved so well. I want ye over my knee so I can begin your arse training, not to spank ye."

"My...what?" Her eyes were wide, her mouth open.

"We Scots – Brits, too, like Kane – say arse, but you can say ass instead. Say it, lass." When she didn't Ian's eyebrow went up, all but daring her to be contrary.

"Ass," she whispered, looking down at her toes.

"Very good. Now come over here." His tone dropped an octave.

Emma glanced at both of us, considering her options, the consequences. She was a smart woman, well educated; I didn't need to *know* her to recognize a well-bred woman. Moving slowly, her bare feet silent on the wood floor, she came around the bed to stand before Ian.

He cupped the nape of her neck and pulled her into a kiss. I pushed off the wall to stand directly behind her, my cock nudging against the small of her back. Lowering my head, I kissed her bare shoulder, sliding her curtain of hair out of the way, slipped my hands up and down her arms. Just because she didn't want to come didn't mean we were strong enough to keep our hands from her.

As soon as Ian ended their kiss, I returned to my place against the wall. Ian tugged, pulling her across his lap, her upper body on the bed beside him, as she gasped in surprise.

"Ian!" Pushing up on her elbows, she turned and looked over her shoulder, fire swirling from the blue depths of her eyes. Ian's large palm rested at her lower back, ensuring she could not rise.

Ian dipped two of his fingers into the jar of ointment, coating them with the clear, greasy substance.

"I could kiss ye all night. There's nay chance I will ever tire of your taste, but I want to claim your arse," Ian told her. "We will fuck your there, frequently, but you are not ready yet. Dinna fash," he replied in a soothing tone when she began to squirm. "We don't want to hurt you and it is our job to get you ready. To train your arse to take our cocks."

When his fingers ran over the pink pucker, she bucked and thrashed. "No. This isn't right."

"It is right." As he spoke, Ian circled his fingers over her, slowly pressing inward. "Serving your husbands, pleasing them, is a wife's job. Ye will serve us by offering all of your holes. Your tight pussy, your delectable mouth and your snug arse. It will bring us pleasure for ye to do so and in return, we will give you the most incredible pleasure. We took your cunny and ye loved it. Ye had your first lesson in sucking cock earlier and ye came after. Now, we must ready your arse."

Her body stiffened and she groaned when one of Ian's fingers slipped past the tight ring inside her snug arse. She'd fought valiantly, but her body would offer no contest to our attentions. We would show her all the way, all the places pleasure could be found. She may be wary now, but she would soon love having us play with her arse. That thought had my cock pulsing, throbbing with the need to claim her there. But she wasn't ready and her submission to Ian would be satisfaction enough. For now. Soon, she would trust us, knowing that we would see her happy, sated and well satisfied at every turn.

"We dinna want to hurt you, lass. We're doing this for ye." Ian slowly worked his finger in and out of her arse, Emma's body slumped across his lap, her breathing erratic and loud. As he moved further and further within, she mewled, little sounds escaping the back of her throat.

"Our friend Rhys is quite skilled at carpentry, including the lathe. He handcrafts all of the dildos and butt plugs for us, ye ken? When Andrew and Robert married Ann, he made some to their specifications. Even though we hadn't met ye yet, Ian and I knew what we wanted to train our wife. Rhys made them for us and we've kept them, waiting. Waiting for just this moment. Dinna fash, I will use the smallest size plug."

I couldn't resist any longer, moving to kneel on the floor by her hip. Moving my hand beneath Ian's I slipped my fingers over her pussy lips. "She's dripping wet," I commented seeing her slick pussy lips and thighs. My words elicited another moan from her.

"Do you like this, lass?" Ian asked.

She shook her head but said nothing.

"Your body tells us otherwise, lass. Can you feel all the secret places in your arse awakening to my touch? Kane can feel how slick ye are now. Both of your men's hands are on ye, lass. Poor baby, so needy."

Carefully, Ian slowly worked his second finger in to join the first, slowly fucking her, stretching her open as I easily found her clit, hard and eager for my touch.

"No." Her breath was escaping in little pants. "I...I don't like this."

"What? That you feel pleasure in my touching you here? That Kane is watching your arse be stretched for the first time? That he's playing with your clit?"

She shifted her hips back, not realizing she wanted his fingers deeper, perhaps mine as well. When Ian filled her even further, she began to cry. Not in pain, most certainly not. We would never touch her and cause harm. This was the antithesis of her feelings. She needed to come so much that she was falling into a depth of frustration that had her overwhelming emotions escape through tears instead of release. "This is wrong!"

Using his free hand, Ian picked up the small plug Rhys had so expertly crafted, dipped it into the jar so that it was thickly coated, then gently pulled his fingers free, her body slumping into his lap. The way her body clenched down upon Ian's digits, I imagined the strangling grip her body would have on my cock. I stifled a groan as my cock swelled even further.

Before he nudged the plug up to the opening, I could see her opening wink once as it closed back up. Ian didn't offer her body the chance to do so, moving the slippery plug within in a slow, smooth stroke. She groaned and her entire muscles tensed once again, so I ran my hand up and down her leg in an attempt to soothe her.

Settled in place, the dark wooden handle could be readily seen, protruding only a small bit. She was stretched open slightly, just a start for her to begin adjusting in preparation for our cocks. Her swollen and aroused cunny lips beneath my fingers were hot and slippery. I'd set her body ablaze from putting my mouth upon her just a few minutes earlier. Although she hadn't wanted her arse played with, there was no missing how it had intensified her pleasure, her need to come. Her thighs were slick with her honey and her skin was coated in a sheen of perspiration. Moving my hand down, I flicked her clit and Emma arched her back, crying out.

She sobbed, a sound of need escaping from within that ripped at my control.

"See, baby? Only pleasure," I told her, continuing to stroke her cunny and her leg.

"You may come, lass."

I nudged her clit again when she didn't respond right away.

Sniffling, she said, "I...I don't want that thing in me. It's too big."

She was still focusing on what we were doing to her instead of how she felt.

"Not as big as either of our cocks, Emma," I reminded. We will fuck you at the same time, baby, Ian in your arse while I fill your cunny."

"How...how is that possible?" she asked, breathless.

"It's possible, lass. More than possible. It *will* happen," Ian said.

She groaned, probably envisioning how much more she'd be filled when we finally fucked her.

"You've done beautifully. Come now for us. Let us see. Show us you're such a good girl," Ian prompted.

"No," she sniffed. "No. I can't. Oh God."

She was so desperate, so lost. We were letting her decide if she would come, instead of commanding. It was clear she would need to be told to come, to take the decision to cede to the pleasure away from her. She wanted to submit. If Ian changed his tone, his wording ever so slightly to be less soothing and more demanding, Emma most likely would go off like a Fourth of July firecracker.

It was blatant how inhibited she was. How much her brain was in control of her body. And so another lesson would be taught today. With her answer, Ian carefully and slowly pulled the plug from her arse and we helped her stand, keeping his hold on her until she gained her bearings. We would have kept the plug in longer as part of her training, but she needed to learn that playing with her arse was going to be pleasurable, not embarrassing. It would make her come – we would ensure it – and she was denying herself that release. Both of us had our hands on her intimately, working her, yet still she refused. Therefore, we would give her what she wished. Soon enough, she'd *want* us to touch her there. To be touched by both of us at the same time. Until she recognized that, she'd remain on edge.

I stood. "Let's get you dressed. Everyone will wonder what we've been up to."

It was very hard not to smile at the look on Emma's face. She was so aroused her blue eyes were foggy, blurry with her need. Her mouth was open and she breathed in little pants. A pink flush brightened her cheeks and crept down her neck and to the tops of her breasts. A brighter pink tinged her plump nipples and she squeezed her slick thighs together. "But...."

Ian put a finger over her lips. "Shh. Ye did not wish to come and that is fine. We will always give ye pleasure, lass, ye only have to accept it. It is time to eat."

She frowned, her smooth brow marred with a crinkle of confusion.

Ian left to go into the washroom and return with her blue dress. He lowered it to the floor and I helped Emma step in, put her arms through the sleeves and began to do the long line of buttons up the front.

"As we said in the stage, no drawers for you. It will be quite uncomfortable for me to sit at dinner with a raging cock know your pussy is shaved and bare."

"Aye," Ian agreed.

"This dress is temporary until after the meal when we can ask Ann for some clothes. You are both of similar size and her dresses may work for you in the short term, perhaps with some sewing adjustments."

As I did up the buttons over her breasts, the sides of my hands brushed at her sensitive nipples and a sigh escaped her lips. She would quickly learn that her pleasure came before propriety while here on the ranch. Until she asked to come – begged for it – she would be in quite a state. And so would Ian and I.

12

MMA

The evening meal was not a small affair. Even though the house belonged to Kane and Ian, the dining room was large, the vast table able to seat up to twenty. All of the men I'd met earlier were seated around it and stood at my entrance along with a few new faces, including one woman.

"I am Ann," she said. "It will be very nice to have another woman about." She was perhaps a few years older than me, with a broad smile and a soft demeanor. Her hair was a pale wheat color, pulled back neatly into a bun at her nape. With pale skin and blue eyes, she was quite striking. As Kane had said, we were similar in size, although my bosom was much more ample than her more dainty curves. In my tawdry blue dress with my hair a wild tangle down my back, I looked as wanton as I felt.

I forced a smile to my lips, but it was difficult, knowing everyone in the room was aware of the reasons for our tardiness. If they didn't, seeing me in such a fashion would provide answer enough. My cheeks were red, I could feel the heat, and my nipples were tight little buds beneath the fabric and there was no corset to hide that fact.

My pussy, my cunny as Kane and Ian called it, throbbed and pulsed with unrequited need. It felt...strange being shaved. Smooth and noticeably slick. My bottom was sore from Ian's fingers and the hard plug, but it, too, pulsed and little sparks of pleasure erupted every time I clenched down.

Ian pulled out a chair for me and I sat without thought, my husbands sitting on either side of me. "That is Robert and Andrew, Ann's husbands," Kane said, pointing to two men who smiled and nodded at me from across the table. All the men on this ranch were large, as if the fresh air, hard work and good food made them this way.

The plates and bowls of food were passed around the table, Kane or Ian filling my plate as they came by. I was thankful they were assisting me with this nominal task, for my thoughts were too scattered, yet at the same time too focused on my body and the craving I felt for release.

"The men have houses of their own, but we eat our meals together," Kane continued. He acted as if nothing had happened upstairs just minutes before, although he did say his cock was hard. Perhaps he was just better at hiding his need than I. "Ann will come in the morning to cook along with one of the men, the role rotating daily so she has help. You can offer your help as well, or if you are inclined or skilled, in some other part of the ranch."

I picked at the food on my plate, listening to Kane's words, but focused solely on my body. I couldn't help squeezing my thighs together to lessen the ache, although it didn't seem to help. I was sore, not only from my maidenhead being torn, but from Ian working my bottom. I squirmed on the hard seat trying to attain relief. Nothing seemed to help. I feared the only solution was what the men had offered not once, but twice – sweet release. I needed to come.

"Eat, lass." Ian leaned in and kissed my brow, then returned to his food.

"Are you all right?" Ann asked, seated across from me. She tilted her head and studied me. "You look feverish. Was your journey too arduous?"

I shook my head, having no interest in revealing *why* I looked overheated.

"As you might remember from your first day or two as a bride, Ann, Emma is tending to the needs of two very ardent men." It was either Robert or Andrew who spoke. I couldn't remember which one had the beard and which had blond hair.

Awareness lit the other woman's face. "It's not too terrible, is it?" Ann asked, biting her lip. Her eyes darted to her husband beside her.

"Terrible?" her husband queried. "If I remember correctly, Kane came running because he thought you were being beaten, when you were actually screaming your pleasure."

Kane chuckled. "I remember that quite well."

"Do you remember *why* you came so hard that time?"

Ann blushed to the roots of her blond hair. "I...I can't say."

"It was the first time we stretched your ass. You found it most enjoyable."

"Robert," Ann chided, looking down at her untouched meal. She shifted in her seat.

"I know it is hard for you to voice how you please us, but it is something you need to practice. If you won't tell her about your pleasure, then you will tell her about your punishments." Andrew's voice, although patient and calm, was deep. Neither man had British accents.

"But...I don't want to tell anyone about that."

"There's no shame in making amends. You can tell her about a punishment or she can watch one firsthand." I recognized Andrew's stern tone as both Kane and Ian had used it with me.

"I am spanked," she replied, squirming. The reply was short and met her husband's request, but by the frown on both her husbands' faces that was not the answer they expected.

"Emma has most likely learned about that punishment by now," Robert replied. "Give her a reason for why you were spanked, please."

Ann licked her lips. "I went near the stallion in the outer pen."

I was an accomplished rider, but I did not know how dire her act was.

Andrew clarified for me. "The stallion sensed the mare was in heat and was solely focused on mounting her. Ann did not heed our warnings for her safety and neared the primed animal."

It did sound dangerous.

"Ann is the most precious thing in the world and we can not keep her safe if she disregards any of the ranch rules." Robert ran a knuckle down Ann's cheek. She turned her face and smiled lovingly at Robert. Andrew stroked down her pale hair and she turned her gaze to him next.

Their love was blatant and being punished did not seem to hinder their relationship. Ian and Kane, while stern and clearly willing to guide me to their expectations, did not hold grudges regarding my transgressions either. Once a punishment was meted, all was forgiven. I did not have to worry that they would consider me an unworthy bride – quite the opposite, in fact. They seemed rather pleased with me. It was I who struggled with the arrangement.

The other men around the table ate their meals like men half starved. Utensils scraped across the china as they cleaned their plates, grabbing bowls and platters for additional helpings. But there was no question they followed the conversation.

"Stop squirming, sweetheart," Andrew said to Ann.

"I'm sorry, but it's–" She leaned in and whispered in his ear.

"It pleases us to know you have a plug in your ass. In fact, pleased is not the right word. You are not the only one uncomfortable at the table."

Confusion marred Ann's face and Andrew took the fork from her hand and placed it on her plate, then lowered her hand to his lap. "Oh!" she cried.

Both her husbands were looking upon Ann with very heated, very aroused gazes.

Kane leaned his head toward mine. I noticed his clean, male scent. Soap and something else I didn't recognize, but it was intoxicating. I clenched my thighs together. "As you can see, Ian and I are not the only ones with hard cocks."

I did feel some satisfaction in knowing my men were as aroused as I. "To what are they referring?" I asked.

"She has a plug in her ass."

My eyes widened thinking about having my bottom opened and stretched as it had been earlier during a meal. In public.

"Ye wonder why she has a plug inside her now, at dinner?" Ian leaned in and whispered.

It was as if he could read my mind. I gave a small, curt nod.

"In time, you will keep a plug in your arse for longer durations so that you are able to take a cock, to take both of us at the same time," Kane told me. "Stretching you, filling you with the plug for a few minutes was just a start."

"Surely not at dinner?" I squeaked.

Ian shrugged casually. "We will have to see, ye ken, and before ye say anything further, it is nay your decision."

"We will decide what's best for you," Kane added. "Just like Robert and Andrew decide for Ann."

"It's best to have a...plug in me?"

"To take a cock in your arse, for both of us to take you at the same time, yes. We do not wish to hurt you and will only claim that delectable hole of yours when you are truly prepared," Kane said, cutting his steak. This conversation was preposterous; talking about plugs and bottoms over a meal was unfathomable. Until now.

"Prepared and aroused," Ian added.

I gulped at the thought, remembering the size of their cocks, how big they'd felt when they'd fucked me. How good it had been. They wanted to put them...there? One in my bottom and one in my pussy, at the same time? What had I gotten myself into? And why, *why* was the idea of them taking me in such a way only adding to the need they'd aroused in me?

"Ann enjoys it when we fuck her ass, which we do frequently," one of her husbands said. "We are very careful with her, ensuring she is ready for us. She needs a maintenance plug so that she is stretched enough to take us."

"We are doing it for her," the other added. "Everything we do is for Ann."

"This entire conversation is an odd choice for dinner," I commented. "Odd in general."

"Weren't expecting two husbands?" Rhys asked. I looked down the table at the dark haired man.

"Certainly not," I replied.

"Assumed ye'd be fucked beneath the covers with the lamp extinguished?" Ian asked, light eyebrow raised.

I could feel my cheeks heat. "That is what I'd heard," I replied. I thought of Thomas and Allen and Clara and they'd certainly provided an alternative to a bed. What I'd had to do for my husbands in the stage had also altered my perspective.

"Perhaps, baby, what you heard wasn't normal," Kane said, placing his hand on top of mine and offering a light squeeze. "Perhaps what we do here at Bridgewater *is* normal."

I frowned. "What is normal then?"

"Normal is whatever a husband wishes. Whatever pleases a wife. It could be straight fucking."

"It could be arse fucking," Ian added.

"Ass play," Andrew said.

"Cock sucking."

"Eating pussy."

"Anywhere."

"Everywhere."

The men all added something else to the carnal conversation until my mind was filled with an abundance of variation I never knew were possible.

"Pleasing both your husbands," Ann said. Andrew and Robert turned to her, Andrew tilting her face up to him so he could kiss her, then Robert had his turn.

"See, lass, there is nay need to be embarrassed," Ian said

reassuringly. "Ye only need to be aroused. What we did with ye earlier, starting your ass training–"

"Tasting your delectable pussy," Kane cut in.

"–is all for your pleasure. And you denied yourself release."

"Emma, heed these words from another woman," Ann said, leaning forward. "If your men are offering you pleasure. Take it. Accept it. *Enjoy* it." She grinned.

Shifting in my seat, I realized I ached between my thighs, and not because both men had claimed me. No, it was the pulsing of that little bundle of nerves I'd rubbed and touched until I screamed while riding the stage, where Kane had licked and sucked. Upstairs, they'd left me needy, because I'd asked them to. I longed now for them to touch me, knowing it was the only way for this ache to go away. My nipples had tightened beneath my dress, hardening at my wandering thoughts. As Ann said, I had to accept it and I'd most assuredly enjoy it."

"There were men over in Bozeman asking questions," one of the men said, thankfully changing the course of conversation. I didn't remember his name, but he had dark hair with equally dark eyes.

Everyone stopped eating and the room fell silent.

"How did ye hear about this, Simon?" Ian asked, his tone grim.

"I was in town when you were gone and Taylor at the saloon was blabbering."

"So you got him drunk," Mason surmised.

Simon nodded. "Pulled him into a game of cards. Nothing he said about the men should have piqued my interest, but he mentioned they had funny accents. His words, not mine."

This group of men was the one with the funny accents, but discovering there was another – or a few men – that spoke in a similar fashion, especially in the Montana Territory, would be memorable.

"It was only a matter of time," Ian said, giving a disappointed shake to his head.

"It's been five years," Mason countered, pointing a fork at Ian.

"Evers won't give up."

When the men returned to their food, it seemed the conversation was over. I turned to Ian. "Who is Evers?"

He looked at me and smiled, little crinkles forming at the corner of his eyes. Even in the brief time I'd known him, I could tell the smile was forced, that he was trying to protect me. He wanted me to be burden free. "Just someone we all used to work with. In the army."

"In England?" I asked.

"Mohamir."

Mohamir? "Is that near Persia?" I asked.

Kane nodded. I looked his way. "Yes."

The men finished their food without any more discussion, all clearly quiet in their thoughts. It seemed I was to be kept from the details regarding something that involved them years before. None wished to delve into conversation about it, but it seemed to have affected all of their spirits. Finished with their meal, they stood and cleared the table, carrying all of the dishes into the kitchen to be washed. It appeared Mason was the dishwasher tonight as well as cook's helper; from what was said earlier, they must rotate this task as well. I blushed at how he'd come to the bedroom door earlier and how, at the time, my legs had been pinned back by Ian as Kane shaved me. Fortunately, Kane had kept the man from seeing me naked and lewdly exposed, but he most assuredly knew what the men had done. My cheeks burned.

When Mason caught me looking at him, he gave me a smile and winked. I flushed even hotter and turned away. As I stood in the center of the kitchen, the men swirled around me and I felt overwhelmed. Everyone was so familiar with each other, so organized, so at ease. I felt out of place, on edge and wary of any misstep. Instead of remaining in the throng, I decided I could help by picking up any remaining dishes, so I returned to the dining room only to stop in my tracks just inside the doorway.

In the corner was Ann, hands on the wall, Robert close behind her. Fucking her. Naive as I was, I knew what I was witnessing, although I never knew it was possible to do standing up. Robert's pants were open enough only to free his cock, which from across the room, was quite large. He buried it all the way into Ann, then pulled back, his hands on her hips, pulling them back and keeping her in place, filling her again and again.

Andrew stood beside her, his cock out and his hand stroking up and down. "Good girl, Ann. Neither of us could wait to fuck you as we watched you shift and squirm in your chair knowing your ass was nice and filled, knowing you belong to us."

His words weren't harsh, but kind, pleasing. Soothing. Ann cried out, and most definitely in pleasure. "Yes, oh, Robert. Harder."

"Do ye like what ye see?"

The words at my ear had me jump, my hand flying to my chest. "Ian, you scared me."

"You may think Andrew and Robert are harsh men, perhaps cruel to speak so frankly about Ann. Do they look uncaring to you?"

Ann came right then, her sign of pleasure escaping as a deep moan.

The sound shook me to my core. I wanted to have the attention of my husbands just like Ann did right now. I wanted to feel what Ann was, a bone deep pleasure that couldn't be dampened. I shifted, rubbing my thighs together, which were now decidedly wet. My nipples tightened almost painfully.

"See? They cherish Ann, just as we cherish you."

"Why are they doing this where we can witness?"

"They are taking care of her. You saw that Andrew was aroused at the table. None of them could wait. She needs her men to recognize when she is ready for a good fucking. Most of that squirming she did at dinner wasn't because of the plug, but because her cunny was ready to be fucked. Her needs come first, wherever they are. All of us understand this. Besides, Ann knows how pleased her husbands are with her and they are not afraid to show it."

Andrew thrust one last time, held himself deep as he clenched his jaw, his grip tightening on Ann's hips. After a moment, he pulled out, his cock now replete, white seed dripping from Ann beneath a dark object that protruded from her back entrance. Oh! That was the plug? It looked so big! They could take her with that within her?

Robert took Andrew's spot behind Ann and without ceremony, filled her up. "Ann, you're so tight, so slick with seed."

Ian took my hand and pulled me from the room and toward the stairs as Ann's moans followed us. "Where are we going?"

Kane was waiting for us on the landing. "You've pleased us this meal, so we are tending to you."

13

ANE

Simon's words over dinner had me distracted and agitated. Downright mad. I was leading my wife up to my bedroom to strip her naked and make her scream and I was thinking about the men that were coming for Ian. There was no question it was Evers, or at least men sent by Evers. Once they found Ian, they'd drag him back to England for trial. Or, they'd drag him just over the ridge and shoot him, their own kind of vigilante justice. None of us would let that happen. Ian had done no wrong and Evers knew it. But pinning his own dastardly crimes onto Ian had kept the man in good standing. A duke could not be sullied by the dirtiness of murder, even in wartime. Even in a land, a culture, so different as Mohamir.

As Ian closed the door behind us with a definitive click, I had to put those thoughts away for now. Emma needed our attention. Deserved it. Required it. When Ian's eyes met mine over her head, I could read his thoughts. Whatever happened to him, I would take care of our wife. I would be here for her. Protect her. Even when Ian was gone.

Like bloody hell.

The sun had dipped lower, the room filled with soft evening light, but not dark enough yet to require the lamp. A soft breeze came in through the open window and I could hear the men still working downstairs. Once the cleanup was complete, they'd finish up any remaining chores with the horses and return to their own homes spread out across the ranch.

"Have ye seen a man fully naked before, Emma?" Ian asked, undoing the buttons of his shirt.

She shook her head, keeping a careful watch on Ian's fingers, the expanse of chest exposed one button at a time.

"I was naked but I fucked her beneath the covers at the hotel this morn," Ian told Kane, then grinned sheepishly. "We were short on time."

"You won't be fucked under the covers again until the next blizzard. Your arousal has been taunting me the entire meal."

"My...my arousal?"

"The scent of you. Your hard nipples poking against your dress. Your flushed cheeks. Take off your dress, baby," I said, my voice rough. I'd had to will my cock into submission earlier when I had my face between her thighs, when I'd watched Ian work the plug into her virgin ass. Even through dinner. Now, though, I couldn't wait any longer.

"Doesn't it bother you that Mason knows what we were doing earlier? Shouldn't Andrew and Robert keep what they do with Ann a secret?" she asked, unbuttoning her bodice. I didn't mind the question, just thankful she was taking off her dress without duress.

I paused in my undressing and gave her my full attention as it was a serious question. An important one.

"There are no secrets at Bridgewater, baby."

"Privacy, yes, but nay secrets," Ian added.

"None of the other men will covet you as we do if they know your pussy is shaved and perfectly smooth. They will not think less of you if they hear your screams when you come. In fact, they will be right angry with us if they don't know you're being well tended. Your pleasure only validates our being good husbands."

"Ye belong to us and they ken that," Ian added. "Just as Ann belongs to Andrew and Robert even though we saw them fuck her downstairs. The other men will soon find brides of their own soon enough."

She considered our words as she stood there, her bodice open wide enough to glimpse the creamy swells of her breasts. I needed to calm myself; I wanted to relieve all the tension in my body by getting lost in hers. But that was not going to happen tonight. Her cunny was sore and not an option for relief, however there were many possible other ways to please her, and have her please us in return.

She fumbled with the remaining buttons, distracted by Ian and most definitely still aroused from earlier. We'd left her needy and wanting, her orgasm so close yet unattainable. Only when she accepted the pleasure as her due as our wife would we let her come. It was a self-inflicted punishment all in itself.

"Why does this man Evers anger you?" she asked. I must have answered her previous question readily enough for her to change topics. It did not seem to be in her nature to leave any worries unresolved.

Ian paused as he undid the placket of his pants, frowned. "He was our commanding officer during our time in the Mohamir."

"Our?"

"Don't stop, Emma. I want to see you," I told her, redirecting her thoughts. Her fingers began to move once again, but I could tell by the focused look in her gorgeous eyes that she wasn't to be deterred. I wanted to know her thoughts, share her experiences, learn about her. Evers was just someone neither of us wanted to think about, let alone talk about, especially when a hint of pink nipple appeared as the loose dress started to slip off her shoulder.

"Kane and I. Mason, Brody, Simon and Rhys, too." Ian said the last man's name with the English pronunciation, "Reese." "We were stationed together to guard the British ships in the Dardanelles for a time, then travelled with British dignitaries to Mohamir to meet the religious and secular leaders of the region."

The dress slipped from her body and pooled around her feet.

Both Ian and I paused and looked our fill, watching as her nipples tightened. It seemed I had a slight obsession with her nipples.

I yanked at my shirt, stripping myself of my clothes as quickly as possible. Ian was already naked and positioned himself in the middle of the bed. "Come to me, lass."

Emma climbed onto the bed and Ian tugged her across his chest, kissing her, his arms wrapping around her securely. My mouth watered with my need to kiss her as well. It had been too long. An hour, perhaps?

"Evers doesn't matter now," Ian said, lifting his head to look at her, to stroke her hair back from her face. "Christ, you're so wet I can feel it on my thigh." He lifted his leg up so it pushed against her bare cunny.

Going around the bed, I sat with my back against the footboard, watching, lifting one hand to caress over the long line of her leg.

"Since you're too sore to fuck, I'm going to taste ye. Up ye go," Ian said, lifting Emma easily and turning her around so she faced me, but still across Ian's body on all fours. Grabbing her hips, he pulled her back so she was astride his face.

"Ian, what–"

I knew the moment Ian started to lick and suck at her cunny when her eyes widened and she startled, her breasts swaying beneath her as she did so.

"She's so smooth, so bloody slick. She tastes incredible," Ian murmured from between her thighs.

"Do you want to come, Emma?" I asked her. Her eyes had fallen shut and she was gasping at every expert flick of Ian's tongue.

"Yes!" she cried out.

"You're not worried about it being wrong?" I asked, intentionally prodding her. We'd left her unfulfilled earlier because she considered it wrong to find pleasure in being with both of us, in having us touch her body. *All* of her body in various, very intimate, ways. I hoped not to continue with this lesson, but would if required.

She shook her head, her dark hair a curtain around her shoulders, down her back.

"No? Before dinner you didn't want to come."

"I...I need it."

I smiled at her, although she couldn't see me with her eyes squeezed shut.

"Good girl. Look down, Emma."

Her eyes fluttered open to glance down at Ian's erect cock, just an inch from her chin. "Suck him, baby." I shifted so that my cock was just to her right. "Suck both of us. After you swallow our seed, Ian will make you come."

I could tell Ian slowed his attentions because Emma shifted her hips and mewled.

"Take him into your mouth, just like you learned in the stage."

She did, working Ian with little licks, then taking him into her mouth as far as she could. He was big, too big for her now.

"Put your hand around the base, lean your forearm on the bed. Yes, like that. Now, use your other hand on me. Good girl."

It didn't take Ian long to come; he was no doubt as ready as I. Watching Emma take the plug earlier then seeing her watch another woman get fucked had been my personal torture. The look on her face, the unvarnished need, had had me on the brink of coming in my pants like a randy teenager. Seeing her ride Ian's face wasn't helping matters. Licking up every luscious drop of her honey most certainly pushed him over the edge. I remembered how sweet she tasted from earlier.

His hips thrust up and he groaned. Emma's cheeks hollowed, sucking him, taking his seed, her throat working to accommodate it all. She lifted her head and wiped her mouth with the back of her hand, only a small drop of seed on her lip.

"Good girl, baby. You took it all. Take my seed now and Ian will give you your reward."

Her face was flushed, her eyes half lidded with desire. Lower, her nipples were a bright pink and tightly furled.

"You want your reward?"

She nodded. "Oh yes," she said breathily, turning her head and opening her red, swollen lips to take me deep.

I hissed out my breath at the heat of her mouth, how wet it was, how her tongue stroked over the thick vein along my length. My balls drew up readying for my release.

"There's nothing wrong, baby, with getting pleasure from your husbands," I gritted out through clenched teeth. "Giving it to us. Yes, just like that, now suck. Good girl." I couldn't talk for a minute, watching her head bob in my lap, feel the tight suction of her drawn cheeks. The pleasure was so intense I was on the brink of spurting into her throat.

With Ian recovered, he returned to fervently work Emma's cunny, gripping her hips firmly to hold her in place. As she sucked me, she moaned, sending delicious vibrations up the length of my cock. They were my undoing. Nothing could stop the orgasm from coming and I groaned. As I did so, she too came, screaming around my cock, swallowing my seed voraciously, her hands clenching into fists in the quilt. Once I stopped pulsing in her mouth, she lifted her head and cried out. "Ian, yes!"

Ian flipped their positions so Emma rested on her back and we both began working her. She'd come once, but we weren't done. My hand delved to the juncture of her thighs finding her slick and wet, easily, yet gently, slipping two fingers into her tight channel. I set about to discover her secret pleasure spots, finding that little ridge of flesh inside that made her cry out, as Ian sucked on one nipple, pulling and tugging with his teeth, his fingers working the other.

Emma came again quickly, her body arching like a bow, a rough scream escaping her lips. Ian grabbed the jar of lubricant and dipped his fingers in as I flipped Emma over once again. This time, Ian worked a finger into her tight arse as I continued to fuck her cunny with my fingers. As we did so, we spoke to her. *Ye are so bloody beautiful, Emma. You're so sensitive, look how you're coming again. See, you can come with something in your arse. Oh, it's so much better, isn't it? Soon it will be our cocks filling you. Together.*

We worked her until her voice was hoarse, her skin coated in sweat, her body mindlessly riding our fingers until she wilted in complete exhaustion.

With her on her stomach as she was, Ian retrieved the small plug we'd used on her earlier. Slick from his fingers, the plug was able to slip in easily. She didn't even stir. We admired how pretty her cunny was, especially knowing her arse was stretching in preparation for us taking her together. Pulling her beneath the covers, we let her sleep and I was more than pleased with the progress she was making. Thrilled we'd saved her from an uncertain fate. Touched that she belonged to us.

14

ANE

"Who's going with you?" I asked Ian from the kitchen doorway. He was brewing a pot of coffee. Emma was asleep in my bed, not stirring when either of us left the room. I'd slipped on my pants, but that was all. Ian was dressed, even had his gun belt slung low on his hips. It was late, close to midnight, and we had the house to ourselves. The only sound came from the ticking of the grandfather clock in the other room.

"Mason." Ian's hair was mussed and instead of going to sleep beside Emma, he'd be heading toward Bozeman to find out who had come for him.

"Evers won't come himself."

"Nay. A scouting party." He grabbed a mug. "He won't sully his hands with the dirty work."

I agreed. "The distance is too great, the time too long to be away. How can he justify a trip to America? The Duke of Everleigh going to America." I shook my head. "Wouldn't happen."

"We should be gone a week." He shrugged, took a sip of the hot brew, winced. The man made coffee as thick as mud in the springtime. "Evers' men can wait a day. They've waited five years. One more day willna make a difference, ye ken. I want – hell, need – to take care of Emma's step-brother first."

My ire for the man flared to life like embers on a fire. "Thomas James."

Ian nodded. "Aye. I'll take care of the bastard."

Through gritted teeth, I replied, "Good."

"You'll protect her?" With the change in topic, he turned his head to look at me. His eyes were...bleak.

"Of course. You take care of her step-brother, I'll watch over her."

"I hadn't expected this to happen so quickly. I kent Evers would come after me eventually, but right after we found Emma? A cruel twist of fate. We've only just made her ours. I should be here with you both, as she should be trained by both her men. This fuck-all situation is preventing this."

We learned more in Mohamir than defending the Crown. When we were in charge of protecting a local secular leader – a man with three brothers, all of whom shared a wife. We discovered the staid Victorian ways we'd been raised with were only for the man's gain. In England, a woman was a husband's property, to use and abuse as he saw fit, all the while fucking a string of mistresses, leaving his wife cold and unfulfilled. The Mohamiran leader's wife, when we met her, was a submissive in the five-person marriage, but was quite happy. She was cherished – a word the leader used frequently – and protected by not one man, but several. Her needs were met, every carnal desire fulfilled. When one of the brothers had died in a fall from a horse, she was not left alone, destitute and without a means to support herself or her children. We learned much from the leader, from all of the brothers, and we chose to follow the Mohamiran culture's claiming of a bride.

England was not the place to fulfill this alternative way of life. It would be too hard to hide. America, especially the West, was a new frontier, where open land abounded and men were free.

Ian and I had been close like brothers for years. There had been no question we would share a bride. Until Emma, the woman was just a dream. And now, she was upstairs, sleeping off our attentions. No way in bloody hell would Ian miss out on her. Evers wouldn't take that away from him as he had his rank, his military career and his country.

"Go. Take care of the problem, then come back."

"Her arse is mine, Kane." He looked at me directly. Clearly.

I nodded. "I'll get her ready for you."

I'd taken her virginity, her maidenhead. He would claim her arse.

"I'll be back."

———

EMMA

It was the second morning I awoke engulfed in a man's embrace. This one, however, was not Ian. I'd come to recognize my men quickly – had it only been two days? – and they felt differently, smelled differently, held me differently.

This was Kane. His hands were rougher. His scent was...him. Woodsy, fresh air. Cinnamon. Ian held me like two spoons in a drawer. Kane had me sprawled across the top of him, one of my legs tossed over his, my breasts pressed into him, the sprinkling of dark hair on his chest tickling me. I was comfortably settled with my head on his shoulder, my nose nudging his neck. I breathed him in, relishing his stillness. I could take my time to study him, think about him, what he and Ian had done to me the night before. The last I remembered, I was on my belly, my knees tucked beneath me, both men's hands between my spread thighs. They'd worked both my holes and I came, again and again. I'd been mindless, lost to the pleasure they'd wrung from my body. I hadn't cared that two men were touching me. I hadn't cared that Ian's fingers had penetrated my bottom. I hadn't cared that I'd sucked both men's cocks and swallowed all of their seed. They'd made it seem intimate and special and that my body was made just for them.

For, it seemed, it was. All of my senses awakened when I was with them. The depth of feeling was unlike I'd ever known before. My skin was more sensitive, my body more responsive. I felt delicious and wanton and delicate and brave. The last was more coerced than the others, but nonetheless, Ian and Kane made me *feel*. I had no idea what had been lacking in my life until now. It was early days yet, but I was ever so thankful that Thomas was such a terrible man and chose to leave me at the brothel. If not, I'd still be alone and bored tending to his children and assisting in quilt making and church lunches completely unaware of the bond between a woman and her husbands.

In the safe confine of Kane's arms, I assessed my body. I was sated, relaxed but there was something in my bottom, something hard and it filled me up. Clenching down, I tried to force it out, but it wouldn't budge. It had to be the plug they'd used yesterday before dinner, but put it in me once again after I fell asleep. It wasn't exactly uncomfortable, but it was...there.

His dark chest hair was right there to touch. I hadn't had a chance to lay with him when we were awake. The man was all action and authority. Now, with him asleep, I could feel his heart beating beneath my cheek, watch the rise and fall of his chest. The soft springy hair on his chest tickled and I carefully ran a finger through it. His skin was remarkably soft for someone so strong.

"I can hear you thinking," Kane murmured, his voice rough with sleep.

I stiffened in his arms, but when he squeezed me reassuringly, I relaxed. "I don't remember what happened last night."

"We made you come. Over and over."

I idly swirled my finger in his dark hair. "I remember that."

"Your body was too exhausted from all the pleasure to remain awake."

"Why?"

"Why did you come several times? Because you gave up your inhibitions, at least for a short duration. I assume they are back in full force now."

"Why do believe that to be true?" I asked, although I knew he was right, but I wasn't going to say so.

"Because you realize there's a plug in your arse."

"Yes, that," I grumbled.

He shifted and slid out from beneath me so I lay on my stomach.

"No, don't move," he said, coming up to kneel beside me. I looked over my shoulder and could see his cock, thrusting out fully erect from a thatch of dark hair. I'd taken it into my mouth! It had fit within me...and I'd liked it.

"Tuck your knees under you."

I frowned up at him. He just frowned back, so I complied. There was no question what he could see of me this way.

"Good girl. Unlike Ann, I think it's best for you to have your plug training solely while you sleep. Relax, I'm going to take it out."

I relaxed, perhaps because his hand was on my lower back as he worked the plug from my ass, or because I wouldn't have one filling me during the day. Wincing, I breathed out through my mouth as he gently tugged it free.

Once it was gone, I felt...empty.

"So pretty, baby." A finger ran over the stretched opening and I startled. "Shhh, easy. That worked so well. Tonight, we'll try the bigger size."

He bent his body over mine so I felt the smattering of hair on his chest tickle my back. He whispered in my ear. "Did Ian tell you we'd fuck you every morning?"

I nodded, my pussy clenching, anticipating his cock. If he made me feel like they had last night, I was not going to complain.

"Good. Let's feel if you're ready." That's when I felt his fingers slip into me and there was no question I was eager for him. I sighed in pleasure and felt how easily his entrance was.

"Oh baby, you're so wet. Are you still sore?"

I shook my head. All I felt was delicious heat.

Shifting on his knees, I felt the thick head of his cock nudge my opening when he slipped his fingers free.

"You'll take me like this – from behind?" I asked, surprised as he filled me completely. I groaned.

"Oh, baby. Just like this."

15

MMA

Breakfast was much like the evening meal with everyone eating around the large dining table. Ann was smiling at her husbands and did not seem in trouble or embarrassed by what had occurred the previous night, nor did she shimmy or shift in her seat.

"Thank you for letting me borrow some of your clothes," I told her as I sat down, Kane holding out the chair for me.

Ann smiled. "That dress looks lovely on you, although you seem to fill it out a bit better than I." The bodice *was* quite snug but Kane did not seem to mind as his eyes kept drifting down to the strained buttons.

Kane leaned down and whispered. "I rather like the dress as it is. Perhaps a few of these will pop off?" His finger flicked over the top button.

I rolled my eyes and grinned at him knowing how much he liked my breasts.

Once seated, the platters of eggs and ham being passed to me, did I realize we had some empty places. "Where's Ian? And, um...Mason?"

Sitting next to me, Kane took the platter of ham and put a slice on my plate, then another on his. "He's gone to Bozeman."

Gone? I paused. "I thought he had work or chores to do. He left because of what you said last night?" I looked to Simon.

The man nodded.

"Why?" I asked.

Everyone glanced at Kane. Perhaps, as my husband, he was to answer. "I told you some of us were regimented together in Mohamir under the command of a man named Evers. An incident occurred and Ian was implicated. He was innocent, but framed."

"Framed?" I asked, worried for Ian. "For what?"

"Killing a number of women and children."

I sat wide-eyed at Kane's words. Ian wouldn't kill women and children. I hadn't known him long, but could vouch for his character nonetheless.

"Yes, what Brody said is true. Evers killed a family. I won't go into detail of why or how as it is too gruesome to share."

I put my fork down, my food having lost any appeal.

"When word spread of the horror, Evers pinned the crime on Ian."

I frowned. "Why would he do that?"

"He's a Scot, not English."

"So?"

"You are not familiar with English history," Andrew said in his American accent. "Neither was I until I met up with this group." He tilted his head indicating the Englishmen around the table.

"The Scots have wanted their freedom from the English for hundreds of years. The Battle of Culloden in the past century finished off the clans, but hatred still runs through the veins of men on both sides. Returning to England, Ian could be tried and convicted for Evers' crime for being a Scot alone; the hatred is that strong."

Panic flared. "We must go to him. Keep this man from taking Ian!" I pushed back my chair, yet Kane's hand on the high back halted me.

"Emma, stop." Kane's voice was deep and clear.

I shook my head furiously. "No, we need to help him."

He lowered his head so his dark eyes met and held mine. "I do not wish to spank you for disobedience when you are clearly thinking of Ian's best interest."

"But–" He put a finger over my lip, his brows raised.

"Do you think I, or any of these men, would sit here eating breakfast if we truly thought Ian was in danger?"

When he put it that way, I saw that I was acting rashly.

I let my shoulders slump in a very unladylike way. "It's just that...."

Kane kissed my brow, his lips warm. "I know."

Did he really know how much Ian was coming to mean to me? In such a short time, I cared for the man. Love? Perhaps not, but I didn't want to see him come to harm. He'd only treated me with the utmost of care. Tender, even. The idea of someone using him falsely, and in such a cruel, ruthless way left a bitter taste in my mouth.

"Does Evers have this much power?" I asked, needing the details. "He was stationed in Mohamir, a small country far from home. I beg your pardon, but that must not have been the most plum position."

I glanced between the men, a little fearful I spoke out of turn.

"We found it quite enlightening, until this event," Kane took my hand in his, reassuring me my words were not taken more deeply than deserved. "As you are well aware, being married to several men is not a Western custom."

"This man Evers has come all the way here to take Ian back to England?" The idea made the breakfast unappealing.

He squeezed my hand. "Evers wouldn't come here. He's too important in England, or at least he thinks that of himself. Besides, it's half a world away. We chose this location well. Once we learned of Evers' intentions to implicate Ian for his crimes, we banded together and departed Mohamir and worked our way here. To remain safe and keep Evers' secret."

"Here, we found a place to settle, to begin lives like the families in Mohamir," Simon added.

"A woman with several husbands," I finished.

"It's not something I was raised for," Ann told me and she looked to Robert, then Andrew. "But my straits were dire and I had to marry.

Robert promised he would take care of me, to protect me and ensured I would never see my father again. He was a...cruel man."

A look of old pain crossed her face.

"I wanted her the moment I saw her," Robert said, lifting Ann's hand and kissing the knuckles, which made her brighten remarkably.

"It was quite a surprise when I learned that Andrew claimed me as his wife as well. It was...complicated." She chuckled and the other man smiled. They were clearly happy now, infatuated even and I remembered how they'd taken her together, all of them verbose in their pleasure.

"What are we to do, sit by idly while we wait for their return?" I asked, feeling helpless.

"There are no idle hands here on the ranch," Simon said, returning from the kitchen with a platter refilled with ham. "We work for the common good. We rotate turns cooking and tending to dishes as you saw last night. It is my task this morning. There is ample to do. Horses, cattle, fences, building maintenance, the list is never ending."

"What do you think would interest you, baby?" Kane asked.

I thought for a moment. I'd grown up with a cook, a housekeeper and other people to take care of the more mundane tasks. I was...had been a society woman and was not adept at ranch life.

"I can ride. Perhaps I can offer assistance in the stables?" I looked to Kane, then at the other men around the table.

"Then we shall begin the day there."

———

"Relax, Emma," Kane said in soothing tones. I was on my stomach, knees tucked under me in the usual position for having the plug put in or taken out. It was morning, so the latest plug had been in all night.

"I...I'm sorry," I replied, taking a deep breath, although it did nothing to settle me.

"You've only been awake a minute. What can you be so tense

about?" He'd moved his hands from between my thighs and ran one up and down my back.

I sighed into my pillow. "Ian. I worry about Ian."

His hand continued it's slow, soothing motion. "Baby, there's no reason to worry. He's fine."

I looked over my shoulder at him, once again in awe. His shoulders were broad, his chest solid and with dark hair that tapered in a line below his navel to the thatch of hair at the base of his cock. His cock was always erect; there wasn't a time when I saw it at rest, even after a good fucking. Unruly locks of hair fell over his forehead. Sleep had softened his features, if that were even really possible. I was...enthralled.

"It's been five days," I pouted. I missed Ian. I had to admit to myself that I wanted both men. I wanted Kane...and Ian. It seemed like something – someone – was missing with Ian gone.

"I thought all the time with the horses would have distracted you."

I shook my head dejectedly. "I've enjoyed it, especially riding astride instead of sidesaddle. That seems so paltry though in comparison to what Ian's challenges."

His hand slid down my back to cup my bottom. "Take a deep breath and push out. That's it. Good girl." He slipped the plug from me and didn't delay working me with his fingers. This had been the routine in the days since Ian left. "You've done so well. I can now fit two fingers in you."

I breathed heavily from his ministrations; his two fingers – very large fingers – scissored and stretched my ass even more than the plug. The feeling wasn't something I would ever become used to. It was foreign and uncomfortable, yet the sensations elicited as his fingers brushed against the ring of muscle there had me panting and even coming. I disliked it, but loved it all the same.

"Ian will be so pleased when he returns. He will want to see your progress, to see you taking the progressively larger plugs. You will be ready for his cock. Why will he be pleased, baby?"

I moaned as he pushed the fingers in deep, the greasy lubricant from the plug still kept me slippery. "Because...because he will fuck me there."

"That's right. He's going to claim your virgin arse. After, we'll both fuck you. Together. Ian will fuck your arse while I fuck your tight cunny. What will that mean?"

He'd said these words to me every morning as he worked my body. It was a daily reminder as to Ian's inclusion in our marriage, that we would not be complete until he returned. That he was training my ass for Ian.

"That we are one."

Kane moved behind me and nudged the head of his cock at the entrance to my pussy. It was so broad, so flared that every time he filled me, he opened me so wide. "It will be like this, only better. My fingers are most certainly a poor substitute for Ian's big cock."

With those words, he thrust deep, filling my pussy, his fingers in my ass, coaxing me into complete submission. Kane was correct. With Ian missing, I came, but the pleasure I knew would not be the same until he returned and his cock was deep within me as well.

16

MMA

One challenge of ranch life I discovered was the lack of solitude. Kane remained close to me at night from dinner until breakfast. After eating in the morning, he went off to do whatever needed to be accomplished that day. Repairing a well, a breeding of a mare to the very eager stallion, stringing barbed wire, going into town for supplies. The list was never ending. When Kane was not about, I usually worked in companionship with at least one other man in the stable, if not more. Ann enjoyed working the garden, the immense patch of land that held all kinds of vegetables and fruit that would sustain our larder for the winter.

Today, however, the men were off working far afield and I was alone in the stable. I'd ridden each day, with the promise to remain in sight of the buildings when alone for my own safety. Fortunately, I'd done nothing to warrant a punishment from Kane while Ian had been away, which only helped me to settle into my daily tasks.

After saddling the horse Kane had chosen for me, I led the animal out of the stable and into the bright sunshine. The air was warm and fresh; a rain shower overnight left everything verdant.

I was just pulling a carrot I'd stolen from the kitchen out of my pocket to give to the animal when something in the distance caught my eye. It was a group of men, four of them, on horseback, although who they were was unclear. They were on a rise to the south, in the opposite direction of town.

A bad feeling settled in my stomach, knowing none of the men on the ranch had gone that way. Kane was with Brody and Simon tending to a sick calf in the north pasture. Rhys and Cross were stringing barbed wire to a repaired fence to the west. Ann was most likely in the garden at this hour.

Slowly, they came closer, their horses plodding over the terrain as if they had all the time in the world. Recognition was swift, even from such a distance, for I knew Ian's bearing, the breadth of his shoulders. He was with three other men. Strangers. Oh, dear lord.

Dropping the horse's lead, I sprinted into the stable to grab the rifle, locked and loaded, perched upon pegs in the wall, ready for use at any sign of danger. Kane had pointed it out to me the first day, ensuring I knew not only the dangers that abounded, but also how we protected ourselves from them.

I was surely familiar with a rifle. Before my parents died, my father had instructed me to shoot until I was competent in using one. He'd also provided a lifestyle that did not require doing so. Until now.

Returning to the horse, I mounted carefully with the loaded weapon and a long skirt and nudged my heels into his sides.

"Ann!" I shouted as I came upon the garden, dirt kicking up around me in a soft swirl.

She stood from her crouch by the summer raspberries.

"Ian is on the rise with several men."

Her eyes widened beneath the brim of her sun hat, from my words and most likely from the gun I had slung across my body. "Surely you aren't going to meet them?"

"He is with the men who sought him. I know it."

"How do you know such a thing?" she asked, her head turned in the direction of the rise, her hand on her forehead to block the sun.

I shook my head. "I just do." My heart raced and I was breathing as if I'd run the distance to the garden instead of riding.

"You can't mean to approach them yourself!" A look akin to horror crossed her face.

"What if they are here for the others?" I looked in the opposite direction to see if any of the men could be seen. "Do you want them all to be taken? Killed?"

"*You* could get killed," she countered, pointing at me.

"I have the rifle."

"Emma!" she shouted, but I'd already spurred my horse into a full gallop.

My bonnet slipped off my head from the brisk pace, bouncing against my back as it dangled from the ribbon about my neck. Ian was back and he was in danger.

When the men saw me approach, they stopped. I slowed to a trot, shifting the rifle so I could aim and fire at will.

Ian was indeed one of the men, Mason, I now recognized, on his left, two strangers on his right. They all appeared travel worn, with dusty clothes, skin tanned from the sun. The length of the scruff on their cheeks indicated several days in the saddle. To my eyes, Ian looked heavenly. He was whole and appeared uninjured. The look on his face, however, indicated his situation to be dire.

"You're not welcome here. Let Ian go and I won't shoot you," I warned.

The other men stared at me with mixed looks – amusement, anger and surprise. None held weapons as I did, however rifle butts protruded from two of the packs. They sat relaxed in their saddles, hands resting on the pommels.

"Would the lass shoot us?" one man asked Ian. His accent matched Ian's brogue.

My husband hadn't taken his eyes from me, although they narrowed at the question.

"I dinna ken," he replied. "Emma, put the gun down."

"No," I replied, shaking my head. "I won't let these men take you back to England." I lifted the rifle so it pointed at the man on the far right. His hands came up slowly, and so did his eyebrows.

"I assume this is your wife," the man commented.

"Aye," Ian replied, his voice in that stern, low octave. "Emma, put the gun down." His repeated words were more insistent.

"We aren't taking your husband to England," the other stranger said. I shifted the gun his way.

"They're not, Emma," Mason added.

"How do I know you aren't lying?" My palms were damp and my shoulders began to ache from holding up the heavy rifle, but I held true.

"Because I said so," Ian said. He nudged his horse forward until he came along side me and grabbed the weapon from my hands. I exhaled at the relief of Ian taking charge and so did the other three men. "So did Mason."

Up close, a tick pulsed in his jaw, his eyes narrowed not in lust as I so wanted to see from him, but in anger. "Are ye daft?" he asked, his voice loud. "Waving a gun around, approaching men ye dinna ken?"

His Scot's brogue was stronger than usual.

"You're innocent," I affirmed.

"He is," a man behind him said.

I paused at the words, looked to Ian for confirmation.

"These men are MacDonald and McPherson. Scots like me. They were part of our regiment in Mohamir and have come to join us. They have surnames, but they've never shared them."

I looked around Ian and to the men. They tipped their hats at me and I blushed. Mason just gave a subtle shake of his head as if he were in disbelief.

"Oh dear," I whispered, my shoulders slumping.

Ian turned and tossed the rifle to one of the other men, caught easily and readily in the way only those used to such weaponry did. My husband slid from his horse, came around and stood at my side, arms out. "Get down, Emma."

"Then why are they here?" I asked, ignoring his order.

He sighed, but did not dim his anger. "As I said, they've come to live here. They emigrated to America."

"What?" That was the last possible scenario I'd expected. Turning my head to the men briefly, I saw the truth of the words with slight nods from each.

"MacDonald, the lug, is Simon's brother. Now get down from the bloody horse."

Now that it was made apparent, the resemblance was clear. Oh dear. I was in dire straits.

I looked down at Ian for the briefest of moments, knew from the look in his eye, the set of his jaw, the timbre of his voice that I was in the worst kind of trouble. Tossing one leg over the saddle, I let Ian lower me to the ground, take my hand and drag me several feet away to a large boulder, one of many that dotted the rugged landscape. He sat and abruptly pulled me over his knees, my belly down.

"Ian!" I shouted, right before the air escaped my lungs in a loud oomph. I'd expected him to pull me into a hug, a kiss, something to end the drought of attention and affection his days away had brought.

Unceremoniously, he hoisted my skirt up and over my back, exposing my naked ass to the air, Ian and the three men. He did not talk, did not delay, only spanked me – hard – all over my ass so that the flesh there and on the upper part of my thighs prickled with heat.

"Ye will nay approach danger with complete disregard."

Smack.

"Ye came alone."

Smack.

"Wielding a gun that could have been taken from ye and used on your person without effort."

Smack.

"Did ye ken Mason and I that weak that we couldn't protect ourselves against two men?"

Smack.

"Where the bloody hell is Kane?"

Smack. Smack. Smack.

I started to cry, my hands gripping the tall blades of summer

VANESSA VALE

grass. The searing strikes had me wilted and contrite. I *had* ridden into presumed danger without a care to my safety. I *had* aimed a gun toward men who had outnumbered me and could have overpowered me readily enough. I'd been headstrong and desperate.

"They were going to take you away!" I shouted, then sniffled.

"She's a little hellcat, lad." The voice came from behind me. Oh, the men! I forgot they were there and most assuredly watching my punishment.

"I'd like a little lassie to defend me like that." Another man's voice broke through the sound of Ian's palm striking my already tender flesh.

"You would, but then you'd spank her arse just like Ian."

Tears ran down my cheeks as Ian continued, my humiliation complete not only from these strangers commenting on my misery as if it were nothing, but by the sound of horses approaching and knowing the men from the ranch would see me this way as well.

I heard the men talking, but couldn't hear the words, dipping into a place where the spanking had switched from painful to a fog, although each strike was still filled with vehemence. I had succumbed. I was out of control, at the mercy of Ian and his palm, his anger, his fear. Wait. His anger was because of his fear for me. His punishment was to ensure that I was whole and hale, but also to soothe his frazzled nerves that I could have been harmed if I had approached more nefarious men.

"Are you finished?"

Kane.

"Aye."

"Good. It's my turn."

The spanking began once again in earnest, this time it was Kane's palm, although he only added about five swats to the tally.

My world upended and I dizzily landed on Ian's hard thighs. I hissed out a breath at the contact. Using my hands, I wiped the streaks of tears from my cheeks as I sniffled. "I'm...I'm sorry," I mumbled, still recovering.

Kane knelt down beside me. "You scared ten years off my life when Ann told us where you'd gone."

"Are you going to spank me again?" I asked, glancing between both men. They looked at me with a mixture of fear and anger. Kane was breathing hard and sweat dotted his brow.

"Nay," Ian said. "I'm going to fuck you." I felt the truth of his words hard beneath my bottom.

"Now? Here?" There were the two strangers who who'd arrived with Ian, plus Mason. From the ranch were Brody, Simon and Cross. Simon and his brother were hugging and smacking each other on the back congenially, clearly pleased to be in each other's company after so many years.

"Now. Here," Ian repeated, shifting me on his lap so I still sat astride his thighs, but this time with my knees on either side of his hips. Kane grabbed the tangle of my dress and pulled it up around my waist and out of the way. Reaching between us, Ian undid the placket of his pants, his engorged cock bobbing free. Without a chance to even consider what we were about to do, he hoisted me up by my waist and lowered me directly onto his cock, filling my pussy in one smooth slide.

"Oh!" I cried out, feeling so full and surprised by how wet I was for him. I wanted to lift and lower myself on him, to use his cock to seek my pleasure, but he wouldn't let me. His hands, banded tightly about my waist, held me in place as he shifted his hips, thrusting up into me, using me.

"No! The men are watching," I pushed on his shoulders, frantic to rise. The feel of him inside of me was...delicious, but I did not wish to be watched, exposed as we were. "It's...it's private!"

"Stop, baby." Kane's voice cut through my panic. "The men, they're gone." Gripping tightly to Ian's shirt, I turned my head and saw the backs of the retreating men upon their horses. "This is not a theater show. Your punishment was warranted for your reckless behavior and they observed it, knowing now you are contrite and will not put your life, or those of anyone else, in danger. But fucking, they did not need to see."

I relaxed every tense muscle, which had me sinking lower on Ian's cock. He nudged the very entrance to my womb and I moaned.

"Ye are nay to come, Emma." Ian took me hard, filling me roughly. My breath escaped with every thrust. "Open her dress. I want to see her breasts."

Kane stepped behind me, reached around and ripped my bodice open, little buttons flying through the air. Dipping his hands into my corset, Kane lifted my breasts free.

"Oh, look at ye. I love the sight of ye getting well fucked," Kane said in my ear.

I cried out from one adept stroke.

"You're so beautiful. Can you feel how much Ian wants you? How much he's missed you? How desperate he was when you wanted to rescue him?"

My breasts jiggled with each hard slap of my thighs against his. The sound of my arousal, slippery wet and slick, filled the air.

"Dinna come, Emma," Kane warned.

My head fell back, my eyes squeezed shut as I panted. "Why?" Ian sucked a nipple into his mouth, drew on it, tugging the tip into a tight furl.

"Ye must ken how frantic I felt when you charged up the hillside," Ian growled against my breast. His short beard was soft and prickly at the same time, only heightening my sensitivity. "How desperate I was. So out of control. It is nay your job to rescue me. It is your job to remain safe or you will make me insane."

His hands tightened about my waist just as he pulled me down onto him, his cock swelling inside of me as he came, his hot seed coating my womb.

His sweaty forehead pressed against my breasts as he recovered, his breath soughing out of his lungs, but he loosened his secure hold. Not that I had any intention of moving. I had his cock filling me up and I wanted completion only he could give me. Clenching my inner walls around him, I felt tremors of my desire, but it wasn't enough to make me come. It seemed it was not to happen. Even shifting my hips offered no relief.

"Is she ready?" Ian asked, his hot breath fanning my chest.

"Yes," Kane replied.

He lifted his head and looked at me. Desire was still etched in the hard line of his jaw, his pale eyes hooded from his release. "Your arse is ready for me, Emma?"

I clenched his cock once again, the idea of him taking me as they'd planned, now, had my arousal simmering. I was so desperate, so needy for my release, Ian's cock buried within me while remaining still was torture. "Yes." I repeated Kane's words.

Ian plucked at a long tendril of my hair.

"Then it is time."

17

AN

I scrubbed the dirt and sweat from hard days on a horse. The water in the hip tub was cold, but it didna matter. Emma's cries of pleasure and begging wafted through the air from Kane's bedroom. After I'd recovered from fucking her – and the scare to my heart when I'd seen her galloping and gun wielding – I'd tossed her onto my lap for the ride back to the house. I hadn't been afraid for her safety as we wouldna hurt her, but knowing she would have done something so dangerous if I really had been in trouble had my ire rise. She had nay thought to her safety. She dinna ken what she meant to me.

Mason had been waiting to take care of the horses as Kane and I took care of our wife. Once upstairs, we stripped her bare and unceremoniously tied her hands to the brass headboard.

This hadn't been done without questions or opposition from Emma, who vehemently apologized and protested. She was not going to go off and do something dangerous like that again. While I bathed, Kane worked her body, keeping her arousal elevated, yet not allowing her to come. The spanking had been her punishment, rightly enough, but torturing her with pleasure was a perk I relished as I scrubbed my body clean.

When I'd come across MacDonald and McPherson in Bozeman, I'd expected a kill-or-be-killed situation. There was nay chance of my return to England. There was nay chance, if Evers had indeed tracked me down personally, he would have let me live to make such a journey. When I'd found my friends to be the men Simon had heard about, the relief had been immeasurable. Discovering they wished to live in the Montana Territory, start anew as well, only made me happy. I ken Simon must've felt the irony at discovering one of the men who he'd alerted me to was indeed his brother.

And so we returned as a merry group, until Emma rushed up the rise like Boadicea, all beauty and fierce protectiveness. This lack of personal safety proved to me that she considered me hers just as much as she was mine. The revelation had me grinning, sitting naked in a small tub with my knees practically by my ears. She hadn't said that she loved us, but her actions spoke for her. She would not have ridden into potential danger if she didna care. I felt at peace for the first time in...years. Evers was still a threat, but I could not live my life in constant fear of the man. I could, however, live the rest of my days with Emma with me, between me and Ian. I was possessive of her, perhaps excessively so, but that was what a husband felt for his woman. Protectiveness, possessiveness and the stirrings of love. I finished my bath with additional haste and returned to my family.

Kane had her legs spread, knees bent. His hand between her thighs, two fingers filling her arse. From where I stood in the doorway, drying myself, I could see he was ensuring she was completely slick with the lubricant.

Emma was stunning. Her eyes were closed, her head back, mouth open. Chestnut locks fanned out on the pillow behind her head, her arms over her head with her wrists secured. This placement forced her breasts up, her nipples tight and a cherry red. Perhaps the moans I'd heard from the tub had been Kane playing with those sweet tips. There was additional length in the rope, but the knots securing her were sufficient. She was just where we wanted her.

Kane looked to me, his gaze hooded, his desire evident in the rigidity of his cock. At some point, he'd stripped as well. "She's ready."

"Yes, please. Ian, I need to come!" Emma begged, her breathing ragged and deep.

Kane moved to lie next to Emma, side by side. I knelt on the bed, lifted Emma up and flipped her over so she was astride Kane's waist, one of her knees on either side of his hips. With her wrists tied, she couldna move. Kane slipped his head between her arms. As I reached for the jar of lubricant, Kane shifted Emma as he wanted, forcing her down onto his cock. My seed from her earlier fucking made the action easy and both of them made sounds of pleasure.

Coating my fingers, I tested her tight pink pucker. It had been days since I'd touched her here, but Kane had assured me of her readiness. I took a moment to play, circling my fingers over the slick opening, pushing against the tight ring. When my fingers slipped in without much effort, I knew he was correct. The feel of her, so tight with Kane's cock right there, separated from my fingers with just a thin membrane, had my balls tightening and the need to claim her intense.

"Oh God," Emma moaned.

"It's time, baby. Time to make you ours. Together."

"Yes!" she cried as Kane rocked his hips up into her.

Coating my cock with additional lubricant, I nudged the broad head to her virgin hole. I took her only a short time ago, but my cock was pulsing, aching to feel her walls around it once again. Carefully, slowly, I pressed forward, knowing my cock was larger than any of the plugs Kane had used on her while I'd been away. She might have adjusted to accept something filling her, but a cock was different. Bigger, deeper and most certainly harder.

Stroking a hand down her back, soothing her, I murmured words of encouragement. *Good girl. You're ours now. Ah, my cock's in you. Relax. You took another inch. Such a pretty sight taking both our cocks. Breathe, baby. That's it. I'm in all the way.*

She was completely filled. Little mewling sounds escaped her throat as she held perfectly still. I met Kane's gaze. His jaw was clamped tightly, undoubtedly struggling to hold off pumping into her just as I was. We both took a moment to let her settle, let her adjust to having us cram her so bloody full. Her back was so silky smooth against the hard line of my chest. Kane lifted his hands to cup her breasts, rub his thumbs over her sensitive tips. With her hands bound, she could do nothing but accept whatever we gave her.

"You're so big. I'm filled so deep. I...I don't know what to do," she whimpered. Her pale skin was coated in a sheen of perspiration, her hair clinging to her damp skin. She licked her lips, her eyes closed.

"You don't have to do anything, baby. It's time for us to take care of you," Kane said. He offered me a brief nod and he moved, pulled back so he almost withdrew, then slid back in. As he did so, I pulled back, so we worked in opposition, one filling her as the other retreated. We kept a slow pace, a consistent, mind-numbing pace. "This is where you belong. Between us. You were made to be filled by our cocks. You're ours, baby."

"Ours," I repeated on a growl.

Emma was lost, wild, abandoned. She cried out, tears sliding down her cheeks as she pushed her breasts into Kane's palms. We didn't stop, didn't let her catch her breath. "Yes!"

"Come, baby. Your pleasure belongs to us. *You* belong to us."

At my command, she came, screaming so loud the men in the stable had to have heard. Her body squeezed and pulsed around my cock, which had me falling off the cliff directly after her. I couldn't hold back with the tight constriction of her arse. My seed filled her up. Kane followed directly after, pulling her down onto his chest, letting her recover as we were connected as one.

———

EMMA

I must have dozed, for when I came awake, I was curled into Kane's side, Ian pressed against my back, my body feeling empty as their cocks were gone. I did, however, feel the remnants of their releases, sticky and warm coating my pussy and thighs. My hands had been released. The room was bright with daylight, only just shy of the noon meal. We were in bed, lounging during a busy summer's day on the ranch. It felt...decadent. I reveled in the feel of both men surrounding me.

Ian was home. He was safe.

Kane kissed my forehead as I felt Ian's hand stroking my back.

"Ye willna go off trying to save me again, Emma," Ian said, just before kissing my spine.

"We are here to protect you. There are two of us, yet only one of you," Kane added.

"But you are irreplaceable!" Didn't they understand that I wanted both of them?

"Ah, lass," Ian breathed. "It's our job to protect ye. To possess ye just like we did."

"I can feel your possessiveness dripping out of me," I replied dryly.

"Mmm, yes. It's a beautiful sight."

I idly swirled my finger through the soft hairs on Kane's chest. "If your job is to protect me, what is my job?"

Kane retreated and turned me so I was on my back between them. He delved his hand between my thighs and through their mixed seed. I looked into his dark eyes. All hints of anger, of lust, were gone. In its place was most definitely the possessiveness he spoke of. "To take our seed. Again and again until it takes root and you swell with our child."

Ian came up on an elbow on my other side and looked down at me. "Do ye ken this is enough to make a baby, lass? We are a family, and soon, hopefully very soon, a growing family. Nothing will separate us."

"Nothing," Kane reiterated.

"What of the others?"

Kane frowned. "You ask after the other men while Ian plays with your cunny?"

"They need to find their own wives," Ian muttered. "Perhaps, Kane, we have not done enough to make her remember to whom she belongs."

He slipped a finger into me and I sighed. "I...I remember."

"I'm not so sure," Kane countered. "Since it is your job to make the baby, it is most certainly your men's job to fill you with seed to do so."

"I...I would not want you to be remiss in your duties," I said, my eyes falling shut as my legs fell wide.

Ian moved between my legs and filled me in one easy stroke. "I will never get enough, lass."

His breath fanned my neck.

"Never," Kane added.

"Never," I whispered, as my husbands claimed me once again.

THEIR WAYWARD BRIDE - BOOK 2

1

AUREL

I'd never been so cold in my life. My fingers had gone from cold to painful and now they were numb. My legs were warmer where they squeezed the horse's sides. I'd thrown my scarf over my head and tied it beneath my chin an hour ago, but it offered no real protection from the snow. It had only been light flurries when I left the stable, but now the flakes were thick and came down so heavily I could see nothing in front of me. The wind had picked up and it blew the snow sideways, the chill biting into my very marrow.

I was lost. Completely and absolutely lost, which meant I was going to die. Virginia City had been my destination when I'd set off, the town only two hours on horseback from home, but I'd been out for so much longer, and the town was nowhere in sight. Of course, nothing was in sight. My eyelashes were coated with snow and it was getting harder and harder to remain awake. Falling asleep would be bliss, especially with warm, thick blankets, a roaring fire and hot tea. Dreaming as I was did nothing to change my predicament. I was going to die. Foolishly.

But what had I been expected to do? Stay at the house and let Father barter me off as part of a business transaction? Mr. Palmer had dangled the sale of his land, along with several thousand head of cattle, for me. Yes, I was the price. Perhaps not all of it, but the man had made the financial amount reasonable enough for Father to be hooked like a fish with a nice fat worm. Then, once he had my father eager, he'd given him the true price. His daughter. I'd lived at a school in Denver since I was seven, shipped away and forgotten for fourteen years. Then, two months ago, a letter requested my return. I'd thought, after all that time, my father had wanted me and I'd foolishly grasped onto that hope. My illusions were shattered yesterday when Mr. Palmer had arrived to meet me and the men had told me their plan.

It was then I realized my true value for Father. I wasn't his *daughter,* but a prized mare he'd sold to the highest bidder. He'd sent for me only to marry me off to Mr. Palmer and finalize his deal. I was to be traded for a swath of land, cattle and water rights. I'd been nothing to him all along, for I was the one who'd killed his wife. She'd died birthing me so it had been my fault.

Marriages of convenience happened all the time in the Montana Territory. A woman couldn't survive on her own without a man; that was a given. But I hadn't even been in Simms, let alone Montana Territory. I'd been a ward of the school in Colorado. Regardless, my life was not my own; I would not be a pawn in Father's land negotiations. Especially not when the price, for me at least, was so high.

My prospective groom was at least fifty. He had three grown children, two who were married and lived in Simms, the third in Seattle. It might have been tolerable to be the man's wife while being younger than his children, but the man was shorter than I, had a belly that reminded me of a whiskey cask and had more hair on the back of his hands than on his head. Worst of all, he was missing teeth, and the ones that remained were yellow from chewing tobacco. And he smelled. The man was repulsive. If he'd been tall and handsome and virile, making my heart race and my cheeks flush in his presence, that would have been something else altogether. Father had said the deal was done, the contracts signed. The only legal work left was acquiring a marriage license—and with tomorrow being Sunday, would be resolved at the morning church service.

So instead of marrying Mr. Palmer, I was going to die. I, Laurel Turner, chose to freeze to death over marrying an unattractive, unappealing, overweight geriatric. My anger toward the man, and my father's lack of consideration for what I wanted, had me spurring the horse harder. Perhaps I could see a light, a house, a building, anything in this frozen squall where I could seek shelter. Numbly, I wiped my hand over my eyes in disbelief. Was that a light? A yellow glow, muted and soft, appeared briefly through the snow, and then disappeared.

Hope shot through me and I turned the horse in that direction.

———

MASON

"I'll get more wood for morning," I told Brody, who was working at his desk. We were in the parlor, the fire in the hearth heating the room and the house beyond against the bitter cold night. Wind and snow rattled the windows. I went to one and pulled back the thick curtain. All I could see was my own reflection and snow blowing sideways. "I imagine the wood pile will be buried by then."

Brody looked up from some papers he'd been studying. "Is the box in the kitchen full?"

"I'll check and stoke the stove before bed."

My friend just nodded and returned to his work. There wasn't much ranching to be done in the dead of winter beyond making sure the cows didn't drop dead out in weather such as this, and tending to the horses. The days were short, the nights long. Only the heartiest of men survived in the Montana Territory, but for me, for Brody and the rest of the men from our regiment who built the Bridgewater Ranch, it was home.

For Kane and Ian, they had their wife, Emma, to help them pass the time, and with the noticeable way her belly was growing, they'd been quite busy. Andrew and Robert had Ann and their infant son, Christopher, to keep them quite occupied. It was the bachelors of Bridgewater who endured the long winter nights, alone. I sighed, wondering if Brody and I would ever find the woman for us. It wasn't an easy task, finding a woman who would marry two men, for that was what we'd have—a wife for both of us. That was our way, the way of the men of Bridgewater—find a woman, make her ours, cherish, protect and possess her for the rest of our lives.

I sighed to myself as I shrugged into my shearling coat, flipped up the collar and slipped on leather gloves. A woman wouldn't be appearing tonight, no matter how much I wished for it. As I opened the back door, a blast of frigid air struck me full force, swirling snow into the kitchen. I stepped outside quickly, shutting the door behind me, keeping the warm air inside. On more clement weather, I could see the lights of the other houses off in the distance. Tonight, however, there was nothing but black and white. Stacked beneath the eaves of the house was a pile of wood big enough to sustain us for the winter. Grabbing a few logs, I piled them in my arms, went inside, carried them into the parlor and piled them on the hearth.

"Need help?" Brody asked, still at work.

I shook my head. "Another load here and one in the kitchen. I'm going up to bed when I'm done."

"'Night," Brody replied absently, focused on his work.

Once again in the bitter outdoors, I piled more wood on my forearm. It was as I picked up the last log that I heard a horse whinnying. I paused. All the horses were in the stable for the duration of the storm. They wouldn't survive outdoors on a night like this. No doubt we'd have a cow or two dead by morning. The wind kicked up as snow slid down my neck. Lifting my shoulders, I winced at the coldness against my skin. I was hearing things.

There.

I heard it again. It was a horse. This time the whinny sounded more like a scream. I'd heard it before, a horse in pain. Injured. I looked out into the darkness, but could see nothing. No animal, nothing was in sight, just snow. It was up to my ankles; no doubt the accumulation would build overnight. By morning, the drifts would be waist high if the wind sustained. Had one of the other men missed a horse? Was it wandering out in this weather?

I put the pile of wood back, opened the door and yelled for Brody. He came quickly.

"I heard a horse. I'm going to go look for it."

Brody was surprised. "That's odd. Could be the wind."

"Could be," I agreed. "I have to check. I don't want to lose an animal to this."

He held up a hand. "You'll need a lantern, and take the rifle." He went to the gun rack where six rifles were vertically aligned on the wall, ready for any kind of emergency. On Bridgewater, there was always a chance for danger. Brody picked one and checked the barrel before handing it to me. He picked up another for himself.

"Give me five minutes, then fire a shot," I told him, ensuring I knew which direction to turn to return. "I won't go far."

"Don't get lost because I don't want to go out in that bloody weather to find you." He grinned.

I couldn't blame him. I didn't want to go out in this weather either. But I *had* heard a horse. I wouldn't be able to sleep if I didn't check.

After slinging the rifle over my shoulder, I tucked my collar up around my neck again and forged a path out into the snow. After about ten steps, I paused, listening. Wind, nothing but wind. Wait. There. I turned toward the sound, walked in that direction. One minute, then two. Then another. It was slow going in the deep drifts, fighting the wind. I finally saw it. The animal was only about ten feet in front of me, lying on its side. Thankfully it had a dark coat, otherwise I might have missed it. I squatted down by the head, heard it breathing heavily, eyes wide and wild. Sweat coated the animal's fur, even in this weather, and the snow was beginning to cling to it, pile on top of him. The sound that escaped the animal was of pain, almost a tortured scream. It had a bridle, the reins beginning to be covered with snow. A saddle. Which meant there was a rider. Somewhere.

I stood and ran in a quick circle around the animal and found a dark mass in the snow. A man. Was he dead? It would not be a surprise, either from the elements or being tossed from the horse's back. Thankfully, the snow was fairly deep and cushioned the fall. While the horse made agonizing sounds, I put my hands on the dark coat of the silent rider. It was not a broad man's physique I felt, but a narrow waist, flared hips. A woman! Holy hell. A woman was out in weather such as this.

I rolled her onto her back and her full breasts were beneath my gloved palms. I could tell they were full, lush mounds even through the layers of clothes. Her head had been protected by a tightly wrapped scarf, but she'd been laying there long enough for an inch of snow to cover her. I didn't even know if she was alive or dead. I wouldn't waste time finding out now. She had to be out of the elements and quickly.

The horse, however, was another matter. Leaving the woman, I went back to the horse, looked down at his front legs. There, as I'd suspected, was a nasty break, the bone sticking through the flesh in a white jagged edge. He must have stepped in a prairie dog hole. It was not uncommon and unfortunately, deadly. Cocking the rifle, I went back to the horse's head, stroked its sleek coat, and aimed.

The shot rang out in the night, but was muffled by the snow and blown away with the wind. I doubted any other men besides Brody would hear the shot. If they had, they'd wait for two more, three in a row being our signal for an emergency. No one would venture out in this weather otherwise. It was clearly deadly.

I couldn't take another moment over the horse; the woman was now my concern. Lifting her easily, I turned and followed my tracks back to the door. It would only be a matter of time before they disappeared. The wind wasn't as strong returning.

"So...cold," she murmured.

She was alive!

"I've got you," I replied. "In just a minute you're going to be nice and warm again. Just stay awake for me, sweetheart."

"You...you smell good," she slurred.

I couldn't help but chuckle at her words. Clearly, she was out of her mind, for what woman would admit that while in such a predicament?

She wasn't a slight woman. I could feel her curves beneath my arms. It was her stillness that had me hastening my steps. Finally! The warm glow of the kitchen lantern came into view.

"Almost there, sweetheart."

I kicked the door with my foot. Once, twice.

Brody opened it right away. "Holy bloody hell," he muttered, stepping back to let me enter.

"Here. Take her."

I handed her off to a surprised Brody, his eyes widening when I'd said the word *her* and even further when he, too, felt her woman's shape.

2

RODY

I stood in the kitchen, holding a woman. Stunned. Mason had gone back outside because he thought he heard a horse—I figured it had been the deceiving sound of the wind—and came back with a woman. Yes, she most surely was a woman. The size of her, the feel of her soft curves, even through her coat, provided no doubts. She was covered head to toe—boots, long dress, wool coat, a scarf that came down low over her face. I could see nothing of her skin, only *feel* her femininity. Her attire was no match for the fierce weather. What was she doing out in this storm? Why was she here, on Bridgewater? Where had she come from?

"Is she dead?" I asked Mason, who stripped off his gloves and coat. She was freezing cold and the snow that covered her began to dampen my shirt.

"No," he replied, breathing hard.

This spurred me into action. Spinning around, I gently placed her on the large kitchen table and started to rid her of her layers of clothes.

I worked the scarf from her head, unwinding it and dropping the damp item to the floor and she moaned. It made me pause. "I just want to sleep," she mumbled.

Her face was pale, so pale, and her were lips leeched of all color. If she slept now, she might die. We had to warm her up and keep her awake. "Oh, no. No sleeping," I said.

Her hair was a fiery red, a bun at the nape of her neck with wild tendrils falling over her face, the tips of some coated in snow and ice. I touched her cheek. It was icy cold.

"Mmm," she said and tilted her head into my fingers.

I looked up at Mason, who'd come to stand across from me, the woman between us on the table. "Get a quilt from the other room. Sit it on top of the stove to warm. It's not hot enough now to burn."

Her life was in our hands. I went down to her feet to take off her boots, but ice encrusted the laces. I grabbed a large kitchen knife and cut through them. I tossed the knife onto the stove with a clatter, tugging one boot off, then the other.

"Wait," she called out, shifting on the table. "What are you doing?" Her eyes opened and she looked at me, confused and lost. Her eyes were so green, so clear.

"You're cold and wet, and some of you clothes are covered in ice. We need to get you warm."

I didn't wait and discuss this further; it was a matter of life and death. Next came her heavy stockings, tied with a ribbon just above her knees.

Mason returned with two quilts, one he laid on the stove, the other on the chair beside him. He nimbly worked the other stocking free, as I undid the buttons of her coat.

"Who are you?" she asked, starting to shiver. That was a good sign.

"I'm Brody and you are on our land. Mason found you."

"Thank you," she said. "I thought I would die out there."

"No dying on us, sweetheart," Mason told her. "But we're going to have to take your clothes off."

She looked between us as she shook her head. "No, I'll do it myself." Her fingers worked at the buttons on her coat. "I...I can't feel my fingers. They're numb."

"Let us help." I gently nudged her hands away and finished her task for her.

"Jesus, you're beautiful," Mason murmured, helping me to prop her up and slip the coat from her arms.

"I don't think I've ever seen hair that color before," I responded.

"It's red," she grumbled.

She spoke the words as if the color was terrible. It was like fire, with burnished gold and bronze mixed in. The places that were damp were darker, yet it was clear it was quite curly, even with the length of it tucked up into a bun.

Mason held her upper body as I struggled with the buttons down the front of her dress.

"You shouldn't be—"

"What's your name?" Mason asked.

"Laurel."

"Laurel, your clothes are wet and you must get warm. Aren't you cold?"

She nodded and another shiver wracked her.

"Then let us take care of you," I soothed. "You're safe with us."

I began once again, but was quickly frustrated it took so long, so I yanked at the material and the buttons went skittering across the room. Underneath, she wore a corset and I worked the stays free.

"This isn't appropriate. I've never...I'm cold." She was confused and tired and clearly affected by the cold. Her modesty was a sign that she was thinking somewhat clearly, but her need for warmth overrode her anxiety.

"Shh, it's all right. We'll have you warm in just a minute," Mason told her, going to the shelf and pouring out a small portion of whiskey. "Here, drink this." He propped her up with his arm as he held the cup to her lips. She took a sip, then coughed and winced at the pungent taste. "More." She shook her head but he insisted and was able to get two swallows down. "Good girl."

Beneath the corset, she was covered—barely—by a thin shift. The lower half of the dress was sodden now, the snow that had clung to it melting in the warm room. The dark green wool accentuated her hair color, made her skin even paler. As Mason held her, I worked the garment down over her hips and onto the floor.

"Shit."

I couldn't have agreed with Mason more. We were in big trouble here. Our gazes met over the woman's head. We'd been waiting for her. *The one.* She was barely alive and I knew it to be so. How? I had no idea, but I knew it to the very marrow of my bones.

I looked to my friend and he gave me a quick nod.

Relief coursed through me at his tacit confirmation.

The skin of her leg was icy beneath my fingers. "Almost done, sweetheart."

"Her fingers and toes aren't black, so frostbite hasn't set in. Thank god," Mason muttered.

I tugged at the hem of her shift. "This is damp. It has to go."

"No, I need my clothes," she replied, trying to hold the shift down.

Mason stroked a hand over her hair. "Shh, we've got a warm blanket for you."

"Oh," she moaned, clearly the thought appealed to her.

"No wet clothes, sweetheart. We'll get the shift off you and then wrap you in a nice warm blanket." I tried to make my voice as soft as possible, but I wasn't known for my gentleness. Laurel required it, though, so I tempered it for her.

I quickly stripped her bare and I couldn't help but look at her luscious form before Mason wrapped the quilt around her, rubbing her with the soft material to warm her more quickly.

"That feels so good," she sighed as she curled into Mason's chest from her position on the table. She wasn't as small as she seemed in my arms. I estimated her to be of average height, and with ample curves. There were no sharp bones with her, only very plump breasts, her nipples tightly furled and the color a pale coral. I'd seen them in the few seconds before she was covered. Even her hips were lush and full as if made for a man's hands to grip. I'd even caught a quick glimpse of the hair that shielded her pussy. It was a shade darker than the hair on her head, a striking contrast to her pale skin and the pink flesh just peeking out. Mason lifted her into his arms and she rested her head against his shoulder as he carried her into the parlor. He sat in the chair directly by the fire as I followed with the heated blanket.

Unfolding it, I tucked it around her until she was completely covered with only her face showing. Beads of sweat dotted Mason's brow, which meant his heat would be seeping into her. I took the seat across from them, leaned forward with my forearms on my knees.

"Is that better?" Mason asked.

"Yes, you're so warm. You saved me."

"We'll keep you safe, sweetheart," Mason soothed, stroking the back of his knuckles over her cheek. "Her color's better," he told me.

Pink tinged her lips now instead of blue. A good sign. Her eyes drifted closed.

"I'm so tired," she said. The whiskey most likely helped with this.

"Sleep now. I've got you. Brody and I will take care of you."

"I'm safe?" she asked, her voice soft.

Mason kissed the top of her head. "We'll let nothing happen to you."

Both of us watched her for a minute, her muscles going lax as she dipped into sleep. She was past any danger now and needed to warm up and rest.

"I heard a shot," I lowered my voice.

Mason lifted his gaze from the woman to meet mine. "She was riding a horse. Looks like the animal stepped in a hole, broke his leg. She was thrown. A snowdrift softened her fall. I had to put the animal down."

"How far from the house?"

He shook his head, considering. "One hundred meters, maybe further. I couldn't see anything out there to know. I followed my tracks back."

"I wonder where she came from, and why the bloody hell was she out in this?" I looked down at her. Long lashes fanned across her pale cheeks.

"We'll have plenty of time to find the answers. The way this storm is blowing, she's not going anywhere for awhile."

"She's not going anywhere. Ever. Agreed?"

Mason nodded. "Agreed."

LAUREL

Curled warmly on my side, I was reluctant to wake up. Miserable as I'd been gripping the reins of the horse, I'd been correct to fall asleep. The coldness was gone. My fingers and toes were no longer numb. Snow and wind weren't stinging my cheeks. My clothes were no longer wet. In fact, I was no longer wearing clothes. Then why was I so warm? Something hard pressed against my back while something warm touched my front.

I stretched and bumped into a solid, very warm, slightly hairy—

My eyes flew open and there, just a few inches from my face was a man. Blond hair that was a few months past a haircut, blue eyes, full lips.

"Oh!" I gasped and backed away and as I rolled over was surprised to find myself face-to-face with another man. My heart leapt into my throat. "Oh!"

Men surrounded me! It all came rushing back. Falling in the snow, being carried inside, men talking to me, taking off my wet clothes, warming me. I remember the whiskey, the hot blanket and being held. I'd felt safe in the man's arms, so warm and comforted. They had been concerned and focused solely on warming me up. They'd been...kind and protective.

"It's all right, you're safe." The man I now faced had short black hair, a neatly trimmed beard and equally dark eyes. His voice was deep, yet the tone soothing. And he was in my bed.

"We won't hurt you," the other man said. I turned to look over my shoulder at him. "Do you remember us from last night?" He held my gaze and I nodded. They spoke with unusual accents, nothing normally heard in the area. No one I'd ever met. I didn't notice this the night before, but I wasn't completely coherent.

I couldn't stay here. I needed to get up, to get away. This was not proper, being in bed—naked—with two strange men!

I sat up, both men lying on their sides facing me. My movement exposed the expanse of their broad shoulders, naked chests, and muscular arms. Tugging the sheet and quilt over my breasts to keep my modesty did nothing to cover my back. I felt cool air on my skin and watched as their gazes lowered.

"Oh!" I moved to my knees and tried to crawl from the bed between them, only to quickly realize two things simultaneously. The first was that they held the bedding securely, keeping me from moving. The second was that I was showing them my bottom, and if they could see that, they could see my womanhood.

I could have climbed from the bed naked, but realized if I did I'd have nothing to cover my nakedness. I could not run out of the room as I was. So I had no choice by to lie down once again, tugging the quilt up beneath my chin with a little squeal. I decided to try and talk my way out of this unseemly situation.

I needed to stay in the bed to keep my virtue. *They* needed to leave. I told them so.

"No." The blond one shook his head slowly. His eyes were heavy lidded and his cheeks had taken on a ruddy color. "You were half frozen when Mason found you. Nearly dead. We warmed you and watched over you all night." His voice was rough as he stared at me. No, he was staring at my lips.

"We need to ensure you are well, for you fell asleep on us." The dark haired one propped his head up on his elbow and looked down at me, the quilt not covering his body as much as it did mine. A smattering of dark hair covered his chest and I wondered if it would be soft to the touch. It narrowed and tapered into a line that went to his navel before being covered up. "Did you hit your head when you fell? Do you have pain anywhere? Your fingers and toes, are they numb?"

Realizing my eyes were wandering inappropriately, I lifted my gaze to meet his. "I am quite well now, thank you. No damage done," I replied, trying to distract him from my actions.

It didn't work. He smiled very knowingly. I'd been caught. My cheeks flushed hotly. Instead of being cold, I was overly warm. These men were like cast iron stoves, ample heat radiating off of them. The quilt was becoming too much, but I could *not* lower it.

He lifted a hand toward my face and I flinched as his fingers ever so gently moved over my hair. He didn't stop as he spoke. "Shh, don't be afraid."

"I am Mason," the bearded one said. His hand slipped beneath the blanket and I startled when his warm fingertips brushed over my shoulder. "And that lug is Brody."

"How do you do?" I asked politely, then cleared my throat. "Thank you very much for rescuing me, but I should be on my way." I spoke as if they blocked the door at the mercantile, not surrounded me in a bed.

Mason's restraining hand on my shoulder was insistent, although gentle. Brody continued to touch my hair, as if he'd never seen the color before. Their touch was as tender as it had been the night before, their voices soothing me in a way I'd never known. It was all surprising to me, this tenderness I found in two strangers.

"Which way is that?" Mason's brow rose in question.

"I...um, well, toward Virginia City."

Brody frowned, his hand stilling at my nape. "That's several hour's ride from Simms, and we're further to the north."

"Then I must certainly make haste, being late as I am." I was a terrible liar, especially under duress. Being naked in bed with two men was most certainly under duress.

"Is someone expecting you? No one would assume you would travel in such a blizzard," Mason commented. "They will think you home safe and anticipate your arrival after the roads are passable."

Both men's hands were moving over me once again, Mason's sliding up and down my arm, Brody mimicking him with the other. I clutched at the bedding by my neck and tried to ignore how their hands felt. I'd never had a man touch me in this way before, clothed or not. Of course, I'd never been in a bed with a man before, let alone two.

Mason's hand stilled on my elbow. "A husband? Was he traveling with you? I didn't find anyone else."

Brody stopped moving at the question and they looked at me closely.

I could lie and say I was wed, but then I'd have to create a spouse and that was why I'd run away in the first place. Or they'd venture out in the dangerous and inclement weather to find an imaginary person because of a lie.

Besides, I did not wish them to think I was a loose woman, falling into bed with men all the time. This situation was...highly irregular. "Oh, no. No husband. That would be highly inappropriate of me to be married to one while in bed with another...two."

Both men visibly relaxed and their hands began stroking over my skin again, causing goose bumps. Their motions were meant to be soothing, but it was quite hard to relax in a situation such as this.

"Um...where am I?"

"Bridgewater. It is our ranch."

"Why am I in bed with you?" How did I word this delicately? "With...both of you?

3

AUREL

I remembered being wrapped in a warm blanket and comfortably tucked in one of their laps. I remember a hand stroking over my cheek, over my hair, a kiss on the top of my head. It had felt so good, deep down knowing I was safe. Even now, between these two I felt safe. Still, they would think me forward. "Besides being unseemly, this is quite odd."

"Here at Bridgewater, it is not odd for a woman to be cared for by two men. In fact, it is the norm. We believe in the ways of the East where a woman has several husbands."

Several husbands? "I've never heard of such a thing," I replied.

"As you can tell from our accents, we're British. We were stationed in Mohamir with our regiment. It was the cultural norm. The marriage protects the woman. It keeps her safe and cherished, having multiple men to possess her," Mason explained.

"Cherishing a woman is her husbands' job," Brody added.

I felt obscenely uncomfortable. Adding their surprising tale of multiple husbands made the situation even more unusual. "You both share a wife? Won't she...um, find it odd for you to be in bed with me? Or is that also a cultural norm?"

Mason's eyes narrowed. "I will forgive your words out of ignorance, but do not think to besmirch our character, our honor, by insinuating we would shame a wife by being in bed with another woman."

"We are bachelors. No wife," Brody clarified.

Did that make it reasonable then to be in bed with me? This was a topic of conversation that was not only unfamiliar, but also very uncomfortable.

"If I could just get my clothes, and perhaps if you would be so kind to offer a simple meal, I can let you return to your tasks." I just needed to get away from these handsome men. Their touch should have been repulsive, just like the very idea of Mr. Palmer's hands on me, but it wasn't. In fact, it was having quite a different effect entirely. It felt good. Gentle. Warm. Kind. *Very* attentive.

"It is still snowing and is unsafe for travel. We just saved you from the cold, sweetheart. We aren't inclined to let you out in it once again. Besides, your horse...I'm sorry to say, I had to put him down." Mason's voice was gentle and he watched me closely. Worry made him frown.

In my distraction, I'd forgotten about the animal. "The horse, oh. What happened?"

"It looks like he stepped in a hole. It was covered in snow and easily done. Broke his leg. It was his cries of pain that I heard when I went out for more wood."

"The horse saved your life," Brody added.

The poor thing. He should have been safely in the stable with a bucket of oats and yet he'd ventured out with me because I wanted away. Now he was dead, and all because I'd gone foolishly out in the poor weather. Tears knotted in my throat, stung the back of my eyes. I had been given no choice. If I'd remained abed, I most likely would be standing at the church alter right now with Mr. Palmer. No matter which way my mind turned, there was only crisis. Mr. Palmer. Two strangers in a bed. The horse being hurt. Dying. It was all too much. I started to cry. Brody turned me and pulled me close, letting me cry into his shoulder. His hands ran up and down my back soothingly and both men whispered to me. Although my crying too loud for me to hear their words, it was soothing nonetheless.

Brody's skin was warm against my face, the pale hairs on his chest tickling my nose. His scent was clean, dark. Manly. Hands ran through my hair and tilted my head back. Soft lips grazed over my forehead, my cheeks, and my jaw and then settled on my mouth.

I was being kissed!

His lips were warm, soft and they brushed over me gently, before his tongue licked over the seam of my mouth. Surprise had me gasping, which allowed Brody's tongue to slip inside and touch mine. My hands roamed over his hard, chiseled chest. His hands slid down my back to cup my bottom. No. That couldn't be possible because his hands were in my hair. Then that meant....

Mason.

Brody angled my head to the side and plundered my mouth. There was no other word for it. My senses, too. I'd never been kissed before and I'd imagined it to be a dry, staid peck. No tongue. I had no idea a man would kiss you with his tongue in your mouth. It was...incredible.

Why was I feeling this way? I shouldn't be all hot and tingly and achy from these men. These *strangers*. But they didn't feel entirely like strangers, for although I was quite confused and listless the night before, I could sense them taking care of me, protecting me. Warming me. I'd been held close and it had made me feel safe, safe enough to fall asleep in a stranger's arms. A stranger was someone unknown, someone with whom to maintain a cautious and wary distance. With these men, there was no distance. The wariness was there, but it wasn't for the men, but what they made me feel. Pulling my head back, I sucked air into my lungs that Brody had kissed away. "We need to stop. This...this isn't right. It feels...."

I felt more than saw Brody's smile. "No, sweetheart, this is very, very right. Didn't it feel good when I held you last night? Remember I said you were safe with us?"

I nodded.

"You're still safe. We'll still take care of you, but here in this bed, we'll take care of you in different ways." His thumbs moved to brush the tear stains off my cheeks before lowering his mouth to mine once again. Mason moved closer so that his front was to my back, his lips sliding over my shoulder. I felt the soft bristle of his beard against my skin. Completely different than Brody's mouth. His hand rested on my waist.

I don't know whose touch was whose; their hands were everywhere. A hand went behind my knee and lifted my upper leg onto Brody's hip, pulling it close and holding it. The grip didn't let go.

One finger ran over my womanhood and I cried out in surprise. I tried to close my legs, but Brody's hand—it had to be his—held me securely.

"What...what are you doing?" I asked against Brody's mouth. His taste was as appealing as his scent, the combination softening my resistance, the muscles in my body.

"I'm playing with your pussy," Mason murmured as he nipped at the spot where my shoulder and neck met. His beard was soft, rasping against my skin.

A moan escaped my lips.

"W...why would you want to touch me there?"

"You offered us a little peek and I couldn't resist. Those pretty red curls only showing a hint of your pussy lips."

His words were carnal, crude. Honest. But I couldn't think about that further. Somehow, his finger—his one blunt finger—was doing things to me that had my mind turning to the consistency of oatmeal.

A hand cupped my breast. "Ah, Mason, you're going to love her breasts. So full, and her nipple, it just tightened against my palm."

"I can't wait, but I'm busy with her pussy. She's dripping wet."

I startled in alarm. "I'm wet? What's dripping? Something's wrong. No. You should stop."

"Sweetheart, nothing's wrong with you." Brody's fingers tugged on my nipple and I arched my back into it. "You're aroused and your pussy is readying for a cock."

I shook my head. "No. No...cocks. I'm a virgin. I can't allow that, no," I sputtered.

"No cock until you're married," Mason agreed, his voice deep. "Nothing in your pussy at all until then."

My muscles relaxed. "Then we are done."

Brody pulled his head back enough so I could see his face. Pale eyes that showed tenderness, eagerness. Need. "We are far from done."

As Brody said that, Mason touched me in a place that felt like I was struck by lightning, a searing heat shooting through my body. "Oh my god," I moaned.

"Her clit is hard."

"Her nipples tightened in my palm. Do it again."

The men spoke of my body as if it belonged to them, as if it was theirs to touch and work. For they were most assuredly working my body. I had no idea such feelings could be elicited. And there, between my thighs, I was wet. The sound of Mason's finger slipping through it was loud in the room. When his finger brushed over me there again, my clit he'd called it, my eyes slipped shut and my head fell back against his shoulder. All of a sudden, I felt overheated.

"See, so perfect," Brody commented, continuing to play with my nipple.

Mason kissed the length of my neck and shivers ran down my spine. I didn't know I could shiver and be so warm. How could a beard be so...carnal? He must have been glancing down at what Brody's hands were doing. "Gorgeous. So responsive. Pinch it."

Brody did and I groaned. The feeling was a mixture of pain and pleasure.

"She likes a little bit of pain," Brody commented.

I was lost. Completely and totally lost to whatever these two men were doing to me. I knew it was wrong, I'd been told by the teachers at school not to succumb to a man's attentions, knew even more that *two* men should not be touching me in such a way, let alone at all. But there was nothing I could do except succumb, not because I didn't think they would stop, for I knew deep down that these men would halt their attentions if I truly wished it. I could only give in because it felt...so...good. Mason's finger continued to flick over my clit, to rub the side of it in a way that had me shifting my hips as if trying to reach something. My mouth fell open and my breath escaped in little pants.

"It's too much. Oh. Please!" I stiffened in their arms, unfamiliar with the overwhelming feelings they wrought from my body. I'd never felt like this before. I was out of control; my body climbing and climbing toward...something and it was scary. I clawed at Brody's arms.

"That's it, sweetheart. Shh. We've got you. You're going to come and we'll be here to catch you," Brody murmured.

"You're safe," Mason added as he worked my clit with even more vigor. I couldn't take it any longer. Their words of holding me, watching me, keeping me safe helped. I relaxed enough and the pleasure so intense that I shattered into a million pieces. It was as if my body had been held together and their touches had broken me apart. I couldn't do anything but succumb. The feeling was absolutely amazing and I never wanted it to end.

4

ASON

She'd come apart in our arms so beautifully. Her arousal coated my hand, so hot, so slick. I shifted and pulled Laurel with me so she was once again on her back between us. Propped up on my elbow, I raised my dripping fingers to my mouth and licked her essence off the tips. Her taste was so sweet it made my mouth water with eagerness to slide down her body and taste her arousal directly from the source. My cock was so hard it throbbed, desperate to sink into her, to claim her. Not now though. I'd have to wait. *We'd* have to wait. Like she'd said, she was saving her virginity until marriage. That would happen as soon as the weather cleared and we could get the justice of the peace or the minister out to the ranch and the "I do's" spoken, and not five minutes more.

The blanket had slipped down her body as she'd cried and I'd pulled it to her waist when Brody had distracted her with his nipple play. Her skin was so pale that pale blue veins could be seen, so silky soft I was afraid I'd mar her with my calloused palms. When she'd inadvertently shown us her arse and a hint of her pussy, I'd almost come then and there. Her hair was the fieriest shades of red. Everywhere.

And now, now she lay with her eyes closed, replete, a small smile curving her full lips, completely unaware of anything but her first orgasm, even the fact that she was bare to the waist. There was no doubt that had been her first pleasure. She'd been too scared of it, too overwhelmed by its intensity for it to be a familiar occurrence.

Her hair was a tangle on the pillow, so long, so thick. Her eyelashes so long, her.... I was turning into a romantic, all at the sight of a naked woman. She wasn't the first I'd seen, but most definitely the last. She was ours.

"What was that?" she asked, her voice as soft and slow as honey.

"That was your men pleasing you."

Her eyes opened and panic flared the moment she returned to herself. The moment after that was when she realized she was uncovered to her waist. To say her breasts were lovely was an understatement. They were large, easily a handful, with plump coral nipples. Her figure was lush, ample and when I'd slid my hands over her, her curves were soft and plentiful, something to hold onto when fucking.

She sat up and crossed her arms over her chest to cover herself. Her hair slid long and wild down her back to touch the sheet behind her. "I shouldn't have allowed you such liberties. It isn't right."

Brody lay back on his pillow, tucked an arm behind his head. I pushed up to sit beside her, much less concerned for modesty than she. "Why isn't this right?" I asked.

"I don't know you and we just...you...." She couldn't find the right words to explain the emotions and the reasons for why what we'd done was wrong. She just knew it to be so.

"Last night, when I held you, did it seem wrong?"

She shook her head.

"Were you afraid?"

She licked her lips. "No, I was so cold, so afraid I was going to die and then you were there."

"It felt right, didn't it, sweetheart?" I asked. "There's something special here, between the three of us. You felt it then and you just felt how good it can be, how we can make you feel. It's not wrong."

Tucking her hair behind her ear, she looked up at me with her green eyes, unconvinced. She was a well-bred lady, not a woman from the brothel in town. She'd been told all her life to protect her virtue. Thankfully she'd heeded those warnings, for she'd saved herself for us, but she would have to fight those social standards perhaps more than Brody or I. It would take time and gentle coaxing and persuasion. "Please get me my dress."

Because of her skittishness, there was no time like the present to continue her lesson. If she was to be our wife, she needed to become familiar with her husband's bodies, and teaching her when she was sated from her first orgasm was the perfect time. It was her job to tend to our needs just as much as ours to see to hers. Tossing back the covers, I stood, offering her the expanse of my back first, then turned to place my hands on my hips. My cock was hard. Hard enough to pound nails. The blunt head was an angry red color, and it pulsed, eager to fuck. It curved upward toward my navel and my balls hung heavily below. If she hadn't seen a cock before—and the way her mouth hung open and her eyes were wide and ogling it—she was in for quite a learning experience.

"Your dress is most likely still sodden from the snow. You may wear a shirt of mine."

She wasn't listening, wasn't doing anything but staring.

"What's the matter, sweetheart?" Brody asked. He pushed the blankets down to uncover his own cock, equally aroused and ready as mine.

Laurel shook her head and glanced over her shoulder at Brody, only to see his cock. She scooted back on her arse toward the end of the bed and faced us both, pointing at our cocks. "They're really big. Um...they couldn't...I mean....never mind."

We'd stunned her speechless. Brody grinned wickedly, keeping one hand tucked behind his head, as the other gripped his cock at the base and started stroking it up and down as a drop of clear fluid seeped from the tip.

"Have you ever seen a cock before?" I asked as I took mine in hand. She shook her head, then licked her lips. Brody groaned.

"Then we'll give you a lesson in cocks, shall we? Our cocks are ready for fucking. They're big. They're hard. See the veins running up the length? Seeing your gorgeous hair down makes me hard."

"Seeing your nipples does it for me," Brody added. "Your breathy little pants almost had me coming."

"Feeling your pussy lips and strumming your clit almost finished me off. Everything about you, Laurel, makes us hard."

Brody pushed up onto his knees, working his cock. "Seeing you like this, in my bed, looking at us with those gorgeous emerald eyes, I'm going to come. Do you want to help me, sweetheart?"

Her mouth fell open. "Help? How? Will it hurt?"

Brody indicated with his chin. "Give me your hand." He released his hold on the base of his cock and held his hand out to her. After biting her lip and considering, she placed her hand in his.

I groaned at her innocence. "Move closer to Brody, Laurel. You're safe."

She looked up at Brody's face then closed the distance between them. He placed her hand on his cock and her eyes widened.

"It's so hard and hot and smooth."

Brody grinned, but his jaw clenched tight. My cock ached just seeing her tiny hand on him. "Like this," he said, placing his hand on top of hers and moving them in smooth strokes.

"Such a good girl. Your hand feels so good. I'm going to come all over you."

I continued to stroke my cock as I watched Laurel's face when the first pulse of Brody's seed coated her breasts and belly. Brody groaned as her hand continued to pump up and down his length, his cum landing on her in thick ribbons. Laurel looked down her body at the white viscous seed.

"I love seeing my seed on you, sweetheart. Marks you as mine." Brody breathed heavily, yet his muscles had relaxed, his body sated.

He took her hand off his spent cock. "Let Mason feel your hand rubbing the cum from his cock. It's his turn."

She glanced at me over her shoulder, then crawled over to me. Like Brody, I took her hand and placed it on my cock, hissing out a breath as her fist squeezed by dick. Unlike Brody, I didn't have to show her how to move her hand; she was a fast learner.

I took in the thick ropes of cum on her breasts, the furled pink nipples, her fiery thatch of hair. I'd been ready since I felt her woman's form for the first time in the snowstorm. Now, seeing her naked and feeling her hand work over my cock, my balls drew up tight as my orgasm came from my spine and into my cock, forcing my seed out in thick jets, crisscrossing and covering Laurel's breasts with my cum. Pulse after pulse I coated her, my seed copious. I couldn't escape the groan as I thrust my hips forward, the pleasure overwhelming. I put a steadying hand on the headboard as my senses returned.

———

LAUREL

I was hungry, ravenously so, my last meal a hasty slice of bread with cheese as I left Father's house yesterday. It was this need and this need alone that had me seated at the kitchen table in a man's shirt. And only a shirt.

After Mason had come, the men had me spread their white, thick seed over my breasts and belly, as if coating myself with something as everyday as lotion. I'd wanted to clean myself of the residue, but the men had refused, offering me not a wet cloth but instead a soft flannel shirt. Brody had rolled up the sleeves to my wrists as Mason buttoned it, covering me down to my knees so that my modesty was intact. Barely.

The food Brody served had my stomach grumbling and I relished every bit of the eggs, ham, bread, sliced potatoes and coffee, but it was hard to stomach my predicament. I'd done things with these men I never knew possible. I'd behaved wantonly, and they must consider me the lowest of the low. I was a fallen woman. My virginity was maintained, but that was really all. If I continued to allow them liberties, would they let me go once the snow abated?

I glanced out the window to see white. Only white. The wind had tapered to nothing, but the snow still fell. It was much improved from the night before, but I was not interested in going out in it any time soon. I shivered at the very possibility. There was no escape, at least for the moment, even if I wished it. I didn't even know where my clothes were. The kitchen's stove made the room warm and I was not chilled in just Mason's shirt. I'd most certainly learned my lesson about being unprepared outdoors.

I was trapped. Trapped with men who thought I was a slattern and were using me thusly. Once I was able to depart, Mr. Palmer most assuredly wouldn't want me any longer. That was an unforeseen perk. However, my chances for any other man were gone as well. I was used goods.

"How was it that you were out last night?" Mason asked, cutting a thick slice of ham.

I looked up at him, patted my lips with my napkin. I couldn't tell him the truth, at least the whole of it. Even though they'd rescued me from certain death, I didn't know the reach of my father's control. If they worked for my father, or *with* my father, they'd have me thrown over a horse and hauled to church to marry Mr. Palmer in a man's shirt. No. I couldn't risk it. It was safer to lie, at least in part, to protect myself. I could maintain most of the tale, but couldn't risk a connection with my father. I was not known in Simms, or anywhere in the area, by sight. Nolan Turner had a daughter, but the last time anyone in the Montana Territory had seen her was almost fifteen years ago. Unfortunately, I'd told them my real name in bed, but only my first name. The men looked at me, waiting, so I kept as close to the truth as possible, while staying safe.

"I...I was to marry a man I did not wish."

"You are affianced?" Brody questioned.

"Not officially. I learned my father arranged the marriage as part of a business contract. He gained a long term alliance and the other man gained a wife."

"What was so lacking in this man?"

"Youth, agility and kindness," I replied succinctly. "You find it odd I have qualifications for a husband?"

Brody shook his head. "Some women don't."

I pursed my lips. "He's well over twice my age, is rotund and has jowls from overindulgence and shared some less than pleasant plans for me."

"What kinds of plans did he share with you?" Brody asked, his jaw clenched tight. He ran his hand over the shadow of pale whiskers.

I blanched at the memory. Mr. Palmer had leaned in close enough for me to smell his foul breath and whispered tawdry things in my ear. "He...he intended to tie me to the bed and take me until his seed took root." I kept my gaze pinned to my hands folded in my lap.

"That idea repulses you?" Mason asked.

I whipped my head up and narrowed my eyes, shocked. "Yes! Everything about that man is repulsive."

"It isn't the idea of being tied up and fucked that bothers you. You've thought about his words, being fucked hard and long, over and over, filling you with seed until your belly is ripe. You're squirming in your chair so it's obvious to me—"

"Me, as well," Brody cut in.

"—that it is something that interests you. But not with this man."

I opened my mouth to argue, then closed it. Was this the case? Were the man's words so awful just because *he* would do those things to me? I glanced at Brody and Mason who were awaiting my answer. If these men had me tied to a bed, the idea held...appeal. I did squirm, my...pussy awakening once again at the very idea. I refused to admit the truth, although they seemed to recognize it before I.

"When was this marriage to occur?" Mason asked.

"Today."

"You went out into a blizzard, risking death, because of your impending wedding?" He looked at me with a combination of surprise and anger.

Folding my hands in my lap, I straightened my posture. "I did not know it was to be a blizzard. It was barely flurrying when I rode out, so do not think me insane. Would you wish to be married to a man who was cruel, unappealing and old? I assure you, his actions would be akin to rape."

"He will not touch you," Mason growled. He stood, the feet of his chair scraping across the wood floor. The adamance of his words sounded possessive. "You almost died out there. The man almost drove you to suicide." He waved his hand toward the window where the snow still fell. It had lessened over the course of our meal, but it was still a winter wonderland.

"Your father will search for you. Without you, there is no deal." He gripped the back of his chair, his knuckles white.

"Both men will search for her," Brody added.

"Yes, I do not know who has more at stake." Mr. Palmer's interest was greater than avarice. He saw something in me that set me apart, a condition in a contract unlike any other. When he discovered I was tainted goods, my father would become irate. There was no chance I could make either man happy.

"Who is your father? Surely if you're from Simms he is familiar to us." Brody set his forearms on the table. "*You* should be familiar to us."

Here is where I had to lie. I couldn't tell them my father's name. I'd been back only a week and in that short time I knew the man's power. He'd held me prisoner at a school in Denver for almost my entire life. I knew more than anyone his control.

"Hiram Johns." It was the first name that came to mind, the name of the riding instructor at school in Denver.

The men looked at each other, but said nothing.

"The snow is to our advantage. They will not search for you until the weather improves. Any trail you may have made is buried under a foot of snow." Brody tipped his chair back onto two legs.

"They will search in town and toward Virginia City, not this way. At least not to start," Mason added.

"We have today at least, I expect, before they show," Brody replied. The men glanced at each other briefly and seemed to speak to each other without words.

"There is much to do."

I had a suspicion they weren't speaking about ranch chores.

5

RODY

I was standing at the pump sink washing the breakfast dishes while Mason showed Laurel our collection of books. Our library wasn't extensive, but something should interest her on a snowy day. The idea of spending it with her was a perk neither I nor Mason, had anticipated. *She* was a perk we had not anticipated.

The story Laurel told was a mixture of truth and lies. It was obvious to me, and Mason as well, that she was hiding something. Her name *was* Laurel. She'd told us when we first brought her in from the cold without a chance to think. I believed she was intended to marry a man not of her choosing. I believed her father had made a business arrangement of it. But that was all. There was no man named Hiram Johns in Simms or even in the outlying areas. No one moved into the area without the news of it spreading like wildfire at the mercantile. Everyone at Bridgewater had a vested interest in keeping abreast of the latest news, especially relating to new faces. Evers, our former regimental leader, was always at the back of our minds and whether the bloody bastard would track us down halfway around the world and find us. He'd pinned his heinous crimes from our military stint in Mohamir, a small middle eastern country, on Ian and it was only a matter of time before the past returned. We'd fled to the United States, traveled all the way to the Montana Territory to find a swath of land we called Bridgewater. We ran it together, our common home. We were always vigilant for danger of any kind.

That was why we knew Laurel was not who she said. Pushing her would not bring answers. Well, it could, but then we'd have a woman who hated us and that was most certainly *not* in our plans. We wanted Laurel to like us. Very much. She would be our bride as soon as the weather cleared. She'd tell us the truth, in time. I chuckled to myself. She was a terrible liar. She'd most likely slip up soon enough.

Rinsing the coffee mug, I turned it upside down on a cloth to dry.

As for the man she was to marry, Laurel's reaction to him was enough for us to keep her as far away as possible. A fifty-year old man only wanted a young woman, a virgin, like Laurel for only one reason. Hell, all men wanted Laurel for the same reason, including Mason and me. I wanted to fuck her over and over again until my need for her was sated. I'd even tie her to the bed as she'd said the man would do. Even keep her there until her belly swelled with a baby we'd made.

We weren't sadistic. We weren't thinking only of ourselves. Mason and I were thinking of Laurel, of her pleasure. Her needs. Her desires. I doubted the bastard would think of her at all after he fucked her, or during for that matter. In fact, knowing his kind, he'd have a mistress or two on the side, ensuring Laurel's value and self-worth were always in question.

Running away had been her only option. If both her father and intended husband were as committed to the business arrangement as she'd said and she hadn't run off, Laurel would be married right now. The thought of that had my breakfast settling in my stomach like a heavy river rock.

She could have died. She *would* have died if Mason hadn't gone out for firewood. I wasn't a man to think of things like fate or destiny, but she'd literally fallen at our doorstep. She was ours.

I wiped down the table with a damp cloth, thinking of our time in bed. Although Laurel was clearly unaware, we'd claimed her then and there. Her body was so lush and curvy my cock was rock hard. Again. She'd tasted as sweet as her breathy little moans of pleasure. Her skin was silky soft and I wanted to learn every inch of it. Seeing her come for the very first time was something I'd never forget. So was the look on her face when she'd seen her very first cocks. Ours. Knowing our seed coated her breasts and belly was akin to marking her, branding her as ours.

With these thoughts running through my head, I scrubbed the table with a little extra vigor. Glancing out the window, I watched the snow fall, but it had tapered off to just flurries. The sun was brilliant and sparkled on the thick, fresh coating of white. Looking outside was almost too bright for my eyes. Squinting, I could see across the ranch to the other houses. In the near distance, I could see someone approaching. He was on foot, trudging through the deep drifts, coat collar lifted up around his neck, hat low over his face. It was only when he stomped his boots on the back porch that I could see it was Andrew.

Tossing the dishcloth over my shoulder, I opened the door for him. The man stepped in with a swirl of cold air behind him. He shut the door firmly to keep the warmth inside. Placing his hat on a peg by the door, he looked up at me and smiled.

"Quite the storm," he commented.

Andrew and Robert also lived on Bridgewater. They were married to Ann, who'd given birth to their first child only two months ago. They were the Americans of the group; we'd met them in Boston directly after our arrival in the country. Besides them, Bridgewater was home to Ian and Kane, who married Emma over the summer. Other members of our regiment were Simon, Rhys and Cross. MacDonald and McPherson were new to Bridgewater, having arrived just last summer. It was quite the week when we'd thought Evers had found Ian. Instead, it was Simon's brother and friend.

"Two feet?" I guessed, glancing out the window.

"Easily."

"Is everyone all right?" I asked. Ann was well after birthing Christopher and the lad was thriving, but it was a vulnerable time for both of them.

He nodded. "Besides being tired, everyone is well. I should be asking that of you. I heard a shot last night. You're the closest house and thought it would have come from here."

"It did. An interesting turn of events."

He ran his hand over his beard and watched me closely, unsure if it was good news or bad.

"Take off your boots and I'll tell you."

I told him about Mason's trip to the woodpile, the discovery of Laurel and her predicament.

"I've never heard of a Hiram Johns."

"Neither have I," I replied.

"Then who the hell is she? She didn't just fall out of the sky."

I shrugged. "Based on the weather, she couldn't have been riding more than a few hours, so she had to have come from somewhere near Simms. Don't worry, the story will come out."

Andrew grinned. "I have no doubt of that."

I patted the man on the shoulder. "She's the one, Andrew.

His eyebrows went up in surprise. "You're sure?"

"We're sure. I'm not going to punish her for her secrets. That will gain us nothing. I want her biddable. If she's going to be ours, she needs to start her training now."

Andrew's eyebrows went up in surprise as he placed his boots in front of the cast iron stove to warm. "You've fucked her?"

I frowned. "Hell, no."

My friend held up his hands in surrender.

"We're honorable enough to wait until she's truly ours before we claim her. That doesn't mean we can't show her our ways."

MASON

There was no way in bloody hell I'd let her put her dress back on. Seeing her in just my shirt only made her even more mine. Ours. Knowing she wore nothing underneath, that her pretty nipples were poking against the material, that the red curls on her pussy were easily accessible, had me hard. Hell, even after I'd spent my seed on her I was still hard. She was marked. Besides her unique floral, sweet scent, she smelled of fucking. I couldn't wait to mark her on the inside as well by filling her delectable pussy with my cum. I knew Brody felt the same.

Before Andrew left, he'd invited us to their house for the evening meal, which was good because Laurel would see the dynamic Ann had with two husbands. Regardless of her past, Laurel was going to be our wife. She was a horrendous liar; every emotion she felt flitted across her face—indecision, wariness, even deceit. She *was* deceiving us by keeping secrets.

"What do you think?" I asked Brody, my voice low. Laurel was in the bath in the washroom. We were downstairs adding logs to the fireplaces and stoves to keep the house warm.

He glanced up at the ceiling as if he could see her through it. "I believe everything except her father's name. Never heard of him."

"Neither have I. If she ran away, she can't be protecting him. She's protecting herself. But why? We saved her from certain death. We wouldn't hurt her."

Brody shrugged. "She doesn't know that."

I frowned at the thought. We'd never hurt a woman. Never. Everyone at Bridgewater protected women. Cherished them. "Then we must show her. She's so bloody beautiful." I ran a hand over my beard. "Her hair is memorable. If she's been living around here, we'd have known."

Brody nodded. "Every man within a hundred miles would be after her."

"Good thing she ended up here."

"Where did she come from?"

I didn't have an answer. Only Laurel would be able to tell us.

"She's ours," Brody growled.

"No question. So we wait for her to tell us?"

Brody opened the door on the stove in the kitchen, stuffed a log in and shut it. He tossed the cloth he'd used to protect his hand on the table. "Does the past really matter?"

I shook my head. "I'd rather train her than question her, wouldn't you?"

"Hell, yes. I spoke to Andrew before he left. They'll help any way they can."

———

An hour later, I carried a bundled up Laurel into Andrew and Robert's house. Her coat was still damp and I'd cut the laces of her boots so we wrapped her in a blanket to keep warm on the walk. It was a short distance, only five minutes, but the air was crisp and the sun had set offering no additional warmth. The trio met us at the doorway and took our things, the scent of stew and baked bread filled the air. There was a roaring fire in the hearth and it was warm and comfortable. Since their marriage to Ann, the house had turned into a home.

"It is good to see you again, Laurel," Andrew said. "May I introduce Robert and our wife, Ann? Christopher is in the cradle near the fireplace, napping."

Robert had dark hair and a beard similar to mine, although he was shorter and stockier than I. Ann was petite with pale blond hair. Since the birth of baby Christopher her slim figure had filled out and was quite lush.

"Hello," Laurel responded shyly. She stood there in my shirt and a pair of Brody's socks, her hair pulled back into a long braid down her back with a piece of rope as a tie.

"I've heard you've had quite an adventure," Ann said, looking to Laurel with frank interest. Women were few and far between in these parts, Ann only having Emma nearby.

"We were hoping to borrow some clothing, if you wouldn't mind," I told her.

Ann smiled. "Would you like to come upstairs and see if something might work? The baby should be asleep for some time yet and the men will watch him."

Laurel looked to Brody, then me, for assurance.

"The others will be here soon." When she frowned in confusion, I added, "The others that live here at Bridgewater. The meals are usually at Ian and Kane's house, but we've shifted here because of the baby and the weather. You can go with Ann, sweetheart."

Brody nodded his agreement and the two women left the room and we heard their footfall on the stairs. It pleased me to see her look to us for approval, although we weren't the kind of men who expected their wife to cede to them with their every decision. We wanted Laurel to be submissive to us, not meek.

"She's lovely," Andrew commented.

"Know a man named Hiram Johns?" Brody asked.

Robert led us to the chairs that faced the fire. As we sat, he answered. "Andrew shared Laurel's story. The name is not familiar to me."

The other men agreed with me that she was lying. It wasn't just a feeling on my part. It was obvious to all. I rested my forearms on my thighs. "If she's lying, it could be to protect him." I didn't want to believe this, even assume it.

"She ran away. I think she's protecting herself," Brody added.

"If she really is part of a business contract, they'll come looking for her," Robert said.

"Whoever *they* are," Andrew grumbled.

"We'll be ready," I vowed.

6

AUREL

"I was surprised at first. I thought I was married to just Andrew and I soon learned Robert was my husband as well," Ann shared, taking a dress from a hook on the wall and bringing it over to me. We were in her bedroom, the room I assumed she shared with both men. The room didn't appear out of the ordinary, although their marriage certainly was.

"Did you grow up dreaming of two men?"

She shook her head and smiled dreamily. "Oh no. Here at Bridgewater is the only place I know of where a woman has multiple husbands. I...like it. Very much. My husbands are *most* attentive." She handed me the dress.

"Thank you. Mason and Brody ripped the bodice of my dress when they rescued me last night." Lord, that sounded wicked, so I added, "The dress was covered in snow. I fear it is irreparable." I held up the dress to my front and looked at Ann. "You're much smaller than I. I don't think alterations are going to help."

"No. I suppose not. You're so tall, curvy too, although now that Christopher is born I've yet to regain my shape."

I didn't know what shape she had before but she was beautiful now. Her features were fine, almost dainty, her skin so creamy pale. She was so calm, so mild, so comfortable in her life.

She went to a dresser and opened the top drawer, then a lower one. "Here are a blouse and skirt. They may work better being separate pieces."

I heard doubt in her voice, the same doubt I felt about her clothes fitting. I folded them over my arm as she spoke.

"Brody and Mason are fine men. You will be happy with them."

My mouth fell open in shock. "I'm not married to them, nor marrying them. They rescued me from the blizzard."

Ann frowned. "Yes, Andrew told me of your predicament. You were most fortunate. The men, though, they are honorable."

"I...I can't be as confident as you in that, for I hardly know them," I answered. We'd done things in bed together that created a deeper level of intimacy than should be expected considering.

"You can trust me on this. Brody and Mason are quite honorable and they will take good care of you." She beamed at me. "Then that's settled. I mean you were with them overnight and—oh!" She lowered her gaze to the front of her dress. There were two wet spots.

"Is something the matter?" I asked, unsure of the extent of the problem.

"My milk has come in. It is so plentiful that I have more than little Christopher can eat. Bring the clothes and we'll go back downstairs."

I followed Ann and when we returned to the main living room, the men stood at our arrival. There were two new faces in the group.

"My milk," Ann said breathlessly.

Andrew and Robert encircled Ann. "Let's go in the other room." Even though they'd moved into the nearby office and we couldn't see them, Andrew's voice carried. "Sit on Robert's lap and he'll take care of you."

Mason and Brody approached me, Mason taking the items of clothing from me and placing them across the back of a chair. "Laurel, this is MacDonald and McPherson, two other men from our regiment."

Both stood tall and broad, as if they could block out the sun with their bodies. Their hair was unruly and long, with hard features yet kind eyes. They each gave me a simple nod in greeting before sitting.

I felt a little silly standing in the middle of the room in just a Mason's shirt surrounded by a group of men. Glancing left and right, I looked for a place to sit. Before I could move, a hand came out, took my hand and pulled me down onto hard thighs. "On my lap," Mason whispered in my ear, the soft hairs of his ears tickling my jaw. His arms came around me and held me in place.

"Do they hurt, baby?" Robert said from the other room.

"Yes, they are so full they ache and the milk won't stop."

"Then I'll take care of that."

Ann groaned and I looked to Mason.

"She has too much milk and it must be worked from her. With Christopher sleeping and his belly full, it is Andrew and Robert's job to relieve her."

I frowned in confusion.

"Robert is drinking the milk from her breasts."

The idea should have been uncomfortable, but instead it was quite erotic. That Ann had a need that only her husbands could help with formed a bond between them that was quite appealing. Brody had played with my breasts earlier and the idea of his mouth there instead of his fingers made my nipples tighten beneath the soft fabric of Mason's shirt.

"We shouldn't be listening to this," I whispered to Mason. "This is private."

He shook his head. "They took her to the other room for privacy. Remember, the woman's needs come first."

I wasn't sure how having us listen put her needs first, but Ann didn't seem to mind we were nearby, nor the other men. In fact, based on the sounds drifting from the other room she seemed to like it very much.

"Her pussy's dripping, Andrew," Robert said about Ann.

This time I did squirm, for Mason had told Brody the exact same words about me and I remembered where his hand had been, how it had felt.

"We haven't fucked her since the baby was born. Her pussy needs time to heal before we take her again."

"Please, Robert. Having your mouth on my breasts always has me so needy. I *need* you to fuck me," Ann moaned, her desperation evident.

I felt uncomfortable listening. Actually, it wasn't just discomfort I felt. I also felt...aroused. Listening to Ann find her pleasure in Robert's touch reminded me of how Mason and Brody tended to me earlier. They'd been gentle, yet very persuasive, my...pussy tingling now at the memory of what Mason's fingers had done. They'd said nothing would go in my pussy until I was married, but the way Ann begged to be filled had my inner muscles clenching down, my core aching for something. As a married woman, Ann knew what she wanted. What she longed for. She'd experienced a cock, no, two.

I hadn't. I felt a keen longing that I'd never known before. Brody and Mason had awoken something within me. They'd made me crave their touch, crave what I didn't know. I wanted what Ann had, although their connection, their bond was greater than I could imagine having with Brody or Mason.

"No, baby. You don't decide," Andrew told her. "Your men decide when you will be fucked again. We are being careful, as we don't want to hurt your pussy. You gave us the best gift in the whole world and we will take care of you. Haven't we pleasured you other ways?"

"Yes," she replied, her voice forlorn.

"You are so beautiful like this with your milk dripping, your men taking care of you. I'm going to drink the milk from your other breast while Robert makes you come."

It didn't take long for her to cry out her pleasure. Had I sounded like that?

"Isn't that a beautiful sound?" Mason whispered in my ear. "A woman's needs being met by her husbands? She was uncomfortable and they soothed her. Her happiness and her pleasure are their only desires." His breath was warm, his lips running over the upper curve of my ear. He kissed me there, then to my jaw, then lower to the curve of my neck. My eyes slipped closed and I reveled in the gentle feel of him.

Ann's throaty cries of pleasure broke through the haze of my own need. I blushed realizing how I'd settled in to the unusual openness found at Bridgewater. I knew this wasn't the way of the rest of the world; Denver was a big city and I knew nothing about having more than one husband or any of the more delicate tasks within a marriage.

A minute later, Andrew came into the room wiping his mouth with the back of his hand. "Dinner's warm on the stove." He spoke as if he hadn't just suckled at his wife's breasts. I was taken aback, but it seemed a common occurrence for me.

"I'll help," Brody offered, following the man out of the room. The other men followed him, leaving Mason and me alone.

Mason shifted me in his lap so I looked at him. His hands cupped my breasts and I gasped, knowing he could feel how hard my nipples were. "What Ann's men do for her, it arouses you."

He stated it as fact, not a question. I felt my cheeks burn and I glanced away from his piercing dark gaze. I gave a little shake of my head.

"Laurel, your head might be denying it, but your body doesn't lie."

How could he know my body's desires? I was just discovering them.

"Look," he said, glancing down at his lap. There, where I'd been sitting just a moment ago was darkened and wet. "Your pussy is dripping onto my pants."

I gasped and stood, trying to get away, to hide somewhere in shame, but he hooked an arm about my waist and held me in front of him so I stood between his knees. His hands lowered to the backs of my thighs and slipped upward to cup my bottom. From this position, I couldn't miss seeing the spot on his pants, felt the air cooling the wetness on my pussy and thighs. I *was* wet. The proof couldn't be denied. I didn't *want* to be aroused. This meant I liked listening to others doing carnal things. This meant I wanted those same things done to me. That meant I liked having Mason touch me intimately. It shouldn't be so!

I was holding on to a terrible lie. If they knew who I really was, they'd send me back to Father. Surely no one would want me after Mason and Brody told them what kind of woman I was. I'd be an outcast. It was better to deny the feelings, to show that I didn't like it, that I was unaffected, so when the time came they could only state that I'd been under duress. Perhaps then I'd be able to find a husband that would still be interested in me. I was being delusional. *No one* was interested in me. Everyone had their own needs at heart, their own gain. My father. Mr. Palmer. I was a mere pawn.

Perhaps the reason I reveled in the sound of Andrew and Robert pleasing Ann was because they put their needs second. For the first time, I witnessed selflessness instead of selfishness.

———

MASON

"Don't be ashamed, sweetheart. I love knowing having two men appeals to you." I gave her waist a gentle squeeze. "Do you know how hard my cock is?"

Her eyes widened, clearly surprised to find I was aroused as well. I adjusted myself, my pants a strict confinement for my swollen cock. When she saw the size of me through my pants, she licked her lips. I would come in my pants if I didn't redirect my thoughts. Feeling her hot pussy against my thigh had been torture, feeling her nipples tighten beneath my palms had been delightful, but seeing her juices staining my pants was so damn hot. I couldn't resist looking at her.

Catching my long shirt she wore on my thumbs, I worked the material upward so it slowly revealed her gorgeous pussy. Once my hands rested above her hips, she was exposed from the waist down.

"Mason," she hissed, looking left and right.

"You are so beautiful, all aroused like you are. Your thighs are coated with your juices. Do you know what I want to do?" Her eyes met mine. "I want to taste you there."

"Hello!" Simon called out. I heard the front door close behind them, boots stomping off snow.

"In here," I called. Laurel's body stiffened within my hold and her eyes widened in panic. I let my hands drop, the shirt lowering with it to cover all of her secrets. Her shoulders slumped in relief and her hands smoothed the soft fabric down over thighs, as if assuring herself she was modest.

Out of the corner of my eye I saw the men enter. "Simon, Rhys and Cross, this is Laurel."

"We heard about your brush with death," Rhys said to Laurel. "We are glad to find you well."

Laurel nodded, but didn't say anything.

"I saw Kane. They'll stay at home for dinner tonight."

I heard Simon's words, but I was focused on Laurel. The look on her face reminded me of a child who was caught with her hand in the cookie jar, for the men just missed seeing her body. The men were seeing her in my shirt alone; I wasn't about to share any more of her.

Andrew stuck his head into the room long enough to speak. "I've ladled out the stew into bowls, so come to the table while it's hot."

"I might just stay here and make a meal of Laurel's pussy." Laurel pulled against Brody's hold, but he wouldn't relent.

"Come, sweetheart, you can sit beside me." Brody stood and smiled at her, relaxed, calm, almost soothing in his voice. She gave a simple nod and he led her from the room, her hips swaying as she went.

Ann and Robert came in from the other room. Ann's appearance was slightly disheveled and she had a pink glow to her cheeks. They both peeked at the baby in the cradle, assuring themselves he was settled before leaving the room.

Simon, Rhys, and Cross remained behind with me.

"You're claiming her then?" Simon asked, referring to Laurel.

I nodded. "Wouldn't you?"

"Hell, yes."

"Andrew told you the details?"

All three men nodded. "A woman doesn't run off like that unless she's flighty or fearing for her life," Cross commented.

"She's not flighty," I answered.

"Then someone wants her, besides you," Simon finished.

"They can try." I patted Simon on the shoulder as I walked toward the dining room. "They can try."

7

AUREL

I spent an uncomfortable dinner with a room full of men wearing just a shirt. It had been silly to think Ann's clothes would fit. I'd certainly try to alter them, but it was of no help at the moment. Somewhere along this journey I'd lost all control of my body. My body was literally dripping wetness! This had never happened before I met Mason and Brody. Surely this wasn't normal.

Conversation weaved around me as I had nothing to add, nor did I wish to focus any kind of attention on myself. I felt exposed enough with my legs bare. The group was congenial and seemed to be a family in their own right. Lighthearted humor and jovial stories went around as fast as the basket of bread or the pitcher of water. Only Andrew and Robert spoke like Americans, the rest with accents. McPherson and MacDonald had much stronger burrs. When Brody leaned in and told me that McPherson and Simon were brothers, the resemblance was obvious. I wasn't sure why one went by their family name and the other the surname, but I wasn't going to ask.

The stew was delicious, but I did not have much of an appetite. I'd saved myself from Mr. Palmer and my father's plans, but I'd fallen into an environment where it wasn't just one man, or even two, that I had to extricate myself from now. These men had a bond that, from what Mason told me, was forged in the military. I couldn't stay here on Bridgewater and lie to all of them. Mason and Brody seemed to find enjoyment in my body, but it could not be long term. I was just a loose woman, complying readily with their wishes. I'd been in bed with them naked! Even worse perhaps, I sat in just a men's shirt at a dinner table full of men. Strangers!

I wanted to get up, run out of the house, but I had no real clothes. No shoes. Not even a coat. I would get ten feet in the snow and have to return. That was an impossible scenario. Tears clogged my throat, making it impossible to swallow the bite of stew. I sipped from my glass and looked across the table at Ann, who sat there smiling as she talked with Robert. She seemed happy with her life with her two husbands; she didn't find the arrangement odd at all. Was I the odd one here then?

Was this what a wife was supposed to do? Everyone seemed accustomed to these different values, these Mohamiran ways they'd taken as theirs. Everyone but me. Society dictated certain social mores and life at Bridgewater contradicted them all. I didn't fit in here. I didn't belong here.

I didn't belong anywhere. I was too old for my school, knowing now I remained solely because my father paid generously. I'd recently discovered he'd even paid extra to ensure I did not have any suitors, knowing at some point he would need me to return to Simms. Finally, he did and within the week of arriving I'd learned I didn't belong there either.

I was truly lost with nowhere to run.

I blinked at the tears that formed in my eyes, tried to keep them from spilling over. It was no use. They slipped down my cheeks, fell onto the fabric of Mason's shirt I wore. Quietly, I placed my fork down, looked down at the plate, although the food blurred.

"Sweetheart, what's the matter?" Brody asked. He leaned in and whispered in my ear, his breath warm, his voice soft, concerned.

I shook my head, but the tears continued. Glancing up into his pale eyes, I told Brody, "I...I can't do this. I don't belong here."

The table got quiet. Tears fell faster when I knew I'd drawn the attention I didn't want. I pushed my chair back and stood. All of the men around the table stood as well, but only Mason and Brody followed me out of the room. Seeing the baby still asleep, this wasn't where I could speak freely either.

I wiped my eyes with my fingers as I whispered, "Can we leave? Please?"

Both men stood before me formidable and tall. So handsome, especially when they looked at me with a mixture of male dominance and concern. "Of course," Mason replied. They moved quickly. Brody returned to the dining room, Mason to get on his coat. Moments later, Brody came back and donned his own coat, taking it from the peg by the door. Mason picked up the blanket and wrapped it around me. Brody placed the blouse and skirt Ann gave me over his arm, which looked so incongruous to his large, very male frame.

They worked quickly and efficiently as a team and in only a minute, Mason had me in his arms and out the door. As the men's boots crunched through the deep snow, I thought about what they'd said about Robert, Andrew and Ann. Ann's needs came first. They took care of her before anything else. They'd stopped in the middle of a conversation to help ease the engorgement of her breasts. Nothing, and no one else, mattered. It was a very appealing concept to me. No one, ever, saw to my needs first. No one had ever cared for me. The love I saw in the trio was heart warming and heart rending, for I knew now what I'd been missing.

BRODY

Laurel had panicked. She'd been aroused, there was no question about that but perhaps we pushed her too far, too fast. The Mohamiran customs definitely required some adjustment of thought.

Perhaps something else was on her mind that had upset her. Until we stripped her bare, physically and mentally, so we knew all of her, we could not help her. Instead of putting her down in the doorway to remove his coat and boots, Mason carried her directly up the stairs and into his bedroom, placing her on the bed. Gently. Carefully.

I followed directly, both of us shrugging out of our outerwear to sit on either side of her. We worked the blanket from around her to reveal her luscious body, Mason's shirt riding high on her thighs.

She tugged at the material but we stilled her hands. Her green eyes flared with a mixture of anger and trepidation.

"What has you so upset?" I asked, running my hand up and down her silky thigh.

"I...I don't like to be seen like that," she murmured. "I've never even shown my ankle in public before and it was too much."

"We appreciate your honesty." Mason gave her a small smile. "You enjoyed listening to Ann with her husbands. Your body never lies."

Her cheeks turned pink at his words.

"Perhaps, but I don't like to share that...with others." She pushed the bottom of the shirt between her legs and kept them there. It was like a shield, protecting her virtue as best she could. We'd already taken it—her virtue, not her virginity—so it was just a show of modesty. We let her keep it. For now.

"You didn't like knowing the other men found you so beautiful?"

She turned her head away from me at my words.

"A woman's needs come first, sweetheart. We do not want you upset, therefore we will ensure you are more modestly covered from now on. Know this, we will not share you with the others. Ever," Mason vowed. He pried her fingers from her shirttails. "Your body will be for us alone."

Starting at the bottom button, he worked the shirt open, revealing first her pussy, then her navel, and then the swell of her full breasts. When he parted the two sides, she sat there between us on full display.

"So beautiful, sweetheart. Lay back," I murmured, gently pushing on her shoulders so she fell back onto the bed. She was skittish, fearful even. It was our fault she was this way, not realizing her modesty was stronger than her arousal. Therefore, it was our job to fix it. I slipped from the bed and knelt on the floor. Grabbing her behind the knees, I tugged her toward the edge of the bed. Lifting one leg, then the other, I placed them over my shoulders.

Laurel came up on her elbow to look at me. Her green eyes were wide, confused. "Brody, what are you doing?"

"Tasting you." I didn't say more, just parted her with my fingers, lowered my head to her pussy and licked her there. Her folds were slick and she bucked at the slightest touch of my tongue. Working my way upward, I easily found her hard clit.

"Brody!" she cried when I flicked it. Again and again. Her fingers went into my hair, tangled in it, pulled on it, pulled me into her. Mason took hold of her right knee and placed it on his lap, opening her even wider for me.

We'd agreed to keep her pussy empty, but it didn't stop me from circling the very tip of one finger around the opening, teasing her. The combination had her thrashing on the bed.

"Do you like having your pussy eaten? Do you like how Brody makes you feel? Oh, yes, you like your nipples tugged, don't you?" Mason had moved his hands so he plucked and worked her nipples, only adding to the level of stimulation.

Her heel dug into my back as she screamed her release, so easily brought to climax. Her pussy clenched down on the tip of my finger as if it wanted to pull it in, desperately needing to be filled. Her juices seeped onto my hand. She was so hot as I continued to lick, to suck on her tender flesh until her muscles relaxed and she lay there panting, trying to catch her breath.

I kissed her thigh as I sat back on my heels, taking a hold of her ankles and placing her feet on the very edge of the bed. I glanced at Mason and I nodded. He stood and went to the dresser, bringing back the hand carved butt plug and jar of ointment. We switched places, Mason moving between her spread thighs, getting a very direct view of her needy pussy.

"See this, sweetheart?" I held up the thin plug for her to see. Her eyes were foggy still, her skin flushed a pretty pink, a hint of perspiration covered her breasts. "This is going to make you feel so good."

A little frown formed in her brow. Dipping my fingers in the ointment, I coated the end of the plug. "Rhys makes these. Besides being an exceptional carpenter, he's very adept at making dildos and plugs. He's a master at the lathe." Her frown grew. "It's not just for spindles."

I passed the plug to Mason.

"This one is very small, very thin, but it has two round areas. See that?" Mason held it up for her before placing the round tip at her back entrance.

She wasn't confused any longer. "Mason!"

"We can't fill your pussy, we promised you that. Your arse, however, is going to be breached and this will help to stretch you."

Laurel shook her head in disagreement. "Why would you want to do that?" She winced when Mason pushed the plug against her ring of muscle.

"Because arse play feels good and when a cock fills you there, you're going to love it."

Her eyes widened as she considered my words.

"Relax, sweetheart. Look at me. That's it. Take a deep breath, now exhale. Good girl."

"Just like that, Laurel," Mason added as the top slipped in. The plug was long and thin, narrower even than my smallest finger. The end had a round tip so it flared slightly, then had a second round section about two inches down the length. We'd asked Rhys to create a plug that was more of a toy than something we'd leave inside her, just an introduction into arse play. "You took it so well." Mason ran a finger around the plug, touching the slightly stretched ring and letting the nerves there awaken.

Laurel's eyes widened in surprise.

"See?" I asked her. "It feels good, doesn't it?"

She didn't answer, only started to breathe hard once again when Mason started moving the plug in and out, letting the round part at the tip bump her in one direction, the secondary round section nudging in the other. He continued to slowly work her arse as I lowered my head and kissed her. I couldn't resist. She was so sweet, so innocent; I could feel every intake of breath, every soft moan at every step of her awakening. Her tongue met mine, tentatively, then carnally as her mind let go and her body took over. I cupped a breast in the palm of my hand and brushed my thumb over the distended tip at the same time as Mason's own thumb circling Laurel's clit.

She shuddered once and cried out against my mouth, her body arching and her breast filling my palm. Her orgasm went on and on and I lifted my head to watch her. So beautiful, so perfect. Mason's hands slowed, then stilled on her body. I couldn't wait any longer. My cock was angry and pressing painfully against my pants. Coming up onto my knees, I undid the buckle of my belt, opened the placket of my pants and my cock bobbed out.

"Up on your hands and knees, sweetheart." My voice was rough and dark. Mason helped her roll over and pulled her hips back. The plug was still deep within her and I could see a short length of it sticking out from her arse. I shifted so the head of my cock just brushed her lips. "Open up for me."

Laurel's eyes, so green and a tad blurry from her pleasure, focused on my cock.

"Open your mouth," I repeated. "Lick the head."

"Why? Why are you doing this?" she asked. There was no heat to her words, just confusion as to how we could work her body in such a way.

"To make you feel good," I told her. "Don't we make you feel good? Do you want to come again?"

She nodded, the tip of her nose bumping my cock and I hissed out a breath. "You'll come from being played with and fucked in so many different ways. Not just our fingers on you. You'll come with something in your arse. You'll come with something in your mouth. Ultimately, you'll come with something in your pussy. Just trust us to always give you your pleasure. Good girl. Suck my cock and Mason will make you come again."

He carefully fucked her with the plug once again and she groaned, Mason's free hand slipping through her folds. "She's so wet."

Laurel groaned. I groaned, gripped the base of my cock in my hand. "Suck me off, sweetheart."

"I...I don't know how."

"Just put me in your mouth and lick me like a candy sucker. Trust me, you can't do it wrong." Just the idea of those luscious lips around me had me ready to come.

Tentatively, she took me into her mouth, the hot, wet cavern so amazing I felt my balls draw up. It wasn't going to take much for me to finish. Just seeing her like this, full breasts swaying beneath her, hips wide and perfect for holding onto when fucking, the flare of her full arse, the plug sticking from it. Everything about her made me hot. Made me hard. Made me just...about...come.

She took me to the back of her throat and she cried out in surprise at how I filled her. I groaned from just the vibration. I put my hand on the back of her head to guide her, to stroke over her silky hair so she knew I was pleased just as Mason fucked her arse with the narrow plug. I closed my eyes, gritted my teeth as she licked the underside of my dick. That was it. "I'm going to come, Laurel. Swallow it all."

I pumped my hips forward as my cock swelled even more, filling her mouth as pulse after pulse of my seed filled her mouth. She made a soft sound of surprise and I watched her throat work as she swallowed it. Mason must have touched her clit because Laurel came, her mouth opening around my cock as she cried out her release. I pulled from her lips and let her savor the amazing feeling that was washing over her.

Laurel dropped to her forearms, her head resting on the quilt. It was the perfect pose of submission and Mason growled deep in his throat. He was worked open the placket of his pants and pulled his cock free. We traded spots and I took over the enjoyment of playing with Laurel's arse. Mason had had all the fun so far, but then I'd come.

"Up, sweetheart. It's Mason's turn to feel your sweet mouth." Mason helped her up and fed her his cock. She was a fast learner and knew what to expect. Two orgasms in quick succession also made her quite pliant and eager to please.

"You're going to come one more time for me, sweetheart."

Her pussy lips were red and swollen and dripping wet, her clit a hard pearl just begging to be touched again. And her arse! It was a stunning site. The ointment glistened around her back entrance, her body clenching down on the slim plug. It was beneficial I'd just come or I'd reject our earlier promise not to fill her pussy and fuck her. As Laurel moved on Mason's cock, I started to work the plug. This time, instead of letting it slide between the two broader curves, I pushed it in deeper so that the ball shape stretched her arse wide, then closed around it, taking both of them—the one at the very end and this second one—deep inside. Carefully, I pulled the round part so it popped out, and then pushed it back in. This caused her arse to stretch so much more than ever before, over and over again.

Laurel froze in place, Mason's cock filling her mouth as she adjusted to this new assault. I grinned, thrilled by her response. She wasn't avoiding it and shifting her hips away. She groaned, a deep body sound of sheer pleasure. Mason began to move, fucking her slowly and carefully with his cock, allowing Laurel to remain still as I popped the round part of the plug in and out. In. *Plop.* Out. *Plop.*

I didn't even have to touch her clit to make her come. She was so sensitive from her previous orgasms and the awakening of new feelings elicited from the plug in her arse that she came again. Mason was ready, more than ready and came at the same time. When he pulled his spent cock from her mouth, Laurel slumped down onto the bed. Carefully, I worked the plug completely free and watched her arse clench closed. She didn't move as I did so and realized she'd fallen asleep, so I shifted her up onto a pillow and beneath the covers.

If this was what it was like when we played with her arse, I could only imagine how incredible it would be when we were both finally able to claim her together, her arse and pussy filled with our cocks simultaneously. It would be the ultimate claiming, the ultimate pleasure.

8

AUREL

I awoke, for the second day in a row, in the arms of two men. It was early, the light through the window only the slightest hint of pink. The sun had yet to rise.

"Sleep, sweetheart," Brody murmured, his voice deep.

Mason—I was beginning to tell the men's touches apart—stroked a hand down my arm. I was warm and I felt safe and protected. I knew that nothing was going to harm me with these men surrounding me. They'd given me pleasure, perhaps in ways I never imagined, but it had been incredible. I doubted their every action when it came to touching my body, for I knew they were pushing me, teaching me carnal activities that I should consider unseemly. Now, though, after they gave me the most amazing orgasms after giving in to their demands on my body, I couldn't question them. They'd put a hard object in my back entrance! I'd objected, for the idea had been ludicrous. But when I came so hard, so intensely from the jangly, sharp feelings the plug had elicited, I couldn't question any longer. I craved.

Soothed by their continued gentle attention and caring, I closed my eyes and did as Brody said. When I awoke again, I was alone in bed. Sitting up, I found my dress, the one I arrived in, laid out at the foot of the bed with my corset on top along with Ann's skirt and blouse. I readied myself for the day at the ewer and pitcher, tidied my hair in the mirror above it and tried to put on Ann's clothes. The waist was too snug on the skirt and not only were the sleeves too short on the blouse, but I could not button the front. Abandoning those options, I donned my own dress. The bodice was terribly ripped, half the buttons missing, but with the corset on securely, only my cleavage above the white material was visible. Pulling the two sides of the bodice together, I had the least amount of skin showing since I arrived.

I found the men downstairs, the smell of coffee and bacon luring me to them. They were at the table eating when I entered and they stood. I gave them a small smile, but didn't know what to say. The last I remember from the night before was taking Mason's cock into my mouth. Brody had been playing with the plug in my...ass. I'd come for the third time and the pleasure was so intense, so sharp, it was like a knife piercing through my reserve.

"We have a plate warming for you." Mason went to the stove and took a covered dish from the back corner and brought it to the table. "Coffee?"

I sat and the men followed. "Yes, thank you."

"Today we thought you might want to spend the day with Ann and Emma. They will be together at Ann's house and you can join them." Brody spoke as if I hadn't run out of the group dinner the night before.

"Won't they be upset to see me?" I asked tentatively, taking a sip of my coffee.

Both men frowned. "Why?" Brody asked. "You've done nothing wrong."

"But last night—"

Mason held up a hand halting my words. "Last night we did not recognize your true concerns until it was too late. It is our fault, not yours. Although your dress needs mending, it is a better choice than my shirt, although I do find you wearing it quite appealing."

"Perhaps you can wear our shirts here in the house?" Brody asked, one pale eyebrow raised.

He looked so eager at the idea, like a schoolboy, and I couldn't help but smile. I remembered about how they made me feel so good, again and again. "Just for you?"

"Just for us," Mason said and Brody nodded.

They were so handsome when they grinned, pleased about something so simple as my clothing compromise. So thoughtful and...kind. It was a strange, unusual sensation to feel safe, happy even, with them.

———

Andrew opened the door for us an hour later. I was once again in Mason's arms and I felt quite the invalid, although my coat had dried and I was able to wear that for warmth instead of a blanket. I held my boots in my hands.

Ann met us at the door along with another woman who I assumed was Emma. She was quite the opposite of Ann, taller and with dark hair. Both of them smiled at me and I felt reassured.

Brody held out Ann's borrowed blouse and skirt and the woman took them and set them on the banister leading upstairs, then took my coat and hung it on a peg by the door.

"I'm afraid the fit was too small." I lifted my boots. "Perhaps you have some spare laces?"

"Of course. In the kitchen. We will just fix your dress and it will be as good as new," Ann said very cheerfully, perhaps a little worried I might start to cry on her once again. "You have not yet met Emma. She has been very eager to make your acquaintance."

Emma came up to me and hooked her arm through mine. "Come, let's let the men go about their day."

I turned and looked back at Mason and Brody standing with Andrew. A smile was all I could offer as I was whisked away.

In the kitchen, Ann took my boots and sat them by the back door next to another pair. "I should be civilized and offer you tea, but we are both coffee drinkers. Is that all right with you?"

I nodded. Emma ran a hand over her belly. It wasn't overly prominent yet, but she would soon need to alter her dresses. "When will the baby come?" I asked.

"Summer," Emma replied, smiling.

"She never was sick in the mornings as I was, which makes me furious," Ann chided.

Emma grinned and waggled her eyebrows. "You were as lusty as I."

Ann blushed, but did not deny it. "Enjoy it now." She pouted and looked down at the sleeping baby in the cradle. "Your men won't touch you again for weeks and weeks. Perhaps not ever," she grumbled.

"What? I've seen them touch you and you seemed quite pleased."

Ann pursed her lips. "True, but they haven't *fucked* me since before the birth. I'm healed. Truly. Yet they insist on pleasing me in other ways."

The way they spoke of what she did with her husbands so openly and easily surprised me.

"Oh, I'm sorry, Laurel. You are not familiar with such ways," Ann replied.

I shrugged and felt my cheeks heat, my virginity a hindrance in participating in the conversation.

"Surely Mason and Brody have showed you *some* of what they will do with you?" Ann looked at me so hopefully. I was discovering she was quite the romantic.

"All of the men at Bridgewater are lusty and those two certainly can't keep their hands off you. Your red hair is so pretty," Emma added.

Lusty wouldn't begin to describe Mason and Brody. They were...dominant, possessive, potent, thoughtful, demanding, considerate. Kind.

Both women looked at me expectantly. "You saw me last night, Ann, wearing just Mason's shirt. Obviously *something* has happened with them, but...I...I can't share." I was too mortified to even think about it, let alone share it with others.

Emma's eyebrows rose and Ann told her the details, including my hasty retreat. "They are being very protective with you."

The baby started to fuss so Ann picked him up, tucked him into her arm and opened her blouse for him to nurse, the boy's chubby hand patting her absently. She seemed quite adept at being a mother, even with the baby so young.

Emma took a sip of her coffee. "Within the first hour of arriving at the ranch with Kane and Ian, Mason came to the bedroom door to announced dinner as they shaved my pussy and stretched my ass for the first time. I was completely naked and although he couldn't *see* what they were doing, he *knew*. For me, it was mortifying."

My mouth fell open and a strange feeling washed over me. Mason had been a part of that, even only tangentially? He'd known what her husbands were doing to her? I didn't like it. I didn't like it one bit. I pulled out a chair and sat down. Did that mean Mason was just using me to pass the time? To use for pleasure during a blizzard and that was all?

Ann placed her hand over mine pulling me from my thoughts. "You look as if you want to scratch Emma's eyes out." That had me stirring from my jealous thoughts. That was what I was. Jealous. "Emma had no control over the situation, as you can imagine. Do not think poorly of Mason either. As you learned last night, the men have different ways. Honorable ways that perhaps go against how we were raised, the town, everyone, but honorable nonetheless. Perhaps even more so. Do not worry over Mason's devotion, for he will tend to only you."

I frowned. "This word, tended, is used often around here."

Ann shrugged. "That's because it's what our husbands do to us. They tend to our needs. Theirs as well, but ours always come first. Last night, my milk was overflowing and my men eased the discomfort, regardless of whether dinner was ready or we had guests." She smiled. "I've grown accustomed to orgasm when they drink from me. They've trained me to respond this way because they want me to feel pleasure from my body, from what they do to it."

It made sense. "Aren't you embarrassed?"

"At first I was, when we were just married. But I've learned that everything they do to me is *for* me. I might not like it, at least at first, but they know what is best, and they always pleasure me."

I thought of how they'd filled my back entrance the night before. At first, I resisted, questioned their every action. But they'd done it for me, to make me feel good. I'd doubted, but they'd met their every vow, every promise of pleasure. Ann's words hit their mark and only eased my mind. It made me think that what Mason and Brody did with me was...normal.

"Even in punishment. Or at least after," Emma added.

"Punishment?" I asked, wary. What did they mean punishment?

Both women nodded. "We are punished for indiscretions, but it's for our safety, for our own good."

"They beat you? The teachers at school would smack our palms with rulers."

Both women looked aghast. "They spank me," Emma replied. "It isn't a pleasurable experience...at first, but something about it always makes me wet."

It was my turn to look stunned.

"As I said, they always make us come...eventually." Ann grinned.

I couldn't see how a spanking would bring about arousal, but I had to cede to their expert judgment on it.

Emma lowered herself into a chair in the awkward way of expecting women. "All this talk has me eager for my men."

"They'll be here for lunch and can tend to you then," Ann replied, a sly smile forming on her lips. I recognized it as I'd had a similar on my face after the men made me come.

"Perhaps Mason and Brody can tend to you over lunch as well." Emma grinned, quite the matchmaker. She was striking with her dark hair and pale eyes. Unfortunately, she didn't know I had no intention of staying at Bridgewater and wasn't the one for Mason and Brody. I was just a passing fancy, a woman they had a short dalliance with in a snowstorm. If only I could come up with a way to leave, I'd let them all return their unusual, yet idyllic, life.

9
———

ASON

With Laurel settled with the other women and the weather much improved, we were able to see to tasks that had been set aside. Horses to feed, stalls to muck, tack to mend. Even at the house, wood boxes needed to be filled. We were eating a hasty, cold lunch when we heard the horses. I looked across the table at Brody. His jaw clenched.

We stood in unison, and grabbed our coats. Brody took the rifle from above the door and we met the group of men on horseback. The sun was at our back so they had to squint against the bright snow. There was Sheriff Baker, Nolan Turner and three men I didn't know. The only man with a gun was the sheriff, and his was sticking out the back of his saddlebag.

"Gentlemen," I called out.

Brody stood at my side. "Shit," he muttered.

I was thinking the same thing, but didn't let any emotion show.

"Seems you've got a dead horse on your property a ways back," Harding said. He leaned forward on his pommel, his hat shielding his eyes. I knew them to be crafty and downright mean when he set his mind to it. Nothing good happened when the man was around.

I'd learned his ways a few years back when he approached me in town, offering to buy me a drink. Since I'd never laid eyes on him before, his false friendliness had me wary. I accepted just to suss out the man's intentions. Our ranches were miles apart, several smaller spreads between. Over the first shot of whiskey, Harding told me of the plan he'd devised to force those in the middle to sell, leaving our enlarged properties touching. After the third shot—the man wasn't one for moderation—he'd even mentioned an alliance via marriage; his daughter was just coming into her majority, he'd said. I'd never met the girl, hell, no one had. She'd been shipped off to—

Oh shit. Laurel's identity wasn't that much of a mystery any longer. Hiram Johns was none other than Nolan Turner. That meant she was Nolan Turner's daughter. His runaway daughter. And the man in the horse next to his was the man she was to marry. The description she'd provided yesterday over breakfast was pretty damn accurate. I wouldn't let my neighbor's rabid dog marry him.

The other two men must be either Turner's or Palmer's goons.

"Broke its leg," Brody replied.

"That much is obvious," Turner muttered, clearly not amused. "What I'm missing is a daughter."

I looked to Brody, then back to the men. "Never seen her."

It may have been the truth, but Laurel had never actually said she was Turner's daughter so God wouldn't strike me dead, at least today.

"He's lying," the fat man said. There wasn't a better word for him than that. The man was plain old fat and I felt sorry for his horse.

Sheriff Baker shook his head and held out his hand to stop the man. "Now, Palmer, don't go accusing people of things you have no proof over."

"To make your job easier, Sheriff, you're welcome to search the house," Brody offered.

The man looked to the others. "I find that mighty obliging, don't you, Turner?"

"This ranch is large. She could be in any one of the houses," Palmer blustered.

"If I fire three shots with my rifle, the others on the ranch will head this way," Brody said. "You can ask them all about your missing daughter and go from place to place looking, but I don't want to be shot for being hasty with my weapon. Sheriff, if you can fire the shots, then no one will get hurt by some uneasy trigger fingers."

The sheriff did just that, the loud reports of his weapon cracking in the still air.

In the distance, I could see the others leaving their houses, the stable, the barn.

"Here they come now," I said, trying to be amenable when all I wanted to do was shoot the bastards. "They'll work their way here as quickly as they can with the snow."

"In the meantime, go on in and search," Brody offered.

Turner and Palmer were quick to start to dismount. "Only one. I don't need all of you tracking snow and mud through my house."

"Now see here—" Palmer spouted.

Brody held up a hand. "What's the matter, Turner? You need help searching for one woman in a house?"

The barb hit its mark. Turner stopped Palmer from getting down, but climbed down himself. He was in his late fifties and still spry. "I'll find her," he vowed.

Turner climbed the steps and we moved back out of his way, allowing him a path to the door.

"Stomp your feet," I reminded.

He swore as he did so.

A minute passed and we stood patiently on the porch. The other Bridgewater men were approaching now, rifles in hand. Both Brody and I were sure of what he'd find, or wouldn't. Palmer and the others seemed uncomfortable and impatient.

Finally, Turner stepped back out holding up a pair of ladies drawers. "She's here."

Brody made a big show of sighing, scratched his face and tried to look contrite. "Now Turner, you found those on my dresser?" He shook his head and grinned. "Don't you ever collect a prize from when you're at Belle's? That sweet Adeline with the long blond hair and big tits, I talked her right out of those just last week."

Turner actually blushed.

"What's going on?" Kane said, rifle slung over his arm. Beside him were Simon, Rhys and Ian. The fight, to Turner and Palmer's eyes, had become evenly balanced. However, Brody and I could have taken them all ourselves. I had an itch to do so. Just the sight of Palmer was revolting. *He* would have married Laurel if she hadn't ventured out into the storm? No wonder she'd risked her life to escape.

"Seems a woman's missing. Turner's daughter."

"That your horse over there, Turner?" Simon called out. "Terrible losing a horse to a break. I heard Mason put him down, so you must be thankful he didn't suffer."

"Who the hell cares about the horse? I need to find my daughter." He placed his hands on his hips, the delicate drawers blowing in the slight breeze.

"A pair of ladies unmentionables does not a woman find," Sheriff Baker commented. "Especially since we know we've all partaken of Belle's girls a time or two."

"Then we'll continue our search," Turner added.

"What has you so hot under the collar for this lass?" Ian asked, his Scots brogue thick. I knew this meant he was angry, but Palmer didn't.

"She's my fiancée," Palmer said.

Fiancée. Not a chance. Laurel was ours and he wouldn't lay a finger on her.

"I told the men they could search the entire property," I told the others and they nodded their agreement. "If you're satisfied your daughter's not in my house, can we move on? Andrew's house, ah, here he comes now, would be next."

Andrew approached, rifle in hand, Robert next to him. Turner's party was now certainly out gunned. We had two pompous windbags, a small town sheriff whose gun rested in his saddlebag and two henchmen. They were no match for a group of regimental men with a woman to protect.

"We heard the shots."

Turner stomped over to his horse and mounted, the entire group working their way to exactly where Laurel was. I was confident she was well hidden, for we'd planned for such contingencies. Regimental men planned for all situations, especially dangerous ones.

When we were in front of his house, Andrew stepped forward, held up his hand. "Sheriff, I will permit *you* to search my home. My wife, Ann, is inside with our new baby and I don't want her scared."

"My wife is visiting with her, and I agree," Kane added. "I do not want her fearing for her safety on her own land."

Sheriff Baker nodded his head and dismounted.

"Wait, I don't think—"

The sheriff cut off Turner. "Don't trust me to do my job, Turner?"

That had the man huffing, but didn't say more.

He turned to Andrew. "I heard about the baby. A boy?"

Andrew nodded and smiled with paternal pride. I saw, too, that Robert was pleased by the Sheriff's concern, but held back. Our ways weren't the ways of Simms, of the sheriff and we intended to keep it that way. Andrew was the man legally wed to Ann and would then be the baby's sole father—in the eyes of the sheriff.

"Christopher."

Andrew led the lawman up the porch steps and went inside, both men removing their hats as they did. I could see Ann through the open doorway, the baby in her arms with Emma standing next to her.

They closed the door behind them to keep the heat within. While we waited, it was time to get some information out of the other men. "It's right noble of you to be worried about your daughter," I said neutrally.

Turner's gaze shifted from the closed front door to me. "When you have a child, you'll understand."

"Oh? Didn't you send her off to school when she was just a child?" Kane asked, crossing his arms over his chest. His breath came out in puffs of white.

"You wouldn't know the ways here, Mr. Kane, being from another country and all," Harding countered.

"Oh, I think we Englishmen take the prize for boarding schools," Brody added. "Why'd she go out riding when the weather was so poor?"

Turner whipped his head around to Brody. The tendons in the older man's neck stood out. "She might be a tad insane," he lied, albeit poorly.

"Then, Palmer—that's your name?" When the man nodded, I continued. "If the girl might be a tad insane, why are you marrying her?"

He stiffened in his saddle. "I'm not marrying her for her mind."

"Don't you worry about daft bairns then?" Ian asked, putting a little extra emphasis on his accent.

"There's more at stake here than that," the man admitted.

"Oh? And what's that?" Robert asked. "When you don't find her at Bridgewater, where are you going to search next? There's plenty of land for her to be."

"Her horse," Turner bit out, "is laying dead on your property."

"Then the girl, could be laying dead anywhere between your ranch and here," Simon added.

The sheriff came out then, Andrew following behind. Ann stood in the doorway.

"She's not in there, Turner. Hell, she's not here. These men would have brought her to town when the weather cleared or at least handed her over when we first arrived." The sheriff sighed. "We aren't going to search every building on the property, are we?"

"Did you search the Carter's house? How about the Reed's? You passed both their ranches are on the way here," Kane asked.

I could tell by the angry looks on Turner's and Palmer's faces that they hadn't.

"Is there some kind of bias at play here, Sheriff?" I asked.

Sheriff Baker held up his hand. "The animal is on your land," he offered.

"As I said before you came out, she could have fallen off anywhere between Turner's spread and here. The storm was mighty fierce, and for a woman to go out alone? You think she'd make it this far? Alive?"

The sheriff nodded sagely. "Let's go, gentleman. We've wasted enough of their time."

The men didn't look happy. Turner and Palmer didn't have the business deal without Laurel and the two goons didn't have any faces to smash in. Sheriff Baker climbed up onto his horse, tipped his hat. He was the first to turn his animal around and the rest, grudgingly, followed.

It wasn't until they'd gone over the slight rise in the distance, indicating they were on their way back to town, did we go inside. It was time to get the truth, all of it, from Laurel.

10

AUREL

When we heard the shots, the ladies froze in place. They'd told me that three shots meant something was terribly wrong and indicated that men were needed to help immediately. Within a few minutes—which felt like forever—Andrew had stormed into the kitchen through the back door and led me to what he called a Priest's Hole. It was a secret space to hide built beneath the stairwell. A secret latch opened the door and I easily fit inside.

Andrew, in no uncertain terms, told me that there were men at Mason and Brody's house and were most likely searching for me. He'd recognized the sheriff, even from a distance, which meant there was no real danger. Only to me. He would have pushed me out of the way to get Ann and the baby in first if there was truly a danger.

Of course it was my father. Mason and Brody assumed they'd come searching for me and I knew it as well. I just didn't want to believe they'd actually come. It only meant I was still of value to them. They didn't *care* about me, only needed me for their own personal gains, whatever they were. My stomach lurched at the idea of Mr.

Palmer or my father finding me and went into the hidden space without complaint. Ann gave me a blanket to sit upon and I was comfortable enough, but time moved so slowly in the dark.

I heard the women's voices, although muted, the baby fuss, then settle. I focused on my breathing and staying as quiet as possible. The sound of men's voices had me listening intently. One voice was Andrew's, the other one I didn't recognize. They spoke of the baby in easy, congenial tones.

"You're welcome to search the house, Sheriff," Andrew said.

"I don't care if she's here or not. In fact, if she were here, I'd hide her. Turner's a pain in my...," he coughed, then continued, "I beg your pardon, ladies. He's quite difficult to deal with. Add that man Palmer and those two are like rattlesnakes. Vicious. Mean. Wily. They're up to something else they'd leave that poor girl alone."

"Poor girl? What do you mean, Sheriff?" Ann asked. "Have they hurt her?"

"Mrs. Turner died while birthing the girl and the man has never gotten over it. From what I remember, he probably blamed her for killing her own mother, then shipped her off to some school far away. Haven't seen hide nor hair of her since."

"Then how do you know she's actually missing or even back in Simms?" Andrew asked.

There was a pause. "I don't. If you hear of this girl, you send her to me, not back to her father. I wouldn't wish that on my worst enemy."

"Thank you, Sheriff, we'll do that."

"Ma'am."

I only heard silence for several long minutes, assuming they went outside. Then I heard footsteps. The door opened and I jumped, the light blinding me.

"Come on out, sweetheart. They're gone." Mason.

I gripped his hand and stood, blinking against the bright sunlight. I held onto him tightly not only because I had prickles in my legs from being sedentary, but because I needed the connection. Everyone was there and they were staring at me. Mason and Brody. Robert, Andrew and Ann. Rhys, Simon and Cross. MacDonald and

VANESSA VALE

McPherson. Emma with two men I assumed were her husbands, Ian and Kane.

"Laurel, would you like to introduce yourself?" Brody asked.

I glanced at him and then at everyone else. Although they weren't outwardly hostile, they certainly weren't happy. Swallowing, I knew I had no choice but to tell the truth. All of it. "I'm...I'm Laurel Turner."

"Why didn't you tell us that before?" Mason asked, his mouth a thin line.

"I was afraid, afraid if you knew who my father was you'd send me back."

"Send you back, to that bloody bastard?"

"I...I didn't know you. He has power and reach in this community and didn't know if you were friends."

"You brought danger to my door, to my family." Andrew frowned.

"Our wife as well," Ian added, his voice deep.

"For that alone, you will be punished," Mason said.

———

MASON

"Punished?" Laurel asked.

I nodded and led her to the same chair I sat in the night before. "You lied, Laurel, which put us all in danger. If you'd told us the truth from the start, we would have protected you."

I pulled her between my wide knees and held onto her thighs.

"I thought you would return me!"

"Have we given you any indication we are in any way similar to Nolan Turner?" Brody asked.

She shook her head.

"Over my knee, sweetheart." I patted my thigh.

"Why?"

"You're going to get a spanking."

"No!" she cried, trying to step back.

"You endangered everyone at Bridgewater and you must face the consequences."

If I let her, she'd stand in front of me and argue all day long. Instead, I easily maneuvered her into position. Brody knelt down and worked the length of her dress up over her hips. With her drawers dropped on our front porch, she was bare beneath.

"Everyone's watching!" she cried, shifting and squirming on my lap.

"They are."

Spank.

"They need to know you've learned how one person's actions can affect everyone else here on the ranch. They need to be reassured you will not do something like this again," Brody replied.

Spank.

"You put women and a baby in harm's way, Laurel."

Spank.

"I'm sorry!" she cried.

I looked up at the others, each giving us a reassuring nod before leaving the room. Robert, Ann and Andrew went into their kitchen with the baby. The others left out the front door.

They were content that the consequences were meted out appropriately, but neither Brody nor I were done. I continued to spank her in earnest for she needed to learn her place.

"We will protect you, Laurel. You will tell us if there's ever any sign of danger, whether it be a severe storm or a bastard father."

"My turn," Brody said.

I put a hand on her lower back as Brody spanked her next. "No lying, sweetheart."

By now, Laurel was crying, her body slumped over my thighs.

"We wouldn't give you back to Turner. Don't you see? We're never giving you back. You're ours."

Brody's hand soothed over her red arse.

"I thought you were using me," she sniffed.

Carefully, I righted her so she sat on my lap. She hissed out a breath as her punished flesh made contact. "Using you?" I wiped the tear stains from her cheeks.

"You...we've done things...and now I'm used goods. My virtue is in tatters. No one will want me."

Brody turned her chin so she looked at him. "Used goods? You belong to us, Laurel. No one else. You *gave* us your virtue, no one else's, just like you will give us your virginity. Not just your pussy, but your arse as well."

"But...you said you'd save...filling my pussy for when I married. That you'd pl...play with me and then give me back." She looked so lost and confused.

"I should spank you further for thinking us less than honorable. We didn't fill your pussy because you weren't married to us. Yet. Now that we know the truth, there's only one way to truly save you from your father and Palmer."

Brody nodded his agreement.

"How?" she asked, her voice hopeful.

"We're getting married."

"Married?" she gasped. "You're going to marry me just to save me from Mr. Palmer?"

"Hell, no," Brody added. "We're marrying because we knew you belonged to us the first moment we saw you, unconscious on our kitchen table. But first, you're going to tell us everything." When she remained silent, he added, "Now."

She took a deep breath. "My father is Nolan Turner. Obviously, you've heard of him."

"We've had run-ins with him in the past. He wants to dam up the creek that runs through his property, which means all the ranches and farms downstream will not have water." Brody stood, went over to the window, looked out, then returned. "We're not affected here as we're on the river and our water rights trump his, but I know many other landowners who are fighting him."

Laurel nodded. "I have learned he is not well liked in the community, which means I am not either. Being his daughter eliminated a number of prospective suitors which only helped Mr. Palmer's—and my father's—case toward marriage."

"We've heard he had a daughter, but she was sent away to school in—"

"—Denver," Laurel said, confirming the rumors. "Since my mother died birthing me, Father placed the blame on me. A nanny raised me until I was old enough to be sent away to school. Thus my poor lack of knowledge of the area and a terrible sense of direction. I have only just returned a month ago."

Brody looked her over carefully. "You are well past the schoolroom."

"Quite." She sniffed. "My father paid handsomely for my continued stay. Out of sight, out of mind."

"Until he needed you," I commented.

Laurel looked wounded at my words. They weren't meant to be hurtful, but they *were* the truth and she already knew them to be true.

"I'd thought—assumed—my father had sent for me to return because he'd had a change of heart. That he wanted me. He'd wanted me all right, for all the wrong reasons." She looked down at her hands folded in her lap. "I have not seen my father since I was seven. I do not feel closeness with the man. I'd had hope, brief hope, that he wanted me." She shook her head and I could see the sadness and shame on her face. Sadness for the false hope he'd given her, shame at believing she was wanted. "I was silly to even consider."

I pulled her into my arms, tucked her head beneath my chin. "We want you, sweetheart."

"Hell, yes," Brody affirmed.

11

AUREL

"But....but why?" I asked. I felt lightheaded from everything that had happened in the past ten minutes. Everyone had been so upset with me, and now that I think on it, rightly so. I should have let them know who my father was, but I was protecting myself. I wasn't used to considering others, nor did I think there actually *were* others on the ranch when I'd originally lied, especially a baby. "Marrying me will only make an enemy out of my father. He'll know you were fooling him today and will make him angry. Besides, you've met Mr. Palmer. He's not one to trifle with either. Marrying me might keep him from doing the same, but he'll exact revenge somehow."

Brody placed his hands on his hips. "Your father already is an enemy, sweetheart, and that started long before your return."

"Oh?"

"He approached me to try to squeeze out the smaller ranches between ours."

My eyes widened as I thought about the distance. "That's miles and miles of land!"

Mason nodded and I looked to him. "Those families in between are friends of ours. We stand behind them, help protect them from Turner now."

"They're both very powerful," I warned.

"Mr. Palmer is no match for us. You don't think we can defend what's ours?" Mason asked.

I considered his words, took in both of their very large bodies, the way they were dominant and commanding. With them, I felt safe and protected. Did I think they could shelter me from my father's wrath? Yes.

"Why would you want to protect me? I've lied to you and you can have any woman you want."

"Do you want me to turn you over my knee again?" Mason asked, his voice deep. His dark eyes narrowed.

I bit my lip. "For what reason?"

"You think we would have touched you as we didn't consider you ours, if we hadn't intended to marry you?"

I paused. "Well, yes."

Brody exhaled and shook his head slowly. "You either have never come across honorable men before or have been cloistered away from all of them."

"Perhaps both, Brody," Mason said, keeping his eyes on me.

"We're going to town," Brody replied. Mason lifted me off his lap and led me to the door and helped me into my coat.

"Why?" I seemed to continue to ask the same question over and over.

"To prove that we truly are honorable."

Two hours later, standing before the minister at the altar of the town's small church, I married Mason. Brody and the minister's wife stood as witnesses. How they decided which man I would legally wed was not shared with me. The kiss had been brief and chaste, but Mason's eyes held unspoken promises I knew he—as well as Brody—would fulfill later.

I wore no wedding dress, but my ripped dress, my coat remaining on and buttoned to prevent any questions. We didn't linger in town, for the men seemed eager to return to the ranch before nightfall, which came early this time of year. Making our way out of town, I rode with Mason, but once we were a fair distance away, Brody came beside us and pulled me onto his lap. "You may have married Mason, but you are mine as well," he said, his breath warm on my ear. "I'll prove it to you once we are home."

The journey went quickly, for I spent the time wondering exactly *how* he planned to prove it.

———

Mason helped me off with my coat and he hooked it on the peg by the door.

"Perhaps I might have some other clothes?" I looked down at my ripped dress. "This dress is beyond repair and I don't have any drawers."

"Mmm," Brody said, hanging up his own coat.

"Dress, yes. Drawers, no," Mason said. "I'm sure Emma or Ann will be happy to select some new dresses for you at the mercantile. For the next week or so, however, you won't need any clothes at all."

The look in his eye as he came toward me had me believing him. He bent at the waist and before I wondered his intent, I was over his shoulder and being carried upstairs. "Mason!"

His hands firmly held my thighs in place and I lifted my head to look at Brody as he followed behind. The corner of his mouth was tipped up and knew he would offer me no assistance.

"It is time to make you ours, wife," Brody said.

Wife. That one word was daunting and devastating and nerve wracking all at the same time. I was married to two men! It had been one thing to consider them a blizzard dalliance, but this was something else entirely. The way Brody was looking at me I knew this was so much more.

Mason didn't place me back on my feet, but instead dropped me onto my back upon the bed in his room. I bounced once, but didn't have time to even come up on my elbows before he was upon me, kissing me. This wasn't the chaste peck from the ceremony, but a real kiss. Mason's lips were soft yet intent, his tongue delving into my mouth to tangle and play with mine. With his hand at my nape, he angled me as he wished, plundering. His beard was soft against my skin, scratchy yet silky at the same time. I felt the bed dip on my side.

"My turn," Brody murmured.

Mason lifted his head and I met his dark eyes. *Oh.* He'd looked at me before, but this was different. Deeper, darker, powerful. It was as if he'd held a part of himself back and now that we were wed, he'd unleashed it. He sat back and let Brody turn my head toward him. He kissed me as well, but he kissed entirely different. His mouth was more insistent, rougher and definitely more demanding. He even tasted different.

My fingers tangled in the silky strands of his hair and every time I breathed, my breasts bumped into his chest. All the worry and fear ebbed from me, my body relaxing and softening beneath him. My blood heated, my nipples tightened and my thighs became damp. My body recognized both of these men and readied itself for them.

"Brody....I...more," I whispered against his mouth. Kissing wasn't enough anymore. They'd been preparing me for days for this, whether by touch or by word, they'd promised me...more.

I wasn't sure when, but Mason had stood by the bed. He took my hand and tugged me up to stand beside him. He easily stripped the dress from me as Brody removed my boots with the new laces.

"Should we allow her to wear a corset or let her be bare beneath her dresses?" Mason asked as he undid the stays on the stiff fabric.

"The idea of her being completely bare beneath a prim and proper dress is very appealing," Brody replied. "I haven't had much opportunity to play with her nipples, but I will rectify that now."

Mason dropped the corset to the floor as Brody turned me to face him. As he sat on the side of the bed, my breasts were directly at eye level. He cupped a breast in each of his hands, the rough callouses brushing against my sensitive flesh. "They're perfect, sweetheart."

His thumbs ran over the tips and I cried out as the feel of it spread all over my body. My pussy was wet, the juices of arousal coating my thighs as my inner walls involuntarily clenched in anticipation. He didn't stop there, for he began to pull and tug and pinch.

I couldn't balance and had to place my hands on his shoulders for support. "Brody!"

"Do you need my mouth on you?" He didn't wait for me to answer, just lowered his head and took one nipple into his mouth, laving at it, letting the flat of his tongue lick over the tightened peak before sucking on it.

"Does that feel good, sweetheart?" Mason whispered in my ear, standing directly behind me. He trailed kisses down my neck and across my shoulder, his hands sliding up and down my sides. "Your skin's like silk."

As Brody tended to one breast with his mouth, he used his fingers to play and work my other nipple before switching. I don't know how long he remained focused there, but by the time he lifted his head, my hips were shifting of their own accord into him.

"Let's see if she likes a little bite of pain with her pleasure," Mason said.

Before I could even think of what he meant, his hands came around from behind and took over from Brody, his big palms cupping my breasts. His skin was so dark, the hair there making him seem so manly and rugged in comparison to my pale, sensitive skin. Fingers took hold of my nipples and instead of just playing as Brody had, Mason slowly tugged the tips outward, stretching them long and not...letting...go. I thrust my chest out to relieve the painful pleasure as I cried out. He didn't relent, just held a constant and steady pull, and then pinched.

"Mason!" I groaned, my fingertips clawing into Brody's shoulders. My eyes widened as I looked into Brody's pale eyes. I saw heat there, need, desire. He was watching me closely, perhaps ensuring I wasn't truly being hurt. It *was* painful, but Mason's rough touch wasn't hurting me. It just...was.

Mason let go and lifted my breasts up so Brody could suckle gently at one tip, then the other, soothing my enflamed skin. He only remained until I was soothed, my heightened arousal tapered slightly, only for Mason to repeat his rough attentions. As I held Brody's gaze, he lowered a hand between my legs and a finger slid over my lower lips. I couldn't move, couldn't do anything except take what they were doing, for Mason would not relent.

"She's very wet," Brody said. "She likes it. Do you like how Mason makes you feel, sweetheart?"

"I...oh," I sighed. I couldn't respond for Brody's finger ran over my clit and flicked it. He must have been using two hands on me for I felt a finger circle the entrance to my pussy. They'd made good on their promise to keep it empty until marriage.

"We're married now. Please, Brody," I begged. I tilted my hips toward his fingers and I saw him grin.

"Please fill you, sweetheart? You want a cock in your pussy?"

I nodded.

"Let's see how tight you are." The very tip of his finger dipped inside and I clenched down on it.

12

AUREL

"Ah!" It wasn't enough. Just the feel of being filled even the smallest amount had me eager for more. But his finger was big and my body was untried and it was very snug.

"So tight. Jesus, Mason, she's going to strangle our cocks." He slipped in a little further. "I want you to come for us now. With Mason tugging on your nipples, I'm going to stroke over this special spot inside you...right...there and you're going to come. Now."

I could do nothing but follow his command for my body had been well primed by Mason's insistent fingers on my breasts. Somehow Brody knew of a place inside me that would make me come instantly. Perhaps it was the combination of his finger and the almost painful tugging of my nipples. Whatever it was, I screamed, the feeling so intense, so hot, so different that I never wanted it to end. I shifted my hips, rocking them onto and over Brody's finger. He didn't let it go up inside me any further, only rubbed over that place he'd found. It was...delicious, that place he was rubbing over.

Mason's mouth kissed across my sweat dampened shoulder as he let go of my nipples and just cupped my breasts in his palms, holding them as if they'd ache if he didn't. Brody leaned in and kissed me, slowly yet deeply. When he pulled his head back, he met my eyes. "Undress Mason, sweetheart."

He took my wrists in his hands and turned me about. Mason stood there, tall and broad and waited. I looked him over, from head to toe, every virile inch of him, and could see the hard, thick outline of his cock pressing against his pants.

"I can't wait to fuck you," he said. The idea sent a shiver through me. I undid the buttons down the front of his shirt as he toed off his boots. He stripped the shirt from his body as I undid his pants and pushed it down over his hips. His cock sprang free, red and thick and eager. Clear fluid seeped from the tip.

I glanced over my shoulder and saw Brody finish removing the last of his clothes so he, too, was naked. "Lay down," Brody said.

I sat down on the side of the bed, and then lay back, slowly, tentatively. I was still so aroused, even after the pleasure they'd just given me, perhaps even more so. Seeing their cocks so eager and ready proved to me how much they wanted me. They'd been correct; my body didn't lie. I wanted them so desperately and the slickness between my thighs was one of the many giveaways.

"You may have married Mason, but I'm going to take that perfect maidenhead of yours. I felt it inside you against my finger. It's mine, sweetheart, and you're going to give it to me. Now spread your legs so we can see your pretty pussy."

My eyes widened at his crude and carnal words. I lifted my legs from where they hung off the side of the bed and bent my knees, pulling them back so my feet were planted on the bed. When I didn't part them wide enough, Brody just raised a brow and waited.

Both men stood staring down at me. They were naked and so handsome. While Brody was taller, Mason was broader in the shoulders. The hair on their chests was of strikingly different colors, but both had muscles rippling beneath their skin. Their cocks both were aimed at me, both thick and hard and almost angry in readiness for me.

I licked my lips remembering the taste of their hard yet satiny soft skin, the salty flavor of their seed. Parting my legs, I opened myself to them in more ways than one. I was not only giving my body to them, but I was opening up my heart to them as well, for I had to trust that they would protect me and keep me safe, to treat me well and cherish me. They said they'd guard me from the likes of Mr. Palmer or my father and I had to believe them. I had no choice, just like I had no choice but to spread my legs wider, then wider still, beneath their lusty stares.

Their eyes shifted to between my thighs.

"Her pussy's dripping. I can see it from here."

"Those curls are so striking."

I wanted to close my legs, but knew they'd just have me open them again.

"We'll shave her later."

My eyes widened at their words, at their frank discussion of my body.

"We must leave at least some red down there. Later. Now I need to make her mine," Brody said, placing a knee on the bed and positioning himself between my thighs.

My skin was warm and flushed. I could feel it. The quilt beneath my back was soft, the room lit solely with the soft glow from the bedside lamp. Their tastes mingled in my mouth from their kisses. Brody gripped his cock in a tight fist, came down to support himself on one hand and lined himself up. He slid the broad head back and forth over my slick folds before catching it at my opening, pressing slightly forward.

The hint of stretching had me wince. He was so big, so much bigger than his finger that he'd just inserted a tiny amount. I knew he would put his entire cock inside me and I tensed, knowing it would hurt and questioning if the action was even possible. My eyes widened and my fingers clenched in the quilt.

"Wait," Mason said. Brody froze and I tensed even more. My breath came out in silent pants. "She's not ready."

Brody looked up my body so our eyes met. "Ah," he said, his

voice gruff and deep. Letting go of his cock, he placed his other hand by his head so he was directly over me, our noses practically touching.

"Shh," he crooned before dipping his head for a kiss, this one a light brushing over my lips. "Listen to my words, sweetheart."

He was so close I could see the rough stubble of his beard, the gold flecks in it.

"Do you know what makes me so hard for you?"

I shook my head but held his gaze.

"The little sound you make in your throat when you come. The way you bite your bottom lip. The color of your nipples."

"Oh," I whispered, almost an exhale.

"I like the way your pussy tastes," Mason added. "The way your eyes widen in surprise when you come, then they slip closed as you succumb."

"We'll never hurt you, sweetheart," Brody murmured.

"You're...you're too big," I admitted. "I don't think you'll fit."

Brody stroked my hair back from my face in a soothing gesture. "Let's work up to my cock, all right?"

I nodded, soothed by his words, by his gentle tone.

He shifted and reached down to run his fingers over my lower lips and the sound of my wetness filled the air. A finger slipped inside and my hips arched off the bed. It went in farther than when he'd done it before and I clenched down on it.

"Right there, that's your maidenhead. That's for my cock." He pulled his finger out, but only for a moment and this time two fingers worked into me. My eyes widened at the feel, a slight burning, yet it felt...good.

"All right?" he asked, concerned.

I nodded. I was more than all right. His finger felt incredible.

"That's right, move your hips to what feels good. Just like that. One more finger, sweetheart."

When he had three fingers in me, I cried out. It was tight, so very tight, yet for the first time I felt filled, but he wasn't deep enough. I couldn't stop the movement of my hips and soon I became frantic. I needed more. I felt hot all over and I heard the little sound that Brody mentioned escape my throat.

"Are you ready for more?"

Brody, too, was breathing hard and I could see that his patience was costing him. A bead of sweat dripped down his brow and his cheeks were ruddy.

"Yes. Please."

"Ah, I love the sound of her begging," Mason said. He'd moved to sit beside me and tucked his hand behind my knee and pulled my leg up and back so I was spread so incredibly wide. "Brody's going to take your maidenhead now, sweetheart, and I'm going to watch."

His words eased the last of my fears, although my arousal was so intense I could barely remember why I didn't want Brody's cock inside me.

This time when I felt the broad head I wasn't scared. Instead, I shifted my hips toward him, letting him slide in a little.

"She's...Jesus, Mason, she's so tight." Brody gritted his teeth as he forged ahead, then pulled back, slowly, again and again until I winced. He was so big, so wide I felt so full and he wasn't even in all the way.

"You're ours, Laurel. Ours."

Brody sucked in a deep breath and shifted his hips forward, breaking through the thin membrane and seating himself all the way. I cried out at the twinge of pain but also at being so completely full. I felt as if he was splitting me in half, yet also forging us together into one.

He held himself still and looked at me, waited until I met his gaze. "All right?" he asked.

I clenched down on his cock and he groaned. "I want you to take a moment to adjust, but if you do that, I won't be able to do so."

I arched a brow. "There's more?"

Brody grinned wickedly. "More? Sweetheart, there's so much more."

Slowly, he pulled back, then slid in. "Oh," I cried.

"You are so beautiful, Laurel. Brody's going to fuck you now. Nothing will stop him. There's nothing between us any longer."

Brody moved his hips so that his cock worked me, stroked me, filled me, and then claimed me. The hint of pain dissipated quickly and only pleasure took over. I moved my free leg up and down Brody's side, the inside of my knee touching him from torso to hip to thigh. The spot he'd discovered earlier that had me come so easily was rubbed by the flared head of his cock. My eyes slipped shut, my head tilted back as new places flared to life by his cock. Mason's grip on my leg tightened and he pulled my knee back even further. Reaching between Brody and me, he ran his finger over my clit, and then pressed down.

I came in one violent rush, the intensity of it surprising me. My back arched and I screamed, most likely deafening Brody in the process.

Brody didn't slow his thrusts, but instead quickened them as I convulsed around his cock.

"So good," he uttered as he filled me all the way then held himself still. I felt him swell within me, then his pulsing hot seed.

When the last of the pleasure ebbed, I lay there wilted, sweaty and very, very happy. Mason had released my leg and my knees rubbed against Brody's ribs. I had no idea it would be like this. So connected, so carnal, so wonderful.

Brody's breaths fanned my neck and once they evened, he slowly pulled out of me. I felt empty and still aroused, as if I needed more. Hot seed dripped from me and onto the blanket below.

Sitting back on his haunches, he looked down at my pussy. "So perfect," he uttered, his expression now relaxed and pleased. "I love seeing my seed dripping from you."

"My turn," Mason said, his voice not containing any notes of pleasure. "My cock aches to be inside you, Laurel. Just watching your face when you were filled for the first time almost had me coming."

Brody stood and Mason took his place. "Roll over, sweetheart."

My eyes widened at his request, but did as he asked. I looked over my shoulder at him, confused. "Why am I like this?"

Mason grinned as he gripped my hips. "I'm going to fuck you from behind."

"From...." When his cock slid over my wet folds, I understood. He curved his body over mine and I felt his chest hair tickle my back. He kissed my nape as his cock rooted and found my opening. In one slick stroke, he slid all the way in. There was no pain this time, only a stretching that had me groaning. When his hips pressed against my bottom I knew he was all the way in.

"You're right, Brody. She's so tight. Do you like it this way, sweetheart?"

He pulled back, the slid in again, the wet sound so loud. I felt Brody's seed drip down my thighs. The feeling of Mason's cock was so different, the angle of his fucking completely different than when Brody took me. "You're...you're so deep."

"I know. Every inch of my cock is surrounded by hot, tight pussy."

His hands stroked over my bottom before he brushed a thumb over my back entrance.

"Mason!" I tried to shift away, but his cock was embedded deep within me and he held me securely in his tight grip.

"We're going to take you here too, sweetheart. Not today, but soon. We'll get you ready for us, but for now, I've got to fuck you. I'm going to move now and you're going to come."

He was so demanding, so confident he could make me come again. The feel of the pad of his thumb brushing over my back entrance was surprising, yet the sensation of it had me clenching down on his cock. It was intense and hot and I couldn't stand it any longer. I ached for him to do...something. When he began to move, I groaned, relieved. His hips began to thrust and he used his cock as a weapon against any type of resistance. I knew his words to be true; I was going to come and I couldn't stop it.

Hands cupped my breasts and played with my nipples. Brody. When his fingers pinched the tips, I tossed my head back and came, sublime heat washing over me. My scream was caught in my throat, my body tightening and I knew I cinched down on his cock. He didn't stop moving, only rammed into me harder than before. His thumb moved from my ass and his hands gripped my hips tightly.

It was as if the pleasure couldn't stop, for his cock continued to rub over spots inside me that felt so good. Perspiration coated my skin as my hands clenched in the quilt. I felt Mason's cock thicken and swell within me as he bit down on my shoulder, his cock bottoming out in me. He groaned as I felt a gush of hot seed fill me and seep out around his cock and down my legs.

Brody turned my face to kiss me. I looked into his eyes. "You're ours, sweetheart."

Ours. I liked the sound of that.

13

RODY

"Where is Mason?" Laurel asked. She was bent over the side of my bed, her feet planted on the floor but spread wide.

"Sweetheart, I have my thumb in your arse and you're asking after Mason?" The slick ointment I was working into her made my thumb's entry easy. It had been three days since we first fucked her and since then we'd taken her together and on our own, like now.

Her hips shifted back onto my hand and she groaned. "It's just that...you always take me together in the morning."

Three days did not a routine make, but she was quickly adjusting to having two husbands. We'd been training her arse these past few days, preparing her for taking both of us together. While we'd fucked her in turn, it wasn't the same. Having me fill her pussy while Mason took her arse would be the ultimate claiming. She would have no doubt that she belonged to both of us, although she didn't seem to question it even now.

"You may be married to both of us, but we will not always take you together. I may want to play with you as I am now. Does Mason do work your arse like this?"

She shook her head against the bed. "He...he has me on my back."

"Oh?" My cock was already hard enough to break ice on a frozen pond, but listening to her tell me about how Mason worked her body had my balls drawing up, ready to spend my seed.

"Tell me, sweetheart, what he does to you." I continued to collect more ointment and work it into her, slowly moving my thumb in deeper and deeper.

"I hold my knees up and back. He...says he likes to see my shaved pussy."

I did, too. We'd kept a little red patch of hair on her mons, which was hot as hell, but the rest of her was shaved. When we ate her sweet pussy now she was slick and smooth and nothing hid those pretty pink lips. Just like now, they were always slick and coated in her cream.

"Does he play with your nipples when his finger is in your arse?"

She sighed and I was able to slide in past my knuckle. She was so hot, so tight that when I got my cock in her I wouldn't last.

"Yes, and it hurts."

"Hurts bad or hurts good?"

I couldn't hold off any longer. Stepping close, I aligned my cock with the entrance to her pussy and pushed in, holding my thumb still and deep within her arse. It was a tight fit and I hissed out my breath.

Laurel groaned. "Hurts so good."

I grinned and let go. She might be small and dainty compared to either Mason or myself, but she could handle us. In fact, we'd discovered she liked it a little rough, which was good because I couldn't hold back any longer. I rocked my hips into her, over and over, my balls slapping against her pussy. Since I'd been playing with her for some time, she was close and I could feel her inner walls clenching down as if trying to pull me even deeper. She came on a scream and I followed directly after.

"So good," I repeated, pulling from her body and tugging her into my arms so we lay front to back.

This was where Mason found us an hour later.

"It's after nine," he grumbled. "Some of us had work to do this morning."

Laurel stirred in my arms. She was no longer modest about being unclothed in front of us. No doubt Mason could see every delectable inch of her. I kissed her shoulder, and then stood to put on my clothes.

"I went to Ian and Kane's house to collect the clothes Emma picked for you at the mercantile."

Her eyes lit up.

"You don't like being naked, sweetheart?"

"I just don't want to wear the ripped dress again."

"Here." He tossed a new cream-colored corset onto the bed. "You may wear this today."

She came up on her elbow and fingered the lace edging, but frowned. She had no idea how decadent she looked sprawled across my bed as she was. "And a dress?"

Mason slowly shook his head. "No dress today. Tomorrow I will give you another article of clothing to add."

"Her stockings," I told him.

He nodded. "Good thinking. Stockings it is tomorrow."

"I want at least some drawers!"

Both of us shook our heads and replied at the same time. "No drawers."

"But—"

"No drawers," Mason repeated. "Eventually you will wear clothes, sweetheart, but for the time being, we are enjoying our bride being scantily clad. See what you do to me?"

He pointed to the thick line of his cock pressing against the placket of his pants.

She grinned then, recognizing her power over us.

"Did Brody play with your arse this morning?"

Her cheeks flushed a pretty pink. She might no longer be a virgin, but she was still innocent. "Yes," she whispered.

Mason directed with his chin. "Show me."

Slowly, she turned onto her stomach.

"Not like that. You know how I like to look at you."

She rolled over, placed her feet flat on the bed and spread her legs wide, knees bent. If her nipples hadn't tightened into tight little peaks at his command, I'd think she was apprehensive, when in fact she most likely was afraid of how much she actually liked it.

"Knees back, please."

Mason stood, legs shoulder width apart, arms across his chest. He didn't look forbidding, but formidable.

Hooking her hands beneath her knees, she pulled them back and wide so they were up at the sides of her breasts.

"Good girl." He knelt down on the floor directly in front of her pussy. "You're still slick with ointment and I can see that Brody fucked you well."

"Mason!" Laurel cried out.

"Here." Mason held out the larger sized plug we'd used on her before. "Let go of one knee and play with your arse, sweetheart. I want to see you work the plug inside."

She lifted her head from the bed and looked at him, mouth open. "What?"

"You heard me. Do it, please."

She took the plug from me, the broad head of it slick with additional ointment, reached around behind her leg to press it against her little rosebud. My cock rose to attention once again.

"Now work it in. Fuck your arse with the plug."

"But—"

"If you please me, Laurel, then I will please you. Brody will as well. I'm going to rub your little clit the way you like it and Brody's going to play with your nipples, but only once the plug is filling you up."

"Oh yes," she sighed.

I moved into position on the bed and watched. Laurel bit her lip as she slowly began to work the plug into her arse. It stretched open around the broad head and she cried out when it breached the tight entrance. It closed around the tapered wood and it was lodged in place between the wider section and a small handle that protruded from her. When she took a deep breath, settling into the feeling of having her arse nice and crammed full, I began tugging and playing with the already hard tips.

Mason's finger slipped into her pussy to collect some of her juices and coated her pink pearl, then began to give it the attention she wanted.

"Such a good girl. Now work the plug in and out. That wide section is going to stretch you open in preparation for our cocks. It's going to make you come right away."

Mason was right. It didn't take long for her to climax; she'd pulled the flared section back to stretch open, then pushed it back in deep. That was all it took. She came, her eyes falling closed, her mouth open and her skin flushing a bright pink. It was an amazing sight, seeing all of our hands on her, working her, pleasing her. The knowledge that she enjoyed arse play made me want to claim her there now, but it was too soon. She wasn't *quite* ready. Soon. Very soon.

Once her pleasure ebbed, Mason worked the plug from her. She lay sated and open, completely uninhibited.

"Who gives you your pleasure, sweetheart?" Mason asked.

She licked her lips. "You do."

"Yes, that's right. Brody and I. Who do you belong to?"

Her eyes open and she looks at both of us. "The two of you."

"Such a good girl."

LAUREL

In the morning Mason finally gave me one of the pretty dresses Emma had picked out for me at the mercantile. It was a dark green that he said matched my eyes perfectly. My men—I enjoyed calling them mine—had continued to lavish attention on me, either by themselves or together. When Ann had said her men cherished her, she hadn't been boasting. Mason and Brody were attentive, not only as lovers, but as husbands. It had been a game to them, watching me spend a day in solely my corset, then my corset and stockings before today allowing me to cover my body modestly. It did feel nice to be completely covered once again, but when Brody's hand had dipped beneath the fabric of my long skirt to cup my bare bottom, I'd seen the heat in his eyes. It thrilled me to know that what they were thinking; my pussy was bare and wet for them to take whenever they desired.

It had been a week since we'd married and I had yet to leave the house, but I'd most certainly been kept occupied. Today, however, had both men going to the stable, for a new colt was born overnight and they needed to take over the chores of Ian and Simon who had stayed up all night for the birth.

I didn't mind the quiet of the house, but it seemed strange. One perk of being married to two men meant I was never lonely. Even when I was alone and reading a book in a comfortable chair by the fire, they were with me, for I could not forget either man or what they did to me only an hour before because of their seed continuing to drip from me.

When I heard the front door open and close, I smiled, thinking one of them had returned to make good on their promise to bend me over the sofa. When I stood and walked across the room to meet them, it was not Brody or Mason, but Mr. Palmer.

I froze in my tracks and my hand came up to my chest. My heart pounded in my chest at the sight of the man. "What are you doing here?" I questioned.

"Claiming my bride," he said. His voice was nasally and weak.

"Your bride?" When he continued to stare at me, I added, "I'm already married. You'll have to find yourself another woman."

"I heard about your wedding. It's the talk of the town. Turner and I looked mighty embarrassed after coming out here looking for you and all. You were hiding somewhere all along." He shook his head slowly, his jowls shifting as he did so. "It doesn't matter if you've given yourself to another man or not. I don't want a different woman. I want you."

I pointed at myself. "Me? Why are you so keen on me? As you said, I've already given myself to another." He didn't allude to the fact that I was married to both Mason and Brody. Clearly that knowledge did not reach town.

He pursed his lips. "I don't want *you*. I want your land."

What? I frowned and shook my head. "My land? I don't have any land."

"You own the entire Turner parcel and it was to be mine."

His eyes narrowed and he moved a step closer. I retreated keeping the distance between us as great as possible.

"That land is not mine. It belongs to my father."

He closed his eyes briefly and clenched his hands into fists. "Your father had a gambling problem and I won the property in exchange for monetary debts."

"What?" My father was a rich man, wealthy enough to keep me at a fine boarding school for thirteen years. His house was immense and surrounded by Turner land as far as the eye could see.

"He gambled and owed me more money than he had in the bank." He shrugged. "So I claimed his ranch...and you, in exchange."

"I'm not for sale."

"No, you're not for sale, for you were won fair and square."

14

AUREL

I took another step back.

"There must be some mistake."

"The only mistake is allowing your bastard father sign all of his property over to you in his will."

"He...he did what? He doesn't even like me. I haven't seen the man in over ten years!"

"Doesn't matter. He made you the beneficiary of his estate."

Where were Brody and Mason? How I wished I wasn't alone right now! There was nothing to do but try to escape this man for he was clearly irrational, so I tried to run past him but he caught up with me in the hallway, grabbed my arm and spun me around to face him.

"I'm married to Mason. You can't have me!" I tugged against his tight hold.

"I can." He reached into his jacket pocket and pulled out a folded piece of paper. "A marriage license that says we were married two weeks ago. *You* are Mrs. Palmer."

I shook my head. He *was* crazy.

"No, that's not true. It's not real. We were married in a church."

"It's real. The circuit judge signed it, therefore your supposed marriage to the Bridgewater man means nothing."

Means nothing? My marriage to Mason...and Brody meant *everything*. They were the first people to see me as a person, as a woman, not a pawn or a tool to someone's advantage. They hadn't married me then sent me off somewhere. I knew now what it felt like to be cared for, for someone to care about me. They'd shown me what love was.

"No." I shook my head. "No. You need to talk to my father. If he signed the ranch over to me, just have him change it. I want nothing to do with this. As I've said, I barely know the man, so why would he listen to me?"

His grip tightened on my arm at the mention of my father.

"I know him rather well, actually, and he can't change it if he's dead."

I stilled in his hold. What did he mean? "Dead? My...my father's dead?"

Something dark and evil flared in his eyes and he grinned. "He tried to cross me, to keep me from getting the land that rightfully was mine. From *you*. He was stupid to think he'd get away with it. Of course he's dead. I shot him...right...between...the...eyes." He tapped a finger to his forehead. "Just like I'm going to do to you."

He'd killed my father and now I was alone in the house with him. The wild look about him had me panicking, fighting against his hold.

"I can't help you with whatever your plan is if I'm dead, too." I needed to escape! Being alone in the house with him was not going to keep me alive. He'd plotted this all along. When they'd come to the ranch the other day, Palmer had been the one in control. My father only wanted to find me because he owed Palmer.

"I wanted you, at first. The idea of a meek virgin who'd been sheltered as if she were a nun held appeal, but you've been a whore here on Bridgewater. I don't take sloppy seconds." He slowly shook his head. "No, my plans for you have changed. I don't need you alive to inherit your land with this marriage license. In fact, I need you dead."

My eyes widened and blood roared in my ears. "What? Why?"

"Marriage makes the land rightfully mine regardless of whether I'm your husband...or widower. Since you're used goods and worth nothing to me, widower is more appropriate. I want the land. It's more valuable than you."

He carefully put the supposed marriage license back in his jacket pocket and pulled out a gun. A gun! I didn't think, just reacted. I grabbed his wrist in both my hands, fighting with him to keep the weapon from pointing in my direction, but he was stronger and bigger than I. Twisting and turning, I used all my might and struggled with him, but a shot fired. Fortunately, it went wide and into a wall. I gasped at the shock of it, the nearness of the bullet to my head. The sound was deafening and my ear rang.

I remembered the words of a teacher at school, who mentioned a way to defend inappropriate advances of an overeager suitor. At the time, I didn't imagine it would work for I barely had contact with men to even consider the idea, but I now knew a man's physique. I brought my knee up as hard as I could, sliding it right up the man's inner thigh and I connected squarely with his...man parts. I couldn't think of it as a cock, for that was what Mason and Brody had and theirs were hard and thick and ready for me. This man...I swallowed back bile at the very idea. He made a high-pitched squeak and bent at the waist. His arm went lax and I was able to grab the gun from him.

I was breathing hard, sweat coating my brow. I kneed him one more time before I dashed out of the room, my long dress tangling around my legs. All I could think of was getting to Mason and Brody, having their arms around me, protecting me, sheltering me from everything bad. With fumbling fingers, I opened the front door and dashed out onto the porch. I held the gun up into the air and fired a shot, the kick from it reverberating up my arm.

I remembered what Emma and Ann had said. Three shots meant help was needed. I fired again, my eyes squeezing shut and my body tensing.

"You!" Mr. Palmer was hunched over, but approaching quickly down the hall. His eyes were narrowed and an evil gleam showed. It was as if I'd poked a hibernating bear and not only did he have intent, he was now very, very angry. "You bitch. You are going to—"

As he came through the door with his arms out to grab me, I turned and aimed. It was him or me. *Bang.*

———

MASON

That morning we had given Laurel one of the pretty dresses Emma had picked out for her. It was a dark green that flattered her hair and matched her eye color perfectly. Both Brody and I had enjoyed her walking around in just a corset, then just her corset and stockings over the past two days, but I also thrilled to know that I could just toss up her dress and find her bare and ready beneath. I liked knowing that all of her hot, wet secrets were hidden for Brody and me alone.

We were both in the stable, mucking out stalls when McPherson came in leading his horse. "I see you've left yer bride." He grinned at us as he patted his horse's side, and then worked the buckle free on the saddle. "Took ye both, what, a week for yer cock stands to go down?"

I looked to Brody who was shaking his head slowly, but he had a grin on his face for he was well pleased with his new bride—as was I. We knew we'd get some grief from the others, especially the unmarried men, taking so long to tend and fuck our new wife. "No chance in hell of that happening. I just have to think of her and I get hard."

In fact, I shifted my cock in my pants to ease the growing ache as we spoke about her. It had only been two hours since we fucked her last, but my cock didn't care.

"Have ye heard the news?" McPherson asked, lifting the saddle off the animals back and placing it on a rack. He removed the blanket next.

"News?" I rested my forearms on the top of the pitchfork I held.

"Turner's dead."

Brody stilled, glanced at me. "Dead? How?"

"Shot in cold blood."

I shoved the pitchfork into a pile of straw and walked over to McPherson. "What do you mean cold blood?"

McPherson's eyebrows went up. "Don't know. Saw the sheriff at the livery and he said that after they left here last week, Mr. Palmer, the bastard that was in the group, was right pissed at Turner. They argued, mentioned something about a debt being paid. Turner replied that it was all taken care of."

"What the hell does that mean?" Brody asked.

McPherson held up his hands in front of him. "From what I heard at the mercantile—word spreads fast and the sheriff isn't the only one with news—Turner was a gambler. Bad at cards. Lost everything."

"To Palmer." I gritted my teeth. Something wasn't right. I had a bad feeling in my gut.

"If Palmer collected his money, why was he so bloody pissed?" Brody asked.

"Right. Palmer was angry enough to kill him," McPherson stated. "Why?"

We glanced at each other and the reason became clear. "Laurel." Brody and I said it at the exact same time.

McPherson's head came up, his eyes sharp. "Where is she?"

"At the house. We need to—"

A shot rang out, coming from a distance, but clear and loud in the still air.

My heart seized at the sound and we ran to the stable door and threw it open.

Bang. A second shot.

"Shit," Brody muttered. "It's coming from the house." He grabbed the reins on McPherson's horse and led it outside and mounted deftly.

McPherson grabbed the gun from the pegs above the door. "Brody!"

He tossed the rifle and Brody caught it before he spurred the animal into motion.

McPherson and I started running in the direction of the house and Laurel. What the hell was going on? Was it Palmer or something else? Was Laurel the one firing the shots to call us to help or was she defending herself? Or worse, had someone shot her? I picked up my pace, running as fast as I could through the deep snow. I needed to get to her, but was relieved to know Brody would almost be there by now.

"The others will come, too," he breathed. He kept pace with my sprint. "It's only been two shots so that doesn't mean anything."

Bang. A third shot, which meant—

"Laurel!"

15

RODY

I barely slowed the horse before I jumped down. Laurel sat on the porch floor in the cold, her hair wild and half down from the pins, a gun held tightly in her hands and aimed at a body lying on the ground. Based on the blood beginning to pool around him, he wasn't getting up again. I dashed up the stairs, my footsteps loud and skidded to a stop in front of the man. I aimed my rifle at him as I nudged him with my foot, and then pushed him over onto his back.

Palmer. His eyes were open and staring fixed at the ceiling of the porch, a crimson stain of blood spreading across his white shirt. He was dead.

My heart pounded and my muscles were tense and ready to kill. I wanted to shoot him myself, to relieve some of this pent-up angst and fear. Swiveling, I dropped to my knees in front of Laurel, put the rifle down gently beside us on the floor.

"Laurel," I said, my voice soft. I held my hands out by my sides not wanting to startle her.

She hadn't moved since I came up, her eyes focused solely on

Palmer, the gun still raised and aimed at the man. The strong tang of blood filled the crisp air.

I reached out slowly and took her hands in mine. They were so cold, icy even, and not from the freezing weather. I doubted she even knew I was there. "Laurel, give me the gun. Laurel," I repeated, louder this time.

She shook her head slowly. "No. He's dangerous. He'll hurt—"

"He's dead, sweetheart. He can't hurt you now." Her hands relaxed enough for me to take the gun from her and place it beside the rifle. "Look at me."

She was in shock, stunned and petrified, but whole. What had the man done before she'd fired the shots? Clearly one of bullets had killed him.

"Laurel," I said one more time, my voice deeper and more commanding.

She blinked and turned her head to mine. I saw the moment her eyes focused and she *saw* me.

"Brody!" she cried, hurling herself into my arms, burying her face in my shoulder. "He...it was awful. I remembered to fire the three shots, but he was coming after me and I only fired two." Her voice was high and she was on the verge of hysteria. I didn't blame her one bit, for I was a little unsettled as well. I couldn't go crazy, though; it was my job to soothe, to make her safe. I'd done a fuck all job of it, having to defend herself from the bloody bastard, but she was safe now. I hugged her tightly.

"No. No, sweetheart. You fired all three and we heard you. We came as fast as we could, but you took care of yourself. I'm so proud of you." I stroked my hand over her hair, again and again, hoping my warmth would seep into her.

"I thought...he had a gun and—"

She shuddered once and then began to sob.

I pulled her up onto my lap and tucked her head beneath my chin, my arm about her waist holding her securely. I did nothing but rock her and let her cry, all the while staring down at Palmer's lifeless body.

I could feel her heart beating, savor the sharp grip of her fingers in my shirt, inhale the floral scent of her hair, and yet I couldn't get her close enough. The thought of losing her, of how close she'd come to being killed had me want to shoot the bastard all over again. She'd literally fallen into our life by the hands of Fate and I wasn't prepared to lose her now. I *couldn't* lose her.

Mason and McPherson ran up then, the snow crunching beneath their feet and breathing hard. They took in the situation and I met Mason's gaze over Laurel's head. I gave a brief nod and his shoulders dropped in sheer relief. He bent at the waist and lowered his hands to his knees to take a moment to breathe. He mounted the steps and came down on his knees in front of me, stroking his hand down Laurel's back.

"Everything's fine now. You're safe. Mason's here with me and we're going to take care of you," I murmured, although we'd done fuck all to protect her from Palmer.

McPherson came up the steps. "I'll take care of the bastard," he growled, nudging the man's leg even though he was obviously dead. "You two take care of your woman."

Mason took her from my arms and stood, carrying her into the house. I followed, slamming the door shut behind us, blocking out Palmer, the closeness we'd come to losing our wife, to everything.

McPherson and the others would deal with Palmer for us. Laurel needed her men.

I followed Mason up the stairs and into his bedroom and I closed the door behind us. Lowering her to the floor, Mason set her back from him so he could look at her. I moved to stand directly beside him.

"Sweetheart, did he hurt you?" he asked.

My gaze raked over her body. Her dress wasn't torn; it was only dirty in spots from where she'd been sitting on the porch. Her hair had come undone and tears stained her pale cheeks, but otherwise she looked...whole.

She shook her head. "No. He...he just grabbed me, but I'm not hurt."

Mason's hands went to the buttons on her new dress. "We're going to take this off you and take a look and make sure. You've had a scare."

"We've all had a scare," I added. "Let your men make sure you're not hurt."

She glanced between us and nodded. "For you, yes."

Mason's hands moved quicker now. He stripped the dress, her corset, even her stockings and boots so she stood before us naked. I ran my hands over her shoulders and down her arms as Mason worked his way up her body. There were red marks above her elbows that might bruise, and my jaw clenched at the sight. I moved to stand behind her so she was surrounded by the two of us, my hands moving up and down her back, past the little dimples at the base of her spine, over her lush arse, then back up again. We needed to touch all of her, to ensure she was whole, real and ours.

"He...he said we were married. He had a license." Even though we touched her, she was distracted.

My hands paused. "A marriage license?"

She nodded. "A judge signed it and it looked official. He said my marriage to Mason wasn't real."

Mason shook his head. "Our marriage is real, sweetheart. There's no question. Palmer could have bribed a judge, but God joined us. Before that, were joined when we took your virginity. Hell, we claimed you the first time we saw you."

He said just what I was thinking.

"I...I shot him. I didn't mean to, but he was coming toward me. I...kneed him in his...there, and then I ran but he recovered and—"

Christ. She'd have to live with killing Palmer for the rest of her life. Every man at Bridgewater had killed before; it had been our job to do so. But not Laurel. She'd had to shoot a man dead or die herself.

"You were defending yourself. You did nothing wrong. He was a bad man." Mason stroked her arms.

I leaned forward and kissed her shoulder. "Shh," I soothed. "Mason's right, he was a right bloody bastard and he can't hurt you ever again. You took care of that yourself, didn't you, sweetheart?

We're so proud of you. No more about Palmer. I don't want him in this bedroom with us."

Hot tears rushed down her cheeks again, but this time it was more from overwhelming emotion than fear. "I...I didn't think I would see you again. Oh, your hands feel so good." Her head tilted back and I kissed up the nape of her neck. "All I thought about was you. Getting to you. Being with you. I...I need you. Both of you."

She became bold then, empowered by the threat that danger had held over her. She reached up and worked at Mason's shirt. Her overwhelming emotions shifted to frantic need and her fingers fumbled. "Please, I need you. I need you both. Make Palmer go away. Take me."

Fervently, she kissed Mason's chest that had been exposed. "I know...you have been waiting...." Each pause in her words was a kiss. "I need both of you. I want to truly be yours."

I tugged on Laurel's hair, forcing her head to turn. It wasn't rough, but I wasn't gentle either. Her wild eyes met mine. She needed this. She needed someone to be in charge, to make her forget. To make her let go. She'd taken care of Palmer, and now we'd take care of her. "Together? You want to take us together, sweetheart?"

Instead of answering, she took my hand and put it between her thighs, my fingers slipping over her slick folds. She was dripping wet and I could feel her clit, hard and pulsing. She looked over her shoulder, took Mason's hand and brought it between her legs from behind. A gasp escaped her lips as Mason must have brushed a finger over her sensitive rosebud.

She pressed her hand over my cock through my pants, but I had a clear enough head to tell her no. "You're not in charge, Laurel, your husbands are. We decide when we fuck you and how." I didn't move her hand away, but curled one finger just inside her opening to make her hand fall away. Her eyes slipped shut and she moaned.

Her nipples hardened at my stern words and the touch of my finger.

"Do you want me to fill your arse with my cock?" Mason asked as he nipped at her neck, leaving a trail of reddened skin in his wake.

Laurel angled her head, offering Mason better access, and nodded her head.

"Then we should see if you're ready. Up on the bed on your hands and knees, arse up in the air."

Mason made space for her to move and she readily complied, settling onto the middle of the bed on her knees, then lowered her cheek to the quilt, her green eyes on us. It was the perfect submissive pose, her pussy and arse on perfect display, showing us what was ours. Her pussy lips were the prettiest pink and furled open, exposing her narrow passage and pale pearl. The lovely thatch of fiery red hair was directly below. Her back entrance winked at us, still a hint of slick ointment from our play earlier. With the way she took the plug this morning, I knew she'd be ready for us, but since Mason would claim her arse, he would take the time to ensure she could take him.

I stripped off my clothes with haste and took in the sight of Laurel's perfect body. Her breasts hung down heavily, the nipples plump. My mouth watered wanting to taste them again. My cock bobbed and ached for her. Mason's eyes met mine. He nodded. It was time.

I moved to sit on the bed, my back propped up against the headboard, spreading my legs so they were on either side of Laurel's shoulders. She looked up at me from her position on her forearms; she was so eager, so ready. I crooked my finger. "Come here, sweetheart."

She pushed up onto her hands and she crawled toward me, her breasts swaying beneath her as she did so. She stopped with her mouth just inches from my burgeoning cock. I grabbed hold of the base and stroked up and down the length, clear fluid oozing from the tip and down over my fingers. Just seeing her mouth there, her lips wet from her tongue had my hips shifting.

"Suck my cock, sweetheart."

Her eyes held mine briefly, then dropped to my cock. She licked her lips, then lowered her head, licking the broad head clean, but didn't linger, taking the entire length into her mouth. I hissed out a breath at the hot, wet feel of her mouth. Her tongue flicked over the head, then swirled up and down the length.

I saw Mason grab the jar of ointment and dip his fingers in before running them over her arse. With Laurel's head dipped down over my cock, I could see what he was doing, watch as he easily slipped a finger in. She moaned around my cock, the vibrations making my balls draw up tight.

"She easily took one finger. Take a deep breath, sweetheart, I'm going to add another," Mason told her.

I felt her hot breath on my fist as she breathed in, and then exhaled. Mason worked the second finger in beside the first and Laurel wiggled her hips. She moaned around my cock again, eyes widening at being stretched so.

"Jesus, Mason, I won't last if she keeps making noises like that." I was breathing hard and my hands were clenched in the quilt; she was that good.

I saw his fingers scissor and stretch her open even more, then slip in to the first knuckle. Mason met my gaze.

"She's ready."

Cupping her cheek with one hand, I lifted her bobbing head off my cock. I slipped down the bed so my head was on the pillow and her face was directly above mine. "Climb up and ride me."

She looked down between us at my cock, which was pointing straight at her navel. She put one knee by my hip, then the other so she straddled my waist. Slowly, she lowered herself down onto my cock, seating herself directly onto me so I filled her completely. She was tight and wet and hot and...perfect. This was where I wanted to be, where I belonged.

"Brody, oh, you feel so good, but I want both of you."

Mason leaned forward and kissed her shoulder.

"And you will. Right now."

16

AUREL

This was what I wanted, to be surrounded and know that my men wanted me, needed me and that I was not alone in my feelings. Coming close to death made me realize how keenly I needed Mason and Brody, and I knew that giving myself to both of them, at the same time would forge a bond between us that could not be broken. I was the missing connection that forged us all together. And as Brody pulled me down onto his chest and kissed me, I knew it was time.

His hands gripped my head, holding me just where he wanted me so his tongue could lave mine. He nipped at my lower lip, and then soothed it with a tender kiss all the while shifting his hips and filling me. While he couldn't take the deep strokes I was used to at this angle, just the slight rubbing had me moaning. I was so wet for him he moved easily within me. My clit rubbed against him and it was a slow, sensuous torture. Even my nipples rubbing against his chest were sensitive.

I felt Mason's large hand on my bottom, parting me, then the broad head of his cock pressed against me...there. He slipped out of place, his cock obviously slickly coated in ointment. They were both so considerate, thinking of me, tending to me. There was that word...tending, just as Ann had said. Mason didn't want to hurt me; he wanted to make me feel how good it was for all of us to fuck as one.

They both said it was going to be good and I could not do anything but trust in their words. Once again, his blunt tip pressed in, then back. In a little more firmly. I remembered Mason's words, to exhale and push back. I did both, letting my forehead rest on Brody's chest as I pushed back against Mason. His cock was broader than any of the plugs or even their fingers and I began to stretch wide, wider, wider still.

"Oh," I moaned at the burn, the incredible stretch.

"Almost there, sweetheart. It's so hot seeing you being stretched wide for my cock. Push back once more. That's it....yes. Oh, I'm in. God, you're so tight."

I groaned as the head of Mason's cock fit just past the tight ring of muscle that had been fighting his entry. I felt so open, so wide. With Brody's cock filling me as well, it was such a tight fit. It burned, the intense stretching, but it also felt...amazing. The combination was like when Mason tugged and pinched my nipples in the past, painful yet so good. I winced at first, but as I relaxed, it morphed into something different, something more.

Mason's fingers gripped my bottom as he began to move. Slowly, very slowly he pushed forward, then pulled back. Brody shifted his hips as well, but in opposing directions so that one of their cocks was filling me up as the other retreated. The feelings their cocks elicited were overwhelming. I thought of nothing but how these men made me feel. My clit was pulsing, my inner walls clenching down on both their cocks. My fingers clawed at Mason's shoulders as I breathed into his sweaty skin, then bit him lightly as Mason sank in all the way.

"You're ours, Laurel," Mason said, his voice rough as he breathed hard. Our bodies clung together, slick with sweat, and yet we were already one. I was finally joined with both of them. I knew now that they belonged to me as much as I belonged to them.

"She's so tight, Mason, I'm not going to last," Brody said.

"Her arse is strangling my cock," Mason growled. "Are you ready to come, sweetheart?"

I nodded against Brody's chest.

"Good, because you're going to come like never before."

With that vow, they started to move. Mason pulled back as Brody tilted his hips up so he nudged my womb. Then Mason slid in slow, but sure, filling me up all the way as Brody pulled back. Again and again they moved in this fashion. I couldn't do anything but feel. I couldn't move, couldn't even shift my hips and yet the pleasure built. I'd thought it had felt incredible when they'd made me come before, but it had never been like this. The feeling of two cocks in me was so intense, so overwhelming that I couldn't hang on to the thread of reality anymore and let go. I fell into the pleasure so hard, so fast, that I screamed. My clit was rubbed with every move Brody made. The head of his cock nudged against the incredible places inside my pussy and Mason awakened places deep inside me I had no idea existed. All of it coalesced into a bright ball of flame that burst, exploded through my body to the tips of my fingers, to my very toes and everywhere in between.

I heard Brody groan as he held his hips still, his cock embedded deep within me, the hot wash of his seed coating my womb. Mason plunged into me one last time and squeezed my hips almost painfully as he exhaled a breath and filled me, marking me as his.

I lay slumped and exhausted on Brody's slick chest, too wilted to move. I could feel their cocks pulse within me as they began to catch their breath. Carefully, Mason pulled out and I winced, for while he'd been gentle, I'd been well claimed. Brody lifted me up his body enough to pull me off his spent cock and place me at his side so I used his arm as a pillow. Their seed mingled and dripped down my thighs. I felt Mason's hand on my hip as he kissed my shoulder.

"There was no question, Laurel, from the first time we saw you, that you belonged to us," Mason told me, his voice soft.

"You may have doubted, but we never did," Brody added. "Not once."

I tilted my chin up to look at Brody. "How?"

I felt him shrug his shoulders. "It was love at first sight."

I was so replete before, but now, my heart filled. I couldn't feel anything more for these two than I did in this moment. I turned so I lay on my back and could look up at both of them.

Mason was nodding his head in agreement. "It was Fate, our wayward bride."

I thought about that. I'd gone out into a blizzard aiming for town, but somehow became so lost I went in the wrong direction and ended up in front of Mason and Brody's house. Not Andrew and Robert's. Not any of the other men's. It had been Fate.

They'd found me, not only lost in the snow, but inside. They found the real me and loved me. Wanted me. Cherished me.

I smiled up at them, knowing this all to be true. "Yes, yes, you're right. I am your wayward bride."

THEIR CAPTIVATED BRIDE - BOOK 3

1

ROSS

The first time I saw her I thought her a vision. In the lantern light of the hall, her hair was as black as pitch, artfully pulled back into a bun at her nape, but with loose, soft curls that made my eyes follow the graceful curve of her neck. Her skin had a golden glow to it, as if lit from within. Her pale blue dress was modest, yet hinted at every one of her curves, and those curves were quite appealing. I was not the only one who noticed them, for men's eyes turned her way as she danced, walked past or even smiled in their direction. It was her eyes though, that drew me in completely, for when she turned those pale blue eyes my way, I was lost.

She had the look that Rhys or Simon would call Black Irish: black hair and light blue eyes. I'd never met someone with the combination before and it was striking. In fact, I couldn't look away. The public dance in celebration of the country's independence was a well-attended affair, especially in a town the size of Helena. It wasn't often any of us from Bridgewater made it to this town; only ranch business brought us this far afield. Our ranch kept us well occupied and fairly self-sufficient. While Ian and Kane had made the last cattle contracts, it was our job—Simon, Rhys and I—to purchase a stud horse needed to improve already superior bloodline of Bridgewater's horses. It was one of our goals to make the sturdiest, fastest and best horses in the Montana Territory.

To hell with the horses. I wanted—no, needed—to know who this woman was. I couldn't leave the dance without hearing her voice or feeling her waist beneath my hand as we danced. I wanted to know her scent.

"Ask her to dance," Rhys said, coming up beside me. We didn't look at each other, but at the lovely woman who was right now sipping lemonade and speaking with two other women. The others were of similar age, perhaps early twenties, but neither even sparked my interest. Had I turned around and been quizzed as to their appearances, I doubt I could have warranted a fair guess. It was *she* who held my regard.

We stood on the outer fringes of the dance floor, the music—two violins, an accordion and a piano—not so loud here as to make speaking with others difficult. Several sets of doors were open to the cooler evening air and I saw one of *her* wayward curls shift in the breeze. I spared a glance at Rhys. He was taller than I by an inch or two, but trimmer of build. His hair was as dark as the mysterious woman's, yet his skin was much darker from time spent outdoors and natural inclination. He might look the part of a Montana man, but he was not born, nor bred, in the Territory, nor even the United States. He, as well as our other friend Simon, were both from the United Kingdom - Simon from Scotland and Rhys from England. In fact, the Englishman's name with the strange spelling had a simple pronunciation of Reese. Why it wasn't written as such was just another British anomaly I could never comprehend. One only had to hear the duo speak to know they were foreigners.

The woman smiled.

"You do not find her...."

I couldn't think of the right word.

"Unique?" Rhys asked. "I find her unique." That was true. She was unique that she had captured my attention, and it seemed his as well.

"Simon would think so as well if he were here instead of at his meeting," I considered. We were in Helena for the horse purchase, not a dance, but as it was decided that Rhys and I remain separate from the arrangement, we'd chosen to spend our idle evening at the town function.

"Meeting? It's a bloody game of Poker."

"Business arrangements are forged over liquor, women and cards."

"He may have the liquor and cards, but we have the woman," Rhys stated.

He was the quiet one of the three of us, a man of few words, but when he spoke those words were well chosen, and his statement was correct. Just looking upon this dark-haired beauty had me readily agreeing.

Simon, the Scot, was more brute strength than emotion and handled brash deals with ease. It was a good thing he was not here, for he would have knocked down everyone in his path to get to *her*, regardless of her married state or inclination towards foreign men. This method would have worked had we not been at a town dance; this environment took finesse and he was not known for that.

"She has not been with a specific man most of the evening, so I do not believe her to be claimed," I commented, placing my hands in the pockets of my pants. No man held her attention for long. Her smile, which was now given freely to the women she was with, was offered sparingly to men, and then only in a polite fashion. While I wouldn't pick up a woman and toss her over my shoulder like a caveman claiming his woman, I had no intention of idly standing by and watching the one I wanted slip through my fingers like sand. The band ended a song to scattered applause and I took the opportunity that presented itself. I approached her with my gaze fixed and when she saw me coming, it was as if she were trapped in a spider's web, unable to look away or move. The ladies at either side of her were still talking, however, she'd lost their attention in exchange for mine.

When I stopped beside her, the other ladies ceased their chattering and all three tilted their heads back to look up at me, for I was almost a head taller than all of them. I nodded at them in greeting, but kept my gaze fixed upon *her*. "May I have this dance?"

The band began to play a new tune and couples moved out onto the floor. Not wanting to give her an opportunity to say no, I took her hand in mine and led her out to an open spot. Perhaps I was part caveman after all. Her skin was warm, her fingers gripping mine. Turning to face her, I stepped in and placed my free hand on her waist to begin our dance. It fit in the delicate curve there, my little finger wedged against the flared bone of her hip, my large fingers almost touching the bumps of her spine. I could feel the stiff stays of her corset and wished I could instead learn the feel of her soft flesh. "My name is Cross," I said as I began to lead her around the dance floor. The steps were not complex and needed little to no thought as to the movement, which was well and fine, for my attention was focused squarely on her.

Her eyes had been on her hand at my shoulder, but she flicked a glance up at me. "I am Olivia. Olivia Weston."

I offered her a smile and her eyes widened in surprise. Was I that forbidding?

"Are you from Helena, Olivia?" I asked, hoping to make general conversation and set her at ease. I cut a formidable figure; I was taller than most and had thirty pounds on many a man. Women certainly looked at me twice, but often not because they were smitten, but fearful. The tight grip of her hand was the only indication as to any type of concern coming from Olivia, which was good, as I did not wish her to fear me. In fact, I wished her to find our dance quite pleasing, for I was enjoying holding her petite frame as I let her sweet scent entice me.

She gave a short nod, a curl bouncing as she did so. "Yes, and I assume you are not, for I believe I would have remembered you."

Her voice was soft, yet had almost a husky quality to it that had my blood stirring.

"I am that memorable then? That is good to know and quite a compliment," I replied.

"No, I mean...it's just--" she stuttered, then seeing the teasing gleam in my eye, pursed her mouth closed, although a corner tugged up and I knew no harm was done.

"I definitely would have remembered you, Olivia, if I had seen you before. In fact, I would have been quite attentive and you would not have forgotten me."

Her cheeks turned a pretty shade of pink and she gazed upon the buttons of my shirt.

"To answer your question, no. I hail from my ranch, Bridgewater, which is to the east of here."

She stiffened in my arms and at first, I thought it was the mention of Bridgewater, but then I took in that she was staring fixedly just beyond my left arm. She stepped in a touch closer and turned her forehead in toward my upper arm, as if using my body as some form of a shield.

"Something troubling you?" I asked, not looking in the direction that held her concern. While I maintained a calm demeanor and kept dancing, I was vigilant to any kind of bother or danger to Olivia.

She relaxed, forced a smile upon her face and replied, "No, everything is quite fine."

Something, no, probably someone, had bothered her, but she had no interest in sharing with me.

"We may have just met, but please consider me a protector, Olivia. I wish you no harm and I will see none come to you."

Surprise widened her pale eyes. "You say that as if you believe it."

"You don't think I can protect you?" Her words surprised *me*.

"Look at you." She indicated with a tilt of her chin. "You are...very large and could be quite an adversary."

I grinned again. "Yes, I am very large, and can put the size to good use." I doubted she understood my secondary meaning. "You have no male protector?"

"I live with my uncle, who is a dragon and protects me fiercely. I also do not lead an extravagant life and am in no need of much of a defender."

"Oh?" I replied neutrally.

"My uncle raised me and I have taken on his tendencies of

educational pursuits, reading and remaining at home. I am fairly sheltered and not one for parties."

"You seem quite settled at this event," I countered.

She frowned briefly. "It is a holiday and besides, my uncle insisted."

"Then I will have to offer him my thanks."

"Why?" she asked, tilting her head slightly.

"I never would have met you otherwise and I am quite pleased." Again, her cheeks flushed prettily. "But you never answered my question regarding a male protector."

"As I said, my uncle is quite enough. I am not in need of additional protection."

From the way the men at the dance were watching her, I disagreed, but was not going to waste the dance arguing with her. I gave her hand a light squeeze so she looked to me. "Very well, but I am Cross from Bridgewater Ranch if you ever have need."

The song came to an end and while we stopped moving, I did not release her. "Promise me, Olivia."

People milled around us, chatting amiably while we stood still and I pinned her in place with my words.

"You are not in Helena and cannot offer any kind of shelter, regardless of the storm, however from the serious look upon your face, you will not release my hand until I agree."

I grinned at her savviness.

"Very well, I agree. I will call upon you if ever I have a time of need."

The definition of the word 'need' offered more than one connotation. While I would protect her from any type of harm, I also would gladly fill the role of any other kinds of needs she might have. From the look of her, from the type of rearing she had, she led a sheltered life and did not know of a woman's needs. The idea of any other man teaching them to her was off-putting at best.

Unfortunately, I had no choice but to release her. I was averse to do so for she felt...right in my arms.

2

LIVIA

I had enough male interest to keep me dancing for most of the evening, which was quite surprising. From his place in the corner chatting with his friends, Uncle Allen watched with a broad smile. We'd wagered the last slice of cake that I would not be a wallflower at the event. Unfortunately for me, I was the loser and would not enjoy the dessert.

The attention was surprising, for my day-to-day life was quite tame. I had male callers, but none were of interest to me. Some were handsome even, but they spoke of insipid things as if I had an empty head. I did enjoy a discussion about ribbons and the latest dress patterns, but I also liked to engage in debates over statehood and other civic concerns. However, when I broached such a conversation, I was either rebuffed for not knowing my own head or scorned for sharing it.

It was Clayton Peters who had been subtle in his attentions but warranted the most concern. He was appealing to the eye, but his character set me on edge and made me feel quite uncomfortable.

Each time I saw him, his attentions became more aggressive. He'd not physically touched me more than a shake of the hand; the aggression was verbal, proprietary. *When you are mine.... It is only a matter of time before you relent to my expectations.... My plans include you....*

He made my spine tingle and not in an appealing way. Although I rebuffed all of his attentions, he did not seem to recognize my disinterest or he did not care about it and continued to seek me out. Just a day earlier when we'd sat in my parlor and I'd told him I no longer wished to see him that he changed before my eyes. The attentive suitor was replaced by a man scorned - a sinister man who refused to take no for an answer. He was angry, his skin flushed and mottled, and he'd grabbed my wrist quite painfully until Uncle Allen hastily entered the room at the sound of our raised voices. He'd been stunned and angered by the other man's altered demeanor and had bodily removed him from the house.

After we'd calmed down—Uncle Allen vowing to 'kill the bastard' if Mr. Peters got anywhere near me again—he reminded me, "You will feel as if you were struck by lightning when you find the right man." That had never happened in my twenty-three years, especially not with Mr. Peters, and I started to feel concern that it never would. My uncle, while only in his early fifties, was a confirmed bachelor and clearly had not had such an occurrence, so I couldn't guarantee the veracity of his words. But at the dance it happened not once, but twice. Surely Uncle Allen was in error if I felt lightning two times within a short time span.

The first had been with the man named Cross. I wasn't sure if that was his given name or surname. He hadn't said, and my mind had not been clear enough to ask. To say the man befuddled me was an understatement. When I'd first seen him from across the room, I thought my heart had stopped for a moment, for it lurched, and then leapt against my breast and I felt hot all over. One time I'd fallen through a rotten board on the porch and I felt flustered and surprised and overheated and fearful and my heart had beat frantically at the jolt of it. Just looking into Cross's green eyes—for they most certainly were a very appealing grass green—had me feeling as if I'd fallen through the porch floor all over again. There had most definitely been a jolt.

He was tall enough where I only came to his chin. When I'd been in his arms for the dance I'd felt so small, his wide shoulders, solid torso and long legs had me ogling and from the closeness, it had been easy to do. His hand had dwarfed mine, all but swallowing it in his gentle grip. I'd expected him to be brash and rough, but he'd been just the opposite. I'd felt almost incorporated into his person, as if the rest of the dancers had disappeared and only a tall, fair-haired man existed. I could barely look past his shoulders. Instead, I had been content to get lost in his words, his deep voice, in his gaze. As he looked at me, I'd felt as if I had all of his attention, and perhaps I had. His jaw was square and his mouth wide beneath a long nose, yet it fit his face. His jaw was clean-shaven and his hair, while reasonably long, was neat and groomed.

When I'd glimpsed Mr. Peters in my periphery I had not wanted the dance to end. I'd felt safe and sheltered in Mr. Cross' hold, clearly protected from Mr. Peters' ire. Heat radiated from Cross' body, the clean, male scent of him enticing me to put my head upon his chest and close my eyes. Somehow, he'd noticed my fear over seeing the other man and offered his concern, even his protection. It had been...kind and I had wanted to revel in it, but the dance drew to an end, for then I worried if Mr. Peters would make a scene and I would have to deal with him once again, this time more publicly.

When Mr. Cross escorted me back to my friends, there was nothing more I could do than to thank him for the dance. Throwing myself at him or calling to him from across the room were things I could not do, regardless of the strength of my desire to do so. The lightning had struck and yet the man departed, and so did my eagerness to dance with others. Fortunately, I saw nothing more of Mr. Peters.

To my surprise, it was an hour later when the last dance was called, that lightning struck again. I was telling Uncle Allen that we could leave early, for nothing could compare to dancing with Mr. Cross, but a different man cleared his throat behind me. Uncle Allen

VANESSA VALE

saw him first and his eyes widened and a soft smile formed on his lips. I spun on my heel thinking it was Cross. Instead, it was the antithesis of him, but equally heart stopping. The newcomer had dark hair, perhaps as dark as mine, and tanned skin that only amplified the brightness of his smile. Dark eyes pinned me in place. Oh....

"Miss Weston, may I have this dance?" His voice was clipped, the words spoken with a strange accent.

Realizing my mouth was open, I snapped it shut. I glanced briefly at Uncle Allen, not wanting to put him out, yet at the same time didn't want him to see any hint of the jolt I felt at just the stranger's simple question, but he nodded readily.

"Yes, thank you," I replied.

He held out his elbow and I wrapped my hand around his biceps. His very thick, hard and well muscled biceps. The cut of his jacket did nothing to diminish it. As he led me out onto the floor, he leaned down closer so he could speak solely to me. "I am Rhys, a friend of a man you danced with earlier. Cross? Do you remember him?"

Remember? How could I have forgotten? But this man, he was so completely different than Mr. Cross. He was just as tall, but leaner. Darker, yet more intense. While Cross had been calm and offered his protection somewhat like a heavy winter blanket, Mr. Rhys was bright assurance and confidence. People parted for us; the man had a way about him that called for deference. When he took my hand in his he was just as gentle as Mr. Cross, but he had much more intent, placing my hand about his waist and the other upon my shoulder just as he wanted. When the music began and we started to move, I felt as if I was being taken for a dance rather than led.

As I glimpsed up at him through my lashes, I realized I'd been comparing instead of considering them separately. It wasn't as if I'd see Mr. Cross again, and there was certainly no reason for comparison. The men were different and just like Mr. Cross, when this dance ended I would not see Mr. Rhys again either. And so I stilled my thoughts and just enjoyed being held in the circle of his arms, knowing that he sought out the dance and had been interested specifically in my attentions.

"Miss Weston, it is rare to see a Black Irish such as yourself, and a quite lovely one at that," he commented. I'd heard the reference to my hair and eye color before, but that was not what made me misstep. A firm hand on my hip held me securely without a chance to fumble.

"How do you know my name?" I asked, cocking my head slightly.

The corner of his mouth tipped up. "As I said, Cross is my friend and he thought I might enjoy meeting you."

How strange. "Why?"

He frowned slightly and a small line formed at his brow. "Why?" he repeated. "It isn't often that either of us see such a beautiful woman, a woman who catches both of our eyes."

I couldn't help but flush at the compliment, but at the same time felt it odd. "You share dance partners?"

He took a moment before answering. "We share many things, Miss Weston."

Another odd answer, but I was intrigued. "Your friend, Mr. Cross, said that he was from a ranch east of here. Do you fare from that direction as well, for your accent is quite unique?" Surely it was idle chit-chat, but I didn't know what else to ask. He had me off kilter and the dance would end soon enough and that meant he would leave me just like his friend. It *was* just a dance. Nothing more.

"I am British, but I have not been there in some time. My home is Bridgewater, as is Cross'."

"Is it quite large?"

He arched a dark brow at my question, but responded easily enough. "I believe it to be one of the largest in the area, but we are a ranch of many."

"You are here in Helena on business or pleasure?"

"This dance and your company, Miss Weston, are all pleasure." The compliment heated my cheeks and I did not know how to respond, nor could I continue to look at him, so I studied the buttons on his dark jacket, just as I had with his friend. He was as neat as his friend. "We are in Helena to purchase a horse."

"You and Mr. Cross?"

The music played and the people danced around us but I, like before, ignored it all.

"Cross and I, as well as a good friend of ours, Simon."

"You have many friends," I added. I had many acquaintants, but no close, bosom friends.

"Not many, but the ones I do have I hold in the highest of esteem. And you? Your chaperone, Cross said he was your uncle?"

"Yes. My parents died when I was small and he raised me."

His hand tightened about my waist briefly. "I am sorry to hear about your parents."

A flicker of sadness appeared in his eyes was quickly hidden.

"You have lost family as well?" I ventured.

He gave a single nod. "I, unlike you, did not have an uncle to take me in and orphans are not held in the highest regard where I come from. Over time, I have learned that a family is one you make, so I have been lucky."

I faltered. "You are wed then?" I glanced around as if I could find a woman on the fringes of the dance that could be his wife. It was a silly act, but kept me from seeing the truth on his face.

"Of course not. I would not dance with another if I were married."

The dance drew to a close and Mr. Rhys led me back to my uncle, his hand upon the small of my waist. The feel of it sent tingles down my spine. Had I insulted him? A crushing feeling invaded my chest at the realization that I'd insulted his honor, for an honorable man would not seek out another woman for a dance or any other type of amusement.

"Sir." Mr. Rhys held out his hand to my uncle and introduced himself. "Thank you for the opportunity to dance with your niece."

"Anytime, young man," he replied. He seemed impressed by Mr. Rhys and was not aware of the gaffe I had made. "You are not from around here."

He shook his head. "No, sir. I am from Bridgewater."

Uncle Allen's face changed then, in some slight way I couldn't identify, but it wasn't disdain. He was...pleased somehow. Impressed, too. "I am familiar with another gentleman from the ranch, a Mr. Kane, I believe."

The dark slash of Mr. Rhys' brows rose in surprise. "Yes, Kane is part of Bridgewater as well."

"He purchased cattle last year from a man in Simms, I believe," Uncle Allen added.

"He did." He paused, then grinned. "Weston, yes. Now I have the connection. They were your cattle then."

Uncle Allen nodded.

"We are in town to purchase a stud horse, however the arrangement has not been as smooth as Kane's dealings with your man last year."

"Oh? Who is your connection here in Helena?"

"Clayton Peters. While he has been somewhat difficult to work with, his horse flesh is quite impressive."

I stiffened at the mention of his name.

"We are quite familiar with Mr. Peters," Uncle Allen said darkly. The curt tone and stiffness in his shoulders were not missed by Mr. Rhys.

"Is there something we should know about the man as part of our dealings? Has he treated you wrongly?"

To my surprise, Uncle Allen took my hand in his. "I have much respect for the men of Bridgewater, and of your ways, so I will share something with you." He lifted my hand and tugged the lace cuff of my dress back to show the bruises Mr. Peters had inflicted.

Mr. Rhys' eyes narrowed and his jaw clenched as he looked at the dark marks about my wrist. "Peters?" When I didn't answer, he looked to my uncle, who nodded. "Did he hurt you in any other way?" he asked me.

The vehemence and anger in his gaze had me stepping back, but I could not move from my uncle's gentle hold. I was embarrassed at my weakness being shared with a stranger and I covered my wrist with my other hand. "No, just wounded my pride," I replied.

"I am in town with Cross, whom you met, Miss Weston, as well as

Simon McPherson. If there is anything you need, please do not hesitate to contact any one of us, now or at Bridgewater."

"Thank you," Uncle Allen replied. "These two men, they are of like minds as you?"

A look passed between the men but I did not know what it was. Mr. Rhys nodded and replied, "Indeed." The man turned to me and offered slight bow. "Miss Weston, the pleasure was mine. I hope to make your acquaintance again soon."

I murmured a soft thank you, but my throat was dry. His dark eyes held mine a moment longer, as if trying to see something deep within. Then he turned and left.

"Lightning, Olivia?" my uncle asked, eyes twinkling, questioning how I felt for the man.

My cheeks flushed and knew I could not hide any emotion from my uncle. "Lightning," I repeated.

"Not just for Rhys, either, hmm?" he queried, then chuckled when I blushed even more hotly.

Hmm, was right. I felt *something* for two men. What was wrong with me?

3

IMON

"By the looks on your faces I missed something," I said to Cross and Rhys, pouring whiskey into three glasses. I picked up my own as I eyed them.

"Not something, some*one,*" Cross replied, downing his shot in one big gulp.

"If it was Peters, I ken. The bastard said he wanted to finish the deal to get to the dance. I believe his words were, 'I've got a fancy piece I want to get my hands on. Her being prim and all, a dance is the only way the virgin bitch will let me touch her.'"

I tossed back my whiskey as I thought about the bastard's words. I didna like to hear a woman talked about in that way, no matter who she was. If I were her father or brother or any relation whatsoever, I would have beat him and left him for the vultures.

Rhys leaned back in his chair and crossed his arms over his chest. "He said that?"

I nodded, placed my forearms on the table. "If he didna have the stud horse we want, I wouldna get near the man."

"He was speaking of Olivia," Rhys shared.

"Olivia?" I asked, my voice loud, even over the tinny piano music. I glanced left and right at the others in the saloon, then leaned forward and lowered my voice. "Who the hell is Olivia?"

"She's the one," Cross said.

"He's right," Rhys added. "She's definitely the one."

I couldna help but look at them in surprise, for having both men agree on a woman had ne'er happened before.

"And Peters talked about her that way?" I asked. "What is the chance he will win her?"

"None," Cross replied.

Rhys looked between us, tilted his chair back on two legs. "Peters touched her," he said.

Cross placed his forearms on the table, too. "What?" he shouted. "How?"

"I don't know the details, but she had bruises on her wrist. Her uncle will keep him away from her now that he knows of what the bloody bastard's capable."

"That fucker's insane. From what I can tell of his character, he could inflict more than bruises." The idea didn't sit well and I hadna even laid eyes on the woman my friends were ready to claim.

Hell, we were more than friends. Rhys was a brother forged by battle, by hardship and life in a corrupt army regiment. We, along with the other men at Bridgewater, persevered and built the ranch on our own. Our safe haven, our land, our family. Together, Rhys, Cross and I would, someday, claim a woman as ours, just as we'd learned from our time spent defending diplomats in the small middle eastern country of Mohamir. Disappointed by the Victorian social values, we adopted the Mohamiran ways where a woman was bound to more than one man, possessing her and cherishing her. Multiple husbands were for the wife's own good, for she, and any children produced in the union, wouldna be without a man's protection.

Rhys and I met Cross when we arrived in America. He'd joined us in a fight to protect a whore against a group of men set on raping her. We'd left Boston together and he'd fled west with us. The journey and the years together since had forged a brotherhood just as readily as had the war. We helped build Bridgewater into the successful ranch it was with the other men and the three of us would claim a bride together.

Kane and Ian had married Emma the year before, Andrew and Robert had claimed Ann prior to that. Over the winter, Mason and Brody had found their bride, Laurel, when they rescued her from a blizzard. We hoped we'd find a woman of our own, but it wasna an easy task. To find a woman that one of us wanted was nae as hard, but finding one woman all three of us longed for was much more difficult.

This arrangement—three men for one bride—wasna something we shared with the world, so it was quite difficult to ken when a woman would want all three of us.

We'd share, we'd claim, we'd possess her together. We just didna ken who she was yet. It seemed, though, that both Rhys and Cross kent this woman Olivia might be the one. It boded well if both of them found her appealing.

"Describe her," I said.

Cross indicated with a tilt of his chin. "Hair as dark as yours."

"Petite," Rhys added, using his hands to indicate her height, then shifted his hands to show off the shape of her curves.

Cross laughed. "It is true, she has very nice curves."

"There are women upstairs with dark hair and curves," I countered, referring to the loose women who worked above the saloon servicing patrons all night long.

Both men's faces hardened and I feared my nose would be broken if I spoke again of this Olivia woman in a disparaging way. "Shit," I muttered, then held up my hands to ward them off. "It's like that."

Both men nodded. "It's like that," Cross repeated.

"I met her uncle," Rhys said. "The name Weston mean anything?"

I thought about where I'd heard the name before, and then it came to me.

"The deal with the cattle?" I asked.

"Didn't Kane say that he...?" Cross asked, but cut off the end of his question, for we all kent the answer.

Both men grinned and I joined them, knowing that Olivia's uncle would approve of our ménage lifestyle, for he lived it himself. Kane had said the man who'd sold us the cattle the previous summer shared a wife with another man, but seemed to have kept that fact a secret from his niece. Kane had only said good things about him, so if he vouched for Allen Weston, then it was good enough for us. It only helped our cause when we wanted to marry her, for her uncle wouldna disparage three men claiming her. He'd see it as a perk.

I poured another round of whiskey. "She's ours."

———

OLIVIA

I couldn't sleep, too restless with the handsome faces of Mr. Cross and Mr. Rhys haunting me as I tossed and turned. I relived every moment of both dances, their words, the feel of their hands upon me, their distinct scents, Mr. Rhys' unusual accent. Everything. I groaned. Nothing would erase their images from my mind so I put on my robe and went to the kitchen for a snack.

"You were quite a catch at the dance," Uncle Allen said, surprising me as I came into the room. I should have seen him there, and it was clear indication my mind was wandering. He had a cup of coffee in hand, the steam rising from the top. How he could drink something so strong and fall asleep afterward was beyond me.

I went to the icebox and took out the pitcher of milk, poured myself a glass and joined him at the table. We took our meals in the kitchen, the two of us simple enough where we did not need to eat in the much larger dining room. While Uncle Allen was quite wealthy, he did not flaunt it and I'd grown up the same. The house wasn't large or ostentatious like others nearby where money was flaunted; it was just big enough for us to be content. We were both simple people with basic needs.

I could feel my cheeks heat and so I took my time drinking my milk to collect myself. "Yes," I replied neutrally.

"Two men especially were very handsome and seemed very taken with you."

Handsome? Mr. Cross and Mr. Rhys were not just handsome. They were stunning, virile, strong, intense. They were...lightning.

He had a hint of gray in his hair, but otherwise his age did not show. He was well connected in the Helena community and beyond through his work. The fact that he knew men from the Bridgewater Ranch was quite a coincidence, yet showed how powerful he was in the Territory. While he was busy with all of his endeavors, I wasn't as settled, perhaps because I'd been waiting for something more. Lightning. I'd been waiting for that.

I could not avoid looking at Uncle Allen any longer. He had always been able to see all of my secrets, although I did not have many. "They are both very handsome, both very...manly," I replied, trying to be as neutral as possible.

He smiled. "They are that. I know some of the other men from Bridgewater quite well. I have nothing but good things to say and if you are amenable, if these men come calling, I will be more than happy to welcome them into our home."

"Them? I doubt one will come, let alone both of them."

"I believe Rhys said there's a third man from Bridgewater here in town as well. Simon McPherson."

A third. Could he possibly be as attractive as the other two?

"Nothing will come from meeting either man," I said, cutting off any hope he may have at making a match. "They are not from here and clearly spent the evening dancing with women to pass the time as they are here on business."

"I did not see either man dance with any other woman," he countered, picking up his coffee and taking a sip.

My heart leapt at that thought, but surely he was mistaken. I shook my head at the silly notion. "It matters not. They are most likely on their way back to Bridgewater as we speak."

"At this time of night?" He shook his head. "I will not force any man upon you, nor will I keep you from one who has captured your heart. As I said, you will know when the right man comes along."

I took a sip of my milk, and then said, "What if it feels right with more than one man?"

I winced, worrying my uncle would think me too forward.

"More than one man?" He considered, but did not seem stunned by my question. "You mean both Bridgewater men?"

I nodded.

"I am not averse to the notion of a woman having more than one man protect her. So, did the lightning strike twice, then?"

He grinned and I blushed.

"You don't think something's wrong with the feeling of lightning striking with two men?" Surely something was wrong with me if I did so, or I'd have to pick one and that would be quite hard.

"Olivia, I have something to tell you. You're well old enough now to know and, hopefully, to understand. I—"

The sound of broken glass followed by a loud crash cut off Uncle Allen's words.

He stood quickly, his chair scraping against the floor as he ran toward the front of the house. I followed along directly behind him.

I smelled smoke before I saw it and then there were the flames.

"Fire!"

4

RHYS

Pounding on my hotel room door woke me with a start. I shot up in bed, noticed it was still dark, and wiped my hand over my face. I hadn't fallen asleep readily; seeing Olivia's face in my mind and remembering the feel of her waist beneath my palm had made my cock rock hard. I hadn't been able to sleep with a bloody cock stand, so I'd made myself come to ease the ache, thinking of her as I did so. Only then, did I fall into a fitful sleep. Unfortunately, I was being roused when I had finally settled in.

"What?" I shouted, tossing my legs over the side of the bed. More pounding. I stood, went to the door and pulled it open, stark naked. Whoever wanted to disturb me in the middle of the night could get an eyeful for all I cared. "What?"

Simon and Cross were at the door, and from the sight of them in the dimly lit hallway, they had hastily dressed. "There's been a fire at the Weston house. Allen Weston sent for us."

I ran my hand over my face again, and then turned into my room to throw on my clothes.

"Bloody hell. Was anyone hurt? Olivia?"

Simon stepped into the room. "We dinna ken for sure, but we've been told they are both fine."

The thought of Olivia being hurt in a fire had me dressing with additional haste. I stood, skipping a tie or even doing up all of my buttons. Tucking my shirt in was wasted effort. "Let's go."

Even if Allen Weston hadn't provided the address, the residence was not hard to find, based on the strong smell of smoke and the number of people milling about at such an hour.

The sight of Olivia, wearing a white robe, her hair long and unbound down her back, had my heart skipping a beat. If she weren't standing in front of her house that had been, from the looks of it, only partially ruined, I'd be quite pleased by her less than modest appearance. But no maiden should be seen in such a way— nor a wife for that matter—by the general public, and the idea of any man seeing her thusly had me stripping off my shirt and giving it to her.

"Take this." Those were my first words to her. Not overly comforting or reassuring, but she needed to be covered. Now. "Please put this on over your robe."

She froze in place as I started to unbutton my shirt, ogling my chest as it was revealed. Probably not my wisest of decisions, but she needed to be covered more than me.

"No," Mr. Weston said, undoing the sash of his dark, long robe and taking it off. He wore pants and a dress shirt, although some of the buttons at the collar were undone. It was as if he hadn't fully undressed from after the dance. "This will be more appropriate for everyone."

Cross took the robe from the man and moved to stand behind Olivia to help her into it.

Simon introduced himself to both of them and shook Allen Weston's hand. "Are either of you hurt? Burned?" he asked, looking Olivia over. It was the first time he'd seen her, and his gaze was more clinical that sexual.

She shook her head and looked over her shoulder at Cross as she slipped her arms through the sleeves. "No, we were both awake and in the kitchen."

"It was a rock. Broke the window," Mr. Weston said, glancing over to his house and where the damage had been done. Besides some streaks of soot on his face, he seemed fine. Angry, but fine. "Then he tossed in a flaming whiskey bottle. The floor in the foyer is stone, but the liquid spread and caught the walls."

I glanced at the house. It was two-story and made of quarried stone. The front door stood open and the front windows on either side of it were broken. The fire did not appear to have spread much, most likely due to sturdy construction. While the house was not overly large, there was no question that we stood in a well-to-do neighborhood. It was much smaller than Mr. Weston's vast means, but he did not seem the type of man to flaunt his wealth. Unfortunately, that wealth was most likely the motive for the fire.

Neighbors—no doubt awakened by the commotion—were standing about in various states of dress, watching and speaking to each other in hushed voices.

"Ye said *he* as if ye ken the person," Simon said. His accent was pure Scot, but when he became angry, the burr was much thicker.

Mr. Weston nodded. "I can't say with complete certainty, but I think it was Clayton Peters."

Olivia held the front of the robe closed, her hands up by her neck as if she were chilled. It was a warm night, so I was worried about shock, but she seemed calm enough. I would watch her closely though and at the first sign of unease, we'd whisk her away.

Cross took hold of Olivia's hand and slid the overly long sleeve of the robe back to look for the bruises I'd mentioned. There, on her slim wrist, I could see them, mottled and dark, even in the night. Her hand was so small, her wrist so narrow and delicate in Cross' hold, he could easily snap her bones. She'd been lucky with Peters. When I got my hands on him, he'd know what it felt like to fight someone of his own size.

"Because of this?" Cross asked.

Olivia tugged at my friend's hold and he let her go, the long sleeve covering her hand once again. Clearly, she didn't want to be the reason for all of the destruction and Cross must have noticed it as well.

"This isn't your fault, love," Cross told her, carefully pulling her hair out from beneath the robe so it hung long down her back.

I was jealous of the man, for he knew what her hair felt like. I imagined it to be soft as silk.

"Oh, no, Olivia. This is Peters' doing. Not yours," her uncle said with certainty.

She nodded and stepped closer to her uncle. "If I hadn't made him angry, then—"

Mr. Weston shook his head. "No," he replied. "The only way to make him happy is if I hand over my money to him and that's not going to happen."

"He won't stop," she said, her eyes wide and wild.

With his hands on her shoulders, he looked at his niece. "No, I don't think he will. While this isn't your fault, I think it's more about you than me. He's angry at being rebuffed and he will, most likely, try something else."

I agreed with the older man.

"Then we must go away where he can't get us."

"I'm staying here, but you'll go."

She shook her head. "No, Uncle Allen, you can't. He's dangerous."

He cupped her jaw so she stilled her motion. "To me, he's not. He could, at a minimum, compromise you and then where would you be? Married to the damn bastard. I couldn't live if something like that happened."

Olivia pursed her lips for she knew the answer. So did the three of us. She would be married to the bastard, stuck with him for a lifetime of cruel treatment.

"If he resorted to setting fire to our house," he continued, "he could want to truly harm you."

"If he wants the money, he could...he could kill you to get it." Unshed tears filled her eyes, made them glisten in the moonlight.

"He won't get a dime, I promise."

I glanced at Simon, then at Cross. Both men nodded.

"She'll come with us back to Bridgewater. No harm will come to her," I said, vowing to protect her.

Mr. Weston looked at me over her shoulder, then at the other men. "Yes, Bridgewater is a safe place for you, Olivia."

"You want me to go off with three men? Three strangers?" She waved her hand in our direction.

"Their reputation precedes them. I know other men from their ranch and I'd trust them with my life. Yours, as well. They are honorable." He looked at me directly. "You have no idea how important she is to me."

"We will keep her safe," I vowed.

"Protected," Cross added.

A horse whinnied in the background, the fire brigade's pumper being pulled down the street and back to the station. With the fire out, there was not much more they could do.

"There is one stipulation." He took Olivia's shoulders and turned her to face us, her eyes wide, her body shrouded in the overly large robe. "You must marry her."

"What?" she cried, spinning back around, the robe swirling about her legs. "Uncle Allen, perhaps *they* are doing this for the money!"

She didn't dare glance at us, for it was clear she knew the words were insulting. The barb did not hit its mark, for we all knew she was under duress.

"We don't need your money. Bridgewater is self-sufficient," I said.

"Yes, but marriage, that's not necessary—"

"Olivia. Stop." At her uncle's words, Olivia quieted, but I could tell she wished to argue. The tone of the man's voice was enough to keep her from brooking further argument. "Lightning, remember?"

She bit her plump lower lip and nodded, glancing at the three of us in turn. I had no idea to what her uncle was referring regarding lightning, but Olivia did.

"But...but how do I choose?" she asked, her voice low, but I heard it readily enough. So had the others. The fear for her safety lessened, knowing that this man was giving his niece to us. He, too, was honorable if he expected marriage before letting us take her. While we'd honor whatever gentlemanly rules existed when it came to being in the presence of a maiden, her virtue would still be in tatters upon her return regardless of our good behavior. Three bachelors didn't just take an unmarried woman to their ranch, no matter the reason.

In this instance, Mr. Weston could feel confident in her safety, Olivia would know our intentions were honorable and we'd know that she belonged to us. I could see his request for more than just honor. If something did happen to him, she'd inherit all of the Weston fortune. But married, it would pass to her husband, therefore preventing Peters from getting a dime. It was an uncle's way of protecting his niece and I had to respect him for that.

We should have run away at the idea of Mr. Weston forcing us to marry Olivia, but for the first time, she was the woman we wanted. I flicked my gaze to Simon, who'd had the least interaction with her, but he nodded his head, his intentions silent but very clear.

"Choose?" Weston asked. "You don't have to."

5

LIVIA

An hour later we were in the home of Uncle Allen's close friends Roger and Belinda Tannenbaum. If they were surprised to see us with three burly men in tow, they did not show it. When Uncle Allen announced I would wed all three of the men, they didn't blink an eye, which seemed quite odd. Was it because it was so late an hour and they were not fully awake? That was doubtful, since they sent one of their servants off to fetch the minister. It wasn't until then that I began to panic.

"I can't marry three men!" I cried, glancing between the formidable trio standing in the Tannenbaum's comfortable living room. "It isn't done."

"Actually, Olivia, it is," Uncle Allen replied.

I frowned, confused. Was I hearing him correctly? Had I hit my head in my rush to leave the burning house and I didn't remember?

He stood and went over to where the Tannenbaums sat across from us on a wide sofa and sat down with Belinda between the two men, placing his hand on top of hers in a surprising move. "This was

VANESSA VALE

what I wanted to tell you earlier before that damn rock was thrown." He took a deep breath, and then said, "Belinda is my wife, too."

He looked at the woman I'd known my whole life and gave her a sweet smile, then turned to me.

I stared at their joined hands, confused. "How can you be married to...to them? You live with me."

I could feel Mr. Rhys, Mr. Cross and Mr. McPherson watching the conversation unfold and they did not seem the least bit horrified by what my uncle was sharing. It was as if they already knew.

Nodding, Uncle Allen continued. "I do. When your parents died and you came to live with me, you were too young to understand the dynamic of two men claiming a bride and besides, the townspeople would not be forgiving. It was important to maintain appearances and give you a comfortable home, yet Roger and I, together, are married to Belinda. Those nights when I went out of town for business and Hattie stayed with you? Remember?"

It was as if a veil had been lifted off my face. "You came here, didn't you?"

"Yes. Do not be mad, or at least do not be mad at me just yet. Think on this for a little while. It's been a long night. These three men," he lifted his hand and indicated the men from Bridgewater, "will be your husbands. You felt a connection, what some call chemistry, with the two at the dance. It's all right to be enamored and attracted to more than one man, as Belinda can tell you. As I said, you don't have to choose one of them. You will have all three."

I glanced at the men. They were all so handsome, so big, so...breathtaking that the idea of belonging to all of them only made me panic more. I stood, shook my head and paced back and forth in front of the cold fireplace. "No, no, this is insane! I would have known, I would have—"

"Olivia," Belinda said, standing and coming before me. She was in her late forties with very pale hair, now pulled back in a simple braid for sleep. She'd donned a modest dress after our surprise arrival and I'd never seen her so simply put together. She took my hands in hers and gave them a squeeze. "I love them. I love them both. I *love* being married to both of them. Remember what your uncle always said about the man you are to marry? What I've always told you?"

She stood so close I could see the blueness of her eyes, the earnestness there. She'd always been kind to me, like a surrogate mother, involved in my life for as long as I could remember. Even as just a family friend, she'd answered all of my questions about becoming a woman. Even though Uncle Allen had been there for me regardless of my need, sometimes a girl needed a woman to confide in. She smiled softly. "What is it?" she prompted.

I pulled my hands free and wrapped them around my waist, as if I could keep myself from falling to pieces. "When I find the right man, it will feel like I've been struck by lightning." I sighed, then glanced over at the three men and I felt it again. They were not dressed as expected out in society, but none of us were. They wore no jackets, only their shirts and Cross' wasn't tucked in, Rhys' buttons weren't done up to his neck and Simon's sleeves were rolled up to show off tightly corded forearms dusted with dark hair. All were tall, serious and handsome. One fair and two dark haired men who intended to marry me. The idea was exhilarating and absolutely petrifying, as I'd never really felt the true interest of one man, let alone three, until now.

"I felt it when I met your uncle." Belinda's words had me turning back to her and I saw the love bright in her eyes, in the wide smile. "And again when I met Roger. I wanted them both and they wanted me."

"But it's so...wrong." I covered my face with my hands, and then pulled them away as I realized my blunder, tears sliding down my cheeks. "Oh, Belinda, I'm so sorry! I didn't mean your marriage was wrong—"

She held up her hands, a simple gold ring on her left ring finger and a similar one on her right. I had never known what the one on her right hand was for until now. She had one for each one of her husbands. "It's all right. This is overwhelming for you. Quite a terrible night, but look." She waved her hand toward the three Bridgewater men. "They are here for you."

"I...I don't even know them," I admitted.

I felt even worse now, for the men just looked at me with seriousness, yet a hint of concern shone in their eyes. While one I'd never even spoken with, the other two *had* been remarkably kind.

"How can you *give* me to strangers?" I asked Uncle Allen as I wiped the tears on my cheeks

"You said you felt a connection, a spark with them, that you were worried about being attracted to two men at the same time. Your head may be telling you it is wrong, but your heart will always tell the truth."

I chanced a glimpse at Mr. Rhys and Mr. Cross, one's eyebrows went up, the other smiled broadly.

"Is that true, love, that you are attracted to me and Cross?" Rhys asked. I noticed the term of endearment he used and it didn't feel dirty like it had when Mr. Peters had called me 'sweetheart.'

"It's all right," Melinda said, urging me to share my feelings.

Reassured by her smile, I nodded.

At that, the three men stepped forward. "May we have some time alone with Olivia before the minister comes?" Cross asked Uncle Allen.

He gave his assent and stood. Melinda gave me a quick hug and left, holding hands with her two husbands. *Two husbands!*

I felt so incredibly uncomfortable standing alone in a room with three men, strangers, who were going to marry me. Not one, not two, but three! I couldn't look at them and had no idea what to say, so I kept my gaze firmly on the Oriental rug at my feet and my hands clenched together in front of me.

"Come here, Olivia," one of them murmured. I looked up and saw that it was Cross who had spoken. He sat down on the sofa where my uncle had been. "Please," he added.

His voice was calm, his eyes gentle. I glanced at the other two who gave slight nods of encouragement. I swallowed at the way they towered over me. I felt dwarfed beside them and should have cowered at their domineering presence, but instead it made me feel as if I was sheltered, that they blocked out the entire world; Mr. Peters, the fire, even Uncle Allen's surprising pronouncement.

I took the final step to Cross, but instead of sitting beside him, he took my hand and tugged me down onto his lap.

"Oh!" I cried at the feel of his hard thighs beneath my bottom. His arms came about me and pulled me in so I was sheltered, my cheek against his chest. I could hear the steady beat of his heart and his clean scent swirled around me. This was the first time I'd ever been held by a man and I felt the hot jolt once again. He was so warm and yet I shivered. It felt so wrong and so right at the same time.

"Mr. Cross, we shouldn't—"

"We should," he countered. "And my name is just Cross."

The other men came closer, Mr. Rhys sat next to us on the sofa and Mr. McPherson moved a desk chair and placed it directly before us. They surrounded me and there was no escape, however they still did not feel threatening and I truly did not wish to move.

"This lightning, explain," Mr. Rhys said.

His dark eyes watched me carefully.

"It's a feeling, when you meet the right person," I replied. "Uncle Allen wanted to ensure I didn't compromise on the man I was to marry."

"You felt it with me?" I could see the hope in his eyes. Was the feeling reciprocated?

I nodded.

"And with me?" Mr. Cross—Cross—asked. His chin rested lightly on top of my head.

Were they always this direct? Always so open about their feelings? Weren't men supposed to be the ones who never shared or showed any kind of emotion?

I scrunched up my face and squeezed my eyes shut, dreading voicing my own feelings aloud. "Yes," I exhaled quickly.

I didn't want to look at them, to see the horror or the amusement or the disgust on their faces at admitting my feelings for two men. Would they consider me loose and immoral?

"And what about me, lass? Think ye can feel something for me as

ANESSA VALE

well?" Mr. McPherson's words were thickly accented, so much so that the word *well* sounded more like *wheel.*

I peeked out from around Cross' arm to look at Mr. McPherson. Gone was the look of a harsh warrior, a man ready to conquer the world and slay dragons as necessary. Instead, it was a man with the corner of his mouth tipped up and question in his eyes. He was the biggest of the three men, with dark hair that was overly long, a square jaw and a blunt nose that had a crook in it. He was handsome in a rugged, brutish sort of way, but when he looked at me so endearingly, I could see he was gentle as well.

I could also discern the worry on his face, for it seemed these men did things together, including marriage, and if I did not like all of them, one would be lost, perhaps cast adrift and alone. Mr. McPherson had much riding on my answer. In that moment I realized perhaps I could hurt him more than someone as sinister as Mr. Peters.

"I cannot say, for I do not know you."

"Then we will change that," he murmured.

"You don't think there's something wrong with me then? I am not wanton," I stated baldly.

Simon's gaze lowered to my lips, then raked over my body. "Nay, lass, we dinna ken a thing wrong with ye."

Cross shifted me in his arms so that my head rested against his arm and he was looking down at me. "You can be wanton for us any time you wish," he offered, then said with more seriousness, "I felt it, too, Olivia, when we were dancing, and having you now in my arms...."

I saw something flare in his eyes, bright and hot, before he looked at my mouth. "I am going to kiss you."

He didn't give me time to think, or to refuse, or to even push myself from his arms before his mouth lowered to mine. His lips were warm and soft and gentle as they brushed over mine as if he were learning the curve of my lower lip, the corners of my mouth. All at once I felt hot all over and I was quite glad he held me so surely, for I would have slid off his lap and onto the floor otherwise.

To my surprise, my eyes had fallen shut and I had to open them to

74

look up at him, at the first man to kiss me and saw him smile. "Again," he murmured, then kissed me once more, this time deeper, which elicited a surprised gasp from me and he used that to his advantage, his tongue slipping into my mouth.

His tongue!

The idea was stunning and yet this was most definitely what wanton felt like. Tentatively, I touched mine to his and it was Cross' turn to groan. The sound had my heart pounding, had me feeling triumphant that I could actually please him with a simple kiss.

"Share," Rhys grumbled.

I felt Cross smile against my lips before he pulled back and propped me upright in his arms. "Ah, it seems I am not the only one who wishes to kiss you, love."

I knew my cheeks were bright red, for it was one thing for a woman to have her first kiss, it was another altogether to do it with two other men watching. So enraptured, I'd completely forgotten they were there.

Was I supposed to just get up and move on to the next man? It seemed awkward and very bold to do so. Before I could decide what I should do, Rhys pulled me out of Cross' arms and onto his own lap. He grinned down at me, the look wicked and friendly at the same time. "I've wanted to kiss you ever since I saw you at the dance."

I frowned. "I thought...I thought you were mad at me for questioning your honor."

"We have a higher standard to which you are accustomed, but no, I was not mad."

"Then you are willing to marry a woman just because you want to kiss her?"

He ran his knuckles over my cheek. "I want to do more than just kiss you."

I had a vague idea to what he referred and I was equally pleased and petrified.

"It's like you said, love. I just knew."

"Really?" I asked, surprised. He'd seemed so indifferent when the dance had ended. Then I remembered his vehement demand that I promise to seek his help if needed, and felt better.

He lowered his head and said, "Truly." I could feel the words against my lips then only the delectable pressure of his mouth on mine. Other than his lips on mine, the two kisses were completely different. Where Cross coaxed and played, Rhys delved and claimed. He angled his lips over mine and plunged his tongue into my mouth as if he needed me to breathe, as if he put his all into the kiss. My hands tangled in his hair, the feeling of silk slipping through my fingers. He tasted of peppermint, completely different than Cross. Even his scent was different. My skin tingled on my chin where his whiskers rasped.

"Does it feel as if we are strangers, love?" he asked, his nose brushing against mine.

I put my hands to my lips. They felt swollen and slick and hot.

"It feels as if you belong to me. To us. You are ours."

My body...it felt as if, as if...I couldn't explain it. I felt...hot and relaxed and tense and desperate and needy and confused and so many other things all at the same time. Beneath that, though, I felt...home. It was as if these men were familiar to me yet completely new all at the same time. It was quite strange and I did not readily understand, and as I felt prone to babble when nervous or overwhelmed, I decided it was best if I remained silent.

"Ye will have three husbands, lass, nae two." Simon murmured, the fiercest looking of the bunch, held out his hand in the space between us and sat patiently waiting. His dark pants were drawn tight over well muscled thighs and his shirt—snug over his broad shoulders—only defined how broad, how big, how, oh, enticing he was. He was letting me decide when, and if, I'd come to him next.

The room was quiet; only the ticking of a clock on the mantel and my soft panting breaths could be heard. Where my uncle and his...family went, I had no idea. I met Simon's dark eyes, searched for something, anything that indicated that he would treat me falsely, that he had less honor or integrity than the others.

I had to trust that these feelings I had were an accurate indicator of these men—*men*—being right for me. I'd waited for it all my life and now, once it happened, I was uncertain. I had to take a blind leap of faith, and Simon, Cross and Rhys were as well. They were sure, so very sure of this match and I was as much a stranger to them.

I climbed from Rhys' lap and placed my hand in Simon's. Placed my faith, my blind trust and hopefully my heart with him. With all three of them.

6

IMON

It was right then, when she looked at me with those ice blue eyes that held such nervousness, fear and hope that I kent Rhys and Cross were correct. She was the one for us. To say she was beautiful was an understatement. The dark hair and light eyes was a striking combination. While she was covered from neck to floor in her uncle's heavy and unflattering robe, I'd caught a quick glimpse of her in her own flimsy nightclothes and had seen her woman's shape. She was so small that I seemed a giant in comparison and I would feel terrible if I hurt her with even the gentlest of touches. How was she going to handle three men whose sexual needs were prolific enough where we would make almost constant use of her body? She would love it, we would ensure that, but just looking at her had a cock stand press painfully against my pants.

There was nae question to her virtue; the woman was a virgin and a very innocent one at that. I'd wager a bottle of the finest Scottish whiskey that she'd just had her verra first kiss, her first contact with a man. With men. Now I knew why my brothers—while our brotherhood was nae from blood, we were brothers nonetheless—

were so adamant about her at the saloon. I would have reacted the same, ye ken. Nae harm would come to her again, nae while I was alive. And if I died protecting her, I would ken that Rhys and Cross would be there for her. That was the way in Mohamir and we respected the practice enough to want to live it ourselves. It had only been a dream, until now.

Now, Olivia's hand was in mine and I knew she was offering up more than just a simple touch. She was giving me things she didn't even know we would take. With that came trust and I wouldna do anything to tarnish that. Instead of setting her upon my lap as the other two had, I pulled her into the cradle of my legs so she stood directly before me, placing her hand on my chest. I wanted her at ease with me, a complete stranger.

As I held her gaze, my hands moved to her waist and they spanned her completely, my thumbs touching in the front, fingers at her spine. Her breath escaped in shallow pants and her eyes widened.

"Perhaps the order was a bit off, but since I'm to be yer husband, I should introduce myself. I'm Simon Angus McPherson of the clan McPherson, although these days I hale from Bridgewater. I may have been a wee lad in the Highlands, but I belong here, in the Territory."

I heard the knocker on the front door and Olivia's body tensed beneath my palms. "Nay, lass, tis only the minister."

She furrowed her brow. "You don't think I should be nervous of a minister at a time like this?"

I couldna help but grin at her sass. "Tis the man who avoids the parson's noose, nae the lady. Dinna worry, for the man will only change yer name, the rest," I paused and brushed her hair back from her face and then cupped my hand at her nape, "we will change as we go along. All four of us. Together."

She eyed me closely, as if testing the truth behind my words. "Surely the minister will not marry a woman to three men. The acceptance of such ways must only have a certain reach."

I offered one curt nod. "Aye." I glanced over her shoulder at Rhys and Cross, who sat casually upon the sofa, watchful yet alert at the same time. "Ye'll marry me to make it legal, but that is just paper, lass."

Voices came from the front entry and Olivia wanted to step away, so I let her.

"This is happening so quickly. It's overwhelming. All of it. I'm—"

I pulled her back into my hold, this time letting my hands roam up and down her back in a soothing way. "Ye are fine. Yer uncle is content as his only worry is for your safety and he's handed that protection to the three of us. Do ye ken we'll let anything happen to ye?" I gestured to Rhys and Cross as well as myself. "Ye are the center of our world now, ye ken."

The Tannenbaums came into the room along with the minister. Olivia stepped out of my hold and took a deep breath. The man of God was in his fifties and wore his white clerical collar along with his dark pants, white shirt and long robe. Obviously, he was awakened and brought from his bed with haste, but his smile was amiable for such a late hour. It was easy to forget everything when I had my hands on Olivia, but the reason for the swift nuptials was not going to go away when the sun rose. We needed to get Olivia out of Helena and away from the bloody bastard Peters.

"...so pleased you could come at such a late hour, especially after the dance. You remember my niece?" Weston spoke with the minister as he came into the room. We stood at their approach and Olivia was pulled into a discussion with the two about some charity luncheon that was to occur later in the month.

The Tannenbaums stood to the side but seemed not the least put out by the unusual evening, even with their wardrobe of nightclothes as a reminder. Perhaps it was that their secret was shed that had them at ease.

"I am quite pleased to be woken for a wedding. Most often it is because someone has passed on in the night, and it is such a sad affair. This reason, however, and for you, Olivia, is very good indeed. Now, then, which man is your lucky groom?"

"I am." I moved to stand beside Olivia, my hand on her shoulder, there for not only reassurance but also to prevent her from dashing off if she decided to change her mind. "Simon McPherson."

I shook the minister's hand as he looked me over. If he had

concerns, he kept them to himself. Perhaps he knew Weston well enough to know he wouldna just marry his niece off to just anyone.

The minister cleared his throat with mild embarrassment. "Your uncle has given me a brief history as to what has happened this evening, therefore I will not need to ask the usual questions as to the reason for a hasty wedding."

Olivia's chin came up and I saw her cheeks flush a bright red. The color crept down her neck and beneath the robe and I had to wonder how far it traveled.

"Shall we begin, sir, for I would like to finally kiss her and I'd like to do it the verra first time with her as my bride."

The minister kept the ceremony blissfully short, only asking the most minimal of questions before pronouncing us husband and wife. Cross and Rhys had stood on my right while Weston stood beside Olivia, but I forgot all of them when I cupped her jaw and lowered my head to kiss her. This woman, she was my bride. She belonged to me in the eyes of God and her uncle and nae one could change that. The thought had pride filling me, and lust as well. Her lips were soft and tentative, yet when I lifted my head from the very brief, very chaste kiss, her eyes were blurry with awakened arousal and that pleased me verra greatly. The fact that I couldn't toss her over my shoulder and carry her to the nearest empty room so the three of us could have our way with her, only had my jaw hardening. Olivia's eyes widened at my change in demeanor, but I ran my thumb over her silky cheek in the hopes to soothe her, and ease my ache to touch.

Hearing Weston thank the minister had me breaking out of my reverie. I turned to the man and thanked him for his service and Roger Tannenbaum led him away, most likely allowing the man to finally get back to his bed.

"May we remain here until the morning instead of returning to the hotel?" Cross asked. "I believe Olivia would be more comfortable doing so."

Melinda Tannenbaum smiled. "Of course. I've ordered a bath to be delivered to the blue guest room. Up the stairs and down the hall to the right. Olivia, you know where to go."

7

LIVIA

Because I knew the house—I'd visited frequently all my life, and now I knew the true reason as to why—I led my husbands to the bedroom where they were going to take off my clothes and take my virginity. How *three* men did that I had no idea, but being the one to voluntarily guide them to my own deflowering made me very nervous. Nervous? No, that wasn't accurate. Petrified, embarrassed, worried. What if they found me lacking? What if I wasn't good at whatever I was supposed to do? How could I please them if I knew I wasn't good at...whatever? How did I make them happy when I had absolutely no idea—?

"Breathe, lass," Simon murmured, stopping before me as he passed through the door I'd opened. "Tis nae a hanging."

While I knew he was trying to make light of the situation, it didn't help. In fact, it only had me bursting into tears.

I covered my face with my hands and couldn't stop crying.

I heard one of the men swear beneath his breath, the door closed quietly and then I was picked up in someone's arms and carried across the room. There, he sat and I was held, hands stroking over my body. The hands had to belong to more than one man, for I felt gentle touches on my legs, my side, even over my hair all the while being held tightly and securely within a snug embrace.

"Shh, it's all right, love, you've had quite a day." Rhys. I recognized his voice.

"Aye, verra brave." Simon's thick burr.

"You're safe with us. All will be better now." Cross. His words swiftly changed my emotion from sad and overwhelmed to anger. I lifted my head and turned toward his voice. I was held in Simon's arms with Cross and Rhys squatting before me. Concern was evident in their eyes, but I didn't care.

"I'm safe with you?" I lashed out, the three men my verbal victims. "I'm supposed to give myself to you, or you, or...or you and I have no idea what to do? How do I please *three* men? And better? How do you know things will be better? Someone set my house on fire and you think because we're married everything is better?"

Two sets of eyebrows went up before me, one dark, one light, surprised by my vehement tone and long windedness.

"Things will be better because you have us to protect you from the likes of Peters. In the morning, we will take you back to Bridgewater where you will be safe." Rhys' words were laced with absolute certainty. "It may not make the problem with the man go away, but it makes your involvement in it end. You do not need to worry any longer, as you need to let your uncle take care of Peters and we will give help to him if needed. I know he is a smart man, for he gave you to us, didn't he?"

I opened my mouth to speak but Cross put a finger over my lips. "How do you please three men? Trust me, love, you've already done that by marrying us. As to the rest, it is our job to teach you." He tapped my lips once then pulled his hand away.

"Ye can do nae wrong," Simon added, using his thumbs to wipe my tear stained cheeks.

His gentle actions wiped my ire away.

"I can do no right if I don't know what to do," I countered, sniffling.

"Are ye afraid?"

I sputtered. "How can I not be?"

The men looked at each other over my head and it seemed as if they spoke without saying a word.

"We will not take you tonight, Olivia, for you are tired and you will need your rest for what we have in mind," Cross told me. "Besides, it will be hard for you to keep quiet and I want privacy for when we take you."

"Why will I make noise?" While I tried to sound calm, I could hear the panic in my words. "You're not going to hurt me, are you?"

Rhys smiled. "No, we are going to do quite the opposite. It's going to feel so good that you won't help making noise."

"Ye are going to scream, lass," Simon finished.

I wasn't sure about that, but I did believe them when they said they wouldn't take my virginity tonight and was reassured and relaxed into Simon's arms.

"That doesn't mean we won't touch you," Cross added.

"What?" I asked, surprised. Simon lifted me with his hands about my waist to stand once again before him. With his hands on the sash of my uncle's robe, he pulled the bow loose. Hands at my shoulders slipped the garment down and off my arms and then off me entirely.

"You've had an overwhelming day and it's time for your men to take care of you. All you have to do, love, is feel," Rhys said, his voice low and gentle.

"It is our job to make you feel good. Let us show you how we can do that," Cross added.

"Trust us in this, lass," Simon added.

Their hands were on me, running over my shoulders through my robe and nightgown, down my arms, over my waist and hips, over the outside of my legs. Three sets of hands could cover quite a bit of my body at the same time. Their touches were all gentle, soft. Easy and relaxed. Soothing. Everywhere they caressed my skin tingled and came to life, even through the cotton of my nightclothes.

"Oh," I murmured, surprised by...by it all. "But...but I'm all smoky."

My eyes slipped closed of their own accord and I could easily do as they bid, for it felt so good. How they could set me at ease after a crying jag and a burst of anger was impressive and I had my first simple lesson; I should not underestimate them, for when they set about doing something, they seemed to do it quite well.

I didn't know how long I stood there as they touched me, but time had no meaning. I focused on the hard press of their palms, the curl of their fingers, the sound of their breathing, even the mingling of their scents.

Their touches had stayed to modest places, but every so often, a hand slipped below my hip to curve around my bottom or a thumb moved up to caress the underside of my breast. My eyes widened at the surprise of that, but the look on Simon's face when I did made me gasp. His eyes were so dark as to be black, his cheeks ruddy and he looked at me as if...as if he were a wolf and I was a very innocent little lamb. Perhaps that was true.

This time, when Simon's thumbs moved over my breasts, they didn't stop at the bottom curve but came up to brush over my nipples, which formed into tight little points. No doubt all three men could see them poking against the cotton of my robe. His large hands stilled, cupping my breasts as if he was feeling them, testing their weight, learning their curve.

"Simon," I breathed, holding his gaze as he began to gently knead my breasts, his fingers plucking at the tight tips.

I didn't remember it happening, but somehow my robe had come off and I stood before them in just my nightgown. Simon's hands were warm, even through the thin layer of fabric between my skin and his. From my periphery, I saw Cross lean in and kiss my neck, then work his way down to the juncture with my shoulder.

"Oh!" I gasped again. I had no idea my body could elicit such feelings, for as my nipples felt the hot sensation of Simon's playing fingers, somehow between my legs I felt swollen and aching and my core clenched in need. Yes, in need.

His lips worked the narrow strap along my shoulder to slip down my arm, the cool air in the room raising goose bumps on the exposed skin. Cross' mouth continued to lave my shoulder and neck as his hand slid over my hip. Rhys was not idle in all this, for as soon as my nightgown fell off one shoulder, he inched the second strap off my other shoulder as well, and the garment was held on my body solely by Simon's hands cupping my breasts.

I placed my hands on top of Simon's to keep him from letting the material fall, for I was naked beneath. He grinned.

"Like having your breasts played with?" he asked.

Cross and Rhys each brought a hand up and gently pulled mine away and back to my sides. While their holds weren't tight, they were insistent. Simon kept my gaze as he pulled his hands back and the nightgown slid to the floor at my feet with the slightest whisper of sound.

The men froze, their gazes riveted to my body for I knew they could see *everything*. With their hands back on my wrists, I felt gently powerless. I closed my eyes, blocking them out, but I could *feel* them looking at me.

Beautiful. Gorgeous. Perfect. Skin so pale I can see little veins like rivers. Coral, that's the color of her nipples, not pink. Nay, she's not pink there, but beneath that dark hair her pussy lips are.

With those last words, my eyes flew open and I tugged at my hands so I could cover myself. I wasn't exactly sure what a pussy was, but I had a strong suspicion.

"Nay, lass," Simon said with a slight shake of his head. "Dinna hide yourself."

"I'm...I'm embarrassed," I admitted. "I must smell strongly of fire."

"Yes, but we will bathe you. Later. First," Cross let go of my arm and undid the buttons on his shirt. "I will take my shirt off as well."

Rhys and Simon followed suit and soon enough they were all bare to the waist.

"I'm fully naked and you're not," I said, my gaze roving over the men's very solid chests. Simon had the most hair there, a mat of it soft and curly between his nipples that formed into a V to his navel, then into a narrow line that dipped beneath his pants. His belly was flat and muscles were visible beneath his tan skin. Rhys was the darkest of the three, his complexion more olive. He, too, had dark hair, but only a smattering on his chest and then nothing but well-defined muscles. Cross had no hair on his chest, only dusky flat nipples and never ending sleek skin.

I had no idea men looked that way without their shirts. Oh my. My fingers itched to reach out and feel how smooth their skin was, whether the hair there was soft, to touch all those hard muscles. These were not men who sat about idly; they worked and worked hard and it showed.

"Love," Rhys admitted, "the only way to keep us from claiming you tonight is for us to keep our pants on. I promise—"

"We all promise," Simon uttered.

"—that tomorrow when we are at home at Bridgewater, nothing will keep us from showing you our cocks, pleasuring you with them, making you ours."

"For now, though," Cross added. "We will please you."

I liked the idea of it, but the doing so was the confusing part. "How—"

I began to ask a question, but Simon leaned forward and took my now plump nipple into his mouth and my words ceased and a gasp escaped. Oh my! Simon's tongue flicked over the tip and I cried out. Men put their mouths there? It was so deliciously wrong, but I didn't want him to stop. Quite the contrary, I needed him to continue. Perhaps I voiced that thought aloud for his hand came up to cup my very lonely other breast and began to tweak and tug at the now distended tip.

That was just the beginning, it seemed, for I felt a hand slide down the bumps of my spine and over my bottom, curving around and back up again. Another hand smoothed over my belly and dipped lower to slip through the curls that covered my womanhood. For a brief moment, I clenched my hands and wanted to push the hands away, but then I didn't. I so didn't. For the light touch brushed over my heated flesh and I groaned, a deep body shuddering groan.

"That's the sweetest sound I ever heard," Rhys said, his voice deep and rough.

"She's so wet," Cross murmured. It was true, I was somehow slick down there and the way his finger moved I could hear it. It was another in a long line of actions I should feel mortified about but the way these men made my body come alive, I just couldn't. It felt...so good. I felt hot and pliant and I could barely breathe. Simon had switched to suckling at my other breast and I arched my back involuntarily for him to take more. I needed it...needed their touch...needed something but I didn't know exactly what.

A sheen of perspiration coated my skin and I felt my long hair cling to my back and nape. Cross' finger continued to slide over me, down the side of one slick petal to move it aside, then did the same with the other before finding my opening and circling, only the very tip of his finger slipping within.

"She's tight."

"Let me," Rhys said and I felt Cross' hand move away, which had a sob tear from my lips, only to be replaced by Rhys'. His touch was different. While he was just as gentle, he was more intent in his actions, his finger dipping in a touch further than Cross had, only to retreat and slide upwards to touch a place that—

"Yes!" I cried.

I felt Simon's chuckle against my breast.

"She tastes delicious."

I had no idea what Cross spoke about and I opened my eyes to see him sucking on his finger, the finger that he'd had between my legs.

"Wider, love," Rhys demanded, tapping me lightly on my inner thighs. I moved my right foot a little bit. "There, good girl."

"Now we can both touch you," Cross said, and I felt two hands between my legs, one running over the place, the amazing, incredible place that had me crying my pleasure aloud and the other dipping into my opening again and again, not far enough for my wants, but enough to make my body light up as if it were set aflame.

"Her clit's so hard, I bet she can come like this. Can't you, love, come for your men?"

I shook my head as I licked my lips, lost in the feel of their hands and I was thankful for their firm hold on the back of my thighs and at my waist. I didn't know what my clit was, but whatever they were doing I liked quite well. "I...I don't know what you mean," I practically sobbed.

"Do ye feel achy?" Simon breathed across the valley between my breasts.

"Hot all over?"

"Desperate?"

"Frantic?"

The men said word after word, all describing how I felt and I could only nod my head, my mouth open. I needed....

"We'll give it to you, love," Cross promised.

Their hands became even more attentive, Rhys' finger on that place that had me climbing higher and hotter and brighter, Simon's almost sharp nip at the tip of my nipple—

"Right...."

—and Rhys' finger that moved inside of me—

"...about...."

—only to slide back and touch me in the most dark and carnal of places.

"...now," Rhys vowed.

That slightest brush of his finger against my back entrance was what pushed me from the mountain I'd been climbing and I did a free fall, falling, falling with the most blissful pleasure coursing through my veins. White light shone behind my eyelids, my muscles tensed and a sob caught in my throat.

The men's hands continued to stroke and caress me until the pleasure ebbed and my body went limp. Simon sat back in his chair to keep his hands on me as Rhys and Cross moved to sit on the bed. I couldn't help the lazy smile that formed on my lips and I looked at each one of them with a blurry gaze.

"What was *that*?" I asked, my voice husky.

Simon's long fingers tightened about my waist. "*That* was yer men making ye come."

"Come?" I repeated.

In one motion, Simon stood and lifted me, carrying me to the copper bath and lowered me into the water, still warm.

"Pleasure. We gave you your pleasure," Cross clarified.

Simon grabbed the soap, rose scented, and began washing me with gentle efficiency, his soapy hands cleaning the stench of the fire from my body. I was lulled by the surprised bout of pleasure they wrung from my body so that I could no longer be embarrassed, even when he lifted me from the tub and dried me as if I was a child. The look in his eyes made it clear he did not think of me as such, then lifted me again to place me down in the center of the bed. It seemed the man enjoyed carrying me about. I felt the cool blanket against my overheated, sensitive skin.

"We gave you your pleasure, love," Cross repeated. "And we're going to do it again."

"And again," Rhys added.

"And again," Simon finished.

"But I'm not standing up," I said, coming up on my elbow.

While they smiled, they didn't laugh or make fun at my lack of knowledge in the ways of men and women.

"You don't have to be standing. Laying down works quite well, too," Rhys told me.

"I loved licking your taste off my finger. Your flavor is still strong on my tongue. I want more," Cross admitted. He stood and moved to the foot of the bed, placed one knee on the mattress and began to crawl toward me. At the same time, Rhys and Simon each took one of my legs in hand, spread it wide and held on.

Cross's green eyes were darker than I'd ever seen them, his cheeks and mouth flushed red, his hair rakishly falling over his forehead. His shoulders were so wide and yet his waist so narrow, and beneath his pants, there was a bulge a large—oh!

"More?" I began to pant in equal measures of anticipation and trepidation. "More what?"

"More *you*," he growled before he lowered himself between my thighs.

8

ROSS

"I don't know if I'll be able to sit on a horse," Simon grumbled as he ran his hand over his face, his whiskers rasping.

It was early, the sun barely up and we stood with our coffee on the back porch of the Tannenbaum house. We'd left Olivia sleeping, naked with the white sheet barely covering her lush body. Her hair was wild and tangled over the pillow, her lips were red and appeared bee stung from our kisses. But that hadn't been the only place we'd kissed. Simon and Rhys had spread her open for me and I'd eaten her pussy until she came. She was so sensitive, her clit a throbbing little bud, her arousal copious and her folds were delectable. Her taste, I couldn't get enough, but once I made her come, we traded places until we'd each had a taste of her and made her come. Her hot, sweet flavor was still on my tongue, even hours later.

While we all knew officially claiming her should occur only once we were back at Bridgewater, it had been hard—no, practically impossible—not to want to pull my cock out and slide it into her slick, wet pussy. I'd been rock hard ever since I saw her at the dance and it wasn't going to go down any time soon. Even if I fucked her, I'd most likely want her again right away. I shifted myself in my pants and agreed with Simon's words. "I'm going to have to take care of the problem before we leave, but as soon as I see her I'll be hard again. Think we can make it home by nightfall?"

"Absolutely." Simon didn't waver in his answer. We *needed* to get home so we could take her. It would be a long night, but we would ensure Olivia enjoyed every minute of it.

Rhys joined us, his usually tidy appearance rumpled. "We need to get our woman out of here. Seeing her in that bed naked and sated has me wanting to fuck her, but we can't do it with her uncle in the house," he said, his voice grumpy.

"Tonight," I vowed.

"Tonight," Rhys agreed. Simon nodded.

Belinda joined us, and while clearly tired, was dressed immaculately. Her gaze was astute and she seemed the type of woman who missed nothing. "You gentleman are either not happy in the morning or are ready to depart. While the house is quite large, it is not as private as you would probably like." Yes, she missed nothing. She understood our predicament but was too much of a lady to say more.

"Yes, we are eager to get home," I agreed.

A small sly smile formed on her lips. "Yes, I'm sure you are. Would it be *easier* for you if I helped Olivia ready herself for the trip?"

Simon was the one who responded. "Thank you. I fear she is quite a temptation and we would be hard pressed to leave promptly otherwise."

She laughed at his words. "I'll have her ready in thirty minutes."

The Tannenbaum house was lavish enough to have its own stable and that was where Olivia found us within the half hour window. She wore what I could assume was one of Belinda's dresses, for her smoky robe and nightgown would not work for travel or anything else, really, for she would not be wearing a nightgown to bed ever again. The dress was forest green and cut well, but the color didn't flatter her as much as it would the older woman. I expected our bride to approach us with a sense of shyness after what we did with her only a few hours before or even a smiling, well satisfied glow about her, but I did not anticipate the fiery anger that shot from her eyes, the stiffness of her shoulders.

"You are done with me now?" she asked.

The sun was working its way up over the mountains in the distance and the air was warming. Only a few scattered clouds speckled the sky; it was going to be a pleasant ride. It was cooler in the stable, the scent of earth and horses strong. Both Rhys and Simon stopped what they were doing when we walked in.

"Done, lass?" Simon asked with an arched brow.

She stepped closer and I could see the bright flush to her cheeks as she placed her hands on her hips. "After...after last night you've had what you want?"

Rhys came up behind her and Simon and I came up beside her so she was flanked between us and one of the horses. "We gave you want you needed, yes," Rhys replied, although he was being neutral in his statement.

What was she angry about? We hadn't even seen her this morning.

"What I needed? I needed to be reassured by my husbands, not left in the hands of Belinda. What did you think I would feel, being abandoned and then told I had to dress to leave? Is this how you plan to treat me, for I will just stay here if you are."

My jaw clenched tightly as I crooked my finger, beckoning her closer without words. She swallowed deeply, but kept her chin raised as she closed the distance, close enough so I took her small hand in mine. With my other, I undid the placket of my pants and pulled out my cock. My rock hard, eager cock.

She gasped and tugged at my hold.

"You're an innocent and do not understand why we did not join you earlier in the guest room." I gripped the base of my cock and hissed, my cock pulsing with eagerness, pointing directly at Olivia. "We should have explained, and for that we are sorry, but did not want to frighten you, but there is no way around it. See my cock, love?

It's hard, hard for you. See that fluid on the tip, it's all but weeping to be inside you."

When I began stroking from base to tip and back, she watched my motions carefully, and then glanced up at me through her dark lashes. There I saw curiosity and surprise and a hint of arousal. I wondered if she was wet beneath the long hem of her dress.

"I want to fuck you, Olivia, and if I had come to you this morning, I would not have been able to stop myself."

"Oh," she whispered, her eyes lowered once again to watch my hand.

My hips bucked involuntarily at the thought of her on her knees before me, her mouth a perfect O around my cock.

"We all want you, lass," Simon added. Perhaps she forgot the others were there, for she startled and turned her head to look at the front of his pants. I could see the clear outline of Simon's hard cock and I knew Olivia could as well.

"We want you too much," Rhys added.

Moving my hand, I took hers and wrapped it around my cock, placing mine on top and then started to move. I couldn't help the groan that escaped at the feel of her palm, her small fingers touching me, sliding up and down my length.

As I showed her how I liked it, I gave her a brief lesson. "My cock's going to fill your pussy all the way up, but for now, you're going to make me come with your hand. Remember last night when you came? That's how you're going to make me feel. This ridge, yes," I hissed as she slid a finger along the sensitive edge of the head. "It's going to rub over all the special places deep inside you and you're going to come again all over my cock. When a man comes, his pleasure erupts and his seed will ultimately fill your belly."

Simon and Rhys stepped close and began touching Olivia. Rhys grabbed a hold of her long dress and slid the fabric up her thigh, higher and higher until he could reach underneath, Simon doing the same on the other side. Soon, her dress was up about her waist in front and Simon tugged at the ribbon of her drawers, letting them drop to the ground. Simon started to play with her pussy from the front, Rhys reaching around from behind.

She stiffened as they began stroking her, but I continued to move her hand over my cock, my desire building at the base of my spine like a ball of fire, getting ready to explode.

"Someone may come in," she replied, skittish feelings fighting with her arousal.

"Nay, lass, we are alone," Simon said. "Ye are so wet, dripping on my fingers."

"Perfect," Rhys added and then her hand gripped my cock tightly as, I assumed, Rhys' finger found her ass and began playing.

"You shouldn't touch me there," she said, trying to squirm away, but she was held fast.

Sweat coated my brow, as I was more than ready to come, seeing Simon's hand glistening with her arousal and knowing Rhys was beginning to play with her ass. I shifted my body to the side so that with the next vigorous stroke of her hand, I came.

I groaned and pulsed my hips as rope after thick rope of my seed shot onto the hay and dirt at our feet.

"Oh," Olivia said in surprise. My eyes fell shut as I savored the intense feeling, knowing I'd taught her how to work a cock. I released her hand, my cock too sensitive now for her to touch it. I sighed loudly, and then grinned, for I couldn't help it. The desperate ache had been relieved, if only temporarily. As for the others, they'd have their turn next. I moved to the side and the men walked her forward so I could place her hands on a hitching rail used while grooming a horse. "Put your hand here, love," I directed. Once she did so, Rhys pulled her hips back slightly and I knelt down before her, Simon at her side.

"What are you doing?" she asked.

"Playing," I said. "I'm going to play with your pussy and Rhys is going to play with your ass. We're going to make you come while you stroke Simon's cock next."

I took the hem of her dress from Simon as the man undid his pants and pulled his cock free, ready for her to practice her hand skills on another cock. It was Simon's turn to direct her, as I was more than content to play with her pretty pink pussy and stroke her to pleasure.

"My...I don't think you're supposed to be playing with my *ass*." She whispered the last word as if it were a dirty word.

"No, love, we will almost always play with your arse when we are with you, for soon you will take all three of us at the same time. One of our cocks will be in that sweet mouth, another in your perfect pink pussy, and the last in this tight, hot arse. Don't panic, we have to take your maidenhead first, but your pretty arse needs to be trained to take a cock."

I was flicking my tongue over her distended clit as my fingers held her open, but when she stiffened against my mouth and groaned, I had to assume Rhys had slipped a slick finger into her arse. I loved the taste of her on my tongue; the scent of her was sweet and so heady my cock was getting hard again.

"She's verra good with her hand," Simon commented, his voice deep and guttural. "I'm nae gonna last, lass, so finish me." I heard him shift, then grunt, a hand slapping against the wooden wall to hold himself up.

"I've got one finger in her and she's so tight. I think, Cross, every time you flick her clit she clenches her arse nice and tight. When we get our cocks in here it's going to feel like pure heaven."

"It...it's too much," she gasped.

"My finger? It's just the beginning. Relax, that's it. It's my turn to come, love, but Simon's going to take my place."

"Oh," she gasped as the men switched places.

"I need a little honey from the honey pot, lass," Simon told her and I saw his finger dip into her pussy and come out dripping wet before moving over the tiny rosebud.

"Give me your hand, love, and show me what you've learned. I bet you can do it without me helping. Ah, yes," Rhys hissed. I glanced to my left and saw that Olivia was stroking Rhys' cock all on her own, one of his hands on the wall to keep himself upright, the other clenched in a tight fist at his side.

"Such a perfect, tight arse, lass. I'm going to start pushing in now, just like Rhys did."

She whimpered, but knew that for Simon's large size, he would be gentle with her. The pain and pleasure mix of ass play had me sucking on Olivia's clit with more vigor and dipping a finger into her pussy. After last night, I had a good idea of how to get her to come and I wanted to do that while Simon's finger was in her ass. I only wanted ass play to be associated with pleasure, right from the very first breaching.

"Cross is going to make ye come, lass. Take a deep breath now, and let it out. Such a good lass," he soothed as she groaned, a mixture of new feelings, being filled in the ass and pleasure of having her clit and pussy worked. "Be verra quiet so no one hears ye being pleased by your men."

When the fingers of her free hand tangled in my hair I knew she was about to come. I could feel her inner walls clenching down on the tip of my finger.

"Now, lass. Come for us now."

She did, right on command, her body dripping its pleasure onto my fingers as she bit her lip to stifle her cry, her body convulsing with her release.

"She's gripping my cock so tightly," Rhys said just before he groaned and I knew he'd found his pleasure as well.

I sat back on my haunches and wiped the back of my hand over my mouth as I looked up at Olivia. Her eyes were closed, her skin flushed, her mouth open and breathing heavily. Simon was still gently moving his finger within her ass until the last bits of her pleasure waned. When she opened her eyes, he stepped away and her dress fell back to the floor.

"That's why we didn't come to you, but instead of just playing, we would have taken you, taken your virginity, and when we do, we don't plan to let you up," I told her. Her pale eyes looked down at me, foggy with her arousal and quite pleased with herself.

"For days," Rhys added as he buttoned up his pants.

9

LIVIA

On our ride to the Bridgewater ranch, I didn't raise the topic of my angry outburst from the morning, for if I did, they might want to talk about the things we did directly *after*. While I now understood their reasons for leaving me alone in the guest room, I hadn't at the time. Fortunately, their tempers were such that they took the reasoning for my ire into account and hadn't yelled or even argued.

Twenty minutes alone in the stable with the trio had me learning there was more to having them take my virginity than I first imagined. It wasn't fumbling beneath the sheets in the dark.

When, to my complete surprise, Cross had opened up the front of his pants and pulled his...his cock out, I had no idea one could be so large. I assumed they were much smaller, for the idea of him fitting within me was preposterous. Then I saw Cross' cock and it was even thicker and at that point, besides being pleasantly distracted, I didn't want to consider it, or the size of Rhys' even further. They'd said they'd wait until we were at the ranch to do more—more of exactly what I couldn't be sure—so I had a reprieve until then.

Reprieve or not, that hadn't kept them from putting their fingers in my bottom, at least only two of them did, and that had been enough. I'd had no idea that was something done between married people; no whispering I'd heard by the younger married ladies had ever mentioned such attentions. It had felt...odd, and when Rhys had first pushed into me, it had burned a bit. But when he began moving very slowly in and out, like Cross' finger had been in my woman's core, it had been completely different. The intensity of the feelings— the *pleasure* there—was absolutely overwhelming. When Cross had licked me on that special spot between my legs, I'd come and come hard. It was as if each time they took me over that brink it was better and better.

I knew men felt pleasure as well, for why else would there be brothels in every town, sometimes more than one? The look on their each of their faces as they came was...powerful, for I knew my hand sliding up and down each of their thick shafts had been what did it. I'd caught on quickly after Cross had showed me how, and the smooth, hot, hard feel of each of them was impressive. Unfortunately, none of the men gave me much time to focus on them, for they'd very thoroughly taken care of me. When it was three against one, I was always going to be overwhelmed.

For the duration of the ride to Bridgewater I sat on one man's lap, then another, as it seemed they wished to take turns holding me. I was too sated from their attentions to truly argue, and perhaps this had been their strategy – to pleasure me so I wouldn't argue. I didn't comment on being shared, as I was quickly learning they were very possessive men and while they worked together as a team, they were individuals and needed their own time with me.

"Is that the stud horse you spoke about at the dance?" I asked, looking at the animal that was being led behind us. After our last break, Cross had climbed onto his animal and took my hand and lifted me up onto his lap. "Why can't I ride him?"

"It is, but while broken, he's new to us and we don't want to risk anyone getting hurt. Don't you like riding with your men?" he asked, running his chin over the top of my head.

I did, actually, enjoy being held. "It is new to me to sit with a man. Well, to do anything really with a man. Not only is it unseemly to do so before now, I was quite independent." The past tense disturbed me, for now that I was married, would I have the same liberties as I had when I lived with my uncle? I hadn't gallivanted all over Helena as my days were structured with social and charitable functions as well as playing hostess for my uncle—

"Oh," I said.

"What is it?" he asked.

"I just realized that my uncle did so much...presentation to keep me from knowing about his relationship with the Tannenbaums."

"How so?"

The horse's plodding gait had me shifting into Cross' body. While I wore a bonnet on my head, his large body shielded me quite well from the sun.

"He had dinner parties and could have done it with Belinda as hostess in my stead. He kept his house just for me. We didn't sit with the Tannenbaums at church and I know Uncle Allen didn't see them all the time, probably not as frequently as he'd liked. He sacrificed so much for me."

I felt Cross shake his head. "He didn't do it only for you. Do you think your friends and the other church members would approve of him sharing a wife with Roger?"

"No. Am I going to live solely with Simon then to keep up appearances?"

"Nay, lass," Simon said, bringing his horse up so he rode alongside us on one side, Rhys moved into position on the other. "At Bridgewater having several men care for one wife is the norm."

I glanced at him, so dark and handsome, his whiskers coming in quickly and black hair now covered his jaw. His hat was low on his head and he rode a horse easily. While he was at ease, I could see his eyes scan the horizon for any hidden threats. Rhys seemed to be the one who was studious and bookish. Cross was more lighthearted, while Simon was the serious one, although the attraction was not any less for it, the intensity of his gaze upon me just as hot.

He seemed to be the one who was the most protective, perhaps even possessive. We'd left Helena without incident but they had wanted to keep watch for Peters or any man he might have sent. So far, nothing.

"I've never heard of several men marrying one woman and I have to admit, am not used to the idea."

"You wouldn't be used to the idea of wedding just one man as quickly as you did either," Rhys added. "It was done with extreme haste."

True, it would have been a surprise even then.

"Simon and I were in the same army regiment. We left England and were stationed in the tiny country of Mohamir."

"Isn't that near the Ottoman Empire?"

Rhys smiled. "You know your geography. It is that country's custom for a woman to be married to more than one man, in some cases brothers, in others, men who have come together and vowed to treasure and protect one woman."

"In England, lass," Simon swore, "those bloody Brits often marry for social standing or money and the men have strict rules for their wives, but none for themselves."

"There have to be some who marry for love," I countered.

"Aye, lass, that is true, but in the circles I traveled, it wasna the norm. We had friends whose wives were neglected and unhappy while they were off slumming in brothels. It disgusted us as to the lack of honor. In Mohamir, however, that honor existed and it was the way we want to be."

"Don't you and Rhys someday want women for your yourselves?" I asked Cross.

I didn't like the possibility of being left for someone else, for they were handsome men and surely women had flocked to them in the past. How could they not be sought after in the future as well?

"No, love. We only want you."

"We will always want just you," Rhys added. He angled his head and looked at me with dark intensity. "You may not think it now, but the Mohamiran way protects the wife, for if something were to happen to one of us, you would still have the others to cherish you - you and children that will surely come. You will never need of anything ever again."

"If you liked their ways so much, why didn't you stay there?"

"Our commander did something...terrible and one of our friends, Ian, was framed for the crime. We knew he was innocent and justice would not be served, so we left," Rhys explained. "As a group, we chose to band together and make a new life. We traveled to America to find a place where we could practice what we learned in Mohamir, while escaping Evans and any repercussions that might follow us."

I turned my head so I could look up at Cross. His eyes were so green in comparison to Rhys and Simon's dark ones. "What about you? You sound as American as me. Surely you didn't spend time in Mohamir."

He kissed the tip of my nose. "I was raised in Boston and that was where their ship came in. I wasn't as big back then as I am now, but I was involved in a fight to protect a woman and these two helped me."

"There's more to the story than that, isn't there?"

Cross put his chin on top of my head once again, forcing me to not look at him anymore. "My past isn't a good story, love." His voice sounded flat at the mention of his childhood. "Bridgewater is my home now. Your home. It is where our future is. *You* are our future."

10

HYS

"You went to Helena for a stud horse and came back with a bride as well?" Kane asked, holding the halter as Simon brushed the animal down. He'd been working in the stable when we arrived and had come to help with our horses.

"Turns out the man who sold us the horse is a bloody bastard and hurt Olivia and most likely set fire to her house." Cross shared the events of our trip with our friend.

"So you married her for protection alone?"

"We wanted her the first time we saw her," I stated plainly. "I knew when I danced with her, had my hands on her. There wasn't any decision to make."

Kane nodded. He was as dark as I, although a few inches taller. He'd married Emma the previous summer, saving her from a ridiculous brothel marriage auction. At the time I hadn't exactly understood the depth of his awareness that Emma was the woman for him and for Ian. They'd had only a minute or two to look at her before the auction had begun, but they'd known. Just like Cross and I had known at the dance.

He and Ian had protected Emma from the other men at the auction, but they'd married her because they wanted her. There was no doubt of the love match. They were very attentive to her, and she'd given birth to their first child not long ago.

Kane smiled and nodded. "Once the women hear of her existence, they will want to meet her straight away."

"Tomorrow," I said.

Cross shook his head. "Two days. We have yet to fuck her."

"And yet you are here talking with me?" Kane asked, head cocked in surprise.

"Simon remains at the house with her." After her enlightening outburst this morning, we agreed one of us would stay near until she became comfortable with us. "She's taking a bath. We gave her one hour of peace before we descend." Anticipation laced my every word.

"Go," Kane said. "See to your wife. I'll have the others help get the animals settled. I give you three days, consider the extra day a wedding present, and then we meet her."

Ten minutes later we entered through the kitchen door. Simon was sitting at the table reading a book.

He put it down on the table. "I have nae read one word as I ken she's up there," he pointed up at the ceiling, "naked and in a bathtub. After helping her with one last night, tis bloody impossible to sit here and give her some time."

"We're done giving her time," I said, turning toward the hallway.

Simon stood, the chair legs sliding loudly across the floor. "About damn time," he grumbled.

It was time to make Olivia ours.

We found her not in the washroom, but in Simon's bedroom, a bath sheet wrapped around her damp, naked body. I almost came in my pants just looking at her. I tossed the bag of my handcrafted dildos and plugs onto the bed for later and closed the distance between us. We'd surprised her, even though we'd clamored up the stairs and down the hall.

"You have a lovely home," she said, glancing around the room. We'd built the house with large bedrooms, for we were large men, and we'd hoped to someday have a wife who would spend the night in each of our rooms in turn. We also had extra bedrooms built with the hopes of children. Perhaps that day would come soon, for if we were skilled enough and the timing right, it could be in nine months or so. The idea of filling Olivia's womb with our seed and having it take root, to watch her belly swell with our child made my cock press painfully against my pants. If she looked, she wouldn't be able to miss it.

I chuckled at how she was trying to make small talk with just a scrap of white cotton covering her. She knew what was coming, for we'd clearly stated we would wait until we took her, and she was nervous. I didn't blame her. Three randy, eager men were going to strip her bare and take her virginity. Because of this, I took a deep breath and tried to will my cock down.

"Nervous?" I asked.

She gave me a tremulous smile. "You are very daunting." Her pale gaze shifted over each of us and widened as she watched Simon undo the buttons of his shirt.

"Nay, lass. We are three men who want to please our wife, to make her ours." He tossed his shirt onto the bed and then began to toe off his boots. I was undoing my own shirt when he spoke again. "We willna hurt ye. Ever. Now drop the covering so we can see ye."

Biting her lip, she considered, then dropped the sheet, letting it swirl to the floor at her feet.

I hissed out a breath at the sight of her creamy skin, her high, pert breasts, the dark thatch of hair at the juncture of her thighs. Her legs were long and she had dainty feet and her hair was pulled back into a ribbon at her nape.

The other men were almost as completely bare while I was still dressed so I, too, stripped. Clothing wasn't necessary for what we were going to do...for the next three days.

"Her pussy needs a shave," Cross commented.

Simon nodded his head. "Aye."

They stood eyeing her, Simon's arms over his broad chest. Their cocks curved up toward their navels.

One of Olivia's small hands moved to cover her pussy. "What? Shave my...my...why?"

"Did you like how we licked and sucked and ate at your pussy last night?" Cross asked, stepping closer. She retreated and the back of her legs bumped into the bed. "The way I did this morning?"

"Dinna lie, for we ken the truth. Ye loved it...three times," Simon said, walking around to the far side of the bed, placing a knee upon it and coming to kneel behind her.

She glanced over her shoulder, then at me and Cross. "Yes, all right, I did. I liked it very much."

Her eyes kept moving, looking us over one at a time, curious and nervous.

"This is your first time seeing a naked man, love?" I asked, brushing a dark curl behind her ear.

"Yes."

"Have a look at Cross while I go get the supplies for your shave. Simon will get you in position."

As I walked down the hall, I heard Cross' voice. "When you're pussy's all bare, the feelings will be more intense. Besides, we want to be able to see all your pretty pink flesh."

I grabbed the soap cup and brush and a washcloth and stopped in the doorway. Simon sat on the bed with Olivia's back at his front, her legs bent and spread wide at the edge of the bed, her pussy on perfect display. Cross had pulled a chair up from the corner of the room and sat directly in front of her.

I offered the supplies to Cross and he quickly settled into his task.

"But I don't want it bare," she replied, trying to squirm. Simon had his hands beneath her knees holding her still. No amount of effort on her part would have her moving.

"*We* want you bare so bare you will be."

Cross paused in his work and with his free hand, slipped a finger down the length of her folds, then slipped it inside. "This is our pussy, Olivia. Ours. Soon enough you will not doubt that."

A slippery wet sound filled the air as he pulled his finger free and returned to his task. She whimpered and we all knew she was not under much duress.

I moved onto the bed and positioned myself so I could play with her breasts. The flesh was so soft and plush, firm yet supply and pliant. The pale nipples tightened before our eyes and she gasped as I tweaked one, then the other.

"Like that?" I asked, her pale eyes shifting to me.

Cross slid the razor lower over her delicate skin and the patch of bare skin grew.

"Rhys," she murmured.

"What, love? Yes, you like it?"

She nodded her head against Simon's chest.

"How about now?" Did she like a little pain with her pleasure when I tugged on the tip, then pinched it? Did she like it soothing and gentle when I took the worked flesh into my mouth and licked over it and suckled? I felt her hands tangle in my hair as I closed my lips around one nipple and worked the other with my fingers.

"She dripping," Cross said, wiping the clean towel over her now smooth flesh.

"Get my bag," I told him as I saw her bare pussy for the first time. Her lips there were dainty and a lush pink, glistening with her arousal.

Reaching on the other side of her, Cross brought the bag onto his lap and pulled out the items I'd made. Winter was long in the Montana Territory and without a woman to keep us warm, I'd discovered that woodworking was a hobby at which I was quite good. I worked many things on the lathe for my friends' use on their wives. Dildos and butt plugs of various shapes and sizes, often made to specification. I'd made some for our future bride so we could play with her, however none had been used until now.

"What are those for?" Olivia asked, crinkle forming in her brow. Simon had not released her legs, which was good, for she was in the perfect position. Cross held up a thin, long dildo for me to see and I nodded.

"Here. Take it," Cross told her as he held it up.

Olivia took the wooden object and inspected it. It was dark wood, very smooth and very narrow, only as wide as my smallest finger, much smaller than any of our cocks. I'd made it just for this specific occasion, for her to take her own maidenhead as we watched. None of us wished to cause her pain and once she broke through with the dildo, we could take her without any fear on her part. Only pleasure.

Cross placed his palm on her lower belly and placed his thumb directly over her pink pearl. We could all see it clearly now and Olivia cried out at his touch. Her hand gripped the dildo tightly so her fingers turned white.

"I've made many things to pleasure you with. Right now, you're going to fuck yourself with the dildo, love, and break through your maidenhead."

"But...oh God," she moaned, Simon doing an amazing job of building her arousal, however she was quite sensitive and very responsive. I began to play with her breasts again, for I wanted her to be completely brainless and only feel. I wanted her to *want* to fuck herself. "I thought, I thought one of you would do that."

"We will, soon," Simon growled, barely holding on to his willpower. Just looking down the length of her body—parted lips, long neck, pert breasts with furled tips, lush belly and hips, smooth and bare pussy, then Cross' thumb working her slippery clit. She was all I'd dreamed of and more. There was just one tiny barrier still in the way.

"It's going to slide in so easily," I murmured. "Once that barrier is gone, we're going to fuck you. One at a time."

"I'm first, lass, and I canna wait. Can ye feel my cock at yer back?"

Simon took her hand and adjusted her grip on the dildo so she held it like a small spear and lined it up with her slick pussy.

"Will it hurt?" she asked me, her head tilted to the side, her pale eyes filled with trepidation. Cross worked her clit and her eyes slipped closed. I kissed her lips, for how could I not, then whispered, "If it does, it will only be for a brief moment. We will be watching, love, watching you ready yourself for us. It is going to be so beautiful to see."

"Now, lass."

_____

11

LIVIA

I was so overwhelmed! For a few minutes in my bath, I'd had private time to think about what was to come with the men, with their taking my virginity, and then they'd all but stomped up the steps, stripped off their clothes and beat their chests like cavemen. I had hoped for a husband who would dote and offer me attention and affection, and Cross, Simon and Rhys certainly did all of that. Their fervent attentions would be something to which I would have to accustom.

They wanted me! Even a very innocent virgin like me couldn't miss that fact. While I'd had my hand on their cocks earlier, seeing them naked and fully aroused was something else. Seeing one virile, well-formed man with a cock that was big enough to curve up and practically touch his navel was impressive, but I had three. Three! Three men and three cocks.

Simon was solid and broad and big and very, very large. Everywhere. His cock was a ruddy red, the head flared and almost angry looking. Rhys, equally dark, was leaner, taller and his cock seemed longer, which should have been impossible because I didn't think Simon was remotely small. Cross, with his light hair and fairer skin, had hard, sleek muscles and a pale nest of hair at the base of his cock that made him so very different from the other two. That was just their bodies. The looks on their faces were almost predatory, as if they intended to circle me, stalk me, then take me.

The way my body heated at the idea, the way my nipples pebbled at the thought; I wanted it. I wanted *them*.

I was also...scared.

I'd forgotten all about being scared when Simon had held my legs open so they could shave me. If their goal was to keep me off kilter, then it was working, for I had never imagined such a thing, but Rhys' words and then his hands on my breasts had distracted me. *Everything* they did was a distraction!

Once finished, Cross began touching me with just his thumb and in a very specific spot. Circling and circling he worked that bundle of nerves that spread pleasure to my fingers, my toes, to my nipples, to every part of my body. Even then, looking down at Cross's cock, rigid and long between his legs, I'd thought he'd lean forward and push it in, but instead they'd pulled out this slim wooden contraption—a dildo, they called it—for me to break through my maidenhead.

My inner walls clenched as they gave me the directions, and again when Cross guided my hand and this wooden phallus to my opening. My newly shaved skin there felt cool, slick and very, very bare. I watched the dildo disappear, little by little as it began to fill me. My body clamped down on it, but it wasn't big like the men's cocks and I was frustrated. When I was able to slide it in so easily and so far, I knew something was wrong. I'd heard about pain during the first time, of some membrane inside ripping and bleeding. A man expected their bride to be a virgin and this barrier was the true sign, the official notice that she was pure.

My eyes widened in surprise when the side of my hand bumped my newly bare skin.

"It...it didn't hurt."

There was something wrong with me and they'd think I was

a whore!

I let go of the dildo's small handle and grabbed Cross' forearms. I had to make him understand, for he could clearly see from his vantage point what was happening.

"I'm a virgin, truly." I tried to sit up, but Simon's hold on my legs prevented it. Slowly, Cross eased the dildo out and I gasped at the feel of the hard wood brushing against my inner walls. He held it up, coated in my glistening arousal, but no virgin's blood.

"Cross, please, you have to believe me!" I cried. I tugged at Simon's hold on my legs and he released me and I scrambled to sit up. There was nothing with which to cover myself and I could not escape the dominating presence of three large, aroused men. I couldn't discern from their faces what they were feeling. Did they think I'd tricked them? Tears welled—I couldn't stop them—and slipped down my cheeks.

Simon took hold of my arm and pulled me into him, his skin so warm and I could feel his cock prodding my belly.

"We believe you, lass," he said, wiping my tears away with his thumbs.

I frowned. "How? Isn't there supposed to be blood?"

Rhys shrugged, but did not seem overly concerned. "I believe sometimes it is just that way. Have you ever played with yourself? Put your fingers inside or used something like the dildo? It's all right if you did, for I would want you to lay back and show us how you pleased yourself."

I shook my head. "No. I've never touched myself like that. Only...only with you have I felt this way."

All three of the men smiled and I felt the fear, the chill of it, ebb away.

"You're not mad?" she breathed.

"Nay, lass. This is so much better, for now we can take ye as we wish."

"I thought that was what you had been doing," I countered. "You even shaved me."

"Aye, but if your maidenhead had been there and it tore, you'd be verra sore. Are ye sore, lass?"

I shook my head. I was...needy.

"Then it is going to be a long night, for our cocks are eager to fill you, to mark you, to make you ours." Simon and Cross traded places, and I remembered Simon said he would be first.

Cross angled me back on his arm to kiss me, his tongue plunging into my mouth directly and I tasted myself on his tongue; it was so carnal to learn the flavor of my own desire. His hand was on the back of my neck, holding me just as he wanted me and he overwhelmed me. His own need was obvious in his touch, his kiss, his very breath.

When he pulled back, his breathing was rough. "Lay back now and let us have our way with you."

I was so relieved they believed me that I did as he bid without question, although the kiss had certainly helped. I wanted to please them and clearly I became upset if I couldn't, or if I perceived some flaw in myself that would have them finding me deficient. But Cross' mouth was red and slick from our kiss and his eyes held secret promises I wanted to learn. The only way to do that was to lay back and let them teach me.

All three of them shifted to give me room, and Cross was kissing me once again, Rhys returned his attentions to my breasts—he seemed to have a slight fixation with them—and Simon nudged my thighs apart with his hands and flicked his tongue over the place where Cross' thumb had been rubbing.

They were definite warriors, all of them, for they gave all their energies to a task and if they wanted to defeat their opponent, they could do so with sheer will alone. While I was not the enemy, they definitely laid siege and I could not uphold any of my defenses against them, not that I even wanted to. My head fell back and my eyes closed as the delicious pinch on my nipples set my body on fire. A hint of perspiration coated my skin as they again built me up to the brink of that sweet pleasure. They'd given it to me several times now and I recognized what it felt like just beforehand. I cried out and I could feel my belly tighten, my knees squeeze Simon's dark head for I did not wish him to move from that pleasure spot. I wanted him to stay right...there...and...lick...one...more...time. Yes!

I screamed my release, every muscle in my body tensing, my back arching off the bed, my inner walls clenching down on nothing...that thin dildo had just been a quick tease. They didn't stop their attentions, only Cross stopped kissing me but instead stroked a hand gently over my hair and crooned to me.

You are so beautiful. I love to see you come.

I felt a dip in the bed just before Simon's knees nudged my thighs wide as he settled into the cradle of my hips, his cock slipping over my slick woman's core. I was still coming, the luscious feelings making my heart pound, the blood roaring in my ears, as the large head stretched my opening as he slowly pushed his way in.

"Yes!" I cried, my inner walls now having something to clench onto.

"Christ, ye are so bloody tight."

I looked up at Simon, his eyes so dark as to be black. His hair fell over his forehead and his face was all hard lines, his neck tightly corded. He held himself up on his forearms, the hair on his chest tickling my breasts and tormenting my nipples. Rhys and Cross were watching, hands stroking their cocks.

Slowly, Simon slipped into me, one delicious inch at a time. While I'd just come, the new sensation of being stretched wide, being filled deeper and deeper had my arousal simmering. My body was soft and pliant and I brought my legs up to Simon's hips, giving him room to go even deeper. Finally, his hips bumped into my bottom and he was fully seated.

My eyes widened at the feel of him and he watched me carefully.

"Am I hurting ye?" he asked, his voice as dark and rumbly as a thunderstorm.

I shook my head and clenched down on him, testing my body.

"Nay, dinna do that unless ye want me to move."

I grinned and did it again. He groaned and gritted his teeth. "I want you to move."

His eyes flew open and he grinned, his blinding smile combined with the dark intent in his eyes had me eager.

"I *need* you to move, Simon."

And so he did, slowly at first, but when I arched up to meet him, tilted my hips into his thrusts, he didn't hold back.

I wrapped my legs around his waist and held onto his shoulders. "Yes!" I cried out, his cock rubbing over new places deep within me that had me back to the brink within seconds. He rubbed over my clit with each stroke and I just broke, coming again while Simon continued to move. It was so much better than ever before, the way his body could make me come, knowing that it was because we were joined, that his cock being so deep inside me. I screamed, for I could not hold it back. I felt my body soften and get even wetter, the sound of our joining loud. Simon's breathing was ragged and all at once he stiffened, embedded all the way and groaned. I felt his hot seed, the thick emission I'd stroked from him in the stable just that morning, flood my womb, coating me and marking me. There was no doubt I was his.

He kissed me gently, his breathing mixing with mine as he settled. While he was still inside of me, I could feel the wetness seeping out around him and when he pulled out, I whimpered.

"I'm speechless, lass," he said standing up before me. I was too replete to close my legs as I looked at his cock, slick and wet from our combined fluids, still hard. His face lost that tenseness and his smile was soft. He appeared very satisfied and I felt a surge of...something at knowing I was the one to make him that way.

Rhys moved off the bed to stand before me, his cock weeping clear fluid from the tip as his hand gripped the base. "I love this view. Our wife, sated from coming, our seed all over your pretty pussy. My turn, love."

He settled in between my thighs, his cock nudging my inner thigh. Up on his hand, he looked down at me. "Sore?"

I shook my head, anxious and ready for his turn. He took one leg and lifted my knee up to his hip, aligned his cock at my entrance and slid all the way in in one long, smooth stroke.

"Oh!" I gasped. This angle was different than how Simon had me.

The feel of Rhys' cock was different and when he began to move, I recognized that he fucked differently as well. Simon had been gentle, perhaps because of his large size he had been afraid to hurt me, but when he let his baser needs take over, he became rougher, but even then he hadn't hurt me.

Rhys' motions were more deliberate, as if he knew just how to use his cock to bring me to pleasure as fast as possible. He was almost ruthless in his attentions, precise in his motions. "So hot and slippery wet. You feel incredible."

I smiled at him and he lowered his head to kiss me as his hips moved, filling me again and again.

"You'll come for me."

He said it as if I didn't have a choice. Perhaps I didn't, for he used his cock like a weapon and I was powerless against it. I could do nothing but give in, and so I did. As I tensed and tried to hold him within me, he came on a harsh stroke, a guttural sound escaping his lips that were sealed over mine.

When he pulled out of me, a gush of seed slipped from me and he stood before me, just as Simon had, proud of that fact.

"It's Cross' turn, lass. Ye dinna want him to feel neglected, do ye?" Simon sat on the edge of the bed, his back resting against the brass railed footboard. Only Cross looked tense between the three of them and I now knew why.

"Up," Cross said.

Slowly, as my muscles were as soft and loose as pulled taffy, I came up and onto my knees, the seed sliding down my thighs. Cross looked down at it and slid a finger through the wetness. "I'm going to add to this," he vowed.

Moving to the head of the bed, he sat with his back propped up against the pillows. "How are you at riding a horse?" he asked.

I frowned in confusion. "Quite well."

He grinned and held out his hand. "Good. Consider me your stud horse and take me for a ride."

I glanced down at Cross' cock, thick and erect and very ready to fuck.

"Straddle his legs," Rhys directed.

I took Cross' hand and crawled up the bed so that I had my knees on either side of his hips.

"Work yourself down onto my cock."

Placing a hand on his shoulder for balance, I met Cross' pale eyes as I shifted my hips so that the tip of his cock slid over me, then settled at my opening. With all of the other men's seed on me, it was not difficult to have him fill me. My eyes widened at the feel of him coming up and into me. This was so different than when I was on my back. I could look at Cross, see his expression as my body accepted him and opened for him. When he was fully embedded, I sat completely upon his thighs and we both groaned.

"Now, Olivia. Please. I've been patient, but no longer, for you feel too damn good. Ride me and ride me hard. I want to see your breasts move as you do, I want to see you come."

Carefully, I lifted back up as I bit my lip, wanting to do it right. I saw the heat flare in Cross' eyes. When I took him into me again, I bumped my clit on his body and I moaned, shifting my hips and almost grinding myself onto him. I wanted not only to be filled, but my clit to be worked. The combination had me moving; I had no choice for my body took over, my needs replaced my thoughts and so I moved blindly, mindlessly to what felt good.

I knew the other men were watching. I knew I was taking what I wanted from Cross. I knew they might think me wanton, my breasts bouncing as I moved so aggressively, but I didn't care. I'd been fucked twice already and knew they were passionate men and that they'd unleashed the passion within me. And so I used Cross' cock to my needs over and over until I was screaming, gripping his shoulders so hard he'd have indentations there surely.

My eyes flew open at the sheer intensity of the angle and the way it rubbed over new places.

Cross hissed. "She's milking my cock. I can't hold back. Take it, love, take it all," Cross growled.

He thrust his hips up and against me, filling me like a geyser, erupting up and into my womb, flooding me in his own wash of hot seed. I fell forward onto his chest, my sweaty breasts and belly slick against his. I tried to catch my breath as I listened to his heartbeat begin to slow. I could do nothing, nothing at all, for I was done in by pleasure. I didn't know whose hands were stroking my back and I didn't care, for I knew that while they were individuals, they claimed me as one. While it may be one man's hand on my back, they were all soothing me. It was my last thought as I fell into sleep.

12

IMON

"Good morning, lass."

Olivia stirred in my arms, her arse rubbing against my already hard cock. After she'd fallen asleep, I'd tucked her beneath the covers and settled in behind her, an arm over her waist, my hand cupping her breast perfectly. I should have had a difficult time sleeping as I was unused to sharing a bed, but I found having her tucked in safely with me was enough to put me into a sound sleep. I was accustomed to being awakened by nightmares, the sheets a tangle about my sweat soaked body as I awoke on a groan or sob, but my night was quiet, my mind at ease.

She stiffened briefly, and then, most likely realizing where she was and who was holding her, she relaxed. "Hello," she replied, her voice shy. "Where are the others?"

"We willna be together all of the time. They are asleep in their own beds."

"You will take turns with me?"

I shrugged, and then frowned at the idea. "You make it sound as if ye are a toy and we are a bunch of children."

She turned in my hold to look up at me, her pale eyes clear and alight with humor. "Yes, I believe that is an apt description."

I could not help but push her onto her back and prop myself above her. As we stirred, her sweet scent along with the tang of sex swirled around us. It was a heady mix, reminding me that she was soft and lush and feminine as well as the vixen we did all of the things to the night before.

"Dinna ye wish to get to know me?" I asked.

She nodded into the pillow. "You're the brawny one." She ran her small hand down over my chest and I sucked in my muscles of my belly as her hand worked lower, but didna touch my cock. She was nae forward yet in her wants, but she would be soon enough. "I also think you are the brooder, the one who worries the most."

She was insightful and that had me looking away, afraid she might see all the answers in my eyes. While Rhys had seen cruelty in the regiment, he hadna been there the day Evans slaughtered that family. I had and it affected me still. Even though our friend, Ian, was man pinned with the crime, the event followed more than just him halfway around the world.

"I take my responsibilities seriously, ye ken, and they now include ye. Are ye sore?" I lifted up off her enough to look down her naked body. Her breasts were coral tipped and just begging to be licked and sucked. The flesh between her thighs, now bare and smooth, surely ached to be stroked.

She cupped my chin and forced my head back up to meet her steady gaze. "You are changing the subject. You don't have to protect me from everything," she replied.

My heart hurt, actually ached at her simple statement. While I always had Rhys and Cross to watch out for me, this tiny slip of a woman was volunteering to be my protector as well.

"My little lioness," I whispered. "Dinna worry, lass, for tis just my dreams that haunt me. Enough about me, ye didna answer my question. Are ye sore?"

She continued to look at me for a few more moments, and then replied. "My body aches...down there, but I'm not sore."

"When I plow a field, me back hurts the next day." I brushed her dark hair back from her face. "When I plow yer field," she slapped my arm and I grinned, "ye are the one who is aching."

"Simon," she replied, eyes rolling.

"I bet ye are aching for my touch, for my cock."

She glanced away, but I turned her chin back. "Nay lass, now it is you who must answer the difficult question. Ye dinna need to be embarrassed. Yer body, when we are alone, it belongs to me."

Her pale eyes widened and she licked her lips. "I...I feel empty."

I couldn't help the groan that escaped and I shifted my hips so my cock rubbed up against her belly. "Do you want yer pussy filled?"

She bit her lip, glanced up at me through her dark lashes, then shyly nodded.

What my wife wanted, I gave.

CROSS

"I don't think three days is going to be enough," I said, washing the dinner dishes. It had been two days since we brought Olivia to the ranch and tomorrow we would have to share her with the others by joining everyone for lunch. "Surely Emma, Ann and Laurel are driving their men crazy with the waiting."

"Making Olivia come is more of a priority than satisfying the other ladies' eagerness to meet her. Each of them only has two men to share; Olivia has three. We *should* get an extra day," Rhys grumbled.

"It isna as if we have to give her up, just take her to lunch," Simon replied. "I'm glad a trunk was picked up in town, for now she has some of her things. The smile on her face when Andrew delivered it was verra pleasing. Now she'll be comfortable in clothes."

I groaned at the idea of her clothed again since she'd been mostly naked for the past two days.

"We eat lunch, then we can bring her home and fuck her," Simon added.

"You two have each had a night with her." I could hear the crankiness of my voice. Hell, it wasn't crankiness; it was unrequited lust. "I had to lay in my own bed knowing she was naked and warm...without me. What the hell did you do with her in the middle of the night?" I asked Rhys, whose smile spread wide.

"She went to the wash room and when she returned, I had her bend over the side of the bed and fucked her from behind. You could have joined us. You could have taught her how to suck your cock."

I could easily picture Olivia naked and leaning on the side of the bed, her ass up, her legs spread so her bare pussy was visible, then taking her. I also thought of her mouth opened wide around my cock. I groaned and turned back to the dishes, washing them with extra vigor.

"That wasn't what you heard, though," he added. I glanced over my shoulder at him and he was now sharing details just to taunt me, his grin a giveaway. "The sounds she made were when I worked the plug into her arse. It was her first one. It wasn't very big, but she's tight there. I kept it in as I fucked her, and then the rest of the night. It's going to be sweet when we get a cock in there. So bloody sweet and tight."

I couldn't handle the torment any longer. I put the dish down, wiped my hands on my pants and stormed down the hall.

"Be sure to use the next sized plug on her tonight," Rhys called to me as Simon laughed.

"We're taking her together from now on. I don't like to wait my turn," I called back.

I took the stairs two at a time to the washroom. Olivia was taking another bath—we were making her dirty quite frequently—and I entered the room with only a brief knock.

She didn't cover herself this time. That was what I noticed first. She'd lost a bit of her inhibitions, but the blush on her cheeks indicated she was clinging to her innocence. After what Rhys did to her last night and what I planned for tonight, she wouldn't be innocent for much longer.

"I heard you are taking Rhys' plugs in your ass."

She flushed even more furiously as she stood in the tub, water sluicing down her body. I held out my hand to help her out and grabbed the bath sheet as I did and began to dry her. "Well?" I asked.

"You seem angry."

I shook my head and knelt down to dry one leg, then the other. Her smooth, bare pussy was in perfect alignment with my face and my mouth watered to taste her. "Not angry. Eager. Eager for you. It's my turn to play."

"Don't I ever get to play with you?"

I paused, my hands on her legs and looked up her luscious body to meet her eyes. "Haven't you been playing all this time?"

"Yes, but you three tell me what to do."

I began to dry her again, my hands slow so I could savor the feel of her. "You mean you want to be in charge."

She thought for a moment. "Yes, perhaps I do."

I stood and dried her belly, then her breasts, where I lingered. I loved the lush shape of them, their weight, the way the plump nipples tightened at the slightest touch. "Your ass training is not up for negotiation."

"But—"

I silenced her with a finger over her lips.

"Don't you want the three of us to take you at the same time?"

I pulled my finger away and she replied, "Yes."

"Then we need to prepare your ass to take a cock. You know we're big. We don't want to hurt you. Remember, nothing but pleasure." With that resolved, I continued, "We will get the next size plug settled into that delectable ass of yours, and then you can be in charge. All night long."

"The plug needs to stay in that long?" she asked, quirking one dark brow.

"At least a few hours. I have needs though, love, so if you're in charge, it's your job to meet them."

13

LIVIA

"How do you handle three men?" Emma asked, all dark hair and wide eyes.

She was married to Kane and Ian, who met us at their front door. From their accents, the men were English and Scot, just like Rhys and Simon and, from what I'd been told, had been in the same army regiment. Ann was equally interested to meet me, along with Laurel, and they'd pulled me into the kitchen away from the men. Ann was fair-haired and petite, while Laurel had fiery red hair and green eyes. They had me sit at the kitchen table and chop carrots as they moved about, cooking, stirring, checking if something was done baking.

I was not overly adept in the kitchen; I could make a simple meal for Uncle Allen and myself, but I couldn't handle a meal for fifteen, so I was content with the basic task they put before me. From what they told me, everyone at Bridgewater ate meals together—except when a group of them got married and didn't get out of bed for three days—and rotated the role as cook and dishwasher. While it seemed odd that they always ate at Kane, Ian and Emma's house, theirs was the largest and had, it seemed, been built with an overly large dining room for just this purpose. The only unmarried men left were Simon's brother and a man named MacDonald, both of whom had not arrived for lunch yet when I'd been dragged off. The ladies volunteered to cook today, clearly in order to get me alone and pepper me with questions.

"I don't know any other way," I replied. While I grew up imagining one husband, having three was the only way I knew.

"True, but men are fairly needy. Aren't you tired?" Ann asked, and then blushed. She had been married the longest to her husbands who were Robert and Andrew. They had an eight-month-old son who had been crawling on the floor under the supervision of his fathers, who'd introduced themselves as I walked by. "Surely you're tired if you are newly wed to those three."

They all giggled.

"Brody and Mason didn't let me out of bed for two days," Laurel said. She had wed in the winter, and from the story she told, was thankful to be alive since her men had rescued her from a blizzard.

"It seems," I started, then chopped through a large carrot with a loud thwap, "while they like to...to—"

I couldn't go on, for it was hard enough to get used to intimacy with the men, let alone talk about it with these women.

"You can share. We are very open at Bridgewater," Emma said. "My first day on the ranch Kane and Ian shaved my pussy and put a plug in my bottom with Laurel's husband right outside the door."

My mouth fell open. "Outside the—"

Laurel nodded and rolled her eyes. "He didn't see anything. If we need tending, our men make us their top priority."

I frowned. "I think my three are more private. While they like to share, they each also like to spend time alone with me," I admitted. "That's why it's been three days. While they...took me together," I blushed, but continued, "they also wanted time alone with me."

"See? They are needy," Ann commented.

"You are happy?" Emma asked. A baby's cry came from upstairs and she smiled. "Ellie's awake."

"Don't you have to get her?"

Emma shook her head and began to undo the bodice of her dress. "No. Kane and Ian dote on her terribly. One little whimper and they are checking on her. One of them will bring her down to me since she's hungry. Now, before they get here, are you happy?"

I thought about that. Rhys, Cross, and Simon had been nothing but kind to me. Attentive, thoughtful, aggressive, dominant, passionate.... The list was long, but none of them, except perhaps them sticking a plug that Rhys had made into my bottom, but otherwise...I *was* happy.

"So far, yes," I replied, for I thought that was a safe answer. There was a niggle of concern though, for the men were quite secretive. They knew much more about me than I did of them. That could be resolved over time, but not if they didn't share.

"I have a feeling they had difficult pasts," I surmised.

We heard heavy footsteps and silly talk at the same time.

"That would be Ian and Ellie," Emma said, smiling as she adjusted her dress and shift so her breast was exposed. "He's a big brawny man but melts as soon as he gets near his daughter."

In came Ian cradling a baby in his big arms. While Ellie was three months old, she appeared tiny being held by such a large man. He was crooning something to her in a different language, perhaps Gaelic. He kissed the baby's dark hair, much the same shade as her mother's, then handed her off. Emma settled her against her breast. Ian watched his wife and baby for a moment, leaned in and kissed the top of Emma's head almost reverently, then left.

Watching Emma with one of her doting husbands made me feel wistful. While Uncle Allen had doted on me and loved me, he'd had a secret family on the side, one he hadn't wished to include me in. Yes, I'd been involved with the Tannenbaums from the beginning, even being friends with their son, Tyler, who had moved to Billings the year before.

Tyler was two years old than I was, and we'd grown up together. His parents doted him on, but the Tannenbaums weren't his only parents. He had Uncle Allen, too. Was he Tyler's father, and I had never known it? They'd kept me on the periphery all this time. Surely Tyler knew the arrangement of his parents—two fathers and a mother, perhaps he'd even known we were actually cousins—while I hadn't known a thing. My parents had died in a stage accident, leaving me behind on their way to Bozeman.

Finding out about Uncle Allen's secret life had left me feeling somehow betrayed, as if I'd been an outsider all along.

I felt like an outsider now as I watched Emma, Ian and their baby. The bond was there between them, and with Kane as well. The other women had a place on the ranch, each of them a loving life with their men. But me? I was lost. I felt...extraneous and out of sorts. I didn't really know anything about Rhys, Cross or Simon and that only added to my discomfort.

Once Emma had the baby settled down to nurse, they glanced at each other, then at me. The meal was forgotten, at least for the moment. "You asked after their pasts. I think they've all had hardships, Ian especially." Emma looked both wistful and angry, probably because she wanted to protect her man from the burdens of his past, but couldn't. "I've heard some of what happened to them— Simon and Rhys—in Mohamir, for Ian is the one wanted for the crimes he didn't commit," Emma told me, her voice bitter. "But none of the men have shared details of what the crimes actually are, other than that their commander, Evans, killed innocent people."

"Simon woke up from a nightmare the other night, calling out the word *alea*, but I don't know what it means, or if it is something in that country's language or a name. When I asked if he was all right, he said 'dinna worry yerself' and held me as he fell back asleep." I shrugged. "He just seems to carry the past with him more heavily than most. Cross, too. He wasn't even with them in Mohamir. He's hinted at a terrible childhood, but again, he won't tell me more."

They all held secrets, it seemed. *Everyone* held secrets from *me*.

Laurel looked understanding. "Your men are more reserved, as we don't know much either. They'll tell you in time, if they choose. Just be there for him, tend to them as much as they tend to you. They might be big and formidable, especially Simon, but they have their weaknesses, they just don't show them often."

"Don't forget the biscuits," Emma reminded Laurel, who went to the oven to check on them.

"Their biggest weakness is now Olivia," Ann said, moving out of the way for Laurel as she stirred a pot on the stove. "They've taken on your enemy as their own."

When we arrived for lunch, Rhys told everyone about how we met, the threat to my life by Mr. Peters and now I felt guilty, for in truth, besides protecting me through marriage, my men would also have to defend against anything he might do. They'd assumed my burdens, even though they seemed to carry plenty of their own. Had they done this because they felt guilt at buying the horse from the man who may have burned down my house?

"I'm glad it doesn't bother you that the stud horse they purchased came from him," Laurel said, passing by me with a handful of cloth napkins to place on a tray.

I paused in the middle of a cut, knife in the air. While I hadn't forgotten that the men bought the horse from Mr. Peters, I'd put it to the back of my mind. It raised questions I hadn't considered before - questions that only now came about as I was married and entrenched in Bridgewater.

I stood and offered a small smile, wiping my hands together. "Will you excuse me for a moment?"

The ladies looked at me with surprise since I'd abruptly stood and wanted to leave in the middle of a conversation, but nodded. I left the kitchen and followed the men's voices to the room off the front entry. Comfortable chairs faced a cold fireplace. With eleven men in the room, they sat in the chairs but also leaned against the wall, relaxed and in easy conversation. When they saw me, they stood. While they all looked at me, the only men whose gazes held heat and possession were my three.

Rhys came over to me first, followed by Cross and Simon. "Is everything all right?" Their gazes raked over me as if confirming nothing had happened to me in the short duration I was out of their sight.

"Why did you keep Mr. Peter's horse?" I asked.

Simon's brow quirked at the question. "Is there something wrong with the animal?" he asked.

I shook my head. "He seems a fine horse, but if you dislike the man who sold him to you so much, why do business with him?"

"We didna know his actions toward ye before the deal was done," Simon said. "Remember, I hadna met you at the dance as these blokes had, for I was with Peters at the saloon." He didn't seem happy about it either.

I remembered the first time I saw Simon—outside in front of my house in just my robe—and how he'd looked at me with worry and something else. I didn't know it then, but the look was most definitely lust.

"Yet you gave your money to a man I dislike, whom my uncle dislikes, and from what I understand, you don't like him either."

Rhys leaned against the back of a chair so we were of similar height. "We wanted the horse, not him. Our relationship with the bloody man is done."

"Why do business with such a...bloody man?" I put my hands on my hips. "You know how I feel about him."

"Do you want us to return the horse, is that what you're asking?" Cross asked. "Are you making us choose between you and the horse?"

Was I? I felt irrationally angry all of a sudden, as if they were content giving money to a man who was so...dishonorable.

"I just didn't consider it before now, as you are all so mind-consuming." Wicked grins spread across all three men's faces. "It just seems as if you are condoning his behavior."

Rhys narrowed his eyes in thought.

"And we are condoning your behavior right now," Rhys countered. "What's the matter, love? You seem as if you're itching for an argument. You've known ever since the dance we bought the stud horse from him and have not mentioned a concern before now. If you need attention, love, all you had to do was ask."

"I am not—"

Rhys held up his hand.

"We are a large group and I would think daunting for you," Cross said. He looked to Simon, who nodded.

"We were going to take ye home and fuck ye good and hard, but it seems ye canna wait." Simon reached for her hand. "Come, we will fuck ye now."

14

LIVIA

Simon tugged me across the room, the other two following. "What? Wait!" I dug my heels in but there was no way I could compete with Simon in strength. "We can't...I mean, the men, they're all staring!"

Heat flooded my cheeks at the thought. Simon pulled me out of the room, down the hall and into what appeared to be an office. I could barely hear the men's voices from the other room and we were on the opposite side of the house from the kitchen. Rhys closed the door behind him, and I was surrounded by my men with nowhere to go. The room seemed so small with them looming.

"I don't need to be fucked now, truly. Let's go back out there before they start thinking that's what we are doing in here."

"Nay, lass, ye're getting your fucking now."

"But—"

"We may be many here at Bridgewater, but the four of us are a family," Cross said. "You are the center of our world even if we are not in the room with you."

While I believed *he* believed in what he said, I doubted him. I wasn't the center of Uncle Allen's world. I thought I had been, but I wasn't.

"We are newly wed and if we must continue to prove this to you until you believe it, then we will," Rhys said, forcing me to walk backward until I bumped into the large desk. "Turn around, love."

Simon stood next to Rhys, but Cross went around to the other side of the desk and moved the chair out of the way. When I didn't respond as he bid, Rhys put his hands on my waist and spun me about. A large hand on my back had me bending forward over the wooden surface of the desk.

Cross began undoing the front placket of his dark pants and his cock sprung free—his hard, thick cock, clear fluid seeping from the tip. The broad head was plush and I licked my lips with the idea of tasting it.

"I told him how you learned to suck cock, love, and how you took me so deep into your mouth I couldn't help but come on your tongue. Show Cross how good you are."

I felt hands on my legs and cool air on my skin as my dress was lifted.

"You sucked Rhys' cock?" Cross asked, moving forward so the tip of his cock nudged against my lips. "Part those lips and take me into your mouth. I've been dying to be inside there."

"The others...they'll know," I said, glancing up, way up at Cross.

"Don't worry, my cock will stifle all of your cries of pleasure when Rhys and Simon fuck you."

Those words had my pussy becoming wet. Wetter, actually, for I was always wet. With Cross' insistent nudging of his cock, I opened and took him into my mouth. The fluid at the tip tasted salty and clean and made my mouth water. I ran my tongue over the large vein that ran along the bottom, and then sucked on him, just as Rhys had taught me.

"Jesus, Olivia, you're going to make me come like a randy teenager."

I basked in the warmth of his words, as well as the way his hand stroked over my hair, knowing I was pleasing him. I heard as much as felt my drawers rip before sliding down my legs.

"No more drawers, lass," Simon said. "They are just in the way."

Hands stroked over my bottom and I felt the slight weight of my dress bunched at my waist just before hands slid over my pussy, separating my folds before he plunged his cock deep into me. My hips arched up at the abrupt, yet decidedly wonderful action, my moan of pleasure and surprise muffled, just as Cross had said, by his cock that was deep in my mouth.

"You wanted our attention, love, so we are going to give it to you. Simon's first."

The finger pulled free with a loud wet sound and I felt the blunt tip of a cock at my opening, but it didn't linger there or tease me, only slid in with one decisive stroke. I moaned at the feeling, so full, so deep, so perfectly fitting.

"If I hadn't told you, love, that Simon would fuck you first, you wouldn't have known. All of our cocks belong cramming you full. You'll take any one of us at any time because you are our wife," Rhys dictated. "We will give you whatever you need, whatever you desire, whenever you need it."

Smack.

My eyes widened and I cried out around Cross' cock. Simon spanked me! While I tried to pull my mouth free, Cross held me in place and began to slowly move his cock in and out of my mouth instead of me sucking on him as he liked.

"We're here, lass, and nae going anywhere."

Smack.

"If ye need me to spank your arse for you to recognize that, then that's what I'll do."

Smack.

"Did it ever occur to ye, lass, that we didn't give the horse back to Peters—" *Smack* "—because he would then know ye are here with us? Keeping a horse belonging to that bastard is like a sliver under a nail, but we will see ye safe first."

Smack.

I didn't have more than a moment to think about his words, for his hips thrust faster and harder and then I couldn't think at all. My hands flattened against the cool wood, but there was nothing to grab on to, to keep me grounded, as I could no longer fight anything they did. I didn't want to.

"I'm going to come, Olivia, and you're going to swallow my seed. All of it. You're going to taste me on your tongue, to know that I gave you what you needed."

He thrust into me gently one more time, and I felt him swell just before a hot jet of seed coated my tongue and slid down my throat. Again and again his cock pulsed in my mouth as his fingers clenched my scalp.

Simon didn't relent on his driven thrusts, the sound of his hips smacking against my bottom loud in the room.

Cross slowly pulled his cock from my mouth; it was slick and glistening, only diminishing in size slightly before he tucked it back in his pants.

A hard thrust pushed my hips into the desk as Simon let out a groan. His seed was warm and copious enough for me to feel it deep inside. When he was spent and pulled free, his essence slipped down over my clit, onto my thighs and most likely the desk below.

I looked over my shoulder and saw Rhys holding his rigid cock and moving into position between my spread legs. He used his hand to scoop up the seed that had escaped, and rubbed it into my swollen, sensitive flesh. They were right; I was so much more aroused by the smooth, shaved skin.

He took his dripping fingers and moved them to my back entrance, began playing with me there, coating me again and again with Simon's seed. I was so aroused, so needy from Simon's cock and expert fucking that I felt empty and almost forlorn without something filling my pussy. But when Rhys carefully worked a finger into my back entrance and the nerves there came to life, instant heat washed over me, and my brow and temples became damp with perspiration. I couldn't help the groan that escaped, for the jangly, dark feelings that came from his ass play felt so good. I couldn't fight him, couldn't fight the feelings he wrung from my body.

"Here," Rhys said. I saw Cross take something from him over my back and hold it in front of my face so I could see it. It was another one of his handcrafted plugs. He'd used them on me before to stretch me open in preparation for all of them to take me at once, but this one was different. While the other two had been fairly thin and meant for them to play with me—to fuck me there with them without much discomfort yet with plenty of sensation—this plug was quite wide in the middle, the flared head just a narrow tip then broadened quite a bit, then tapered in again, a flat flange at the base for Cross' fingers.

I winced when Rhys slipped a second finger in me along with the first. "I was going to save this for later, but I think now is a better time."

Cross handed it back and I turned my head to follow it. Rhys took it and held it up for me to see one last time, for I knew its destination.

"You're going to love this," he promised. I wasn't as certain, especially when he slipped his fingers free. I thought he was going to push it right into my bottom, but he didn't. I heard a jar open and I knew it was the special ointment to coat the plugs and dildos so they could slide easily—easier—into me.

"You aren't the only one who has their arse filled, lass," Simon said. "Good thing Ian and Kane have jars of the slick lubricant all over the house for Emma."

I only thought for a moment about Emma being placed in the same position as I and having her bottom filled, perhaps not with a plug but her men's cocks. They'd been married long enough for her to be able to be fucked there. Perhaps I'd ask her about it when—

"Oh!" I cried, the cold, blunt and very slippery plug nudged against my back entrance.

Rhys expertly twisted and pushed and worked it into me, wider and wider and wider until I didn't think I could take anymore. "Rhys, please," I groaned.

Just after I uttered the words, the plug narrowed again and my muscles clenched tightly around the narrow section. The wide, hard portion filled me so differently than ever before. It was wide like a cock but not deep, and stretched my opening as the other plugs had. Outside of me, I could feel the cool flat wood parting my cheeks slightly but holding the plug securely within. Rhys tugged on the base and I groaned once again. With my bottom so full, my pussy felt empty.

Perhaps Rhys was a mind reader, for he said, "Is your pussy lonely, love? Let's get you all filled up."

Within seconds I felt his cock at the entrance to my pussy and sliding in, much slower than Simon, but there hadn't been a large plug in my bottom at the same time. Simon moved to stand beside Cross and they both squatted down so their faces were right before mine.

When Rhys' cock bottomed out, the flared head nudging my womb, my eyes widened. I'd never felt so full. I moaned. They grinned.

"Like having something in your arse and pussy? Soon enough we'll have one of our cocks in your pussy, another in your arse and another in this perfect mouth," Simon leaned forward and kissed me, my breath coming out in quick pants as Rhys began to fuck me at a vigorous pace.

"The plug is making her so tight," Rhys said through gritted teeth. "I'm not going to last."

"Are you ready to come, Olivia?" Cross asked. I nodded, for the way Rhys' hips bumped into the base of the plug every time he filled me—how snug he was when he did so—had him rubbing and bumping and nudging places inside me that were new, that were so hot, so intense I couldn't hold back.

"You may come." Cross' voice was soothing, yet commanding. "Show us your pleasure. Squeeze Rhys' cock when you do."

Perhaps it was Cross' words or the erotic feel of being fucked and filled so completely, but I came with a scream, so lost in the flood of heat and pleasure that coursed through me that I forgot all about where I was and who might hear. I tossed my head back, my eyes fell closed and my muscles tensed, as if I held still the feelings would never end. Rhys gripped my hips in his firm hold and held me in place as he thrust deep one last time, a growl escaping his throat as he filled me to overflowing. He leaned forward, slapping a hand on the table beside mine and kissed my sweaty neck, nuzzled against my ear before slowly pulling out.

I slumped onto the desk, my heated cheek savoring the cool wood. I could fall asleep just as I was, for I felt boneless and relaxed and blissfully sated. Cross and Simon stood to their full heights and came around behind me. I should be concerned at how I appeared, my pussy dripping with their seed, not doubt swollen and red, for it felt hot and well used. The plug was still tightly lodged within my bottom. I must have been quite a sight, but I didn't care. They were right; I had wanted their attentions, needed to have validation that I was wanted. How had they known even when I hadn't?

I pushed up onto my elbows, and then felt firm hands about my waist helping me up, and then holding me firmly as I settled. Simon looked down at me and grinned, kissing my forehead tenderly. "Let's eat, lass. I'm hungry as a bear."

Then I remembered my scream. "I...I can't go back out there, they'll know," I said.

Simon picked up my drawers from the floor and shoved them into his pants pocket, a hint of the white fabric peeking out, and winked at me. It seemed I wasn't to have them back.

"They do know, love, and trust me, they won't say a thing. All of them, at one time or another, except McPherson—Simon's brother, I mean, and MacDonald—have tended to their wives at one time or another near the others. You come first," Rhys replied.

"You're not embarrassed?"

Cross tilted my chin up. "Embarrassed for pleasing our woman so well that she screamed in pleasure? Definitely not. Quite the opposite, in fact."

Male preening did not help at all. "Can I clean up beforehand at least? Please take the plug out, Rhys, and let me have a cloth."

All three men shook their heads.

"No," Rhys said.

"Nay, lass," added Simon.

"You wanted our attention and you had it," Cross replied. "With the plug in your ass, their seed dripping from your pussy and the taste of mine on your tongue, will ensure you remember that we are always with you."

"Always," Rhys added, opening the door for me.

As we went out to join the others, walking carefully with the plug still settled deep, I wasn't soon going to forget.

15

LIVIA

Over the next few days, the men were extra attentive, ensuring that one of them was with me at all times. I had not recognized my need for their presence, or that I was worried that they, too, might leave me, but they had. While I could not blame my parents for their untimely deaths, I did blame them for leaving me. As for Uncle Allen, I couldn't deny him the woman he loved or the family he'd made. I couldn't be selfish. But what of Simon, Rhys and Cross? Would they want to leave me as well? Did I crave them in a way that had me taking their attention however I could get it, even if it were to bicker?

I wanted to be the center of their focus because *they* wanted to give it to me, not because I was needy, and that was the crux. It was hard to be confident in our slowly forming bond when I was fretting over something that was completely out of my control. And so when the men were all needed to help repair a large section of fence that had washed out in a mudslide overnight, they were concerned about leaving me alone. They even suggested I go and visit the other women, but truthfully, it had been hard to face them after the group lunch. They all might be comfortable with fucking or being tended to with the others nearby, but I was not. It would take time, and my men seemed to understand that and didn't push me.

When they left for the stable to meet the others, I promised I would walk to Laurel's if I got lonely, for her house was the closest. Once they left, I was content to just read, the windows and doors thrown open to the warm summer day. It also left me open to unwanted visitors.

The footsteps I heard in the hallway I thought could be Simon's, perhaps returning to take me one more time. It was his way to come to me, heat and lust in his eyes, because he couldn't wait another moment to have me. It was hot and my heart pounded and my pussy wept just knowing I made him so eager. Frantic, even.

So when I heard his footsteps this time, I started to undo the buttons of my dress in anticipation, for I knew how much he liked to suck and nip on my nipples as he fucked me. But the man that came into the den was not Simon, nor Rhys or Cross. It was Mr. Peters. I tugged the front of my dress together with one hand as I stood and backed away. The look on his face was almost gleeful, which scared me greatly.

"What...what do you want?" I asked.

"I'm not going to hurt you. I just want to talk."

Talk? Why would he come all the way to Bridgewater to talk? The man was lying and definitely insane.

"How did you find me?" I eyed him warily and very cautiously.

He studied me, tilting his head to the side as to look at me better. His scrutiny was hard to stand, but I did not flinch, did not fill the silence as I waited for his answer.

Finally, he spoke. "They haven't told you, have they?"

"They?" I asked, frowning.

"You married Simon, but I know the other two are fucking you as well. It was all part of my plan."

I swallowed down the fear at seeing him as my fingers fumbled with the buttons on my dress. I didn't want to be exposed in any way with him.

"Plan?" I couldn't manage more than one word questions and I disliked that fact. I should have the upper hand, I should show him the door, but I couldn't. I was too afraid. There was something about his voice, the look in his eye, his bearing, everything, that had me nervous and wary.

"Why do you think you're here? Your *men* belong to me."

I frowned even more deeply. "I don't understand."

"You rebuffed me, so I put men who belong to me in your path. You don't think Simon McPherson would be interested in the likes of you if not for a little incentive?"

The disdain in his voice had me flinching and the way his eyes roved over my body in disgust had me questioning Simon's touch, Rhys' words and Cross' wry humor.

He started laughing. "I can see that you did. I wanted your money, sweetheart, not you. If you weren't going to have me—and that crazy uncle of yours wouldn't let me get near you—then I'd get one of my men to have you instead. It was quite simple really. Simon gets a wife who will submit to his sick ways and fuck three men at once, along with a small payment for his efforts. By the look of you and the way you were stripping down just now, they have you well trained."

I wrinkled my nose in disgust. Had Simon only wanted me for some money and to have a woman to bed with his two closest friends? That couldn't be possible. It was obvious that Bridgewater was a successful ranch and wouldn't have married me for a little bit of money. It was possible he wanted a woman to share with Cross and Rhys, but all three of the men surely had never lacked in female attention and didn't need to marry to do that.

"Simon never even met me until right before we wed," I countered, trying to find issue with his account. "How would he have even met me in Helena?"

Mr. Peters looked down at his fingers as if bored. "He didn't have to. He used his friends to lure you in at the dance. I believe there are two men with whom you are shared?"

How did he know all of this? I remembered the feeling when I first laid eyes on Cross, then later, Rhys. Uncle Allen had used the word lightning, my heart lurching, my skin tingling, the feeling that everyone else in the room disappeared. They'd both been so confident in their attentions, so dominant and... so manly that I'd been almost distracted. The lightning had struck and my brain had lost clarity.

When I didn't respond, he continued. "Simon and I finalized the arrangement at the saloon while you were wooed at the dance. I just stopped in briefly to ensure the men were doing their job, but I had no need. It seems you were lured in quite easily."

A greasy feeling settled in my stomach as I remembered seeing him as I danced with Cross. "Simon works for you?"

The idea seemed preposterous, but here Mr. Peters was, in Simon's house and the story seemed...plausible. Doubtful, but plausible. He wanted something from me more than just talk and I had an idea what it was. I'd spurned his advances before, I doubted he'd let me do so now. I had to keep him talking.

"The horse was just a facade for the real business. *You.*" He chuckled. "Do you really think he needs another *horse*? A stud horse? *Simon's* the stud horse and you're the mare." He grinned at his crude words.

I skirted around him and toward the door. I had to get away. "Then why are you here? If you have what you want, my money, then why even come to Bridgewater?"

He was quicker than I expected. His rotund physique hid a quick step and he grabbed my arm in a talon-like grip. "To ensure you knew the truth. I don't allow anyone to say no to me. You did and your uncle protected you, so I have to punish you. Now you will live with the truth—that you're married to a man who only wanted your money, your body. The other two sick bastards? Simon McPherson thinks so little of you that he'll even share you like a common whore."

"How did you find me?" I'd thought I'd been hidden so well.

"I knew all along, of course. I just wanted to wait a few days to ensure the men had well and truly claimed you—which I can see they have." He glanced down at my bodice and my cheeks heated. "Also to let you know what your man is really like and you can live with the knowledge that I orchestrated it all."

His answer had me connecting pieces of the past week together as if it were a puzzle, one piece interlocking into another. His story actually fit, but I didn't believe it. I had to get away from the man but as I struggled, he backhanded me across the face, white spots dancing in my vision and the sharp sting of his strike made me wince.

"I'm also here to take what you refused to give before. If you already fuck three men, you should not object to one more."

I shook my head and fought him, clawing my hand down his face, my nails digging into his jowls. His hold loosened and I remembered Uncle Allen's advice regarding unwanted advances. I brought my knee up with all my might between his legs, hoping his cock would now be useless. He bent at the waist and a high-pitched sound came from his throat, his hand releasing me. I didn't linger, but fled down the hall and out the front door. I ran blindly toward the stable. I had to get away, away from Mr. Peters at all costs. I could go run home to Uncle Allen, but I had no home; it had been burned and Uncle Allen had his own family. My hair came unbound and my breath came out in deep pants. A stitch pained my side but I kept going. My men. I needed my men.

———

SIMON

While we fucked Olivia frequently and with thorough attention, we'd spent more time out of bed than in three days after our return to Bridgewater. We learned she was an accomplished rider and could herd cattle like a ranch hand with years in the saddle. She was well educated and could speak of books in the evening with Rhys, which fascinated me. I wasna book smart, but could appreciate a lively debate. As Cross showed her how to cook eggs without burning them, they laughed. and I reveled in the way her eyes brightened. I watched quietly, biding my time, for I was always ready to rip the buttons from her dress or toss up her skirts to test her readiness for my cock. She took to our rule of no drawers and it was verra pleasant reaching beneath her dress to find her bare, slick and ready.

Olivia and I didna talk much. We mostly fucked, for this was the connection we shared. If we came upon each other in a hallway, we didna speak, but grabbed each other with frantic, hands and kissed carnally, almost roughly, until I could lift and carry her to a place where I could fuck her. She'd even help, lifting her skirts for me or unbuttoning her bodice to offer her plush breasts. It was elemental and raw and when we were joined, we didna need any words. We were frantic for each other, almost desperate in our need to be close.

It wasna a deep connection like she had with Rhys or comfortable as what she had with Cross. We were more heat and fire, not needing to talk when all we wished to do was get naked—or as naked as we needed to be —for us to fuck. On occasion, Rhys or Simon would hear our rough coupling and join us, but it was I who got her hot, who was able to stoke the lust in those pale, expressive eyes.

After a day of moving rock and digging fence posts, we were all dirty, sweaty and hungry. All I wanted to do was bathe off all the mud and then sink into my wife.

Just this morning, she was verra fetching in her pale blue dress, a color that matched her eyes perfectly. I didna comment on it as Rhys had, but I had shown her how much I liked it by pressing her up against the kitchen door, dropping to my knees before her, lifting her skirts up high enough so I could lick and taste her bare pussy, working her with my fingers until she came, dripping all over my mouth and chin. Rhys and Cross had made breakfast and watched, and all of us agreed that upon our return from the repairs, we wanted her breasts out and on offer.

I didna feel right leaving her behind and unprotected, although I kent she was safe on the ranch; the other women remained at home as well by their men without concern. It wasna that they were less vigilant, for all of the men at Bridgewater put the women and children above all else, but I knew first hand what could happen if I relaxed in my duties to protect her.

While in Mohamir, we'd been tasked to watch over a Mohamiran diplomat and his family. I'd been assigned Alea, the sixteen-year-old daughter to guard. I was many years her senior and felt a keen need to protect her. There was no connection as I had with Olivia, not only because she was too young and our cultural differences too vast, but more because her father trusted me with her life.

We were no longer under the command of the fucking bastard, Evers, who'd singlehandedly murdered Alea and her family. I would not let Olivia down as I had Alea, as we all had her family. It was this incident, this dead family's faces that haunted me still. I was older, wiser and no longer in Mohamir. This was my job in this marriage, to ensure Olivia's safety, for she was a part of me. *She was mine.*

As we rode back to the ranch, one of the hands met us, his horse winded from the pace the man set.

He tilted his hat back. "Ann saw a man at your house. She said it could be Olivia's uncle, but she couldn't be sure."

I shook my head. "Nay. He wouldna come here and risk the bastard Peters following him."

We glanced at each other and spurred our horses toward the house. After a swift search, she wasna there. My gut clenched and I knew instantly something was wrong.

Rhys' eyes narrowed and his shoulders went back. His entire bearing changed. "The stables?" he asked.

'Twas possible, so I gave a curt nod and we both mounted and spurred our animals in that direction. When we rode up, dust kicking up around us, I called out to Kane, who was outside. "Is Olivia here?"

He shook his head. "Ian just came from our house. She's not there."

"Bloody hell," I muttered, glancing out and along the horizon. I tried not to clench my teeth, but I had the overwhelming feeling of helplessness. Where the bloody hell was she?

"Is there a horse missing?"

Kane turned on his heel and went to look.

"Christ," Cross muttered.

I looked up at the sky. About two more hours of daylight left. We had to find her, and soon.

Kane ran out, his feet sliding on the dusty ground. "The new stud horse is missing."

"We'll find her," I vowed, my fists clenching. "We just need to ken which way she went."

16

CROSS

If anyone could track Olivia, it was Simon. Not only did he have vast skill at the task, but he had motivation as well. He struggled to communicate, offering more scowls and brash action than tenderness; he was never known for kindness, but he was different with Olivia. He didn't open up to her more than anyone else, but he watched her in a way I hadn't seen before. Reverence, tenacity and a gentleness he may not have known he had. The two of them fucked with wild abandon, their connection deeper than anything I ever had with Olivia. We talked and joked and found a common friendship between us along with being lovers, but it was different with Simon. Because of that, I worried. I knew how he blamed himself in part for the murders in Mohamir; he hadn't known about the intended crime nor took part in it in any way, but he took his role as defender and protector seriously and he'd let his young charge down. She'd died under his supervision, even if it had been during a time when he was not on duty.

It had been over ten years ago and he still had nightmares; I often saw him at the breakfast table with dark circles and misery etched on his face. With Olivia, he took his concern for her safety to an extreme, even going to the greatest length of marrying her to protect her without having known her for more than a few minutes beforehand. He'd do anything for her, and I had to only hope she had come to no harm, for this would be something from which Simon would not recover.

"I'll go back to the house to see if she left a note or some other clue as to her whereabouts." Rhys grabbed the reins of one of the horses, mounted and turned toward the house.

Simon was tense and most likely ready to beat the face in of the mystery man, for he must know as readily as I, he was the basis for Olivia's disappearance.

"I'll confirm she's not at any of the houses. If I find her, I'll fire two shots," Kane said, mounting his horse, which most likely wanted a rubdown and some hay.

That left me alone with Simon.

"Let's start at the stall."

Simon strode off with single mindedness, his steps long. He stopped about ten feet from the door, and assessed the empty stall for a moment before entering. The hay was fresh on the ground, which meant the animal hadn't been in the stall the entire day. Turning on his heel, he went to the back sliding doors and pushed it open, letting the sun stream into the dim interior.

He glanced down at the dirt directly outside, the squatted down. "See this." He pointed to tracks in the dirt. "The horse was led this way."

I came down beside him, met his dark gaze. "You can tell just by looking at the horseshoes?"

He gave a simple nod. "Peters' horse only had them on the front. We put them on all four feet of ours, just havena done them yet for the stud horse. See, these here have no horseshoes."

Standing abruptly, he followed the tracks to the back pasture. "They continue out the gate." This direction wasn't the corral or even the near pasture but the western graze land for the cattle.

"We haven't had that horse this way before, have we?" I asked.

Simon shook his head. "We've kept him separate for now, so he hadna been out this way."

"This means—"

"Olivia came this way."

————

OLIVIA

The men should have returned to the ranch by now, but I was woefully lost. I'd fled, afraid Mr. Peters would follow, so I'd quickly put only a bridle on the new horse and rode it off in the direction I thought the men would be working. I'd been wrong in my direction. Very wrong, for the sun had just set and I had yet to find them.

I fought tears that I'd held at bay but when I knew I would not find my men before darkness fell, they slipped down my sweaty cheeks unbidden. Mr. Peters' appearance had scared me, for I'd been alone and he'd surprised me. I'd remembered the painful feel of his grip upon my wrist, the dark and sinister look in his eyes when I'd spurned him in Helena. The throbbing in my cheek prompted me continually to his danger. All I wanted was to find my men and accept the shelter they continually offered.

While Simon was the least communicative of the three, he was the most demonstrative. I felt a bond with Rhys and Cross as well, for they were able to share and show their connection through debates or humor, but with Simon, who was so staid and reserved, what we shared was...elemental. It couldn't be faked, it couldn't be bought as Mr. Peters had said; it couldn't be anything but real. So when Mr. Peters insinuated the worst, all I wanted to do was to get to my men, to have them hold me, reassure me. *Love me.* My hastiness was costly though. I didn't know where I was and none of the men did either. How could they find me if I didn't even know my own whereabouts?

Once I realized I had misjudged their location, I assumed it would be easy to find my way back, but I must have followed the wrong creek downstream and then became turned around. My dress had been fine for daytime, but the air was quickly cooling and the wind was picking up, whipping my hair into my face. Clouds had moved in, thick and heavy with the promise of rain, just as we'd seen the previous night. I had to find some kind of shelter. Unfortunately, the open prairie was not a safe place in bad weather and the few cottonwood trees that dotted the creek were a definite danger. Based on the severity of the mudslide the previous night, I knew that being near the water was not a choice so I spurred the horse up and away from the creek bed in case it swelled.

Large boulders dotted the landscape and I stopped and dismounted beside one of the larger ones. My first thought when I saw it was that it was the perfect height for my men to bend me over and fuck. While it couldn't shield me from rain, if I sat curled up on one side of it, the wind would be blocked. I shifted to sit sideways so I could lean against it, bent my legs up, wrapped my dress over my legs and put my head on my knees, holding onto the horse's lead with one hand.

I began to think of Rhys, Simon and Cross, their varied smiles, their varied kisses, their varied techniques with their cocks. I thought of their hands on my body, how they felt and the way I was beginning to recognize the differences between them, how they warmed my skin.

At first I thought I heard thunder, but it was actually the heavy beat of horse hooves that shook the ground. "Olivia!"

I didn't believe my ears, but when I heard my name a second time, I lifted my head. A group of men on horseback approached and I stood quickly. Elation flooded me, making me almost weak with relief. When Simon dismounted with the animal still moving, heading directly for me, I started to cry once again. I could tell by the fierce gaze, his clenched jaw and quick step that I'd been right in my thoughts and Mr. Peters was dead wrong.

He pulled me into him, his big hand cupping the back of my head against his chest. "Are ye hurt?" he asked, his voice rough.

The other men circled around me, their bodies blocking the wind.

I glanced up at Rhys and Cross and I could easily read their relieved expressions.

Simon kissed the top of my head before pushing me back enough so that he could lean down and look me in the eye, and when he saw the tears on my cheeks, wiped them away with his thumbs. When he glanced at my cheek, his face hardened, the dark eyes of a warrior appeared. "Who hurt you?" A bruise must have formed on my cheek.

I tensed at the question. "Mr. Peters."

Simon's fingers tightened on my arms as he glanced at Rhys and Cross, then focused on me. "Did he hurt ye anywhere else? Did he—?"

I shook my head fiercely. "No. I got away."

The relief was visible, then his gaze roamed over my face with the tender look I'd been thinking of when I was lost. His dark gaze searching mine, as if he could see all the way to my soul. "He said disparaging things about you, but...but I didn't believe him and then I wanted to be with you."

He cupped my face and kissed me, pent up emotion and longing forged in that kiss. He eventually releasing me so Cross could pull me into his hold. By now, I was breathing hard, as if Simon had taken my breath away.

"What did he say?" Cross asked as he kissed the top of my head. His scent mixed with sweat and horses had me closing my eyes briefly to savor it.

"He said all three of you worked for him and that you made an arrangement so that Simon would marry me and give him my inheritance and you'd get a portion of it, along with me as a bonus."

Cross stilled his hand that was stroking up and down my back. "What else did he say?" His voice seemed to have dropped an octave.

"That you and Rhys were wooing me at the dance while Simon finalized their arrangements in the saloon," I added.

Rhys turned me to him and took my hand. His hold was firm, yet gentle, especially when he lifted my hand to place it over his heart. I felt it beating steadily and it was reassuring.

"He must have said something about the three of us claiming you," Rhys added.

I nodded, remembering the crude words.

"Tell us," he prompted. I glanced over my shoulder at Cross and Simon and saw that Ian was with them as well, although he stood back about twenty paces beside his horse.

"That Simon would share me with both of you as part of the arrangement. Payment."

"Do you believe anything that bloody fool said?"

I shook my head vehemently. "No!" I cried, worried they'd assume the worst of my imaginings. "I discounted him right away, but he grabbed me, said that he'd...he'd have me since I fucked three men already."

The men's spines straightened and their fists clenched.

"I fought him and then kneed him...him in the cock. I got away and took the horse to find you. I needed to be with you." I stepped out of his hold and put one hand on Cross' chest, the other on Simon's as I looked directly at Rhys. "I'm right where I want to be, between the three of you."

They each took a step inward, closing the space between us.

"I love the way you bicker and argue with me," I told Rhys. "I also love the way you have such focus and precision when you touch me, as if every move you make is deliberate and you know just how to bring me pleasure."

I turned to Cross and looked into his green eyes. "I love the way you make me smile, the way you poke fun at my city ways." The corner of his mouth turned up. I felt Rhys' hand on my arm, stroking it, as if he couldn't keep his hands off. "I also like the way you claim me with such inventiveness, eager to show me new ways to...to fuck."

I turned one more time to face Simon as I felt not only Rhys touching me, but now Cross as well. "I can't stay away from you...from any of you. Simon." I met the warrior's gaze. "There's this...bond that I feel with you, as if I can't get enough, as if I take you inside of me, not just your cock, but *you*. Is it that way for you?" I asked, a tinge of doubt in my voice. Thunder rumbled in the distance.

"Ach, lass, ye are mine."

"You are mine," Rhys added.

"You are mine," Cross agreed.

"I don't want just one of you. Combined, all of you are what I want and need." I looked at each of them in turn. While they were big and brawny and brave, they were also flesh and blood with feelings and their own hurts. While they protected and sheltered me, it was my job to be there for them, in any and every way the needed. "I want to be with you, all of you."

The men's hands stilled as Simon tilted my chin up with his finger. "Do ye ken what that means?"

It meant that I would take all three of them at the same time and one of them would fill my bottom. I clenched there at the thought, but they'd been preparing me for this, not only by stretching me to accept a cock, but to accustom me to the incredible feelings that could be found with something there, whether it be fingers, a plug or even a cock. They'd played with me so that I would *want* it, to need to feel that good.

"It means I belong to all of you. Not one at a time, but all of you at the *same* time, for that's how it is, in here." I placed a hand over my heart.

17

IMON

Two hours later we were home with Olivia settled in the bath, steam rising up from the water that didna hide her body from our gaze. This wouldna be a simple fuck up against the wall, this would be a claiming and it needed to be done right. That began with getting our woman clean and comforted after her ordeal first. My cock wanted to rush, but it wasna the time to do so.

She rode with Rhys, sitting on his lap as we rode back to the ranch. While I didna wish to take my hands from her, I knew that my need for her was too great to hold her so close. I was afraid I might hurt her in my intensity. Just the feel of her soft skin, the smell of her would be too much.

Ian had led the new horse—thankfully we hadna shod the horse's back feet yet—back to the ranch ahead of us to let everyone know Olivia had been found. He would also lead a group that would track Peters and take care of the bloody bastard once the storm blew past. I had a good idea what they'd do with the man and would make sure no one would see him again. While I wished to be the one to finish him off, it was my job—*our* job—to take care of our wife before anything else. Besides, if word of Peters' demise got back to Olivia, I didna want her to have the weight of her men committing murder upon her dainty shoulders. Nothing would come between us now. Nothing.

"You have nightmares," she stated baldly, skimming her hand over the surface of the water, her beautiful pale eyes on mine.

Rhys, who was selecting a plug from the shelf, turned.

Cross paused in unbuttoning his shirt.

Keeping my past a secret wasna easy, as Olivia was verra receptive, and also the first lass with whom I shared a bed. I could hide it while I slept alone, but not when I held her all night in my arms. I must have had a nightmare and nae remembered.

"Aye."

"You all seem to be haunted by events in the past," she added. Thunder rumbled in the distance while the rain continued.

"I grew up in an English orphanage," Rhys confirmed, his mouth a grim line. "Life was...bloody horrible. Then, in the army, we saw terrible things."

"I grew up with a father who liked to use his fists," Cross shared. "Then there was the war. I fought for the North." His mouth formed a grim line.

Olivia watched closely as the men—my true brothers—bared their souls. If Olivia wanted us to claim her, then we needed to give her everything, to share our darkest of secrets. It was time.

I picked up the washcloth from the floor and dipped it in the water. "I was responsible for a girl, for protecting her, but I failed. She and her family were murdered by our commanding officer."

Sadness filled her eyes, so I shifted my gaze to the soap, which I picked up. "Alea?"

I lifted my head in surprise, but I shoulda known she'd seen one of my nightmares. "Aye, lass."

"Did you love her?" Olivia whispered, worry etching her face.

"Nay." Shaking my head, I told her, "She was too young to even consider, but she was my charge and I let her down."

"You weren't even on duty then," Rhys added. "It wasn't your fault. It was Evers. You can't let it haunt you this way."

"I canna control my dreams," I replied, knowing they came to me unbidden as I slept.

"I'll be there to help," Olivia offered.

I ran the washcloth over her shoulder at her tender words. "Aye, lass, ye are there to help, but ye canna share my bed every night. Ye have two other husbands to tend."

"Now I know though, and we can share the burden, the pain, together," she added. "And, I will—from now on—be quite easy to keep safe."

She grinned impishly, for I knew her words were in jest, for it seemed danger followed her everywhere.

"Verra well, I'd like that," I replied. Perhaps her knowing my past could help heal it. If not, I could pull her close and hold on. "Ye, lass, have some worries as well."

"We must know all your secrets, love, to make you happy," Rhys added, holding one of the plugs he made in his hand. Olivia's eyes dropped to it and she frowned, but I took her chin and turned her to look at me. Rhys would play with her arse soon enough.

"I worry you will leave me," she admitted.

I couldna felt more surprised. "Leave ye? Impossible."

"Who's left you to make you feel this way?" Cross asked. His shirt was now off and Olivia's gaze raked over his exposed body.

"My parents died. While it wasn't their fault and I was fairly young, and I felt abandoned." She took a deep breath, which made her breasts rise above the water line. Her nipples were plump and full and I was verra eager to taste them. "Uncle Allen, though, he has his own family. Now that he's shared his secret, he doesn't need me. I don't have a home anymore."

I stood and took Olivia's hand, helping her up and out of the tub. With a bath sheet in hand, Cross came over and began to dry her. "Your home is here at Bridgewater, with us. Your uncle didn't abandon you; he kept a home with you until you had another. We'll go see him in the next few days."

Her eyes were half lidded as Cross stroked the bath sheet over her body. "How...I mean, I thought it wasn't safe with Mr. Peters."

"I dinna ken how he found ye here, but dinna worry, the other men will find him. He willna be a problem for ye any longer."

She looked at me in surprise, but remained silent, for she knew she lived now with a group of warriors.

"Enough about Peters. It's time to make you ours," Rhys said with finality. It seemed he was as eager as I to talk nae more about the arsehole Peters.

––––––––

RHYS

We saw the horse from a distance, the prairie so vast and treeless. Even with the roiling clouds and wind, it was like a beacon on the horizon. Thankfully, the storm hadn't delivered any rain, otherwise we never would have been able to see her. I didn't want to think about what could have happened to her if the storm was more severe. When I saw she was whole and uninjured, I was able to catch my breath. And it was only when we had her in the bath and I was readying another one of my handcrafted plugs that I relaxed entirely. Tonight, we would claim her together and there would be no doubt, nothing between us.

We'd worked her arse to accept the smallest plug, then two larger ones and she should be prepared for our cocks, but I wanted to make sure she was not fearful of it, for we only wanted to give her pleasure. That was why I selected more of a play plug than one that was for training her arse.

"Grab hold of the side of the tub, love," I told her once she was dry. Her hair was up on top of her head, secured by pins, but the long tresses would come free soon enough. She did as bid, and then looked over her creamy shoulder at us.

I groaned at the sight of her; the long line of her back, her breasts that swayed beneath her, her lush hips and perfect arse—an arse that would soon belong to us. For now, we would make her come from being played with there, so she would know how incredible it would be once a cock was buried deep inside her.

I held up the plug I'd prepared. It was slickly coated with ointment, a very narrow tip that widened into a small ball shape, then narrowed, then widened into a slightly larger ball shape, then narrowed, then again in the same way two more times so that there were four humps that would stretch her arse wider and wider going in, and when she came as I pulled it out.

Cross and Simon moved to stand on either side of her and began running their hands over her, each cupping a breast, tweaking or pulling on its nipple, kissing her shoulder, running a hand down her back. They lavished her with attention as I nudged her legs further apart so that her pussy was on perfect display. I stroked over her soft petals, opening them so I could dip a finger into her to test her readiness. There was no need, for she was glistening with her arousal and my digit came out slickly coated. Placing that hand on a soft globe of her arse, I spread her open so her rosebud was exposed. So perfect and soon, she'd have a cock there.

I handed Cross the plug so I had my hands free to pick up the jar of ointment. After dipping my fingers in, I began coating her opening with it, making her nice and slick on the outside, then beginning to push a finger in, spreading it within as well. Again and again I did this, collecting more ointment and working it into her until she was slippery inside and out. She gasped as my finger breached her, but quickly started to shift her hips back, pushing me further within. Once she started to fuck my finger, I took the plug back from Cross.

I placed the narrow tip of the plug to her opening and began to push it within, turning it back and forth as I did so. Slowly, her body accepted the plug, stretching around the first rounded shape, then pulling it in as it tapered down. I assessed Olivia's body, her breathing, the way she gripped the tub, the sheen of sweat on her skin. Simon looked at me and nodded, then turned his head back to whisper in her ear. It was too quiet to hear, but she moaned and clenched down on the plug in response to his words.

I continued to push the plug forward, stretching her wider with the next rounded section until she opened even further and then tightened around it when it narrowed again. I did that two more times until the plug was all the way in, perhaps four inches long. While it had a wide flange for me to hold and to ensure it would not go in any further, I would not leave this one within. It was a different kind of training plug. This one would teach her the feelings associated with arse play and fucking and would most definitely make her come.

"Such a good girl, taking that plug," Cross crooned. "When Rhys pulls it out, you're going to come so hard."

Olivia was so responsive and with three men tending to her, she would be well satisfied within a minute. With that goal in mind, I dipped my fingers back into her pussy and found her dripping wet. "She loves it," I told the others, and Olivia shifted her hips, the sway making her pussy and ass moving just right.

"Please," she begged.

I smiled, thrilled that she loved it when her men worked her body.

"Are you ready to come, love?" I finger fucked her, ensuring my thumb rubbed over her clit each time I moved.

"Oh, oh God. I need...I—"

"We know what you need," Cross said and I watched as his fingers rolled her nipple, and then gave it a little tug.

Her breath hissed out, but her pussy clenched down on my fingers so I knew she loved a little bit of pain along with her pleasure.

"I'm going to pull out the plug and you're going to come."

"Rhys, I...it's so big, will it—"

I cut off her question. "You're going to come," I repeated, continuing the movement of my fingers in her pussy.

Tugging on the plug, I watched her arse stretch around the largest of the round sections, then close back up. She tossed her head back, eyes wide and screamed. Her hips thrust up as I pulled on the plug again, this time her body easily opened and closed for the smaller round shape, which I knew rubbed over very sensitive flesh, which prolonged her orgasm.

Cross and Simon played with her breasts as she came, my fingers curling and rubbing over the special spot inside her pussy, tugging once more, the plug pulling out even easier.

"Rhys, I...it's too much, I...oh it's so good," she gasped.

With one last tug, the plug came free and she was still coming. I stepped away from her so she was completely empty, Cross lifting her up and carrying her into his bedroom. When he placed her on the bed she was wilted and still lingering in the glowing after effects of her pleasure. She was so beautiful like this, and it made my cock ache, knowing we could do this to her. It was so powerful to be able to use our dominance for good.

My balls were tight against my body and they ached with need. As I watched her with one leg bent so her pussy was on display, I stripped, as did the others. I moved to lay down on the bed as Simon lifted her up and easily placed her so she straddled me with her knees on either side of my hips. She placed her small hands on my chest for balance and I felt her arousal coating my lower belly. My cock slid up the seam of her arse.

"Lift up, love, I've got to get inside you."

Coming up off my legs, she hovered over my cock, aiming now straight for her slippery pussy. Putting my hands on her hips, I guided her back down and moved her until I nudged at her opening. It was so hot and wet I knew once I released her, she'd sink right down onto me. Lifting her head, she met my gaze and held it, tilted up her chin as she shifted her hips as if to shake my hands off. Gladly, I let go and she seated herself. Her eyes flared as I stretched her and filled her. My belly tensed and I hissed out a breath as her inner walls squeezed me, so hot and perfect. When she sat perfectly upon my lap, she held still and whispered a simple, "Oh."

I grinned wickedly, recognizing that this was the perfect connection, but I couldn't remain still, so I thrust my hips up, nudging her womb. "Crammed full, love." A shy smile formed on her lips.

"Come here." I crooked a finger and she lowered herself down so I could kiss her, cupping the back of her head.

Once she was in position, Cross and Simon moved, Cross behind her—he'd be the one to claim her virgin arse—and Simon off to her side so she could suck his cock. I let go of my hold and she lifted her head so her pale eyes were close to mine.

"Look," I turned my head slightly to see Simon's cock just by her shoulder. "Simon needs you."

She licked her lips and turned toward him, her tongue flicking out to lick over the head, cleaning it of the weeping clear fluid.

"Good girl, lass, open wide to take me. I canna wait to feel your mouth around me, have your moans vibrate on my cock. I'm going to come right down your throat."

"She just got wetter," I commented, sliding in just a little bit deeper and I thought my eyes would roll back in my head. "Cross, get in that virgin arse of hers and join us. I don't know how long I'll be able to hold out."

18

LIVIA

Rhys' thick cock was deep in my pussy and Simon's stretched my mouth wide. I wanted to please them, all of them, and yet they were the ones giving pleasure to me. Rhys knew how to work his cock to make me come and yet he held back as I gladly sucked on Simon, trying to work him and pull his seed from him and swallow it down. I wanted him to be so lost in the pleasure I wrung from his body that he forgot all of his worries. When his fingers tangled in my hair and tugged at the strands, elation coursed through me.

"I'm all slick, love, and should slide right into this delectable ass of yours," Cross murmured, his hand on my hip, his cock pressing against my back entrance. While he stretched me wider than any of Rhys' plugs, he slipped past the fighting ring of muscle easily enough. "Jesus, she's so tight."

I *was* so tight, so full, feeling both Cross' and Rhys' cocks within me was unlike anything I'd ever felt before. Rhys held still as Cross started to pull back then forge ahead a little at a time, and I couldn't help but groan. The sheer bliss of his cock rubbing over the same

362

places as that ridged plug had me ready to come. It was a different feel, an amazing feel and I wanted it so badly. I was close, so very close, but I needed Rhys to move as well.

"Whatever you did, Cross, do it again. She loved it and she took my cock in even deeper. Holy hell, look how full ye are, lass." From his position on his knees, Simon could no doubt see how I was well filled with cock.

I felt Cross press his hips against my bottom.

I was full, so incredibly full. I couldn't be in any more full.

"We're going to move, love," Rhys said as Cross pulled almost all the way out. "You can come. Again and again. Just feel."

I cried out when Cross thrust back in and Rhys pulled back, then alternated back and forth, fucking me in alternating thrusts. I was officially, completely and totally theirs. There was nothing between us, no one to separate us. We were joined and I was the link that connected us all. Mr. Peters nor my uncle nor anyone else could separate us. There was nothing I could do but feel, just as Rhys had said, and I became lost in my men, lost completely. My skin tingled, my body hot, sweat dripped down my brow, my pussy and bottom clenching tightly on the cocks that filled me. One last shift and I went over the cliff, pushed by three strong men into a never-ending abyss of pleasure. My inner walls rippled around Rhys' cock and I clenched hard on Cross with every thrust and it continued my pleasure. I couldn't cry out, as my mouth was full of Simon's large cock. I reveled in it, got lost in it and I knew I had nothing to fear, for my men were there to catch me. They would always be there, always filling me up.

Simon's fingers tightened against my scalp and I knew he was close to coming. I flicked my tongue up and down the bulging vein on the underside, then along the sensitive ridge at the flared head. "Aye, ye are a bonny lass," he growled as his hips bucked forward and I felt his hot seed against my tongue, salty and tasting solely of Simon. Pulse after pulse it filled my mouth and I swallowed to take it all. His fingers loosened on my hair and he slowly pulled from my mouth as he pushed out a pent-up breath.

With my mouth empty, I was able to turn my head and glance back at Cross, then down at Rhys. My pleasure had my eyes blurry, my muscles relaxed. Both men, however, looked tense and driven, as if their pleasure was close at hand and they were using my tight holes to come. I was more than fine with that, for I'd used all three of their cocks for my own. And I wasn't through. As they continued to pummel me, for their pace and intensity had risen, my pleasure, which hadn't fully ebbed, built back to life, like an ember and a strong gust of wind. I was once again on fire, but this time, I could tell them about how I felt.

"It's...oh, it's so much. I'm so full I'm going to...I'm going to come again!"

I tipped right over the edge and arched my back, my muscles tightening as my cry got caught in my throat.

Rhys thrust one last time and grunted, and I felt as his seed filled me. Cross was quick to follow with a shout, both cocks buried deep within. I couldn't do anything but slump down onto Rhys' solid chest and I could feel the frantic beat of his heart.

Cross slowly pulled from me, then Rhys directly after, and I felt both men's seed dripping from me. I was sore, but I knew I was well fucked. I was lucky in that I had not one man, not two, but three who wanted me, needed me, and truly possessed me.

Thunder rumbled, coming closer, the rain still pounding the roof. In my passionate haze, I hadn't heard any of it. Nothing existed outside of these three men's arms.

"I love seeing your pussy like this," Cross said, his finger gently stroking over my tender, swollen flesh.

"We filled you up, love," Rhys said, his hand stroking over my hair.

"We made a babe, lass, there's nae question if it was just now, or one of the many times we fucked ye this week. I canna wait to see you swell with our child, to see the dark haired wee lassie at yer breast."

The idea of making a baby with them warmed me to my soul. Had they filled me with enough seed to make a baby? The vehemence of Simon's words had me believing him.

"What did your uncle call it when you knew you met the right person?"

"Lightning," I mumbled.

Rhys rolled me onto my back so I had three men looming over me, their gazes raking over my body. I could only imagine how slaked and well used I looked and I didn't mind at all.

Rhys' dark eyes held mine as a bright streak of it slashed across the sky, followed a few seconds later with a clap of thunder. "Lightning," he repeated.

I grinned, for he was right. It was as if it was all meant to be.

"Nay, just lightning. Love, too," Simon said, his dark, intense eyes roving over my body then meeting mine. "It's love."

Cross agreed. "Lightning and love."

They were correct. It was lightning and love.

GET A FREE BOOK!

JOIN MY MAILING LIST TO BE THE FIRST TO KNOW OF NEW RELEASES, FREE BOOKS, SPECIAL PRICES AND OTHER AUTHOR GIVEAWAYS.

http://freeromanceread.com

ABOUT THE AUTHOR

Vanessa Vale is the *USA Today* Bestselling author of over 40 books, sexy romance novels, including her popular Bridgewater historical romance series and hot contemporary romances featuring unapologetic bad boys who don't just fall in love, they fall hard. When she's not writing, Vanessa savors the insanity of raising two boys, is figuring out how many meals she can make with a pressure cooker, and teaches a pretty mean karate class. While she's not as skilled at social media as her kids, she loves to interact with readers.

Instagram

www.vanessavaleauthor.com

ALSO BY VANESSA VALE

Small Town Romance

Montana Fire

Montana Ice

Montana Heat

Montana Wild

Montana Mine

Steele Ranch

Spurred

Wrangled

Tangled

Hitched

Lassoed

Bridgewater County Series

Ride Me Dirty

Claim Me Hard

Take Me Fast

Hold Me Close

Make Me Yours

Kiss Me Crazy

Mail Order Bride of Slate Springs Series

A Wanton Woman

A Wild Woman

A Wicked Woman

Bridgewater Ménage Series

Their Runaway Bride

Their Kidnapped Bride

Their Wayward Bride

Their Captivated Bride

Their Treasured Bride

Their Christmas Bride

Their Reluctant Bride

Their Stolen Bride

Their Brazen Bride

Their Bridgewater Brides- Books 1-3 Boxed Set

Outlaw Brides Series

Flirting With The Law

MMA Fighter Romance Series

Fight For Her

Wildflower Bride Series

Rose

Hyacinth

Dahlia

Daisy

Lily

Montana Men Series

The Lawman

The Cowboy

The Outlaw

Standalone Reads

Twice As Delicious

Western Widows

Sweet Justice

Mine To Take

Relentless

Sleepless Night

Man Candy - A Coloring Book

Printed in the USA
CPSIA information can be obtained
at www.ICGtesting.com
LVHW021204220124
769584LV00014B/983